ANOTHER BEAST'S SKIN

JESSIKA GREWE GLOVER

GenZ Publishing

Supervising Editor: Emily Oliver

Front Cover Design by: MiblArt

Hardcover illustration by: Michaela MacPherson

Jacket design by: L. Austen Johnson, www.allaboutbookcovers.com

Please write to the publisher at info@genzpublishing.org

ISBN (hardcover): 978-1-952919-31-2 ISBN (paperback): 978-1-952919-32-9 ISBN (ebook): 978-1-952919-33-6

For Casey
I've left a light on for you

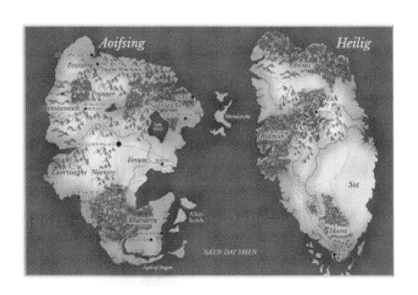

PART I

CHAPTER 1

English pubs really had it down to a science. There was always a level of comfort that places in the States just couldn't master. This one was no different with its cracking plaster, worn floorboards, and large willow tree dipping into the open side garden. The drooping branches shimmied their fingers atop planked tables outside, light dappling through the leaves. I ordered a Pinot Nero and side of chips at the bar and made my way to the patio nearest the beckoning willow tree. Heads turned or politely dipped in silent greeting as I passed. There was no doubt I was the new face.

"You made it out," said a friendly voice.

As I turned toward the sound, a scent of cedar accompanied the breeze as another person slid into the bench opposite. Casting a quick glance over to the man across from me, I took my attention back to Corra.

"Was wondering when we'd see you out. That cottage tends to keep people in," she said, winking. Somehow her words and my earlier uncharacteristic need to be out, left me twitchy.

"Just trying to adjust time zones," I lied, sipping my wine and keeping my eyes down.

She narrowed her own, which I noticed were a sea-glass green. Corra tucked a strand of dark auburn hair behind her ear and gestured flippantly to the man across from me.

"My brother, Silas," she introduced. I turned to a man with short, chocolate brown waves and eyes like polished aquamarines. "Silas, our new neighbor, Neysa." I offered my hand.

"Pleasure." He squeezed slightly before releasing it. "Busi- ness or holiday?" he asked, both palms held out, his thumbs swiping the calluses bisecting them. His accent was rich and lilted.

When I'd met Corra earlier, she hadn't indicated anyone else would be at the pub.

"It's one click to the right on the top lock, one to the left on the bottom," Corra had said outside my rented cottage when I'd first arrived. "The trick is to do them at the same time. The wood sticks after it rains."

After pulling the keys from a coded lock box, I spent a good ten minutes fumbling with the door before she showed up to help. Corra was dressed in running clothes, pulling up the sleeve of her fitted jacket to lift the bottle of pinotage from my carry-on bag.

"Come up the pub in an hour," she said, handing the bottle back as I stepped through the tapestry covered doorway. "The Peasant and Pheasant. Not the Red Lion. I'll see you shortly," she called, jogging away like we had been neighbors our entire lives.

Looking from that woman to the man in front of me now, I guessed that sort of familiarity ran in both siblings.

"A change," I countered Silas' question. He chuckled, again swiping his palms.

"Interesting. I'll come back to that succinctly answered non-answer. However, I was referring to your hands," he clarified.

Automatically looking down at my own hands, my cheeks heated. I needed to get used to English forwardness again.

"Your hands," he repeated. "They are well-callused. Is it from your occupation or leisure activities?"

Ah.

"Leisure," I confirmed, sipping the light red and starting to feel its effects. I opened my mouth to elaborate and was silenced by those damned palms again.

"Can I guess?" He smirked. Beside me, I heard Corra groan.

"Silas, at least allow her the courtesy of finishing her wine before you start."

My demeanor softened hearing the sibling reproach. I met his eyes, the twin set to Corra's, and nodded.

"Let's see," he mused, half standing and leaning in. I could have sworn his nostrils flared.

Self-conscious, I tugged at the strap on my camisole. His eyes locked on my shoulder and bicep, then brazenly raked down my arm. My lips twitched. I was trying and failing to not seem embarrassed.

"Golfer?" he ventured. I choked on my wine, nearly spraying it at him. His eyes twinkled in amusement. I snorted and wiped at my watering eyes. He knew damned well I wasn't a golfer. "I take that as a no."

"You get two more guesses," I said, enjoying the game.

He considered another long moment. "Rowing?" I shook my head, the movement letting my dark hair fall over my collarbone. Silas looked to Corra, who crossed her arms over her chest and clicked her tongue. "What if I'm wrong on the next?"

"You lose," I teased, batting my lashes at him.

He cleared his throat and stood. I followed the movement, watching him. He was built for labor—tall, broad-shouldered, and slim-hipped. Yet his clothes were well-cut and expensive looking. His hand pulled at his chin, releasing a slight scraping sound. This man, like Corra, was perhaps in his late twenties to early thirties.

He leaned down, hovering near my face. I curled my toes in my sandals where no one saw. My blood heated ever so slightly. File that away for later.

"I'll take a break and observe," he huffed.

"Sore loser," Corra poked him.

"I haven't lost," he said quietly, still inches from me. I could

smell his soft woodsmoke-like scent as it wound around me. "I'm calculating." With that, he walked off.

I shook my head.

"Don't mind him," Corra said, waving toward her brother. "He's a terrible flirt and a worse loser. Now, tell me. What's your story?"

I blanched. It's not that I was unprepared for questions. I was a newcomer to a small town, and as far as they could tell, an American at that. It's just that my stomach turned when I had to rehash it. When I was forced to remember my dad dying. The divorce with Caleb.

My chest squeezed as I rallied myself. The simplest version, it would be.

"I got divorced and decided to start over."

She nodded in understanding and pushed my near-empty wine glass forward.

"By the way," Corra said innocently. "I'm truly surprised my brother hasn't guessed about the swords."

I smiled, somehow not surprised by her observation.

"In his defense, I do quite a bit of kettlebell training as well.

. . .

PLUS, I DIDN'T THINK IT WAS NICE TO ALLUDE TO BEING able to gut a fellow when he's just met me."

She leaned back and barked a laugh.

"Neysa, you and I—I think we shall have fun," she chirped.

I started to hope the same. I couldn't remember the last time I'd made friends with another woman.

THE HOUSE I was letting wasn't necessarily unwelcoming. Quite the opposite actually. It felt expectant, as if it was impatient with me. Every creak on the stairs, cold pocket of air in the corners, and pulsating energy from the decorative crystals on the bookshelves, created a pregnant sort of breath within the walls. Was I missing some big reveal of a secret room? The world's comfiest armchair? Auntie Fanny still sweeping the back steps two hundred years postmortem?

The age of the building wasn't to blame, I knew. I'd spent enough time in old, English buildings that they didn't spook me. Whatever was giving me the strange feeling had me needing to get out and put some miles on my sneakers. I nearly sagged with relief as I stepped out to run.

My legs started out stiff and tense to the point of discomfort. Ten hours on a plane the day before does no favors to the hips. My feet moved from the gravel and pavement onto a grassy trail. The ground was softened by a recent rain, the blades of summer grass heavy with the promise of moisture, pushing me further into the woods. Only when I ran could I shut out the despair and loneliness that seemed to seep into my bones. Miles and minutes soldiered on. Tangy scents of greenery crushing under my soles wafted up while I plowed past bramble and thicket. Sticky earth beneath my shoes sprayed up the backs of my calves and even onto the back of my neck.

As a ran my troubles away and felt the muscles in my legs start to relax, I realized suddenly that my whereabouts were unknown. Meadowy wildflowers bordered by bushes had been replaced by wiry trees as tall as they were thin. My stride slowed, and I stopped, looking about. The air was heavier here, the wind picking up. Faint, quickly-fading mud prints were the only indication of the path I'd taken, as the trail had thinned and there was no defined direction to travel. I didn't remember coming through forest, yet behind me, the trees were dense. Canopies of trees with gnarled roots and lush, full leaves engulfed my senses. I held my fingers aloft, testing the wind for direction. Jogging slowly against the wind, the brine of salt spray tickled my nose. Through a line of birch trees, the sky opened to reveal the ocean beyond. I walked carefully to the cliff's edge, in awe at the terrain.

Though the drop below me was unforgiving, I spotted a trail to my left heading toward what looked like a cleft in the ledge. How far had I come? Ten? Twelve miles? The sensation of being completely lost kicked up my heart-rate.

A pulsating ache started between my ribs, and my breathing hitched. Not an ideal time for an anxiety attack. Rationally, I knew I was jet lagged and confused. Irrationally, as panic tends to be, the dense air and sense of being totally turned around, sat on my chest. How did I not know I had come so far? *Keep walking. Fuck. Can't breathe.* Tears streamed down my face, and my mouth felt as though it were filled with cotton. *Keep walk- ing.* My hands clawed at the neck of my shirt, and I ripped it over my head, trying to cool myself down. *Keep walking.* The cleft in the cliff was in front of me. A path descended to the rocky shore below and seemed to wend away toward the wood behind me.

I dropped heavily on a rock. My rational mind realized that had this been California, I would have checked thrice for snakes. If this had been my condo in Los Angeles, I also wouldn't have been listening to recordings of my dad's voice over and over, as I had the previous evening. That expectancy in the cottage had me feeling like it was the gateway to under- standing pieces of me that have been empty for as long as I could remember. I needed to bring myself to the here and now.

It had been a month since my last panic attack. *That* had been stress-induced. The divorce finalized. Dad. *This* was new. My life as I knew it was turned inside out from one foot-fall to the next. I braced my elbows on my knees, head hanging. Breaths were still coming shallow. Spots were forming in my vision from lack of oxygen. *Fuck.*

I sat back and touched the cool rock beneath me and closed my eyes.

"It seems," a cool voice intoned from my left. My eyes shot open. "That you have either lost your way or fancied a tour of the coast."

I made to stand but immediately tipped from a head rush. Breaths became choppier. *Fuck. Think.* The scent of rain in the air increased, as though attempting to soothe me.

"Can I help, Neysa?" the man's voice softened.

I heard the soft rustle of fabric and felt him kneel in front of me. This complete stranger rang every warning bell in my symphony. My feelings were divided evenly between the need to flee and gratitude for the presence of another human being. Slowly, I opened my eyes as I nonchalantly slid my hand into the pocket of my leggings. The brushed metal of my slim knife steadied me. Blinking, I focused on the man before me, strong- jawed and fair-skinned with a crop of night-dark hair. His keen eyes reminded me of smoky quartz, and they immediately noted my movement.

"I won't harm you. Though," he offered a crooked smile, "should I worry for myself?" He sat softly on the damp ground.

I counted. *Inhale for five, hold for seven, exhale for nine. Repeat.* I felt no threat despite the stranger appearing in this wilder- ness. With all my self-defense training, I'd better be right. *Inhale for five, hold for seven, exhale for nine.*

He watched me quietly, then spoke. "I should introduce myself. I am Cade. You are on my property. When you are ready, I can bring you up to the house—if you wish." He must have seen the alarm on my face. "Then we can see about that split lip."

The tip of my tongue darted to the side of my bottom lip and tasted blood. I had bitten it sometime during my panic. The copper tang shook me out of my anxiety. I blinked hard and took a deep breath.

"Well, that was humiliating." I laughed without humor. "Sorry to disturb your home."

"Not at all. Do you get anxiety attacks often?" His question was more clinical than curious, which made me less apprehen- sive of answering, however uncomfortable I felt.

"Yes," I answered honestly. "Though never when I run. I lost my bearings I think."

He made an agreeable huff. "This area will do that. Perhaps it's best to not be alone so far from home?"

Alone. Wasn't I alone everywhere? This was my reality. What a sad case I must seem.

He must have read something on my face. "I only meant," he began. "That the coast trail can be slippery in the best weather. Never mind that the weather can turn quickly here. Come. You're looking quite grotesque."

He held out a hand, which I studiously ignored. I stood swiftly, gathering my discarded shirt. We walked in silence toward a large limestone manor house. The wind toyed at my now chilled, sweaty skin. I shivered. A sidelong glance told me he had noticed and proceeded to deliberately zip his tailored field jacket. A muscle twitched along his jawline, and I wondered if he was that much of an ass, or if he was actually cold.

As we approached the slatted wood door, I stopped dead, hand flicking open the three-inch blade I kept on me. The air seemed to stale between us.

"You knew my name." A statement.

He rolled his eyes. "I did," he confirmed. "I am your landlord. The cottage you are renting is at the eastern edge of my estate." Oh. "Now, as I'm quite certain you know how to wield that knife, and I'm not keen on a new scar, would you care to come in and clean up?"

I clicked the release but kept the closed knife in my fist. I nodded my agreement, teeth starting to chatter.

Cade brought us through the foyer into a comfortably sized sitting room to the left of the staircase. My muddied sneakers left skeletal smudges on the stone floor. I cringed, realizing that my running clothes were sweaty, wet, and had God knows what on them from when I'd sat down in my panic.

"I'll get something for the lip and be right back." He slipped from the room.

I stood awkwardly and took in the details. An ancient-looking kettle hung on an arm from the fireplace. I wondered if it saw any use. My eyes trailed upward to note, with a stirring of excitement, the small cache of antique swords and twin daggers displayed over the hearth. I walked closer. They all had an etching forged along the gleaming length of them. Runes? I couldn't read the lettering from where I stood, several feet below them. These pieces weren't simply left to tarnish. Someone took great care in cleaning the metal.

"You do seem to be drawn to blades." Cade's footsteps moved toward me.

"I am trained in swordsmanship. Most blades really," I admitted, waiting for the shock I normally saw since sword-play was not the most popular sport.

Cade merely raised an eyebrow and placed a few first-aid supplies on a small, brass-topped table.

"Perhaps," he began. "You could keep up your studies whilst you are here." He gestured toward the ancient blades. My eyes widened. "All skills need honing."

"Perhaps," was all I managed as I stood, shifting my weight from foot to foot. His head cocked to the side. Understanding dawned.

"Please sit. This furniture has seen worse wear. I believe the dogs sit on them as soon as I leave." What dogs? I cast a glance around as I sat on the worn leather Chesterfield. "Bixby and Cuthbert are out back." A smile hinted at there being a bit more tenderness in him than the stalwart appearance I'd seen thus far.

He picked up a bit of gauze. He really intended to clean my split lip. I shifted uncomfortably like a scolded child.

"My cousin," that cool, clear voice began, "was always getting into fights as a child. You will likely meet him soon as he lives on property as well. He knew how to get under every- one's skin." He dabbed my lip with the gauze. I winced. "So, I was always patching up his split lip. Or eye. Or knuckles." A searing zap prickled on my face. I pulled back, automatically touching the cut.

"Sorry," he murmured. "The cleansing agent can sting."

There was a lick of warmth that ran through me, ending in another hint of electricity. The lights in the room and the very air itself seemed to pulsate. It was easy to convince myself I had imagined it.

"Thank you. I should get back."

He inclined his head, seeming much older than one whom appeared to be a man in his early thirties. I wondered what shadows dogged his life.

"If you run south and west, there are marked paths. Elderly people walking their spaniels and all that. Should you come north or east, stay on the property. Coming in and out of the estate from the north can be...convoluting."

I nodded and made to leave, exchanging polite goodbyes with him once I reached the front door.

A few hundred meters away from the manor, I was greeted by two shaggy guides. They looked like coonhounds with long, silky fur. The hounds happily trotted along until I reached the short gate, which led into my garden. A scratch at their long, soft ears bid farewell.

I SUNK into the claw footed tub, ready to soak the day away, and fell heavily asleep.

Fast-paced dreams filled my sleep. Scents and colors I couldn't recall upon waking yet seemed so familiar.

Then, my father's voice: *It's okay, Neyssie. You are where you were always supposed to be, my little moon."*

In the dream, Dad held out his aged, golden brown hand, offering something hidden in a glare of light where I couldn't see. I pawed at him, reaching out and asking him what it was. All he did was smile and say something in a melodic language I couldn't place.

The dream object faded from his hands, turning instead, to a twenty something version of him and six-year-old me, seated on my bed in our old home, the one we lived in here in England before we left for Dad's job in California. Dad grasped my tiny hand where it had fisted into the calico quilt. In the dream, I heard him telling me a bedtime story, one I'd all but forgotten in my waking, grown-up life. My consciousness slipped into that of my six-year-old self, becoming a child again.

"Once, in another realm," he began. *"There was a little moon of a child. A girl who would wake up and put on the skin of a different beast each morning."*

"Why did she do that?"

Daddy said, *"She didn't look like everyone else, and she knew the people would be scared of her. They may even try to hurt her. So she used a magical stone to cover her whole self in another skin."*

"Was she magical?" I asked.

"Oh, yes, certainly. She was very powerful, but she couldn't show anyone," he answered. *"So, she had to use the stone to change herself. Like wearing a cloak."*

"What did she look like?"

"She looked like a queen." He tucked a piece of my dark hair behind my ear. *"She had eyes that looked like the forest in summer and pointed little ears that could hear a mouse scuttle in the house next door."*

I made a face at him. I didn't like mice.

"Her family loved her very much, and she was royalty, so they had to send her away for a long time. When she went away, she left behind special parts of her magic."

"Why would she do that? I would want to keep all of mine," I argued, crossing my arms over my chest. He laughed and agreed with me.

"Where she was sent, she couldn't keep these special parts. One magical part of her would act up a little every now and then. Like a certain someone I know," he teased, tapping my nose. *"It had wings and claws."*

"That sounds like a monster," I pointed out, in case he hadn't been paying close attention.

"Indeed it does, Neyssie. But it was a certain kind of monster that lived inside her—a nice one, like you see on telly. But even a nice monster could be scary to some people. As the years passed and she wore the disguise day after day, the little girl grew into a bigger girl and eventually forgot about her original skin. She was able to wear the new skin without the magical stone, and she forgot all about missing her special beast.

"So, the beastie waited until the girl had become what she was always meant to be, and it decided to come back when she needed it

the most. For it knew that one day, there would be another beastie to be with, and together they would create a better world."

"Woah, hang on, Daddy. Where exactly is this other beastie? Does she grow another one? That's kind of gross." He chuckled at the observation.

"No, the gods themselves spoke of someone who would fight along-side her for all eternity, and that partner would have a beastie too. They would defend the world, and yes, get bruised and bloody like you like to hear about. The partner didn't even know his beastie was in him and so, for hundreds of years, he walked the realms, searching."

At that point, I felt myself starting to drift off, dreaming once again about magic, monsters, adventure, and a realm where my father didn't seem so sad.

"It's time for bed now, my little moon," he whispered. "Good night."

As my eyes slipped closed one final time, he kissed my head and said, "Chanè à doinne aech mise fhìne."

I WOKE, chilled to the bone. The bath water had turned to ice; the house was dark. After splashing my tear-stained face, I quickly climbed out of the bath. Six hours. Six hours I had slept in the tub. *God above. What was my deal today?* I pulled on my softest white pajamas, grabbed a cashmere wrap, and tucked myself into an early bedtime, thinking of my dad, this house, and the odd people I'd met since arriving.

As I passed the mirror, I paused and peered closely at my face. I had to admit, Cade did well cleaning my lip. Based on the amount of blood down the chest of my shirt and sports bra, I'd really torn it.

The following morning, there was all but a bit of swelling. Following his suggestion, I decided to explore a running route on the property—bringing my phone this time.

The meadow beyond my willow fence was blanketed in soft, white protrusions of wild garlic flowers. My feet found a comfortable pace through the flowers. The small gravel path wound into a sun-dappled wood, leading me back toward that coastal trail. Only three or so miles in, I decided to take the path through the cleft down to the shore. Mindful of my footing and dodging outcroppings of wild carrot and sea kale, I gingerly made my way down between the stones.

What presented itself to me at the bottom was unexpected: tide pools as clear as glass, bejeweled with smooth rock, stretched from the shore like open arms. Large rocks and seaweed doilies pebbled the shoreline. Of all the times I'd spent at beaches in the UK, I had never seen anything like this. Rocks, grey waves, grey flannel skies lying upon the ashen duvet of water—but not this. This was a fever dream of being inside a treasure chest. Tumbled rocks caught the sunlight as they had in Italy a few years ago. It had been one last attempt at saving the little bit of marriage Caleb and I had left. For that week, it seemed as though he and I could gather the pieces of who we were and make them into what we needed for our theatrics of a marriage. There, the fantasy of who we were seemed plausible. By the time we landed back in L.A., I had enough self-worth to exit stage left when my scene was over.

Then Dad got sick. The polarity of my emotions was staggering. The blessed reprieve from the nagging of an ill-fated union was replaced by a howling denial that I was losing my dad. I was losing the one link to who I was. My dad, who trained me on my first small sword. Who insisted I do gymnastics and ballet even after I was told I was "too tall," "too athletic," by her teammates. For a girl whose mother was non- existent, having a dad who would sit for teddy bear picnics as willingly as he would gift me a black, powder-coated steel hand-and-a-half sword for my sixteenth birthday was everything.

The lapping of waves and frothing of seafoam over

smooth rocks carried my senses back to the here and now. In the distance, voices carried, pulling me from my memories completely. I reached idly into the cool, clear water, letting the ripples caress my fingers. The voices were laughing, coming closer. A female tinkling chuckle made me smile. *Corra.*

After a few moments, three figures rounded the monolith at the tide pool's edge.

"Well, speak of the devil," Silas crooned.

The two siblings were as ill-dressed for beach-going as I.

Like me, Corra looked poised for a run in her black leggings, fitted jacket, and wide running belt. Silas was similarly clad. I opened my mouth to greet them just as my eyes fell on the strap across his broad chest. A small "O" of surprise parted my lips, and he immediately noticed what I'd seen.

Cade sauntered slowly behind; twin swords strapped against his thighs. His look and greeting were bored and self-important, while Silas's eyes scrunched in amusement, lips smirking. Turning to Corra, I raised my eyebrows. She shrugged and introduced Cade as her cousin.

"Silas figured it out last night after Cade told us of your... trials yesterday," Corra explained, referring to my callused palms.

Affronted and more than a little embarrassed for Cade to have divulged my panic attack, I darted an accusatory glance at the dark-haired male adjusting his bootstrap. He glanced up at the weight of my gaze and dismissed me entirely.

Silas pulled his narrow longsword from the scabbard running the length of his spine.

"Care to dance, milady?" A jolt of something part fear part excitement shot from my toes upward.

Cade's face looked briefly alarmed. "Take care, cousin.

The lady is prone to hysteria," Cade warned, his face rearranging itself into utter boredom.

It could have been said in jest, but it came off haughty and rude.

Corra and I both turned to him, disgust limning our features. She opened her mouth, but I stepped forward, ignoring the insult. My own hazel eyes met Silas's glass-green ones. "I find myself at a disadvantage, Silas," I said and held my arms out, anchoring my stance.

He breathed in, pressing his mouth into a hard-lined grin. Without breaking my gaze, Silas snapped fingers at his sister. "Corraidhín, would you kindly lend the lady a blade?"

She rolled her eyes. I felt as though this were a gesture made regularly.

"First off, brother," she began, unsheathing the small sword I had initially thought was a running belt. "Don't snap. I'm not your hound. Next," she said, turning to me. "Have care with my weapon."

With that, she tossed the slim, mirrored blade to me, hilt flipping midair to meet my waiting grasp. Inhuman was the term my previous weapons instructor used for my reflexes. It was a point of pride for me. I smirked in thanks and allowed the steering calm to take over. Assessing the weight and balance of the weapon, I twisted it this way and that, then adjusted my stance accordingly.

Silas struck, laying the weapon sideways and leaning in. I pulled my knee up, pivoting as I turned his blade. My own arm thrust forward and kissed his blade, moving both laterally. We turned in an ellipse, making tracks in the pebbly sand like the tracks of a matchbox car. Sharp edges of the tiny stones were cutting into my bare feet since I'd removed my running shoes as I came to the beach. We truly were in a dance. He wasn't putting his best effort in and, for the sake of my training and audience, I smiled. Bright, wide, and open, meeting his glassy eyes dead on.

"Surely that's not all you have, soldier?" I smirked, and his face changed into overtly male fierceness. "I bet you dance with all the girls like this."

A muffled cough came from Cade and Corra choked on a laugh. Silas stopped, legs wide, and pointed the tip of his blade at the earth. He lifted his proud chin and nodded once. A headiness surrounded us suddenly, clouds forming overhead. I rallied my senses and cleared my mind. Truthfully, I didn't see the sword come up and knock me sideways. Balance catching, I spun and kicked a leg to swipe his shin. He huffed and squatted, one-legged, then leaned toward my hip. I knew before the blade pushed flat against my abdomen that I was in check. My hips bucked, and I was on my back, his sword still laid across me, his hands on the hilt and edge. Checkmate. With one knee astride me, the other bent, he lifted a dark eyebrow.

"Do you yield?" he demanded.

I nodded, stomach tight. I hadn't lost in six years.

He released his damning position, allowing me to sit up. "Cadeyrn." Silas turned to Cade. "I would say she is not prone to hysteria at all." He turned back to me, eyes dancing.

I knew that look. Battle high. I normally needed to run, lift heavy, or have a turn in the sheets to come down.

"Good," Cade spat. "Neysa can train with you lot starting tomorrow. Silas, tend to your hand and, *bloody hell*, take a cold shower."

Silas looked down and had the good sense to look abashed.

His palm was bleeding freely. So *this* was the cousin Cade had likely been patching up for twenty years or more.

Realizing I was an interloper, I stood, grabbing my shoes, and started to walk back up the rock path. Near the top, foot- falls sounded behind me, quick and light. I sucked on a tooth, biting back anything that could have come out of my mouth.

"Are you sore that I won?" Silas asked.

I laughed, only half-amused. "Yep."

"That's a very American form of vernacular."

"Sorry, were you here to patronize me, or shall I get on with my walk home?" I reached the top where the stones were cleft.

Silas scrunched his nose, making his roughly hewn, hand- some features comical. "Your fighting was outstanding. I've been training my whole life and—"

"As have I," I snapped. "My father put a sword in my hand at age four. Thirty-one years ago."

He smiled slightly. My stomach turned as I detected an ounce of pity.

"I meant to say good match."

I stopped walking and took in my surroundings, my companion. What the hell was I doing? So, I had lost to a man twice my size who thrummed with an energy I couldn't place. *Inhuman*, I heard my instructor saying. That seemed an apt term for Silas.

Blowing out a breath, I turned to him, willing a light- hearted grin. "Well met." I inclined my head.

"Cadeyrn said he offered for you to keep up your training while you're here." Not quite a question. "I would happily train with you," he said with a hopeful grin.

"As would I," joined Corra. "Can't let this oaf have all the fun. I would have asked you to spar had we not run into you." She linked a thin arm through mine, leaned her auburn head toward my dark brunette one, and said in a conspiratorial stage whisper, "But tonight we have a bottle of wine with our names on it. We can drink, and I can tell you all of Silas's weak spots."

"Yes, I'm totally useless when my feet are tickled," the oaf in question quipped.

"As long as there is a copious amount of food, I'm there," I said.

CHAPTER 2

The past three weeks had been spent having dinner at the pub, joined mostly by Corra and Silas. I wondered at the fact that they seemed sociable and outgoing, yet apart from friendly banter with the pub patrons, neither sibling seemed to have any friends in town. Sometimes, I watched Silas talk. He was animated to point of being goofy. The juxtaposition of that silliness and the unwavering concentration I had seen in his fighting mode was impressive.

In my thirty-five years, I myself had never had many friends. Being considered "aloof" in my adult life was a graduation from "stuck-up" in my youth. My concentration had always been my academics and combat training. I never felt as though I were unfriendly, and if I were being honest, I had tried to make the effort with my ex's friends. I tried to be the interesting, easy-going wife. We went for drinks and parties, and I let him parade his pretty wife around. So, to see Silas and Corra in their unmasked demeanor was both refreshing and a bit confusing.

Sometime in the midst of a story, I noticed Silas stop

speaking. In the back of my mind, I was aware of him looking at me, an eyebrow raised. Corra waved a hand in front of me, and I blinked. Silas gave me a lopsided grin, which made my cheeks redden. Stubborn to a fault, I met his eyes. Damn it all, they were beautiful eyes. My hazel ones felt muddied in comparison.

The air shifted, and a shadow moved across my side as Cade slipped in the bench.

"Well, look who decided to grace us with his presence." Corra bowed mockingly.

Cade glared, then shifted. He glanced between Silas and me, closed his eyes briefly, and shook his head. *What is it that rubs him the wrong way?*

As if sensing my annoyance, he shrugged.

"I'll head out," I announced, and stood abruptly from the edge of the picnic bench. Something about Cade made me slightly off-center.

The siblings exchanged a glance, then Corra reached over and flicked Cade's shoulder. He again shrugged.

"But you haven't eaten," Corra said.

I picked up my small, pebbled leather handbag and slung it over my shoulder. The sleeve of the grey T-shirt dress I was wearing bunched, and I tugged it free of the strap.

"I'm not hungry, mother hen. Enjoy yourselves."

With that, I walked around the side of the building, out to the country road I would take home. As I made my way out, I heard Corra reprimanding Cade or Silas. Whomever. It was Silas's answering growl I heard. The sound was less than human. Something in it triggered a feeling in me—like a forgotten memory that was too far buried to surface.

I HURRIED HOME, wanting to get back and do some research on market conditions. I had thought that getting away from everything was what I needed, but it turns out that not having a project made me antsy. Back at the cottage,

I opened my laptop and started scanning news reports, international stock markets and analyses, etcetera.

Before coming to the UK, I had pulled my assets out of the Foreign Exchange Market just as I made a 210 percent profit when the Turkish Lira and Iranian Riat jumped. I shorted all my USD accounts, expanded the other two foreign accounts, and gained quite a soft landing spot when I withdrew from my brokerage account in preparation for moving overseas. Within twenty-four hours of my withdrawal, both currencies tanked. It was the only purely intuitive exchange I had made in my Forex career

But I wasn't trading Forex anymore. I had decided during my separation with Caleb to give Forex one month more, then I would move on in every aspect of my life.

"One last heist," Dad had chortled from his hospital bed. *"You're meant for great things, Neyssie. I'm proud of who you are, but I see so much more for you."*

My eyes welled up at the memory of his last lucid day. The next had been the start of his downward spiral. He'd had to be kept sedated after repeatedly yelling nonsense. I recorded his rants partially because in his seventy-six years, he had never said, nor done anything nonsensical, and partially because I knew I was losing him, and I wanted to have his voice some– where. I feared forgetting its sound if left to trust in my memory alone.

I had that recording with me now. Perhaps market conditions could wait.

I put my computer aside and lit a candle in remembrance, then hit play on the recording as I'd done so many times since arriving. As I'd done so many times since meeting Corra and her family weeks ago. It started with cacophony—metal clank– ing, white noise from various machinery, and the gasping breaths of someone who had been screaming. Another intake of air, then:

"Vil! Cab! Amba! Cappa-Cappa! DoKee-Ah! Reela! Gookche Munch Uk!" Heavy breathing. *"Eh-Fa."* Another breath.

I remember him turning to me. *"Neysa, Libellula,"* he mumbled, spittle coming out. The sounds of sleep, then the recording concluded. My father's last words rattled me. Hearing him say my name was a gut-punch, and I was sobbing from it.

Distantly, there was rapping at the door. Not caring if I was fit for company, I went to open it, turning abruptly to avoid Silas's eyes. "Hey," he said softly.

I barely heard him. His hand came down lightly on my shoulder. The contact was my undoing. My shoulders caved in, and my torso went limp with the force of my crying. I had no family anymore. No close friends who reached out. I was a time bomb. Some small part of me said I should be ashamed to be falling apart in a near-stranger's arms. A larger part simply needed the comfort of another person. (Christ, I should have gotten a dog.) So, we stood there in the foyer, his arms around me, half-leaning against the wall.

After a decent amount of time, Silas started small circles on my back then spoke softly. "Shall we sit?" he offered.

I nodded and turned down the hall then left into the sitting room. He kept a hand on my back, knowing I needed that contact. The tears stopped as we sat on a small, stiff settee in front of the fireplace. Fiddling with my fingers, I kept my eyes down.

Strong, callused fingers stilled mine. "If you don't want to talk, you don't have to. But if you do, I'm happy to listen. I don't have anywhere else to be. We could even fight." He smiled, crinkling those clear eyes, making him look older and younger at the same time. "I'll give you a few free shots, too." He nudged me with an elbow, and I laughed and sniffed enough to need a tissue.

He pulled one from the table behind him and handed it to me.

"I'm a gross mess," I said, then blew my nose.

"Nonsense," he argued in an accent not-quite English. Come to think of it, all three of them had a singsong lilt that reminded me of my father. I looked up, my swollen eyes almost painfully raw. He laid a broad palm on my cheek. "You're lovely even covered in snot." He jumped, expecting my half-hearted slap.

I took a breath and began to tell him about my father. About how I'd never known my mother. She had died when I was an infant. I told him about Caleb—about how we had met in grad school and it was wrong from the start. He listened about Dad's illness, his death, and finally, about what set me off tonight. I explained how every time I was in this house, I felt the urge to listen to the recording—as though the house itself pushed me toward it. When I had finished, my head felt lighter. He sat for a few long moments, then got up and walked to the front door and back again. In his hands was a takeaway bag.

"I brought kebabs and rice. Shall we eat and have a listen to those recordings?"

And so we did. Over and over again. I wrote down the ravings phonetically.

Vil, Cab, Amba, Cappa, Cappa, Dokee, Ah, Ree-la, Gook, Che, Munch, Uk, Eh-Fa, Libellulah. The last not articulated as well, as Dad had been spittling whilst saying it. Once they were all written down, Silas stepped back and looked.

After a good ten minutes, he leaned in, chin just over my shoulder. He reached out and pointed at the last word. "*Libell- Libellula*," he read, the song in his accent again, disturbing that buried feeling of memory. His rugged brow pinched together. "That was our mother's nickname for Corraidhín," he explained, turning his head ever so slightly.

I felt his breath tickle my neck just under my ear. A blossom of warmth started in my core. Silas shook head in a slow *tick tok*.

"Corraidhín means 'little spear.' Our mother used to call her *Libellula*, meaning 'dragonfly.'" His hand rubbed over the scruff of his jaw.

The implication sunk in as we sat in silence. It was one thing feeling like I'd known this lot far longer than the month I had. It was quite another finding a stitch in the frayed bits of my life. As children, we hear the stories our parents tell, and bits of those follow us throughout our lives, weaving them- selves into the fabric of who we are. Warnings pepper fairy- tales, and my father was a storyteller to rival all others.

It wasn't the first time I'd thought my father had a kind of second sight—a sensitivity to things not all of us could see. Could he have foreseen my friendship with Corra and her family? There was never a doubt in my mind that magic existed—from seers to astrophysicists. Science and the idea of magic to me was always a duality. Could Dad have been a seer? If not, then could he have possessed a gift for something more fringe than the anthropologist in him admitted?

A tear slipped out as I considered that. Silas remained inches from my face and traced a terribly gentle thumb across my cheek.

"It's a start," I whispered.

He leaned in and slowly brushed a soft kiss to my cheek, just where his thumb had been. "It is, that." He smiled and stood.

In his goodbye, he told me Corra had asked to meet me tomorrow afternoon to spar. My body thrummed with the excitement of sparring. Perhaps from a bit of the past few moments as well. Interesting.

A WEEK LATER, I found myself sparring in the gardens of the estate. My partners alternated between Corra and

Silas. Clouds had been slowly tumbling in since mid-morning, promising a change from the summer weather of late. I pulled my daggers from the drop holsters on my thighs. Corra looked skyward and sighed.

"I'd spar in the rain, but I do have to get some work done today anyway." We pivoted, addressing one another.

"What exactly do you lot do for work?" I asked her.

She pulled at her bottom lip.

"I manage the family accounts. Not terribly interesting, I'm afraid. Come, let's get in a round before that," she gestured heavenward, "takes over."

Anything regarding money changing hands interested me, but I was trying not to pry.

We sparred for a few minutes before sitting on two garden walls just opposite the front of their family home. I laid back and started leg raises, aiming to keep up my core strength.

"What about Silas and Cade?" I asked.

Having been used to the daily grind of currency trading until I cashed in my assets to come here, I was now curious what these three did that allowed so much flexibility. What I was to do next, career-wise, would take some sorting.

Corra paused her plank press and seemed to consider the question. The feeling that this family had secrets they kept buried wasn't a new one.

"Let me guess," I joked. "Cade is the clandestine diplomat to a rogue foreign nation and Silas is his assassin?"

She stilled, then laughed. "Close, but alas, not quite."

A nearby rumble of thunder shook the stone urns. We both moved to gather our discarded weaponry.

When it seemed Corra wasn't going to elaborate, I asked again. She didn't meet my eyes. "Ask them yourself," she answered with a dismissive shrug.

"I'VE BEEN DECIPHERING this gods-damned book

longer than you've been breathing, Ewan. There is something vital I haven't figured out." Cade's low snarl met us in the foyer as Corra and I walked into the manor house and out of the gathering weather.

"Cadeyrn, we have come to an impasse," the stranger said, his voice an echo of someone I felt I should know. Like searching for a word on the tip of your tongue. "If the book indeed tells us what is needed, it is time to reveal that. The Elders are out of patience and have sent me to shorten your leash." This last bit was said softly, reluctantly, as though the deliverance pained the stranger to speak it.

I stood still, not wanting to disturb the conference, shooting a questioning look to Corra. She shook her head tersely and placed a halting hand on my arm.

There was a thick silence in the adjacent room. The formality of the interaction took me aback. It felt like step-ping into a different time period.

Finally, Cade cleared his throat. "Tell the others, Ewan." The slight echo of a glass touching metal could be heard. "I will gladly partake in any solutions they have to offer. I am at their complete behest. Until there is action to take, I will continue my query with the texts."

"My lord," the stranger—*Ewan*—intoned.

At that, Corra pulled her cool fingers from my forearm and moved to step forward. A lithe, brown-haired man, perhaps in his late twenties, rounded the corner. He stood a good head taller than my five-foot-nine height with broad shoulders. His olive-green eyes met mine briefly then shifted to Corra.

"Corraidhín." He nodded.

She leaned against the wall and smiled slowly. "Ewan." A slow, heavy lidded sweep of her round eyes seemed to give him pause. Ewan flicked a speck of lint from his thin sweater and returned the look. "If you're here, it must be getting tense. I could show you back?"

The strange male smiled a bit hungrily. His eyes had an ethereal glow, causing me to blink a few times. "My lady, I shall have to take you up on that at a later date."

The glass from the sitting room set down again, yet this time with a commanding crash. It didn't take a seer to know a few ounces of Cade's annoyance were in that glass.

"Neysa," Cade called. "You are welcome to come in. Gods know we all need escaping from Corra's innuendos."

I moved into the thick-carpeted, wood-paneled room. A clicking sound behind me told me Ewan had left, and Corra was again at my side. Cade gestured for us to sit. Corra fell heavily onto the chesterfield as I sat on the opposite side. Quiet. The manor house was too quiet.

I felt like an intruder in their family home and started to say so when Cade turned, two generously filled cut crystal glasses held out to us. "Please," he said. "Stay."

He met my eyes, and the worry in his had me accepting the glass.

CHAPTER 3

"So, we're doing this?" Corra asked, crossing her legs and sipping at her wine. Cade looked at me and took a long pull from his own glass, holding my gaze. His stare bored right through me. He nodded.

"Shall I leave?" I offered, shifting from one foot to the other. Corra patted my knee and told me to settle in for a long story. Unease prickled up my spine. Cade lifted an apple-sized sphere from the console table he stood beside and placed it on the tufted ottoman in front of the sofa. With a nonchalant flip of his wrist, as though he were waving off a house fly, the sphere turned from grey stone to smooth, smoky quartz.

I blinked and looked to the man responsible, who seemed to have grown taller. Turning to Corra with a question in my eyes, I saw that she too was leggier than a moment earlier. The most noticeable difference was her facial structure. Her fine- boned cheeks were slightly elongated, and her ears came to a soft point at the tips. Cade's did as well.

When my back pressed into the tufted leather behind me, I realized I had instinctively scooted back.

"The stone put a cloak on us. This is our true appearance. More or less." Cade stood awkwardly if a bit impatient. "As Corraidhín said, we have a tale to tell."

The dream I'd had weeks prior pulled at my awareness. *The cloaking stone the child used, the pointed ears...* I looked to my new friends and searched myself for any ill feelings. I found none and met Cade's imploring gaze.

All the tales my father had told, the stories I remember hearing—they all began prodding me with remembrance. Dad had been dropping hints my whole life. There was magic in that room. In those people.

"Your eyes," I stammered. His head cocked to the side, a bit of shock betrayed on his admittedly beautiful face. His smoky quartz eyes had become a more fluid version of his cousins'.

"Did you— was the spell—," I gestured wildly with my hand, "or whatever you did—was it contained in your eyes? In you? The sphere is the exact color your eyes had been."

He smiled crookedly and almost shyly at my question. I cringed a bit, realizing how it might seem that I knew the exact color of his eyes.

Corra squealed. "Och, I knew she would get it right away!" Corra beamed at me.

Cade acknowledged her with a tight upward tilt of his mouth and handed her a fifty-pound note.

My hands shook with a mix of fright and excitement. As the daughter of an anthropologist who had studied the furthest nuances of society, a yawning awakening gave me butterflies of anticipation. There was one thing I needed clarified.

"Did you know my father? Did you know Elías Obecan? Tell me the truth." I directed the question to Cade. Somehow, I felt like Cade needed to be the one to explain himself to me. Had Silas been there, perhaps I would have challenged him too.

"No," he stated, holding my stare. Beside me, Corra opened her mouth to speak several times but held her tongue. "The name sounds familiar though, I must admit. I could have Ewan look into it."

Ewan. That name again, made me feel...what? I didn't know. Sad. Lonely, maybe. As hungry as his eyes had been looking at Corra, they seemed abandoned and haunted. The way my eyes often looked when I saw them reflected.

I pushed aside the thought of a man I'd likely never see again. We sat for a long, awkward moment, the rain outside and the clink of Cade's glass the only sounds.

"What did I miss?" Silas came bounding into the room, his short dark waves glistening with the afternoon rain. He halted and looked around the room. "Och, thank the gods. Cadeyrn, your eyes were giving me the creeps. Reminded me of that time we tried looking for Magnus's hound in that ruined temple in Aoifsing." He shuddered. "Gods-damned ghosts blinked out all the light. I will never forget that place."

Cade shook his head whether at the memory itself or his cousin, I wasn't sure.

"Hello, Neysa," Silas greeted me with a peck on the cheek. He sat back and raised an eyebrow at his cousin.

"We are, what you might call emissaries, or agents, to use a very Hollywood term, from a realm called Aoifsing," Cade began.

I held up my index finger, and he paused. Pulling my feet under me on the sofa and tucking my thick hair back behind my ears, I leaned forward, addressing him. "So, *realm*," I asked. "As in a parallel dimension kind of thing?"

"Well, yes."

"So, alternate Earth?" I opened my hands in question. He rolled his eyes. Christ, this guy.

"Don't you have a graduate degree?" He asked.

My turn to roll my eyes. "Two. Economics and history. Never mind. So not alternate Earth, but sort of parallel dimension. Fine. Go on." I waved in dismissal and picked up my wine.

"In the universe, there are layers," Cade began again and picked up a cashmere throw from behind the sofa. He saw my eyes mark that the throw he held was in fact mine. "You left it here last night. I digress..." Holding the throw over his bent knee, he began to fold it. "This realm—the one in which Earth exists—is the largest. The subsequent folds are the other realms."

"Parallel universe," I pressed. Part of me really just wanted to get under his skin. It was my childish way of deflecting discomfort. My mind was playing catch-up with all I was being told.

Cade squeezed the bridge of his nose. His cousins chuckled, Silas laying an arm along the back of the sofa. His hand rested behind my shoulder.

"Fine. Yes. Though not a full universe. The universe is one, but the realms are parallel," he clarified. The fire cracked and spat behind him, the glow outlining the lines of his face.

"So what separates the realms that are definitely not a different universe?" I asked, my voice wavering slightly through the attempt at a joke.

Corra sat up and held a finger as if to tell Cade she'd take it from here. "A few centuries ago," she began.

"More than a few, sister," Silas interrupted.

"Yes, yes. Time is irrelevant," she said and flicked her fingers toward him. "There were humans who had more magical abilities. These humans found rifts in the Veils that separate and protect the realms."

"You're saying these magical humans crossed back forth between the realms?" I asked, picking at the skin around my fingernails.

"No, darling." She shook her head. "Humans do not cross into Aoifsing, or the fae realm, easily. They weaken. The fae who were able to pass through to Earth were very few, and those whose magic was not compromised by the crossing were sent to try to eliminate the rifts and recon- struct the Veil." She gestured between herself and her family.

"You don't seem compromised," I pointed out. Their strength and speed told me they weren't weakened at all.

"The only fae who can easily cross," Cade cut in. "Are either those who are of a royal line and those who walk in shadows and mist."

"What do you mean, 'shadows and mist'?" Despite the fire, an iciness hung over the room, needling its way into my veins.

Corra held her elegant fingers out over a wine glass, and I watched as the distinction between woman and wine blurred. The particles of her hand pixelated, a cabernet smudge where once was liquid and hand.

"I am assuming you three are a part of the shadows and mist people?" I asked, a tremor in my question gave away my unease.

"We are all that is left of our family," Silas answered quietly. "Cadeyrn is the head, as he is the eldest. We," he gestured to Corra, "owe him everything. It is his power that keeps our family alive. Because of him, we can still become magic itself in its purest form, absorbing energies to move between realms without disturbing the fabrication of the Veil."

Cadeyrn walked to stare out the darkening window. He clenched and unclenched his fist, making me wonder, yet again, what darkness he'd had to shoulder—the same senti-ment I'd always wondered about my dad.

Silas squeezed my own shoulder, and his eyes reflected an unnecessary apology. I found myself having no acerbic feel-ings for these three in unloading their weighted secret on me. If anything, as my father's daughter, I felt a keen excitement at the possibilities this opened up.

"In our realm, most children are birthed in pairs. Twins," Corra spoke softly, gesturing to herself and Silas. "It is normally one of each sex, keeping the balance in our blood-line. We have longer lifespans than humans, you see, so procreation occurs less often than for humans."

"Makes sense," I cut in. "Most species' reproduction rates directly correlate to their lifespan. Like dogs." I wasn't sure if they could tell, but when I get nervous, I get objective. The more logical I could be about this, the more I was able to make it fit into my comprehension.

"Precisely," Corra continued. "As fae, we normally propa-gate our species once in a lifetime. However, as I said, it is nearly always twins." Corra looked to her cousin, who tucked his chin in a single salutation. "There are exceptions. Cadeyrn was the sole offspring of his parents. His birth was marked as the new era for our family, perhaps for most of Aoifsing. As such, he was named, 'Battle King.' It is such a rare occurrence that throughout our history, each single-born babe has marked the beginning of an era." She looked to her cousin, who was pinching the bridge of his nose. "And most live a life under the threat of violence."

Cade paced, moving in and out of the shadows caused by the rain outside.

"As in," I began. "Their lives are threatened?"

Corra answered though I saw Cade nod once as though he felt my eyes on him. "Cadeyrn's father, our uncle, was killed protecting his family. Our aunt hid in the forest canopy until his third year when they came to live with us in Aemes.

"He was such a wee lad," Silas said, stretching his arms out. "He needed us to help him learn to fight." Cadeyrn sniffed a laugh, still turned toward the window. I could never picture Cadeyrn as anything close to small.

"More like I had to keep you wild lot out of trouble," Cade remarked. I sipped my wine, seeing how the three must have been raised as siblings.

"Not me," Corra piped in. "More like the two of you males." It didn't escape me that she used the word male, rather than men.

"All the males in the surrounding villages were spoiling for a fight against us. Especially knowing their 'Battle King' was being coddled by Corraidhín and me," Silas said with a wink.

"They were sick of seeing both your hands up the skirts or under the shift of their females," Corra pointed out mid recollection. Silas feigned offense while Cade still stared through the now-dark glass into an abyss of his own. "Too many village girls were willing to spread their legs for you two once you batted those eyes at them. Fucked off the males enough to get them to start talking on their travels."

"I just want to point out, sister," Silas interjected. "You have the same eyes to bat and our only folly was getting caught. Plenty of those same women and their men were spreading their legs for you just as often." He sat back with a self-satisfied smirk and Corra blushed, not arguing.

Their sibling banter smoothed some of the edges on this new reality I was wading through. I laughed, thinking what these three would have been like as teenagers in a small town. The near normalcy of being fool hardy teenagers juxtaposed the incredulity of this fae tale.

Shaking my head, I said, "That village didn't stand a chance with any of you. Even in this town, minus the teenage hormones, you three might as well have tracking beacons on the way people's eyes follow you."

Corra giggled and toed my knee.

"You don't see the eyes that follow you, Neysa," Cade remarked faintly from the other side of the room, his face half-turned in our direction, hand shoving into his pocket.

I made a face of dismissal and disbelief, cheeks heating, and he rolled his eyes. Again.

"The first night we met you at the pub, as I wandered off to ponder your hands," Silas said, lifting one of the hands in ques- tion and smoothed a thumb over my almost-torn callus, "men at nearly every table were... *discussing* how to conquer you"

My stomach flipped. Between the contact and situation, waves of disquiet rolled in my gut.

Cade turned back to the window, pressed a hand to the glass, and I saw as the glass disappeared beneath his hand and the rain glided over his fingers. Dismissing that as a parlor trick would be logical. That is, if the shift in the room, the hair raising on my arms, and the fact that something buried deep within the walls of my being hadn't recognized that power.

The feel of Silas's hand pressing my own made me shift in my seat, pulling my feet out from under me. He pulled my feet onto his lap and covered them with the cashmere throw. "Your toes are like ice," he commented needlessly.

Cade whistled, and his hounds came bounding in waiting for instruction. He pointed to me and snapped his fingers. Silas pushed to Corra's side of the sofa, and I suddenly had two furry blankets warming my toes. Cuthbert had a stream of dribble perpetually dripping from his whiskered squish, while Bixby was always content to simply press his black and white head against me.

"May I get on with the story so Neysa can decide if she wants to kill us or not?" Silas asked pointedly.

"I don't want to kill you. Yet," I said, stroking Bixby's ears to quiet my shaking hands. "But I would like to know why I am being trusted with all of this information."

They looked to one another. "Getting to that, darling," Corra said, reaching across slobbery Cuthbert to pat my knee.

"Once all of Aoifsing had heard of Cadeyrn's oh so special skill with the sword," Silas continued in a teasing tone. "Saskeia, the queen of Aoifsing, summoned us. We were invited to her summer home to discuss the possibility of a union between the family of mists and shadows, and her own trusted courtiers, some claiming a distant relation to the queen's family..."

Cadeyrn left the room, leaving the rest of the story to his cousins. I watched him go, thinking I understood how he might not want to hear his own story being told.

CHAPTER 4

SILAS

Honestly, I'd wanted to tell Neysa from the get-go that we were more than we seemed. We three recognized something in her and it seemed like a fat waste of time to dance around the important issue for over a month. She was listening to us like we were in a lecture hall. Not that I have ever really been in a lecture hall, you get. But I had watched telly enough to recognize the studious look.

"On the last day of the three-day ride to the Queen's Isle, the forest behind us stilled and the sea to our right seemed to hold its breath," my sister told her, pausing for dramatic effect. I snorted. "We took pause and assessed the change. A howling in the wind was the last warning as both of our parents were pulled from their horses and dragged into the wood by unseen assailants. We hadn't sensed them—they used a type of magic that breaks apart your particles. Silas and Cadeyrn tore after them, following their scents."

She stopped speaking for a moment and stared into the fireplace. I laid a hand on my sister's shoulder and continued for her. "Flickers of magic were all I could feel drawing me to our parents. Cadeyrn and I ran deeper into the woods, trying to keep after them. We were losing their scent, aye?"

I figured it was too much to explain particle transference to her then so I paused, raising an eyebrow at Neysa to make sure she was following the story. Her wineglass pressed to her lips as she nodded, olive eyes wide.

"Cadeyrn was hollering at me to use my shield—my magic shield, but I was trying to track them. I refused to give up, even though I'd lost the trail."

"Stubborn arse," my sister teased.

"I argued that I couldn't shield and track their magic at the same time, but of course, Cadeyrn appealed to my ego and said my shield was stronger than his. That he could take over track- ing. He knew when something needed healing, and he was aiming for that."

"What does that mean?" Neysa asked in a husky sort of voice that undid me a bit.

"Cadeyrn," I said. "Can track that which needs healing. Our parents..."

I drank from my own glass, breaking from the story. I realized then that we had never told this to anyone. It had been so long, yet both my sister and I were getting a bit mind fucked rehashing this part of our past.

"I used aulde magic," I began and Neysa stopped me to ask what that meant. "Magics from a time before fae powers began dwindling. The kind of powers which are now rare in our realm."

"But you three have this... aulde power?" Neysa asked. Her fingers twitched like she was itching to grab a pen and write this down.

"Aulde magic. Yes," I answered, stilling her fingers with my own. My sister gave me a low growl of warning as if to tell me to remove my fucking hands from Neysa. By the gods, she is a mother hen.

"I used the magic to conceal us both, while Cadeyrn ran ahead. I took off at a clip after my cousin and I arrived in a clearing. Fuck, I can still smell the blood in the air. Their bodies—my da and mam—were laying in this tall grass. I stood there like a fucking tosser, staring at them until I heard a clash of swords," I continued.

Neysa set her glass down, looking a bit peaky, then immediately picked it back up, pressing it to her lips without drinking.

"There were four males," I said, holding up my fingers. "Trying to dispatch my cousin, as they had my parents. We combined powers--"

"I'm sorry," Neysa said. "I'm trying to follow, but how do you combine powers?"

I thought about how the three of us can harness each other's gifts. Latch onto them.

"Corraidhín and I can manipulate humidity. We become the moisture in the air, aye?" I looked to see if that made sense to her. I was not a bloody lecturer and I wished Cadeyrn hadn't fucked off, so he could help explain this all. "It was like I let my power slither into my cousin. We created spears of darkness, mist, and electricity. With our rage, you get?" I asked her.

She narrowed her eyes and nodded; the wine glass still flattened to her mouth.

"Those spears punctured the chests of the last assailant. It tore his fucking heart from his chest and left but a husk in our wake." Neysa's mouth was now open, still against the glass, which might have made me laugh, had I not felt sick from the memory. The memory of running back to my sister and aunt.

"Corraidhín had become the sea mist and dew," I explained. "She swelled like a wave and drowned another two assassins, their bodies slumped near the broken body of my aunt."

Her fingers were white, squeezing the stem of her goblet. My sister's were much the same. Even after all these fucking years.

"All three of you lost your parents in the same moment?" Neysa asked, voice barely louder than the rain outside. "I don't...I'm so sorry. I don't know how to process this," she said.

My sister and I both reached over and touched her shoulder which, honestly, was really weird.

"The servants were huddled, shaking and useless near the wagon," I told her, wanting to get this bit over with. "I didn't expect otherwise. They weren't the warriors. We were. And we had fucking failed." I scrubbed a hand over my face. "That's when Cadeyrn stumbled from the thicket of trees, sword arm dragging as he moved toward his mam's body. I'd never seen my cousin look that enraged."

"Well," Corraidhín interjected. "It wasn't all rage. He dropped to his knees before his mam and we saw the injury he had taken." She swallowed a great gulp of wine before telling of the scythe-like hook embedded in Cadeyrn's back. "The flayed open skin and muscle was a mortal injury that nearly took his immortal—"

"Fae are immortal?" Neysa asked.

My sister and I looked to each other. "Nearly. We live indefinite life spans and are hard to kill. But not impossible," I said with a wink. She was pushing at her chest like it ached, and my sister's head tilted to the side which worried me. I jumped back in saying we took Cadeyrn to the Queen's Isle to try to heal him.

"How did you do that?" Neysa asked, eyes bright.

"I rode faster than fucking moonrise and arrived at the

barge to cross the gulf, screaming for asylum and healers, and fuck knows what else. I was in a right state," I admitted.

"Cadeyrn was kept unconscious for an entire lunar cycle to speed the healing process," Corraidhín said. "Once awake, the queen herself wrote to us saying he seemed to have receded into a place no one could reach. He had given up." I knew Cadeyrn could hear what we were saying, so it felt right bloody strange to be talking about him, but it had been a couple of centuries.

"Oh, Neysa," Corra reminisced. "You should have seen it. The balcony of his room jutted out from the cliffs upon which this small palace was built. The sun played note strings along the wall and shone on creeping vines that seemed to stitch the building together. It was enchanting." My sister was lost in the memory like it was a fucking fairytale. I snorted at her.

"As lovely as it all was," she continued, her lips pursed. "My cousin, the one who was born to be Battle King, dreamt of slipping into those waters and never resurfacing. He confessed this to me before sending me away." Corraidhín pinched her nose, a gesture like our cousin.

Neysa again rubbed at her chest like there was a physical ache in it.

"I feel like..." Neysa said, her hand clutched in the folds of her jumper. "None of you would fare very well if one of you —" I understood what she meant and confirmed it with a nod.

"Yet another reason I wished he had never married that toe rag of a female," I muttered.

My sister snickered, but her face looked as haunted I felt. Neysa's eyebrows shot together.

"Toward the end of his stay on Eíleín Reínhe—the Queen's Isle," Corraidhín explained, continuing the story. "Queen Saskeia sent the daughter of her courtier, and distant relative, Solange." It always made me laugh how my sister's lip curled when she said that name.

Neysa was leaning forward, Cuthbert taking the movement to mean it was time for a wet kiss.

"My cousin wrote to me saying he wasn't surprised at the intention behind the girl's presence, but he was not one to be easily amused nor swayed. He had 'chosen his poor disposition and had no intention of altering it,'" Corraidhín said, with air quotes.

Cadeyrn had penned to us that the girl read to him, brought his meals, and always snuck him extra wine. His letters made it obvious he had become more interested in the girl.

"Bait and fucking snare," I muttered. My sister agreed. Neysa looked a bit green listening and I wondered if she'd had too much wine.

"He started writing to me, telling me stories she told him. Like when the servants on her estate were given the day off and she and her brother had to chase the livestock back into the pens. She feigned offense when he barked laughter at her memory of chasing flapping chickens into the hen house and falling into a trough full of freshly laid eggs, breaking them all. It seemed like a load of horseshite to me. I'd heard of Solange, and none of it was positive," Corraidhín sneered. "Oh! There was a drunken letter he wrote talking about the summer equinox, and their engagement."

"Please don't bore Neysa with this part of the story, sister," I groaned.

"*Pshaw*. She needs to understand how he was ensnared."

I put my head in my hands and said under my breath that he was ensnared like every other injured soldier since the dawn of time. Neysa looked a bit murderous, which was almost as concerning as her colour.

"Cadeyrn's back had healed mostly," Corraidhín jumped

back in. "The healers told him he was ready to train. Ready to live again. Solange told him they were to be wed before he was to leave. Silas and I knew it was going to happen. The very purpose of that trip was to forge their match. I mean, don't get me wrong, Solange was stunning," she said and was not wrong. "Her sun-bronzed skin and cascading ringlets of blonde hair caught eyes all over Aoifsing. I just always thought she was more of a one night than a forever-and-always."

I chuckled at that. My sister and I were both more one nights than forever-and-always ourselves.

"We never should have gone," I said.

"You never know what game fate plays, darling," Corra said to me.

"Aye, but in this case, fate was a bucket of shite."

CHAPTER 5
CORRAIDHÍN

I figured it was as good a time as any to take up the mantel and finish this story for poor Neysa. She sat there looking like a deer in headlights. (Is that the phrase human use?) It was quite a bit for her to take in, but really, she was a clever girl.

Plus, I, for one, was done with pretending we're all human.

"So, is Cade still married?" Neysa asked in a pinched voice that almost made me smile.

My brother snorted like a pig.

"Gods, no," I answered. "They were incompatible as soon as they came back to the estate. They argued incessantly. There was something off about that one," I told her. "Like she was always watching and waiting."

"Made my skin crawl, she did," Silas said. "Acted like a bloody princess. Aemes—our village—wasn't up to her standards. I couldn't hack it. Servants couldn't even hack it. Most of them left."

Neysa's eyebrows shot up.

I did wonder if she enjoyed the hounds dribbling all

over her trousers, or if the poor cow was so put off by our family history, she didn't even notice. I wiped my own hands in sympathy. My cousin had stayed out of the room for far too long, and really, it was his idea to tell Neysa today, so I was a bit irritated that he had left simply because he was uncomfortable hearing about his banshee of a wife.

"If she and Cade aren't married still, then where is she?" Neysa asked, twirling Bixby's long black ear. A pop of wood in the fireplace made her jump.

"Mind you," I told her. "This was about—what, Silas? One hundred fifty years ago?"

My brother tipped his head as if to say, more or less. "We were training youth in the village. Combat, defense, the like," Silas nudged in. "I was totally knackered every evening, so I wasn't around for much of the shite Solange put everyone through. I could see, clear as fucking day, though, that thrice, when my cousin became ill, it was no ordinary ague."

"This...Solange made him ill?" Neysa asked, her lovely features contorting to a feral sort of rage that made me pause.

I glanced at my brother, but he was watching the way Neysa's fingers wound over and under the hound's ear. He seemed to stare at a smattering of freckles on her hand. I recognized those. Oh, I must mention something to Cadeyrn. *If he would ever bloody return.*

"We could never find anything incriminating against her," I said, still looking at her hand. She seemed to notice and tucked her fingers under her on the settee. "Until, of course, there was."

"Okay, that's vague and ominous, and frankly," Neysa cut in, taking a healthy sip of wine. "I'm tired and really want to get on with this. No offense."

"*Meow*, darling," I said with a grin. She smiled back

though I could tell she tried not to. See? It was as if I'd known her my whole life.

"By the gods and shite, Corraidhín," Silas said. "We are all tired. Corraidhín woke up sensing the magic that bonds us--"

"You can sense each other?"

"We can," I answered, glaring at my brother. "Our abilities are linked and Cadeyrn's power binds us all. That morning it was as if a hair were being pulled from my head. An uncomfortable pluck that kept on."

"Death by paper cut?" Neysa asked, a small smile playing at her mouth.

"Oh! Precisely, I do hate those," I said. "My brother felt it too and we stood outside in the freezing bloody cold dawn, looking up toward Cadeyrn's rooms." I shivered remembering that, and pat the knife clipped on my boot, just to feel its security. The horror I felt in the moment we turned to mist and reestablished ourselves in Cadeyrn's bedroom.

"I saw Cadeyrn's eyes spring open, a blade at his throat, his wife above him chanting in the aulde language," I recounted. Whatever was in my face made Neysa pull back, pressing into the settee. There was still untapped wrath in me for what was done to my cousin, and maybe Neysa should see that.

"He was savage," Silas added. "Finally knocked her from the bed while Solange was still incanting words to harm him. Fucking creepy."

"My cousin couldn't bring himself to hurt her," Corra said low and dark. "I had no such qualms. Solange intended to control my cousin. Leave him without freedom of choice. A *puppet*. And that was unacceptable. So I followed her to the edge of the sea and slit her pearly throat."

I did not ask if Neysa was okay with this. I would not apologize or make excuses. She looked me dead on and nodded her acceptance.

"Too right, darling," I said.

"Did the queen have anything to do with this? Since she set them up?" Neysa asked, voice shaky.

"We didn't truly know," I said. "So, we tightened our borders for a few decades."

"Decades?" Neysa asked, nearly spiting her wine.

"Mm. Yes, darling. It was then the Elders called upon us to help secure the Veil."

I did wonder if we had traumatized poor Neysa. She looked like there were live wires going through her. I suppose we had to wait and see.

CHAPTER 6

Perhaps the most shocking thing to me as the story concluded was that I was not at all surprised to hear any of this.

Having lived most of my adult life in southern California, there wasn't much room for thoughts of alternate realms and magic. There were stocks and currencies, bills and healthcare reform. I tried to picture Caleb here now. Tried and failed. His West Coast, laid-back attitude would have betrayed his shallowness like a searchlight beacon.

Dad, on the other hand, would have had a million questions and would book office hours to discuss how their tale coincided with that of his folklore texts. He could slip in and out of languages, cultures, and mannerisms like a change of a scarf. He knew the histories of talismans from remote cultures and tribes. Growing up with my father looking for such talismans, we were an oasis for the possibility of magic. He focused his career on the link between science and magic. History and lore. In his storage units on the outskirts of both London and Los Angeles were religious icons, shamanic amulets, and archaic texts in languages I'd never heard of, but somehow, *he* was able to read. Sitting outside his study when I was little, I would hold my blanket and listen to his sing song voice as he read old texts in languages almost beyond the human tongue.

"NEYSSIE?" he called. I poked my twelve-year-old head around the doorway. We had been packing our home in England, readying to move to California. *"What are you doing out there?"*

I remember not knowing whether to answer honestly—that I'd been there since he walked in after dinner or that I'd just arrived. *"What were you reading?"* I asked him instead. *"And what was that white light that glowed from your desk?"*

His face went from its normal golden brown to a reddish flush I so rarely saw on him. *"If I tell you,"* he asked. *"Will you promise to go to bed, little moon?"*

I stood up and nodded empathically as only a twelve-year-old could.

"I was making magic," he said with a twinkle in his eyes. I rolled mine. *"The text I was reading is from a faraway realm. It is a story about a family of deer in a forest of crystals."*

"How do you know how to read the language?" I asked him.

"Magic," he answered, which sent a rush of preteen anger through me. I stormed off to bed, annoyed that he thought me so young he could make up fairytales.

SO, in that manor, with those fae people, I could reconcile the tug of disbelief with the knowledge that my father somehow belonged in their world—or at least knew of it. The others subtly looked to me to gauge my reaction. Pins and needles were biting at my feet, so I pulled them out from under Bixby and Cuthbert. A soft sound of protest came from one of them.

"Yes, I'm sorry, lovey, but I can't feel my feet anymore. Thank you for keeping them warm," I said, scratching at the ears closest to me. This must have been enough, as the large furry heads sat down once more.

Cadeyrn came back in and took his place by the window. A low ticking came from the corner—a clock or radiator. What was I supposed to say? 'I'm sorry your entire family was slaughtered and your wife was a conniving whore'?

Something suddenly hit me, the important item locking in place. "Why tell me?" A sloshing started in my gut. "You barely know me."

I looked at each of the three in turn, settling my gaze on Cade who looked about ready to jump through the window. Too much information was divulged about him, I realized.

"Because," Cade said simply. "You are one of us, and we believe you play an important role in this narrative." His back stayed turned, and Corra and Silas took a collective sharp inhale.

I nearly dropped my glass. "Pardon?"

"What he meant to say in his *delicate, sensitive way*," Silas explained with a glare at his cousin, "is that we sensed you are part fae. At least half, based on your scent." He reached across the mound of fur and covered my free hand with his.

"I thought it prudent to get to the point, cousin." Cade turned and glared right back.

"What exactly is that point, *sir*?" I beseeched him mockingly.

The air in the room became heavier. The welcome warmth from the dogs was suffocating. I stood and poured myself more wine then passed the bottle as if it were a frat party and not a seventeenth century manor house. Their eyes followed me.

"Time is running out to repair the rift in the Veil. We are the last in our line, and your name implies you are pure and good." I snorted but Cade continued. "Your scent..." Honestly, I couldn't decide if the scent bit creeped me out or not. "You have strong fae heritage. I—we—believe you have a well of untapped gifts at your disposal."

"At my disposal or at yours, *friend?*" I asked tartly.

He cocked his head in understanding. "At yours. Of course. My thought is that if practiced, those gifts may give us all a chance to help me heal our realms."

"Do you know if the rift has affected other realms or only that of Aoifsing and Earth?" I hated the sound of saying Earth as a realm. It seemed so sci-fi, but my mind was reaching for an anchor point to reality.

"We can't know," Corra answered for him. "We know of other realms. Yet historically, there has not been access to anywhere else. Where there is a Veil here, there is more of a barrier to other realms. Nothing can pass. The hope is that because of that barrier, any repercussions here or in our realm won't cross."

"What repercussions?" I asked. Mentally, I was moving past the shock and awe of being fae, my logical brain constructing a flow chart of objectives to cross off.

"Piercing the Veil has led to widespread illness here, less children born in our realm. Catastrophic events on both sides," Cadeyrn answered. "We would like to ascertain your gifts, Neysa." He looked at me then, a softening in his features took me aback. "Perhaps hone your skills to use your gifts. If you are willing."

I stared at the ancient blades over the fireplace. The same I had used that day on the beach a month or so ago. A month, yet it seemed an eternity. Every blade my dad trained me on, every hour spent knowing not only how to fight, but to use my intelligence to outsmart the enemy, made more and more sense.

"As far as we know," Cade interrupted my thoughts. I kept my eyes on the swords. "Only our family and those of the queen's bloodline, can pass through. Granted, there are thousands of years of procreation to sort through and there are bound to be illegitimate children here and there, but to be able to ascertain who of those offspring can pass the Veil, seems a small chance." Cade circled the room.

"Who are the Elders?" I asked.

"A group of eight fae who have taken a vow to protect the realm. They have done so for the past eight hundred years and before them, their parents held the position."

"Hereditary monarchy?" I asked.

"More like the convenience of nepotism," he said with a hint of humour I hadn't seen before. "There are five males and three females. Each Elder represents the physical and cultural characteristics of the eight cultural regions of Aoifsing," he answered in more detail than I had expected.

"And who is Ewan?" I asked.

Three pairs of eyes darted to one another. "He is a bastard born of some royal bloodline. He had been left in the temple of the Elders as a youth. There was no sibling, so it is assumed she died. He has been in the debt of the Elders since childhood. They keep him close and hidden from outside eyes so that a lineage claim cannot be made on him and used to surpass the Veil."

The disgust on my face must have shown. Silas snorted.

"I don't even know where to start on that. First of all, to say an orphaned child is indebted to a crusty group of hermits is vile. Second of all, how do you know he wasn't sole born like Cade?" I kept ticking things off on my fingers. "Third, to now keep this orphaned child hidden is criminal. He is being held hostage for political advantage. *Christ*, am I really the only one in this room who thinks the whole thing is abominable?"

I felt close to foaming at the mouth. In the six years I had been married to Caleb, we had tried to have a child. It never worked out and I now see it as a blessing, but the empathy for the abandoned child was soul-souring.

"It is regrettable the way in which he was—*is*—treated. We did not know about Ewan until roughly thirty years ago when the Elders called and placed us here. If it makes you feel any better, Cadeyrn throttled Feynser, one of the representatives, for his less-than-favourable attitude toward Ewan," Corra confided.

I looked to Cade and couldn't picture him stepping out of line. He always seemed like his shirt still had its hanger on.

"He had always been a piece of shit. I had been looking for a reason to hit him for a hundred years. This just tipped the scale." Interesting. Maybe he was less of a boy scout than I had thought.

"And you, Corra?" I pressed. "You and he seemed to...get along."

The males snickered. Corra raised her slightly pointed chin. "I get along with many folk. Ewan particularly pleases me."

"That's because you can't have him," her brother teased. Silas jabbed her in the ribs. "Would you still want him as much if he were released from his servitude? In three hundred years, you haven't been able to stick to just one partner."

Her cheeks brightened, though I barely noticed while I was digesting the fact that they had been alive for three hundred years. I must seem like an infant to them. *Three. Hundred. Years.* World wars, the Industrial Revolution, the bloody Irish potato famine, the sinking of the *Lusitania* and the *Titanic*, the invention of the flushing toilet. This lot had lived through all of it. Though mostly in another realm. A realm which somehow my dad—the only one in the world who I trusted—knew about.

Corra's wind chime voice rang through my reverie. "I get

bored having just one partner. Besides, I would rather have one of each," she laughed. "I would also like to point out, brother, that I do not see a marriage token on your hand either. It seems we both prefer to roam free."

Silas looked slightly uncomfortable and Corra slightly mollified. Cade just looked bored.

"Are they always like this?" I asked of Cade. He half closed his eyes and nodded his head.

"Okay," I began. There was enough wine in me to make this seem like a good idea. If nothing else, I would be paying a sort of closing respect to my dad. "I will help. I really don't think I have any gift, and I can't see how you think I am part fae. I look at you three..." I waved my hand in a broad sweep inclu- sive of all of them. "And I see grace and beauty and strength. I see myself and—"

"Please don't finish that," Silas said shortly. "How you see yourself has been shaped and manufactured by society in this shithole realm."

"Not to mention, living your entire life ignorant of who and what you are," Cade added. "Did you ever wonder why you seemed to stop aging about five years ago? As fae, we reach full maturity just after what humans call the frontal lobe is fully developed. So, between twenty-seven and thirty years of age."

Here I'd thought I just took better care of myself than others my age. It was easy to brush off, trying to keep my cool with these three. However, hearing that I am fae—that I am a part of the utterly ridiculous, fantastical world they described- -made my head swim. Every instance of not fitting in, of being faster and stronger than most people around me, of not being able to truly connect to others, began to make sense. *Inhuman.* Like bricks filling a wall, these bits of myself that I'd accepted as being outlandish and wrong, mortared together to show me that maybe Dad was right. Maybe I was where I was always supposed to be.

"Regardless of what these two said, which is all true," Corra continued. "You are a beautiful female. You do not see yourself as we see you, but I sense your power and see your beauty. Trust me. Takes one to know one." She winked. "Plus, every time your back is turned, I have to wipe Silas's mouth."

There was an uncomfortable silence. I wasn't one to relish in attention, so I was eager to move on. "Tell me what I need to do."

CHAPTER 7

Thousands of years ago, the world in this realm was what we now refer to as pagan. The Veil between realms was but a blur of magic. Different tribes and gatherings had individual beliefs and rituals. Most of these were determined more by the location in which the tribe dwelled. There was a profound respect and fear of the elements. Worship came about as reverence for the bounty received from nature and a fear of an element of nature itself reclaiming its due. People paid respect to the dead for a life well-lived and as petition to those departed to not come back and wander as a spirit.

As societies developed, people began to eulogize deities. Rather than beseech the element of water for safe passage and good fishing, for instance, people began to turn to personifications of elements such as a God of the Sea, rather than the element itself. This started a pivot in the ideologies of the humans. Once that pivot occurred, ideologies and the simple concept of latching onto a doctrine were on a forward track with no end.

At first, there were the ancient Old Gods, most of whom came to this realm from Aoifsing. Not long after, came the adoption of religion. The Greeks, the Romans, tribes in the southern hemisphere, and *many others isolated their beliefs into a system that, while strikingly similar to one another, circumscribed lines to differentiate cultures that were dogmatically drawn. As religions bloomed and people assumed roles in major denominations—Christianity, Judaism, Islam—there became such profound rejection of intrinsic magics that the Veil thickened to protect each realm from the other. The lack of magic and lack of reverence for nature became a blight on the universe. The only way the universe saw fit to protect the other realms was to fortify barriers.*

Sometime in the second century, delegates from both realms decided on a plan to keep a balance of elements here on Earth in order to strengthen the Veil and protect both realms. Crystals were placed in four locations on Earth that harbored special concordance with the elements and linked to humanity and magic alike. Each placement of a crystal embodied a particular affinity for the type of power needed: affinities such as protection, energy conductivity, heal– ing, and releasing of negativity. The placement and type of crystal used was never divulged. The information died with those who forged the solu- tion, leaving the realms to go about on their own. For millennia, the system worked. The Veil strengthened and the realms stabilized.

Five hundred or so years ago, there were people of this realm who began to open up to magic again. Some feared it and began to persecute others. Some revered it. Those with their own accommodation for magic were able to cross through the Veil. Therein the problems began. The realms were too different now. They came back ill in both body and mind. Fae who crossed had weakened magic. Some became so weak that they were unable to cross back over and died of wasting illness in this realm. The strength of the crystals was not holding up. A century ago, it was decided by the Elders that the Veil needed to be guarded and a solution exacted.

Emissaries from Aoifsing, the children of mist and shadow who could become the elements themselves, were sent to guard and fortify this realm. They were tasked to locate, cleanse, and strengthen each crystal and bring them to a centralized epicenter close to the main Veil and refashion the rift between worlds. Thirty years ago, one of the crystals was stolen and the balance of energy plunged from bad to worse. Disease, disaster, and indifference to love has become a blight on mankind. Perhaps reshaping the balance will right the course of humans. Perhaps it will merely steady the fallout of a broken world. For the sake of every realm, the province of these emissaries is imperative.

CHAPTER 8

Reading and listening to the history did not discourage my feeling of inadequacy to face this issue. None of us really knew how to determine what my power might be—or if I had any to begin with. In the week since I learned the truth about this curious trio, I tried to connect to various elements, energies, and finally, the crystals themselves. The hope was that I could channel and strengthen any power through a conduit.

"Why do we need the crystals anyway?" I asked, sitting in the dining room of my cottage a week later.

"They stabilize the Veil. Physics, quantum or otherwise, like magic in Aoifsing, doesn't cross well. When the Veil is destabilized and folk pass through, it weakens it further. There's no telling what would happen if it collapsed completely," Corra said.

"I meant *me*," I said. "Why do I need to use crystals?" I knew I sounded like a child protesting taking out the rubbish bins.

"Och," she said with an exasperated tsk. "You need to tap into what gifts you might have. Your dad had a sort of white light?" She asked. "Maybe focus on that for yourself. Gifts often run in families."

Corra brought me onyx, jade, agate, even limestone. Lime– stone, she explained, had quartz within it and often enhanced quartz reactions due to the sediment and fossilized marine life. It could be a relative time capsule and harness the memories, so to speak, of the composite stone. During everyday events such as a storm, a full moon, an emotionally charged argument, the quartz cannot retain all its recordings, and it replays what is trapped inside. Therefore, people tend to consider the building haunted.

"The limestone absorbs past energies, and the quartz records it," she concluded as she placed the chunk of lime-stone on my dining table.

I focused and even went so far as to sing lullabies I'd been sung as a child, trying to connect my child self with the stone.

It was worse than watching currencies during a global crisis. At least money went up or down. This blasted stone just sat, making me feel like a fool. The lack of change made me tear at my hair. After hour upon hour of sweating in attempt to pull, push, release, or even destroy, I was left with nothing.

Corra sighed, picking at her nails. "When was the last time you had a good seeing to?" she asked.

"A *what now*?"

"A good..." she waggled her full eyebrows.

Oh. That.

"The last time or the last time it was good?" The last time

was at least six months ago. *The last time it was good...* "Three years ago," I admitted.

She whooshed a breath and slammed her empty teacup

down. "You probably have more pent-up energy than all these bloody crystals combined."

That was likely. I pushed the rock away in disgust. "Let's go hit things with pointy objects," I said, jumping up.

"I think you need a pointy object of another sort to help you out," she giggled.

OUT IN THE clearing we used as a sparring ring, Corra and I practiced with our twin swords. My footing needed a lot of work. For a fight with a fae opponent I needed to be much quicker on my feet. I made a note to add agility drills to my cross-training sessions. Shadows moved across the clearing.

"Here come the cavalry," Corra droned. She winked at me and motioned with her eyes dramatically then tapped her swords and jerked her chin.

Blinking once, I got ready for her mark.

"Now," she whispered, and we took off toward the two males.

Silas was in line with me, and I went for him. Only the briefest look of confusion showed on their faces before they braced for the onslaught. Corra hopped in a move that looked closer to flight, and I dropped down, sliding into Silas and pulling him down by his shins.

"Sh-Fu-Oooph," he mouthed, hitting the ground.

"Pestilent children." I heard Cade say as he caught his cousin's landing.

Silas grappled for my weapon, and I pushed him down, one knee at his throat. He yielded with a laugh and put his hands on my hips, lifting me off him. I looked to Corra, who had not fared as well with Cade sitting on the backs of her legs, her arms held behind her. He was so calm he looked like he could be reading a magazine. I wondered for a brief moment, what it would feel like to have his knees pinning me. *Shut it down, Neysa.*

"Well, hello ladies. An invitation would have been nice. Cadeyrn, I don't think my sister will be any more trouble just yet." That sister muttered under her breath.

"She's always trouble, cousin. Isn't that why we love her?" Cade responded, lightheartedly.

"Next time, Neysa, you take this one," she said, jerking her thumb at Cade. Cade turned to me and bowed in invitation.

Not just yet, I think.

"And what, may I ask, was the purpose of this unsanctioned attack?" Cade asked.

"Neysa needed to release some pent-up tension, and she's not into females," Corra answered.

I choked and spluttered. Silas roared with laughter.

"Yes, well, you have me all hot and bothered, Corra, so I shall go home and take a cold shower. Good day, gentlemen," I said, making to leave.

"Need a hand?" Silas called. A sound of a thud and a loud "oomph" came, and I was laughing most of the way back.

FOCUS.

For the third time today I sat, trying to focus my energy on

the crystal in front of me. All of the suggestions I had been given to clear my mind, from sparring to running to eating to bathing, none seemed to help.

The garden door clicked open and Silas walked in, bringing with him a breath of night-kissed, early autumn air. "Any luck?" He set down another stack of books.

I groaned and adjusted the tie of my pewter-colored silk dressing gown. Twenty minutes earlier I had gotten out of the bath, hopeful and eager to try focusing my energy again. My skin had just started cooling off, and my light dressing gown was not quite enough to warm me. Keeping my knees tucked under, I still sat on the floor, fingertips making contact with the crystal. Corra had thought that this bright crystal might be more receptive to my energy than the more opaque ones we had tried in the past few days. It warmed to my touch but nothing else. I whimpered in frustration.

"What if...Let's try combining energy. To start," Silas suggested, placing his hands over my own on the crystal. His thumb was hooked under mine and began to stroke the soft pad of my hand. Warmth bloomed in my core, circling lower. The crystal glowed faintly. Our eyes met, and God help me, I smirked, noticing his nostrils flare. He shifted closer, knees now touching mine. His free hand laid on my knee.

"Perhaps," he began a bit huskily. "All points of contact are key?" His hand swept over my knee and along my exposed calf, then retreated back up across the back of my knee. The fluo– rite had been an ombre of turquoise, cerulean, and purple. It was now glowing, sending its own aura outward. The light glowing around us and his woodsmoke scent filled the room, like a cocoon around us.

Marveling at the ethereal glow, we grinned at one another. "Perhaps it needs you to give it your essence before it can release its own," Silas whispered.

"So," I breathed back. "I haven't let go of my own energy enough?" He nodded.

Silas's fingers squeezed mine as his other hand moved ever so slowly up my thigh, making the silk of my dressing gown bunch. My breathing became a bit ragged, and I noticed his eyes smolder. His hand moved inward; a single finger traced a line toward my apex then came up to my hip bone. I was utterly aching in my groin. That single finger moved up then undid the tie on my robe. The chemise I wore under was the same gunmetal silk with thin straps, one of which had tipped over my shoulder. He traced his finger up my side then across my ribs, under my breast. I felt them swell in answer. He brought the flat of his thumb across my nipple, making us both shudder at the feeling of that thin layer of silk between us.

"Easy now," he huffed.

I had been squeezing his hand and the crystal, so I brought my free hand to his leg wanting to feel more of him. His own cupped my breast and again stroked my nipple through my chemise. He edged closer. The crystal between us began swirling light around it, small sparks of light popping from the chiseled sides. The fae male before me brought his arm around my back and traced my spine down to my backside then circled back to the front. He stilled momentarily as his eyes found mine. I bit my lip, eyes heavy. He growled so low, the bass of it made my blood heat further. His thumb pressed down on the spot where my flesh parted while his other finger dragged upward. I gasped, squeezing his thigh, high enough that I felt the answering throb from him.

The light emitting from the fluorite pulsed. Christ. I wanted all of him. In. Me. Now. I splayed my hand over his inner thigh, hip crease and center, his readiness filling my hand through the too-thick material of his black trousers. Seemingly in tune with our own blood pounding, the crystal kept pulsating. Silas leaned into me and breathed deeply. His mouth moved over my neck and stayed itself over my jaw, those fingers playing at me still. A blinding need had my core pounding as his mouth inched closer to mine, then his fingers plunged into me. I groaned as he crushed his mouth to mine. The crystal evaporated between us. All that remained was a glowing aura. Suddenly, his body was on mine.

He pulled my chemise over my head and immediately fastened his mouth over my breast. I yanked at his trousers, pushing them down, then ripped his shirt off. His tongue flicked my nipple and sucked at it, making my breast harden. His fingers played again as I started to shake from desire. Another inhuman growl reverberated in my gut making me bridge my hips up into him. His finger pulled away as he sat back, and I stared at the length of him then looked up into those sea glass eyes.

Locking on his stare, I skimmed my palm down his smooth, taut stomach and stopped just short of his manhood. My finger dragged a slow trail down his length, an echo of how he'd touched me. I cocked an eyebrow at him and, in a move faster than anything I had seen, he was thrusting inside me. I pulled his face to mine, tasting his woodsmoke skin. I broke and moaned as pleasure overcame us both. His hardline body fell against mine as he gasped for air. Nothing stirred in the air around us. The energy that destroyed the crystal had gone, leaving us dazed, and me a bit out of sorts.

ABOUT THAT PENT-UP TENSION... I lay on my back on the living room floor. Silas was on his side, looking at me. He reached over and pushed my hair behind my ear.

"It's okay, you know," he spoke softly. "You needed this as much as I wanted it." Oh, I'd wanted it too.

"This could potentially be an issue, huh?" I turned to him, utterly unfazed by our naked bodies. He ran a hand along my side and hip. "With the others?" I clarified.

He didn't answer but kept a soft trail along my skin. I placed my finger under his strong chin and lifted his face to look at me.

"I know I'm not the one for you, Neysa. This made me... quite happy. But I am aware that I am not who you need." I wasn't sure I was breathing. I touched his cheek. My friend. "I am happy to have been what you needed tonight. Even if it was just once."

I kissed him chastely—or it would have been, had we not been naked— and put my arms around him in a hug. I had needed him. This.

CHAPTER 9

Autumn arrived seemingly overnight. The tiny buttons of wildflowers, which had covered the ground a couple of weeks ago, were replaced with grass that was turned at the tips like burnt toast. Through the canopy, garnet and topaz leaves were showing up at the top of the ancient trees. I wondered if Cade knew what each type of tree in this wood was. It seemed like something he would know and roll his eyes about my not knowing. Some I recognized: birch, sycamore. Others had leaves that looked like oak but having lived in the Silver Lake district in Los Angeles most of my adult life, my education on plants extended only so far as what to not touch while hiking Runyon Canyon.

Early mornings had always been my favorite time to be outside. Whether I was running or simply having a cup of tea, the watery light and, if I were honest with myself, maybe the chance at a new start, was always invigorating. In this place, so ripe with magic and brimming with the tapestry of fate ready to overflow, I let the weight of it all fill me as I tore through the forest.

Remnants of a stone wall circled a well past its prime at

the western edge of the estate— still inside the wood, but it was pushing toward the cliffs. I slowed to a jog and stopped to catch my breath. Training with fae had shown my weaknesses, making my thirty-one years of handling a blade look like I only just started. Determined to wipe away as much of that weakness as possible, I had been training with Corra and Silas in the afternoons, but the mornings were my cross-training session.

While core strength was a given in battle play, there wasn't a muscle that wasn't used, and as such, each session was full body. Today started with low squats and squat jumps on the wall at varying heights. Following the squats and jumps, were inverted push-ups with my feet on the wall, coupled with pressing a large chunk of limestone overhead in repetition.

Just when I was moving on to do pull-ups on a thick tree branch, I heard distant voices. The wind had shifted enough that the sound carried to me. While the words themselves were unclear, the tone was not. Corra was barking at someone who growled in response. Silas. I knew that growl. I had felt that growl inside me.

I moved silently away from the wood to the cliff's edge. There was a copse of trees clustered on the cliff and within that copse were the twins, faces locked in fury. Fairly certain I was hidden by the boulders and trees, I stood as an unwelcome voyeur.

"You daft, fucking male," Corra spat and whacked her brother on the chest hard enough that the sound echoed. "You can't even pretend to hide it!" She pulled at her own hair in frustration as it blew around her face. Silas looked on, partially like a scolded child and partially unrepentant.

"I didn't realize—I wasn't trying to," he began and was cut off.

"No. Of course you weren't trying, but you did and now

what? Huh? Did you even think this could be an issue for anyone but yourself? Your cousin?" she said sharply, the sound like metal on metal. "We could all see it unfolding but you. You, brother, could exercise a modicum of self-control." They both growled, faces inches apart.

"We agreed to leave it as is. To not make a repeat of it," he said quietly.

Ah. Me. They were arguing about me. Just great. Now my hidden position felt incredibly awkward.

"Fantastic!" Corra exclaimed sarcastically. "Her scent is all over you, and though I haven't seen her, I'm quite sure the reek of you is worse on her. Barring leaving for a few weeks, there is no way to hide this from Cadeyrn. You have misstepped, brother. You should have kept your cock in your trousers." I moved from the boulder, and I knew as soon as the breeze pushed at my back, they were aware I was there. Silas closed his eyes and pulled at his hair.

"Neysa, you should not be here. This is between my brother and me," Corra barked at me. I recoiled like I had been slapped. "It is not. It is between your brother and me," I retorted,

stung by her tone.

"No, *darling*. My brother, Cadeyrn, and I are a unit. With your little tryst, you have become an abscess in the joints between...us." Those were ugly, harsh words. Silas snarled at her.

"Corraidhín." The skies began to darken as they had the first day I sparred with him. "Your disappointment in me is one thing. Do not speak to her that way."

I looked at Silas, avoiding Corra's ire. A curious buzzing filled my mind. Obviously, I had messed up my friendship with Corra by having a night with Silas. Still, we were both adults, and I needed to walk away before I said something I couldn't take back.

"I apologize for putting you in this position, Silas," I spoke carefully to keep my composure. "It was not my intention. You have all been good friends to me, and I regret compromising that friendship."

With that, I turned and left. I needed to find another damned tree to do my pull-ups. Making my way back into the woods, I caught sight of Cade off to the side. He inclined his head to me as I passed, his eyes shuttered after the briefest glimpse of emotion.

FINDING another tree with the correct height and branch width took me longer than I had anticipated, yet it brought me further from the argument that had my ears roaring. Finally, the right tree presented itself to me, and I hopped up. Starting from a dead hang position, I lowered my shoulders and exhaled. In my mind, I zeroed in on each muscle as it packed into position. Lat muscles adducted and I pictured them like wings, lifting me up. The branch was rough and flaking in my pronated grip, but I had enough base layer calluses to keep from tearing.

On my second set of ten reps, the leaves behind me scuffled. I knew from the movement and woodsmoke scent of him that Silas was behind me. His presence was cozy and welcome. I was in a complete bipolarity as to feeling contented that we had both enjoyed one another the previous evening and feeling like I had ruined not only a friendship between us that truly was special but a friendship with the others as well. Especially since I still had to be working with them.

"We made a right mess of it, you and I," he spoke after watching me for an additional set. I dropped down and pulled one arm across my body, stretching the exhausted shoulder muscles. Really, I did not know what to say. Everything seemed trite and redundant, so I simply rehashed an apology.

"Do you regret it, Neysa?" he asked, his tone hesitant. I looked him dead on and blew out.

"No," I answered honestly. "I regret causing friction for you. For me. I know we aren't going to make a go of anything between us and while that makes it okay for me, I see how it muddled up things for your unit. The unit on which I have become an abscess," I said, reiterating Corra's barb.

He winced. "She shouldn't have said that."

"Perhaps not, but it was honest, and I respect that." We stood, close enough to be touching, but a pregnant distant apart. "Do you regret it?" He gave me a sad smile.

"I'd be a right tosser if I did, considering I have wanted you since I first met you. I should have seen that there could be an issue though."

"Why though? Why is there an issue? Especially as we have agreed to not pursue anything. Am I missing something? Some magical clause that says I must remain abstinent throughout this process? Because I sure as hell did not sign up for that."

He laughed at me and playfully hit my shoulder. "It just complicates working together."

Corra's reaction indicated it was a bit more of an issue than simply complicating things, but I just didn't have the head- space to sport it all out.

"Well, I apologize for taking advantage of your chaste nature, Silas. I was in a compromised state of mind," I laughed back. He closed the distance between us and hugged me tightly then kissed the top of my head. No desire muddying the embrace. Friends. At least I had him still.

"I'm going to take off for a few weeks to take care of some things in Aoifsing." Well, there went that idea. "Corra and I need to speak with the Elders, and I think she may need a tumble with a certain fellow," he said with a wink. That left me here. Alone. With Cade.

Silas must have read my thoughts. "You'll be fine here. We won't be gone long. Cadeyrn isn't as much of a stick in the mud as he seems. Promise."

He wrapped an arm around my back and started to walk us off.

CHAPTER 10

The village of Barlowe Combe sat between wooded hillside and the sea. There was very little to do beyond the pub and outdoor activities. Taking the train to London, Manchester, even Edinburgh, were weekly outings. The more time I spent here, the more certain I was that I had no desire to return to the States.

Since Silas had left, I had taken to walking into town every day after my run and getting a cup of tea at Tilly Preston's shop. She had a smattering of small tables in the front of the shop by the curtained windows and trinkets and baked goods in the rear. Tilly herself was a petite woman who had become rounder in her later years. She had a daughter and two sons, she told me one day. One of the boys was in his thirties and never married. With a not-so-subtle wink, she suggested he hadn't met the right woman. Maybe a woman of the world would suit him better than a small-town English girl. Attempting to hide my cringe by laughing it off, I said I was in no hurry to meet a man. I sincerely hoped that would be the end of that discussion, as I had become quite fond of Tilly's little shop.

The last dregs of Earl Grey soothed passage down my throat as I placed my notebook back in the tote bag that had become omnipresent in my village excursions. Standing from my seat next to the window, I saw Cade walk past. He got about a step past the door and backed up as if checking it was in fact me. Now we were in that incommodious state of not knowing whether to stop and chat or get on with the day's affairs. He mouthed something under his breath and opened the door to the shop. Tilly came from the back bringing a fresh scone and teapot to another customer.

"'Morning, Tilly," Cade called pleasantly to the plump shop keeper. "Shop looks lovely. Everything alright?"

I was rooted to the spot. This openly friendly version of Cade threw me for a loop. It wasn't that he had been less than kind to me, but he carried himself in an aloof, disinterested manner. Here, in Tilly's shop, he was warm and animated, and I couldn't help wondering if I had misjudged him. Perhaps I was the one being standoffish with him in a way I wasn't with the others. Maybe I had it all wrong. Or maybe he was just disinterested in me, which tied my stomach in a bit of a vice grip.

"Och, Cade. As good as it gets. Haven't seen you round much lately, love. Got yourself a bird to keep you busy now or are my cakes not in favor anymore?" she teased him.

He lowered his head and gave her a small, childlike smile. He quickly looked to me and back again to Tilly. "No, mum. Your cakes have a special place in my heart," he assured her, placing a hand over said heart. "I was coming to see what you have today and seem to have run into my tenant here. I'd really fancy a Victoria sponge if you've got one."

I knew my mouth wasn't physically hanging open, but the effect on my mind was the same. This was a totally different Cade. Even his accent had lost the lilt of Aoifsing and was solidly English. Plus, he never answered the question about whether he had a girl keeping him busy.

"'Course I do, love," Tilly assured him. "I'll have it out for you directly."

She turned to walk back but not before sending me a knowing glance. Whatever ideas she had about Cade and me, at least it might get her off my back about her son. I pursed my lips in a mock school marm manner and widened my eyes at him imploringly.

He huffed a chuckle. "So, this is where you have been hiding out?" he asked.

"I should say the same of you," I retorted.

He looked confused and I wanted to smack myself. Of course, he would have shops he frequented in town. Why was I stumbling seeing him outside of the manor house? "I only meant that you seem different here. Friendly." He scowled. "Er. *Friendlier*."

Ugh.

"Anyway, I haven't been hiding. Merely getting to know the village and sometimes getting to the cities. I quite like the dog park, though I haven't got a dog. The pub is nice as well, though I haven't got friends to drink with, so I just come here and read the texts from my cottage and write notes. My life is scintillating."

He looked at me a long moment, something like pity in his eyes. That was not something I wanted from him. I should just ask to borrow a dog.

"I take the dogs to the park," he answered my unspoken thought. "Also up the coast trail. You can as well if you'd like. They are always happy to run."

He turned his attention back to the counter where Tilly was packing up his cake. Should I wait for him to leave? Is it rude if I walk out? While I pondered the social niceties of my departure, he paid for his cake and came back.

"Shall I walk you back? Or were you going to go pretend to play with dogs and imaginary friends?" he asked with amusement in his voice. We stepped onto the narrow sidewalk.

"Oh, very nice. Kick me when I'm down. I didn't realize you liked cake so much."

"I don't." He leaned over the box and said close to my ear, his breath tickling me. "I prefer biscuits, but Tilly has always made special cakes for me. She knows I am different and has never told a soul. So, I like to give her business."

My eyes shot to the shop window where Tilly gave us a wave. "Tilly knows you're fae?"

"She knows I'm not entirely human. It's never been discussed but she is aware of our differences."

"Do others know about you all?" I asked.

"Just Tilly. She keeps a quiet life. I like to look out for her since her kids have all moved away." He scuffed his boot on the worn sidewalk.

"So, you get cake."

"So I get cake."

"Which you don't like," I confirmed. He chuckled under his

breath. "Lucky for you, I said. "I like cake, so I can help you out on that one."

"Perhaps come up for tea later then. We can discuss what you've found. I'll send the dogs for you." He may have smiled. Half a smile. I thought to myself he may just need sunshine. Or cake.

I HAD SNUCK out soon after arriving back at the cottage so I could pick up some ingredients to make biscuits to bring to tea. The thought of sitting and eating cake while Cade looked on, nitpicking my table manners while likely daintily sipping his own tea, seemed awkward. Plus, I wasn't too bad at baking, and didn't mind the idea of showing off a bit. Peanut butter cookies were my favorite, but something told me he might not be a peanut butter kind of guy. In the end, I decided to make a batch each of peanut butter and jammy dodgers.

At ten to four, Bixby and Cuthbert showed up at the garden door. I only knew because the soft whine of the garden gate made me look out the kitchen window. "Alright, gentlemen. Lead the way, and mind you don't trip me up as I'm bringing a peace offering to your master."

Both hounds looked to me as if to say, '*good luck.*' Bless their furry bums, the dogs stayed just ahead of me and kept looking back to check I was following.

"Still here, fellas. I should've asked you what biscuits to make. Perhaps I'll see about slipping you a couple peanut butter ones." I could have sworn they glanced at each other at the mention of a reward. We approached the manor and traipsed up the stone steps as Cade opened the door.

"Were you chatting with the dogs?" he asked.

"Of course. Don't you?" I handed him the two plates of treats. He looked at them in question and turned into the house.

"I brought a few books down I thought might help us out."

We proceeded to settle in the sitting room, the fire low and comfortable. To my surprise, a full tea service was laid on the ottoman, complete with sandwiches and the cake. I had never seen a servant in the house, so I often wondered who did the cooking. I suppose my answer was the male perched on the sofa arm beside me. He began to pour two cups and waved at me to take what I wanted.

"This is lovely, Cade. Thank you," I said and meant it.

I couldn't remember the last time someone tried to

prepare a meal for me. Even if it was just tea and sandwiches. Caleb would have starved before boiling water for pasta. All the nights I'd make an effort to cook and he'd come home saying he'd gotten takeout came back to me. I shook my head to shoo the memories.

Cade picked up one of the peanut butter cookies and sniffed it before taking a bite. I cringed a bit, anticipating a snide remark. Slicing the cake, I deliberately did not look at him.

"Peanut butter cookies happen to be my favorite. That's why I made them," I explained, sounding like I was in the principal's office.

"You know, I have never had peanut butter," he mused. "These are quite interesting."

"The others are jammy dodgers. If you don't like the peanut butter."

"No, I like them." He took another. "It was kind of you to make these. It has been some time since someone cooked anything for me," he admitted.

Funny, we both had the same thought.

"Do Silas and Corra not cook?"

His face darkened a tad but shook his head. "Those two?

They would sooner starve than make themselves a meal. I've played nursemaid to them for the past two centuries."

I laughed at that. "You know you just gave me a mental image of you in a frilly apron, right? That's being immortalized up here," I said, tapping my head, still having trouble conceptualizing just how old he was.

"Well, perhaps we will have to change that image and get you back to training tomorrow. With me. We can't have you just sitting in tea shops and baking all day. Neither of those will quell the enemy at our gates."

"Is it imminent then?" I questioned, a heavy feeling in my stomach making the salmon sandwich turn leaden.

"I believe so, yes. I know that's not what you wanted to hear. I wish it were different. However, I do think that together, the four of us can change part of the outcome."

"Do you—is there..." I stumbled around the question, an oiliness sliding into my chest. "Will there be much loss?" My voice broke a bit on the words. A long sip of his tea and a gaze up through his thicket of dark lashes made me squirm.

"It is entirely possible."

We sat in companionable silence for a while, eating the spread before us. At some point, I realized that the plate of peanut butter cookies was down to one. Maybe this was the olive branch we needed.

"Better save that last one for the dogs," I said in warning. "I promised to slip them one."

A SHOULDER I had not seen came crashing into mine.

"Oooph." I stumbled back and swung out with my sword. A

laugh chased my retreat.

We had been going at it for a good hour. My sword arm

was screaming, and I had ripped open a callus on my left hand from gripping my dagger too tight. Despite the chilled after- noon air, sweat was dripping down my face, making me regret the mascara I had applied this morning before heading into town. There was something to be said about making an effort with my appearance.

For the first few months after Dad died and I was just home working and mourning, I hardly got out of anything that didn't resemble pajamas. In coming here, I had told myself it was time to be myself again. So, every morning after my run, I made an effort with my hair and lined my eyes to bring out the olive in them. Small touches here and there. Otherwise, it was all too easy to feel less and less feminine. Less beautiful than that tiny particle within me said I still was. The issue was afternoon training sessions and the unfortunate effect on my mascara.

The sleeve of my athletic jacket dragged across my face, wiping at the sweat streaked with black. Cade rolled his eyes and launched forward with a maddening amount of speed and grace. I barely had time to sidestep, and he swiveled, twin swords pointing at the ground behind me. Any semblance of pride I had vanished at that point as I lost my footing and landed with an undignified thump, which knocked the air from my lungs. That was the third time today he knocked me down. My ego was positively blistered at this point.

I lay there on the damp, leaf-covered clearing, splayed like a snow angel. The sky had clouded over, my vantage point losing light as Cade stood over me, sword discarded, hands behind his back. A single drop of sweat made a lazy path down between his abdominals. Not that I was watching it.

Twenty minutes or so into our scuffle, he discarded his jacket and shirt, preferring to fight bare chested. I refused to admit that the sight of his chiseled chest and abdomen distracted me.

"Do you yield, or are you getting fond of my laying you on your back?"

Whatever he was trying to incite in me with that remark, he accomplished. Sparks of rage and quite conversely, desire, surged in me. My eyes strayed to his chest, igniting a battle of emotions within my mind.

I threw every ounce of my core into kipping up from prone to landing on my feet, daggers out. Adrenaline was coursing through me as my boots took me two paces back. I unzipped and ripped off my own jacket, leaving me to fight in leggings and a sports bra.

Ever so slowly, without taking his aquamarine eyes from mine, Cade slunk backwards to his sword, kicked it into the trees and palmed his own dagger. Both of us were crouched in a standoff, yet I was the only one breathing hard. Damn fae. His boots shifted on the earth and began a predatorial crescent around me. My own feet fell into a dance that matched his. The hairs on the back of my neck were rising, sensing the threat circling me. Goosebumps raised on the rippled plain of my stomach.

He noticed and smirked. "Frightened, Pure One?" he drawled, no hint of a man in that voice—only the essence of pure fire and elemental wrath. This spar was acutely different from those with his cousins. It was as if a beast stood in his place.

I swallowed and wouldn't allow the fright to set in. I was electricity and movement. I tried to channel the amethyst hanging from a silver cord between my breasts. The heat of the stone warmed my breastbone and though my eyes didn't stray from Cade's face, kernels of light refracted in my peripheral. His eyes narrowed slightly, assessing. A slight twitch in his jawline was the only warning I had before he spun for me like a coin on its side.

Split-second decision making at its best, I dropped my daggers in the instant I jumped for the branch a few feet above me and swung myself over, dropping onto him. We both hit the ground. The element of surprise I had died quickly as he flipped me over for a fourth goddamn time. I tipped my head back and muttered a curse. At least I got one good shot in and finally had him breathing heavily.

"Yield?" he demanded, one knee on either side of my ribs, arms pinning me. His stomach pressed into mine, both of us slick with sweat. I nodded. He dragged his leg over and knelt on the ground beside me.

I stayed down. "Even when I fight Corra and Silas, I can gain the upper hand occasionally," I pouted.

He slid his glance sideways and I turned my head, still feeling like, well, like I'd been beaten by a fae warrior. "I am not Corra. Nor am I Silas. You couldn't expect to win."

Cocky bastard. "When I fight Silas, I can at least stay on my feet," I grumbled.

He was pinning me in the briefest of seconds. His sable hair fell forward, brushing my forehead. "One, I am not my cousin, and perhaps he allows you to remain upright because he doesn't want to bruise your delicate ego. Or perhaps he just does not have enough strength to fully take you," he continued. I stared up at the male who was leaning over me, his scent of ice and rain mixing with sweat and heat, washing over my senses, thoroughly intoxicating me.

"Two, you need to be in top form to deal with what is coming. You knew before I moved, and that is how you chan– neled the amethyst. I want you thinking like that all the time. You are a fighter. Act like it. Three," he said, words barely above a growl. "Perhaps my cousin couldn't fully appreciate the sight of you lying beneath him."

With that, his weight was off me, and he was halfway across the clearing before I exhaled. If I got up then, I'd have to interpret just how I felt about that comment, and based on the low gut clenching, I wasn't sure I was ready to face it. Because if I decided I liked the idea of him thinking of me that way, that would complicate things more than it had with Silas. I didn't think there was anything casual about Cadeyrn. So I ignored that clenching.

From a distance away, I heard his voice. "Clean up your hand, and wash that shit off your face," he spat.

"Good match, asshole," I called after him, not caring whether he heard or not.

EVERY BLASTED MUSCLE was aching by the time I

dragged my sorry carcass back to my cottage. It would be an outright lie to say I didn't lay on my back for another few minutes, feeling like I had the wind knocked out of me. Somewhere near the garden gate, my two furry dignitaries made a show of face, and I invited them in for a spoonful of peanut butter each. These two needed to stay on my side. Through the stained-glass paneled window, I watched them trot back home.

After buttering some toast and devouring an apple, I poured a glass of wine and took it into the bathroom with me. The hot water bellowed lavender and eucalyptus steam, and the groan that escaped me was as unrefined as they come. The oils I had added to the bath left a thin layer over my skin, which I used to help massage the tight muscles. Starting at my calves, I worked my way up as I had done since I was a teenager. The only thing I was missing from my life in LA right now, apart from tacos, was the massage therapist I saw weekly. To me, there was no greater advantage to making a decent salary than having someone to work out the kinks in my body.

I sat back in the tub and sipped at my wine, intermittently endeavoring to revive the amethyst on my chest. I had taken to wearing it for its protection and ability to channel energy. Lifting the smooth stone, I brought it to my lips. It warmed against my mouth. How much had changed in my life in a few months.

The amethyst popped from its bindings and glowed in my hands. My heart swelled; I'd finally done it. Not just channeling the energy, but having it contain so much of my essence, that it burst from its casing.

When I emerged from the bath, ready to crawl into the fluffy duvet beckoning from my bed, I noticed a slice of cake sitting on the dresser in my bedroom. No note to say from where it had come, yet a faint scent of rain lingered. A tinge of magic hung in the air, indicating he had somehow made it appear here. Another olive branch, it seemed. I happily devoured the treat without even bothering to fetch a fork. I crawled into bed soon after, holding my still warm, still illuminated amethyst, and wished I could show Cade that I had done it. Maybe I would see that flicker of pride he sometimes allowed to show on his solemn, tragically beautiful face. I knew Silas and Corra would've been, at least before now.

As I drifted off, the weight on the bed shifted and two massive guardians curled up on top of my heavy legs. (I guess, at least for now, I had a dog. Or two. These two hardly left my side.) I dreamt of magic and wind swirling in my cottage, enveloping me in in its embrace. Dreamt of releasing the amethyst from my palm and watching it become a part of the wind and disappear into the night air.

SAINT AMBROSE CHURCH sat the bottom of Barlowe Combe. It had been renovated in the 1960s after a century or so of neglect. The original structure had been built in the early fourteenth century as a chapel for the rectory, which was now nonexistent. The adjacent apiary was still a producer of beeswax candles and honey, which were exported all over the British Isles. In the eighteenth century, following the English extermination of Scottish Highland clans, any remnants of Catholicism in the area were either destroyed or reformed.

Saint Ambrose Church became Anglican until Christchurch Church was built at the head of the town during Victoria's reign. At that time, Catholics had started admitting their faith and moved to reclaim their church. Two world wars saw the building as an army hospital as well as a dormitory for RAF nurses. The church fell into total disrepair until 1962 when the National Trust stepped in to fund reparations for the historical building.

Returning to my exploration of the town, I found myself

in Saint Ambrose for the second time this week. There was a reckoning in the building I could feel from the churchyard. Inside, I felt the urge to touch everything around me but stopped short of the crucifix at the forefront.

I had not been raised with religion being a doctrine to subscribe to, but rather a cautionary tale to study. In university, so at odds with my economics and political science studies, I took up a minor in theology merely out of interest. I found the undertaking and implementation of religion fascinating. The fact that it served a base need of humankind to feel adopted by a community was fundamental to our survival as a species. Religion was not the worship of anything in particular but the congregation of a community to exact axiom over the beliefs and the people in the name of the greater deity. It allowed for the formation of civic and, eventually, non-secular law.

Regardless of my indifference to organized religion, in most places of worship, I felt at peace. In Saint Ambrose, there was a tangible, emotive feeling of otherworldliness. I closed my eyes, tapping into that part of me which burst the amethyst. With that second sight, I could see lines, like star trails, crisscrossing beneath the slab floor. The lines I saw bisected one another and pierced the walls of the building, heading off in four different directions. One line, I noticed, directed toward the estate, and I followed its path through the town, toward the woods that crossed the eastern side of the estate.

The late October sunshine was low and placating to the senses. As I followed the ley line farther into the wood, where I knew the atmosphere became discursive and tangled, I made every effort to keep my wits about me. Emerald shades of mossy outcroppings of rock glittered with autumnal leaves all around as I ambled deeper into the forest. Every fairytale in every culture, everywhere on Earth and likely every other realm, warns of going into the woods alone.

I shook off the feeling and assured myself that I was not a helpless maiden. I was not unarmed, and I was not terribly far from home. The ground dipped, and I laid a hand on a rock to keep my boots from slipping on the slick, leafy ground. From its tiny holster on my knee-high lace up riding boot, I pulled a two-and-a-half-inch double edged fixed blade. The hilt was a loop, which made it easy to hold as well as conceal. This knife I kept on me most times. It was small enough to clip onto my laces and running belt.

I switched the tote bag from my right to left shoulder, freeing my dominant hand. There was a haze. Almost as though looking through fumes from burning gas. I knew better than to walk through it, yet I approached cautiously. Heaviness swelled the air in this mangled corner of the forest where every tree and fern looked like witch fingers.

Someone was watching. I scanned the surrounding area. There were too many shadows. Places where the light could easily conceal someone. Or something. Whatever it was, was biding its time. I was prey, and it had flushed me into its trap. Thankfully, I had this blade, but I really felt ridiculous having come here in jeans with a tote bag full of books rather than any of the cache of weapons at my disposal on the estate.

Once again, I adjusted the tote and nervously pushed at the bottom of the bag, nonchalantly feeling for the phone. I pushed at the outside of the bag, slowly herding the device to the top, like squeezing a toothpaste tube. When it crested, I glanced at the screen for the briefest of moments, allowing the technology to recognize my face. *Please let it work.* The phone opened up. I knew I was out of time as I heard the soft whoosh of air as something jumped from the trees about ten meters ahead of me. I had time to press one call, then dropped my bag to the ground and assumed a fighting stance.

It had been only two days since my spar with Cade. My sword arm was still aching and the skin of the hand holding my small combat knife had yet to heal. I mentally kicked myself for not having Cade heal it, but I had been avoiding him like a child who was trying to get out of homework. Nevertheless, my legs spread wide, I watched as what was unmistakably a fae male came out of the cover of foliage.

He was as tall as Cade but narrower. More like a dancer than a warrior. Hair the color of creamed honey almost clashed with his ghostly pale skin. He wore a close-fitting jacket and leather trousers with a bow strapped to his back and a small sword at hip. An archer.

Christ, he could have taken me out before I had a chance look up. Yet he hadn't. His purpose here was not to kill me. Yet. I raised an eyebrow in question.

"I did wonder how long it would take you to come here," the fae said, accent turning up at the edges like the dog-eared corners of damp paper. "You have been cloistered in that compound for so long. But curiosity finally got the better of you?"

I simply stood, working out in my head what to say, hoping the phone could pick up our voices. He took a step forward, and I moved back a pace.

"Oh, you reek of that blasted family. Well, the males anyway. Both of them. Vixen," he said with an air kiss. "I am surprised Corraidhín hasn't had you yet herself. Few have been able to resist her, male or female. Though," he leaned forward, hinging at the hips and whispering conspiratorially, "I prefer the males as well. Especially those warrior types. Someone who can really use his power against me in the bedroom. Don't you agree?"

"Such honesty for a first date," I drawled. "While I would

love to have a glass of wine and chat about boys, I was only out scouting a more northern running route to take with the dogs."

"Shame. I myself do not have long here. I only came to give you a message." He was standing in front of me in a split second. I'd never seen that kind of speed. "The pathways to all the realms are meant to be open as they were millennia ago. Only the pure and strong are meant to survive. Do not meddle, and you will live." He finished his piece by leaning in and biting my lip with too sharp incisors, catching me by surprise.

Before he had the chance to pull away, I had sunk my small blade into the hollow of his underarm, retracted the knife and held it under his chin.

Eyes wide with pain and surprise, he quirked a smile. "Oh, you *do* taste like them."

I flicked the blade and drew a gash of blood along the top of his throat and kicked him back into a birch tree.

I heard the crash of four sets of paws to my rear and the dogs were snarling at this pale stranger. He touched the wound on his neck then licked the blood from it. We both looked as Cade came out from where the dogs had run. The pale demon put his bony hands together and began clapping and giggling, then ran faster than light itself in the opposite direction. Cade came up next to me and covered the bite on my lip with his index and middle fingers. They tingled as they had the first day I'd met him.

I looked at him and shifted my eyes toward where the male had been. "He's gone. Reynard is ultimately a coward. He is faster than anyone I have met so be wary of him, but he will not challenge me in combat. Nor you now, I wager," he said with that slight glimmer of pride in his eyes. "Let's get back. You did well, placing that call, but the dogs were already out of their minds looking for you. It seems they are as protective of you as...they are of me."

The furry bodyguards flanking us closed ranks a bit tighter. I reached down to scratch Bixby's head and realized I still had my knife gripped so tight in my palm that the looped hilt had imprinted itself into my flesh. The torn wound was oozing again.

"I thought I said to clean that up?" Cade suddenly barked.

Not in the mood to deal with his moody bullshit, I turned away and pressed my palm into my jeans to staunch the blood flow. Then I kept walking.

Footsteps followed me. I could hear him open his mouth, and I held up my bloody hand to stop him. "I don't want to hear it, Cade. I'm not a child, so don't patronize me with your self-righteous crap."

"I was having a laugh. Or trying to," he responded quietly. Oh. "I had thought you might let me heal it. The other day. You never came up. That's all I meant. I'll just see you back now."

My heart sank at his tone, so I stopped walking and turned. The dogs mimicked my motions, then looked from their master to me and back. The blood had started to dry on my hand as I lifted it, shaking, to Cade. He took it in his own and was so gentle I felt awful for snapping. One palm covered mine while his other held my upturned hand. Warmth spread over it, and he lifted his top hand, then brought my palm to his face and kissed the rapidly mending wound. There was a clenching in my lower gut that had me clearing my throat as I thanked him. He merely inclined his head.

"Who was that, Cade?"

"Reynard? My former brother-in-law. He's a right arse and has never really decided if he would rather fuck me or kill me.

Sick really. He is a trickster and always has an agenda, so we need to be on our guard now that he knows you are here."

"Have you ever—you know, not...killed him?" I asked in the most ridiculously immature way.

He looked at me like I was a nut job. Then laughed. I decided I liked the sound of his laughter.

"Have I bed him, Neysa? I have not."

"Do you enjoy both male and female companionship like Corra?" I was fishing. It was almost embarrassing, but I had gotten bored these weeks past.

"While I find both sexes beautiful, I am attracted to only females. Both of my cousins," he said with a pointed glance, "find pleasure in both. Silas tends to gravitate toward females, though. As you know." The last was laced with a sliver of contempt. I refused to acknowledge it.

"Interesting. And do you—" And now I seem like a school- girl. "Do you see someone regularly?" I asked. An eyebrow shot skyward.

"Why?" he asked me.

I had no idea. I'm a nosy little thing I suppose. I just shrugged as if to say I didn't care one way or another.

He sighed in exasperation. "There is no one I see exclusively, as humans say. I do take lovers when it suits me. I find it harder here with humans because we are different species and there are always questions after." I thought back to my foray with Silas and agreed that it was not a human experience at all. He pursed his lips as if reading my thoughts.

"So, really, when you're stuck here all you do is play with swords and read Tom Clancy novels?" I teased him, quirking my lips to the side.

He looked affronted. "They are ripe with militaristic information. I find them fascinating. Are my pastimes so different to yours?"

Not at all, I realized.

"Only in our choices of reading material," I admitted. He sniffed a laugh.

We had arrived back at the manor, and my stomach was growling. I was invited in for a bite to eat and found three jars of peanut butter sitting on the kitchen counter. I doubled over with laughter. He looked around in confusion.

"I see I've created a monster," I said through giggles and pointed to the jars. He looked embarrassed.

"I've always been a monster, Neysa. You just fed it,"

CHAPTER 11

Howling, whipping, lashing winds and rain were the sounds keeping my focus from the detection spell I was attempting. Corra had said they refer to it as a spell, for lack of a better term. It was more of a summoning or reckoning of an object, however.

Two hours earlier, Cade had walked me through the upper levels of the manor house, through the dark paneled walls, scarred with centuries of use and misuse, into the library. He opened the door and motioned me in before him.

Glimmers of luminescence danced from all over the room casting the only light beside the flashes of distant lightning from beyond the window. The storm had been predicted for days and started moving in late that afternoon. I trudged up the property noting the eerie stillness before major weather.

Cade was more than happy to allow me to try the summoning and agreed that during a low-pressure weather system, the electrically charged atmosphere would be conducive to my summoning. "The real weather is still a couple of hours out. Take advantage of the pressure to ground yourself and feel out what you need to do. Use what you need. It's all yours," he said with a broad sweep of his grey sweater-covered arm.

With that, we walked farther into the library. As though a switch was flicked, hundreds of stones became dimly illuminated in the otherwise dark room. He had explained that the room was kept free of artificial light to maintain the efficacy of the stones' powers, allowing them to be charged in the filtered sun and moonlight each day.

My face must have shown my amazement, as he quirked a tiny smile. "Our conductivity allowed them to brighten. Together," he explained. "They will, of course, be a bit brighter. You may find that when I leave, the light will dim."

"Thinking mighty highly of yourself, Cade?" I teased. He rolled his eyes. "One day, those beautiful eyes of yours will get stuck like that."

"No," he retorted, and flicked my chin. "They won't."

Was that a grain of lightheartedness in his carefully honed chrysalis of solemnity? The stones around us glowed briefly. I was momentarily reminded of my night with Silas and the now-missing fluorite.

Cade must have picked up on my train of thought or my changed scent because the sternness clicked back into place, and he started to leave.

"Call if you need anything."

And he walked out, the stones fading to muddy shapes in his absence. Just when I thought we were all getting past the fissure I had caused. I guess that's why there are rules about relationships in the workplace. I blew out a long, steadying breath, then proceeded to look for the amazonite in the extensive cache of precious and semiprecious stones. "I could have used a little help finding the blasted thing," I mumbled.

I heard a soft chuckle and light footsteps. "You didn't

ask," his voice came from somewhere down the hall. "But it's not your style to ask." Damn fae hearing.

"And I suppose it's certainly not your style to offer," I spat quietly under my breath, wondering why I was having a conversation with someone in another room. Footsteps stopped, heels clicked together, and I heard the sound of fingers strumming the walls.

"My offers have always stood. It seems you neither need nor want them," he said, so faintly, I could almost have imagined it. Almost. Bloody hell.

IN THE CENTER of the mostly dark room, adjacent to the library, I had created a circle of clear quartz. Within that circle I sat, cross-legged, holding a chunk of raw amazonite palms up. Eyes closed, I concentrated on the mental image of the blue-green stone in my hand. I sent thoughts of healing and accomplishment. Feelings of gaining what was lost.

The rain was ravaging the sides of the limestone house. Thoughts eddied in, storms and earthquakes, childless mothers. A queen before a stone altar. A natural pool in an underground cavern, covered in mossy rocks and salt deposits. Towering flutes of pale stone, large enough to be turrets. A cloud forest, oppressively humid and green. Leathery, aged brown arms, reaching out to younger, fairer masculine ones on which sat a ring of hammered, oxidized gold. My father's hands, holding something reflecting the sunlight. In my mind, I tried to clear the glare, refocusing.

I was sharpening my inner eye to recognize the item he was holding, my breathing speeding up along with my heartbeat.

As I clenched the stone in my hand, crying out for my father, needing to see what was in his hand, the queen reappeared, turning from her altar, eyes wide as though spooked. Distantly, thunder boomed, and the visions started to ripple away.

The more I tried to hold on to them, the less I could breathe. Sounds of yelling, like the memory of battle sounds, tugged at me.

In an instant, I was thrust back into the manor house with the brightest flash of lightning and a deafening explosion. My back slammed into a wall, and warmth ran down my face before I lost consciousness.

There were no dreams, yet I assumed I had slept, as my eyes opened to a tidy room I didn't recognize. Warm furnishings and simple rugs decorated the space. Across from me, in a winged armchair, large enough for him to sprawl, sat Cade, lids closed in sleep. I didn't dare move as I watched his even breathing and sleep-softened features. He was wearing a different grey jumper than he had worn earlier, now wearing black cotton pajama bottoms. I wondered how long I'd been in here.

Dark, tousled hair stuck up in every direction, so at odds with his normal unruffled appearance. I followed the planes of his forehead and defined cheekbones to his lips, which I had never noticed were full and soft. Their usual guise was either pressed into a hard line or pinched in annoyance. Annoyed with me mostly. A faint scruff of unshaven shadow limned his jaw and upper lip. I wanted to reach out and feel where the stubble met the smooth fair skin. His left hand was on a book. It looked to be a contemporary military intelligence novel. I couldn't help the smile, thinking of this legendary fae male reading Tom Clancy.

As if I had called out, his eyes opened sleepily and met mine. Neither of us moved. The heavy duvet was still tucked up under my chin, his body still half out of the chair, one long leg reaching nearly to the bed. I didn't take my eyes from his face, waiting for a snide remark. Something chastising me for passing out or wrecking the library. Had I wrecked the library? But he didn't say a word.

Unclear of how long we stayed staring at one another, I finally reached up out of the duvet to push a lock of my long hair behind my ear. What my fingers touched was crusted and tender to the touch.

He cleared his throat and sat up, placing the book on a side table. On his left hand, I noted burns and bandages in some spots. "May I examine your head?" he asked clinically, which was juxtaposed by the scratchiness of waking in his voice.

I pushed myself up a bit farther on the pillows. My own grey jumper, though still on, was torn and singed in places. I nodded. The mattress sunk under his weight. Gingerly, he tapped the skin at my hairline, then used one fingertip to lightly tap along my jawline then under, feeling my glands. I swallowed reflexively.

"I had visions," I admitted.

His hands came around the back of my head, probing the base of my skull.

"I suspected as much," he said. "I'm sorry if it was upsetting. I heard—you were screaming for your father."

Unable to turn away, as his hands were still examining my head, I looked to the ceiling. "That was one of them. There were so many images. I'll need to write them down."

Hands pulling back, he looked at me directly. "I came in when I heard you scream. The protection circle became lightning. Literally. I have fire and light in my veins, Silas has control of weather, but I have never seen anything like what you conducted. There was a flash from the window, and the amazonite you held splintered. The refracted electrical beams speared each of the clear quartz. That's what launched you out of the circle."

"And into the wall?" I asked, touching my head.

"Don't worry," he said in a mocking voice. "You'll heal, and your pretty face won't be disfigured." I scrunched my nose in distaste, then rolled my eyes. "Careful," he said. "Your beautiful eyes may get stuck like that." I smiled a little despite myself.

"I think," I started. "I believe I need to take a trip. There is something I need to find. On my own." He dipped his head in understanding. "May I come back here when I have found it?"

The usual cool mask on Cade's face turned to confusion.

"That goes without saying, Neysa. Here...this...please consider it as much your home as ours. You may come and go as you please."

Well, crap. Home is a word I hadn't heard in a very long time. I knew I had a concussion due to the relentless pounding behind my eyes, and I was blaming the tears that threatened on the injury. Cade stood and walked to the door.

"I'll get you something to eat. You need to rest. This is my room, but feel free to stay. The chair," he pointed to where he had slept, "is more comfortable in here for me to read, which is why I put you here. I'll grab you a change of clothes as well. It was a bad night for grey jumpers it seems," he joked.

Joked.

I grinned at the effort. His answering smile made me glad I was sitting. The genuine light that shone from his eyes as they pulled up at the edges took my breath away. In that smile, there was no room for the stern male who normally faced me.

"Do that more," I said on a whim. "You deserve to be happy.

That smile," I said, shaking my head. "That's a face to launch a thousand ships, Cadeyrn."

He hung his head shyly and walked out of the room.

NOW IN POSSESSION of a transcribed version of my

visions, I set out to researching possible locations. Still a bit apprehensive about being in the library among all the crystals, I had spread out all my books and laptop on the floor of Cade's room. He had gone on an errand and not told me what room to switch to, so I stayed put, head still throbbing a bit too much to venture far.

So far, I'd looked up spiritual epicenters and written a list before cross-referencing with my vision transcription.

"Do you always do research on the floor with a sword strapped to your back?"

I hadn't heard him come in. I must look a sight, kneeling on the wood floors in leggings and an oversized T-shirt that hung off my shoulder, spine scabbard along the length of my back, and my hair tied into a lopsided topknot. I hastily spat out the pen I had clenched in my teeth. Yes, that was what made me look like a feral animal. The pen. I squeezed my eyes closed and felt a blush creep up my cheeks. Clearly, I had lived alone too long.

Cade sniffed what could have been a laugh.

"I'd be lying if I said it wasn't more often than not," I answered what I am quite sure had been a rhetorical question. He raised a thick brow and squatted down next to me and my collection of ramblings. Balanced on his heels, squatting deeply, his elbows pushing his knees outward, Cade studied my lists.

"Any epiphanies?" he asked, picking up my list of visions. I could smell heat and rain on him. The scent made me wish I were running.

"Apart from the trip I need to take, not yet. There is a volume in my cottage I'd like to fetch, as I remember reading about a place in South America. Ecuador or Peru. I can't recall. It has one of the last unravaged mines of black tourmaline. Do you think that maybe," I started to ask and turned to him, finding our faces disconcertingly close. Close enough to share breath. Both as stubborn as the other, neither of us looked away as I continued. "Maybe the black tourmaline that contains the electrical charge for the Veil is hidden somewhere there?"

"In possibly Ecuador, possibly Peru?" he asked, and I detected a patronizing tone.

I sighed loudly, sitting back on my heels, then put my palms flat on top of my thighs. "Look, I know you have been looking into this for a long while," I started, and he raised both eyebrows as if to say I had no idea. I really didn't. Three hundred years old, for Christ's sake. "I'm working with what I have. Up until a couple of months ago, I was a broken girl who never even considered realm saving quests..."

He was barely listening, focusing on the map and list. I took a few counted breaths.

"From my research, black tourmaline is found chiefly in Brazil and North Africa," he began. "There are small deposits in different parts of the world: Sri Lanka and Pakistan, even Russia. Most of those mines have either been destroyed, usurped by militants, or I have visited and found naught but child labor and the backwater cronies of organized crime and terror groups." Shadows darkened his features, and he paused, considering. "In Ecuador, I found loads of emerald mines but there is no reason that there isn't any tourmaline hidden there."

He was tapping the outline of Ecuador with his index finger, and I saw the point of his sharp incisor catch his bottom lip. The slight sideburns of his dark hair near the temples were damp with sweat, and I saw for the first time he was wearing his fighting boots. One of what I assume had to be many blades was still strapped to his outer thigh. I didn't like admitting I liked the look.

"Were you training or...problem-solving?"

"Problem-solving," he answered, without looking up. I sat back, bending my knees.

"Care to elaborate?"

"No." Well then. "My cousins will be here shortly. If you need time to do whatever it is you may need to do, I can leave."

I put my hand on his jacket, but he still did not look up.

"I'm sorry for causing you trouble. I didn't mean to create an issue between—"

"You're not broken," he said softly, staring at the map. My mouth hung open a bit as I watched his profile. A muscle feathered in his jaw. "You needed to shed a skin. We all do sometimes. You, however, were wearing the skin of another beast for too long, and it was bound to leave its imprint."

I didn't know what to say.

"I'm sorry," I eventually blurted. Again.

He rolled his eyes and finally looked to me. "There is no need," he said simply.

"What did you do when you saw the militant occupation of
the mines? The child labor?" I wondered aloud.

He looked directly at me and said, "I burned each and every
one of them from the inside out and brought the children to a safer location. After, I tracked down the heads of the militant groups using scent alone and annihilated them. I then spent a week drinking myself into oblivion and trying to cover my tracks."

The frankness. The raw violence of his tone. I knew right then that I would have done the same. He looked away as though preparing for judgment.

Maybe that was what separated me from being human. Or maybe our ability to empathize—to feel so deep about issues and people we didn't know, was where the humanity lived inside us. Or perhaps there was no profound line dividing us as species. There was magic. There was science. The emotional trappings were inclusive of both species.

"Too right," I said, agreeing with what he had done. And that was that.

CHAPTER 12

Dinner outside of sleeping chambers sounded divine, and while I was anxious about the dynamic between us all, I was eager to see the twins. It had been over a month now. The smell of roast chicken and potatoes gave me a gingerbread trail to follow into the dining room where everyone sat. Corra made straight for me and kissed my cheek. I sighed in relief that she didn't still consider me a blight. She was looking casual in over-the-knee suede boots and a blush-colored chunky knit sweater that came to mid-thigh. Her auburn hair fell in waves.

"Gods, your head!" she exclaimed, reaching to touch my wound but pulling back. "Don't worry. You're still gorgeous."

"Why does everyone keep saying that like it would be my first concern?" I tugged self-consciously at my charcoal jumper where it opened in the front to show just a peek of a lace bralette.

"Because it's true," answered Silas's gruff voice. He glided over to me and wrapped me up in a bear hug then pushed my shoulders back to look me in the face. "I can't believe you struck yourself with lightning, you *allaína trubaíste*."

He kissed the top of my head and looked at me as if to ask if we were okay. I smiled genuinely and kissed his warm cheek.

"I think calling her a 'beautiful disaster' is a bit harsh, don't you?" Corra said, looking to Cade who was standing in the corner observing. I hadn't forgotten what she had called me the last time we spoke, but I could see she was repentant. Or at least trying to be.

His shoulders relaxed ever so slightly as his eyes met mine. I quirked my mouth to one side comically and raised my brows, imploring him. His face split into that ridiculous grin. Like his mouth couldn't be contained on his face. The room glowed, and I stood, dumbfounded, staring at his heart-stop-ping smile.

"I don't know, Corraidhín," Cade answered. "I'm still picturing her sitting on the floor shaking her head and spit-ting a pen from her mouth like a dog." Oh, fantastic. I buried my face in my hands, and everyone began laughing.

"Are we eating or just standing around taking the piss with me?" I asked, not stopping my own amusement from seeping out.

A peaceable silence fell as we all tucked into our dinner. Though my healing was remarkably faster, thanks to both my partial fae heritage and Cade's own healing abilities, I could feel the process speed up in my body when I ate. It was as though the tissue and bone were actively knitting together, inflammation reducing while I savored the crispy roast skin of the chicken and the sweetness of the caramelized root vegeta- bles. Once the plates were cleared, we sat back and discussed the issues afoot.

108

"You were in Aoifsing?" I asked Corra. "Is it dangerous?" I fiddled with the stem of my wine glass.

"Yes and no. Those who may hunt us, they are stronger in

the other realm then would be here. So, in that sense, when we are hunted, the danger is greater there. However, it is home, and it isn't as if we are always walking into a trap," Corra explained patiently.

As I did with Reynard, I thought to myself.

"Few are stupid and cocky enough to come after us here. Perhaps our magic isn't as strong, but we are stronger fighters. Warriors," Silas added, his own cockiness exuding.

Something had been bothering me lately, and until this moment, I couldn't put my finger on what that was.

"Neysa?" Cade asked. "Something wrong?"

"That first day I went running here," I began. The day I met Cade and hadn't even realized he had healed my lip. "I had an anxiety attack, yes. However, I've never lost my bearings so completely before. You mentioned things getting convoluted near the northern edge of the property. Is that where the Veil is?"

They all looked to Cade.

"Yes. The Veil lies in several 'spiritual epicenters' as you call them," he said, and gave me a small, amused smile that last week I may have thought to be mocking. "The places we had discussed harboring the crystals. The problem with the one here is that the crystal is missing." Processing this information gave me pause. He seemed to be considering saying more and was weighing my reaction or, who knew, my worthiness.

"Where is it supposed to be?" I asked.

Silas looked to Cade, who assented.

"There is an ancient grotto on the northern end of the property near the coast trail. It is called, *Aoife Gle,*" Silas explained. "Humans had never stepped foot into the grotto... until thirty years ago. That is when the crystal went missing. We had been in Aoifsing, meeting with the Elders when a rift was felt. Upon return, the crystal was found to be missing, and the Veil thinner. There was a faint trace of human scent."

Silas extended his fingers, and a bottle of what I took for brandy appeared before him. Corra flicked hers and four cut crystal tumblers made their way from the sideboard to table. I stared at my hands, at the cluster of freckles that dotted the back of my hand. My vision came back to me.

The same hands, only much smaller, reaching up to pull aside a moss-covered branch. The smell of leaf rot and cold water. A faint blue glow emitting from a pool below. My father, reaching his hand out for me to clasp as we descended. A woman's disembodied voice speaking to him, though I couldn't see her. I was frightened but held still. A featherlight touch on my cheek, and the voice was gone. My father slung the bag he had across his back and walked us back up the mossy cave entrance. Back in the sunlight, I noticed his eyes were red and damp. I had guessed he was scared too.

THE VISION CLEARED. I looked to the others. My friends. I involuntarily placed my hand over my heart and pushed back the lump in my throat. It must have seemed like an odd reac- tion because Silas took my other hand and squeezed it lightly. Corra reached her long slender hand across the table for me.

"It was me," I whispered. The three of them looked at me like I was raving. "I was there. My father and I, when I was very young." I looked to each of them, begging them with my eyes. "I don't know why he would have done it."

Cade crossed one leg over the other. He swirled the brandy in his glass. No one spoke. The others let go of my hands. I felt something like a blow to the gut. I was losing my father all over again and my friends in the process. They wouldn't trust me after this. How could they? My own father had caused a bloody rift in the universe, for Christ's sake.

The air around me constricted. Panic was rising, and I downed the liquid in my glass. I had to get out. Had to breathe. I couldn't remember how to walk without running. Would they chase me? I clenched my hands over and over. In one breath, I was out of my seat and out the front door. Faster than I had ever moved. Once standing on the stone landing in front of the manor, I began to sway from the speed of my departure.

The stone wall was cold as I leaned over and braced my elbows, not caring that the frigid November rain was matting my sweater to my body. Either I was going to die here from lack of oxygen, or I was going to be killed by one of the three fae warriors with whom I had just eaten dinner. Everything I had known about my father was now in question. Had he been working all his life—all my life—trying to disrupt the order of things? All of our trips. All of my training started to make sense. You couldn't have a daughter completely vulnerable when your world was broader and more dangerous than the average citizen's.

"I knew," spoke a rain-muted voice behind me. A warm hand pressed into my lower back. Comforting, yet I stayed where I was, stiffening.

"How?" I breathed, gasping for air. He removed his hand and tugged at my shoulder to turn me. "I can't. Can't stand. Up yet...Can't breathe."

"Use your magic," he said, so simply that I wanted to hit him in the face.

"Hit me then." I was confused. Had I said that aloud? He pulled on my soaked arm again.

"I don't know how. I don't. Know. Anything. Anymore." The stone beneath my fingers was turning to grit. Crumbling. I felt the energy of those who built it hundreds of years ago. Felt their labor, blood, illness, dedication, hatred as it leeched through the grit into my fingers. Absorbing more and more of that ancient energy, I could see snapshots of their lives.

Cruelty from the masters of this place. Love from others. Sick‑ ness and military occupation.

"I understand. Perhaps you could step away from the wall you are now turning to dust. It would be a nasty fall into the roses." The grit was caked under my fingernails as I dragged my hands and eyes from the wall I was destroying as though it were talc. I needed to hit something and run. "Then hit me," Cade said again. My frustration was inching toward madness as I didn't know what thoughts were in my head and which were coming out of my mouth. Shaking my head as if to dislodge a fly, I was panting, trying to make sense of it all.

"I'm not. Not going to hit you." Spots were in my vision again. The dim lights from the door making it impossible to focus. I pushed at his chest, and he grabbed my hands, sending both of us back a few feet.

"You have done nothing wrong, Neysa," he said, trying to capture my eyes, which were darting around like a caged animal. Maybe he read the loss in them because he said, "We aren't going anywhere. It's just a puzzle. A puzzle to fix." He grabbed both sides of my head, forcing my stare, then blew once, lightly. It was like snow-kissed wind. My breathing regu‑ lated. Heart slowed. I closed my eyes. The anxiety eased. That gift of healing pulled the constriction from my chest and allowed my eyes to focus.

"I want to show you," I panted. What a luxury it was to breathe freely. "How do I show you my vision? I feel like I can, or I should, but I don't know how to do it," I stammered.

A long pause. The aftermath of the anxiety left me sway‑ ing. "I don't know. That's not my gift. If it is indeed yours, you may just need to experiment."

The weight of the days, the months, even the years, caused my body to sag. His broad cloth shirt was still pooled under my freezing fingers. His own long fingers still kept my face steady.

"How did you know it was me?" I demanded of him. "Why didn't you say anything? Did the others know?"

"The fracture in the Veil was left to me to heal. The scent of that which caused it committed itself to my being. Almost like a magical microchip. I recognized it as soon as I met you. Before even. I scented it on my cousins. Not wholly, so it was still confusing. But I recognized it nonetheless. I knew you had been too young to have done it yourself. What I had needed to find out is whether you had known." I pulled away and walked off. "Neysa."

"No," I spat, and sliced my hand through the air, a shimmer of color trailed from the movement. Interesting. "I am *done* with being a part of everyone's schemes. There is no one. No one I can trust in this whole fucking universe."

"Neysa. It's not like that."

"Not like what? I am a pawn in this, and I knew that, but I didn't think..." I stammered. "I thought I could trust you. Wanted to trust you."

"Neysa."

"I am so fucking done."

The rain made a job of sludging through the wood to get to

my cottage. I was gone by morning.

CHAPTER 13

Growing up traveling often, Los Angeles never felt like home. The trips I took with my father for his research, and his invitations to speak at museums and educational institutions worldwide had us away more than at home. School was partly home-based, allowing us to be in Europe, the UK, even Asia, as often as we liked. With a surge of resentment and grief, I thought that every trip could have been a ruse. I was an unwitting accomplice.

Landing back in LA made my stomach sour. Dad's house was still on the market, but I knew I wouldn't stay there. I paid through the nose for a hotel in Santa Monica where I could see the ocean and not the blasted palm trees and electrical wires that ran like toxic veins through the breadth of the city. The slower pace and fresh air of coastal England had me wrapped around its finger. Having to be back in this place that had embraced all my pain and insecurities had me aching to be off again. All I needed was a few days to get to the safety deposit box to which I had inherited the key, and God (gods?) willing, remove the item I hoped was entombed. Beyond dumping it back in England where it rightfully belonged, I hadn't a plan. I only knew I was heartsick from being infantry in everyone else's war.

The morning following my arrival in southern California, after a long run on the cigarette-doused beach, I picked up some street tacos and headed to the bank. The box was larger than expected, with a winged opening that held a separate level. On the top trays were a set of wedding rings I'd never seen. Both gold, speckled with chips of what appeared to be aquamarines. Alongside them lay a pendant. It reached from the top on opposite sides like outstretched arms, joining the split silver chain. From the reaching silver arms, aquamarine gems dotted in a sort of sequence until they joined together at a point then extended back out forming an angular kite shape. At each angle was an aquamarine set in silver. The bottom, deeper cavity, contained a leather-bound notebook filled with my dad's scrawl and the item I had been after. A wooden case wrapped in silk. Years I'd spent seeing this sitting on Dad's desk as he scribbled away in his many journals. We had a no touch rule on crystalline objects when I was growing up. Now, I knew why.

Lifting the lid to see inside, I released a breath. There sat a twelve-inch dagger crafted from flawless amethyst topped by a silver hilt bejeweled with two moonstones. The air around me buzzed with energy, and I quickly snapped the lid shut. The last thing I needed was to cause an explosion in a bank in LA. Somehow, in Barlowe Combe, dealing with the complexities of another realm and the magical objects bound to it was easier. Here in the brightness of Los Angeles, this entire task seemed implausible. Foolhardy and utterly ridiculous.

I slumped, thinking I could leave this all. Not try to be this savior. Not have to deal with fae and magic and rifts. I could stay here and forget the past five months and get on with my life. Erase the damage I caused in that family. Erase my night with Silas and my gut-wrenching feelings for...*stop it, Neysa*.

I looked at the wedding rings and the strange necklace and knew. Knew in my soul that not only would I be failing every- one, I would be losing the thread I had started to grasp, linking the me here to the me I truly am. There was so much more I could accomplish and be and hiding here would slowly kill me. Kill me as it did my father. It very nearly could have killed me had I not rented a cottage on the coast of England. I wanted to put the necklace on and feel its oddity against my skin, but wariness nudged me about wearing someone else's jewelry. Dad had always bid me to beware of wearing antiques and even secondhand clothing when I went through my vintage phase. Reading Dad's book had to be a priority. If only to see where this object fit in the puzzle, if at all.

Once the box, minus its contents, which were now in my black ballistic nylon duffel bag, was returned, I set off to fly back to the UK.

THE FLIGHT WAS the worst I had experienced in my thirty-five years. Fretting over whether the dagger would make it back to me, I did not sleep a wink. One obviously could not bring a twelve-inch dagger, no matter the value to the universe, onto a plane. Twice I attempted to reach my power out to the dagger to sense its presence, and both times the plane hit turbulence that had the cabin waking up and praying. Not the best idea then. Knowing the drive north to Barlowe Combe would not happen with the amount of rest I had gotten, I stayed at an airport hotel outside of Heathrow for the night.

CHAPTER 14

Determined and ready to get on with it, I tromped up the steps to the wide double doors of the manor and pounded. Corra answered and started to smile at me.

I cut her off. "Here is the missing crystal from the grotto," I said in a clipped voice so tight I thought I would throw up. I thrust the wooden case at her, pushing her back into the flag- stone foyer of the house.

"Darling, wait," she called as I turned back around to leave. Where? I had no clue. A pub for starters. I hadn't eaten since the tacos the previous day, bar a cup of tea and pack of oatcakes.

I held up my hand to signal I was finished listening.

Silas and Cadeyrn both stood sentry at the bottom of the stairs, dressed in fighting leathers, blocking my path. Fuck. The late autumn air was whipping around me, lashing at the cashmere scarf wound around my neck. Gently, I unwound it and stuffed it into my handbag. Then I stood, legs apart, hands on the short blades strapped to my thighs. The two males looked as haggard as I felt. Their hair, both Cade's silky ebony tousle and Silas's thick brown waves, were in disarray. Their leathers were mud splattered, and Silas had a long slash in his jacket.

"I brought the crystal. I just want to leave. Please." I would fight my way through if I had to, but surely, they had what they needed. My hands twitched at my sides, brushing against the fabric of my pants.

"We don't," Cade said.

"Don't what, Cade? I'm so, so tired." I could barely look at him.

"We don't have what we need," he clarified. "There is a connection between you and...this place. I hear some of the thoughts you have because somehow, we forged a connection. The night you were struck from the amazonite. We need you to be here. With me. With us. To help," he said. I was shaking my head. "Not to be a part of a game. We never meant for that. We need you to be a part of...us." His empty hand grabbed at the back of his neck.

"So, what? You're going to fight me and force me to submit?" I was so very, very tired. Nothing was making sense. They looked to each other, confused. Cade dropped his long sword.

"I wouldn't attack you if you aimed that blade at my heart," Cadeyrn declared, and I sat forcefully on the stone step.

"Nor I," Silas agreed.

"Plus, they would have to get through me, and I'm a right hell cat when provoked," Corra boomed from the door behind me. "Why don't you come inside, Neysa, and let Cadeyrn make us dinner."

"You would think in three hundred years, one of you would have learned to cook," Cade said and walked past me, squeezing my shoulder. I wondered if I had to now be careful of my thoughts around him.

"Probably a good idea," he answered my unasked question with a smirk, as he sauntered into the house, stomping his muddy boots. Well, crap. A chuckle sounded from inside the door.

Silas walked to me and hefted me up from under my arms. "You're dead on your feet, *Trubaíste*."

"I'm guessing that's not the beautiful part," I asked tartly.

Corra laughed and took my bag from me.

THE SITTING room was warmed by the enormous fireplace, currently empty of its crowning weaponry. Weaponry that was now being cleaned on the laps of two large fae males with hounds at their feet. I smiled when I thought of how I had been afraid to sit in here the first time I had come, sweaty and dirty from running. Now, we all sat in various degrees of cleanliness, ranging from Corra, who never seemed less than impeccable, I, who had showered the night before, and these two, who were caked in substances of varying filth.

"Is anyone going to tell me why you two look like you just came off the front lines?" I asked with a yawn.

"It is due to the fact that we just came off the front lines," Cade answered, looking up at me from under lowered brows. Something in that look, the sword, the outfit, made my toes curl in my own boots. I clamped down on the thought before it broadcast unwittingly.

It seems there was a larger rift in the Veil in my absence, which allowed for a band of mercenaries from a festering city in the Realm to come through. Their magic was too weak to normally pass through without it suffocating them. However, in this aberration, they slipped in. The hounds alerted Cadeyrn to their presence, and the cousins tracked the band through the woods. Corra stayed here and captured one who told her they were "*sent by the true ruler of Aoifsing to scourge this plain of the chosen one.*" Silas and Cade managed to slay the remaining five while one slipped back through the Veil.

How very different this was from where I had just flown. The threat of violence had been there since I first found out about all our history. Yet, seeing them fresh from a skirmish made it all too real. The fighter in me was ready to take it on. The woman raised human, still tried to rationalize it all. Tried to tamp down on that inhuman need to engage.

I picked at a cracker from the cheese plate in front of me. The feeling that I was missing something sat heavy in me. I now knew for certain that my mother had been fae. How my father or she had slipped through long enough to conceive and birth me—I knew my father had been present at my birth when she died—was still a mystery.

I pulled the wedding rings out from my handbag and lay them on the ottoman. Corra whistled. "Those are lovely. Fae made," she explained.

"How can you tell?"

"You can't feel it? Interesting," Corra noted. "There is heat coming off them that isn't present in this realm. They were forged from one single piece of gold. Forged to be together eternally." She asked to touch them. "They are stunning, Neysa. Have you put them on?"

Cade looked up with alarm at Corra's question.

"No. I was afraid of what could happen. If I were to trigger something," I admitted.

Cade's shoulders dropped. What I didn't say aloud was that I was afraid of what feeling not only the weight of marriage tokens on my own skin would do to me but tokens of a love snuffed out before it had a chance to blossom. Or decay.

Cade subtly looked at me, still shining his sword. Perhaps he too understood. The warmth of the room and the food finally in my belly combined with the soft brushing sweep of the oiling cloth on metal lulled me into a deep sleep. I did not wake until midmorning the next day.

BACK IN THE DINING ROOM, papers spread out, Dad's journal opened, and laptop queued up, I was prepared to find some– thing linking my amethyst dagger to something of consequence. I wrote down "Vilcabamba, Ecuador, The Valley of Longevity" next to "Black Tourmaline." This would be the energy-harnessing stone. The amethyst was the protection stone, which needed to be near the Veil. The types of gems remaining, supposing I was correct regarding the tourmaline, were still a mystery.

I was looking up crystals for protection circles and magic for reaching "the beyond," but all I was finding were hippie sites run by people with bogus degrees in life studies and archaic texts written by charlatans. Boots scraped behind me, and Silas dropped a scone beside my computer.. I could smell the sea and oak trees on him mixing with his woodsmoke scent. His finger tapped at my short list.

"Vilcabamba," he read aloud. "Vilc..." He began rustling through my papers and pulled out the list we had made together months ago when I had fallen apart in front of him. He read from that list: "Vil-Cab-Amba." We looked at each other, both of our mouths popping into an "O." I half regis-tered the sounds of additional feet scraping in, but I jumped out of my chair and kissed Silas smack on the lips.

"Bloody genius!" I yelled. He looked slightly mortified, slightly cocky. "You're right! What if—what if the whole list..." I spun and saw Cade and Corra standing behind us. I waved the paper at them like a victory flag. "The words my father was yelling before he died. It wasn't ravings. It was—is —a list. Perhaps a list of all the places the stones are hidden." I took a breath, then looked to Cade. He was looking at Silas.

Silas half smiled and shrugged a shoulder.

"Well done, cousin," Cade said and clapped him on the

back. Everyone in the room exhaled. "Let's plug in the rest of the words and see what comes up," he suggested.

I sat back down, and the three cousins crested behind me.

I typed: *Cappado*— The search suggestion came up as Cappadocia, Turkey. Cappa-Dokee-Ah. Bingo. I grinned and peeked behind me. All three were grinning like fools.

"Central Anatolia region. Turkey," Cade said. "That area has been ransacked by every empire and subcategory of every religion in this realm. It sits at a crossroads between Christian, Muslim, Judaism, and the Old Gods. The entire terrain is marked by volcanic flutes in the mountains."

My vision!

"I saw them! The flutes. It should be a blue stone there. I think."

The flutes I had seen are called "fairy chimneys" and drew tourists to see the natural wonders of the area. There are even underground cities within the mountains that remain in use by humans with more affinity for magic. They are heavily fortified as Cade pointed out. The likelihood of our being able to walk right in and grab a protected artifact was next to nothing. Plus, it's a tourist destination. Between the fairy chimneys and the balloon launches, it seemed as though the spiritual marvel of the region had dwindled.

"The likelihood of that particular artifact still being in that location after millennia of war tribes plundering it, is next to nothing," Silas countered. "I would wager the area is a ruse. Just as St. Michaels was here." St. Michaels was known as a spiritual hub of sorts, and this lot used that as a diversionary tactic to keep anyone from sniffing out the amethyst here in Barlowe Combe. We all looked at the screen. Reela. Next on the list. Ree-la. Rila.

"Bulgaria?" I asked. When I was twelve, we took a trip to eastern Europe. My father had been on a monastery kick and the Rila Monastery was a World Heritage Site. "Are you thinking in the monastery? There is a quite a bit of lore surrounding the Seven Lakes as well."

"Giants who protect the land from evil forces?" Silas asked. "Rila was thought to have been named after its founder, Saint Ivan of Rila. He was a hermit who lived in a cave near to where the old monastery was built in the tenth century. They say he had no possessions and was fiercely protective of his cave."

"Do you think that perhaps he was guarding the stone?" I asked.

Silas tipped his head in a *maybe-maybe-not* fashion. I tipped my own back against the chair and blew out a long breath. Cade's hands came down on my shoulders.

"That's a lot of mountain range to be unsure about. I saw the flutes. Maybe we are thrown off," I asked, words slurring a bit. Cade's hands moved on to the back of my neck, kneading the inflamed muscles there. I was shocked at his willingness to touch me so casually.

He leaned down and whispered, "If I don't heal this now, you will tear your shoulder as soon as you pick up a sword." Ah.

Corra was searching on her phone.

"According to this, blue agate is made from volcanic sources. It would stand to reason that it was originally from Cappadocia. Perhaps, when the Armenian settlers began to move out of Cappadocia toward Syria and Mesopotamia, the stone was moved as well, to keep it out of the hands of the crusaders. It could be that moving it then into Bulgaria was a well-intentioned royal disaster," Corra explained.

Cade's thumbs moved up and worked at the base of my skull. An undignified groan escaped me. He really had no idea how much I needed this. And how much he shouldn't be doing this while expecting me to function properly.

"Neysa," Cade began, voice a bit rough. "Are you able to tap back into your vision as you did with your father's? Perhaps try to see further?"

I stiffened. He dropped his hands. I wasn't sure how to do it. In the back of my mind, I remember seeing a cloth-covered arm holding a candle in full darkness. It wasn't enough to venture into Bulgaria in the dead of winter. I twisted in my seat to look at him.

"If I could—or if I could just tap into the memory of what I already saw, do you think I could show you? I don't know how our connection works." I looked to Corra, who was studying me almost too closely, nostrils flaring.

"Perhaps," Cade said carefully, taking a small step back. Corra shot him a look I couldn't read.

"It is worth a go, Cadeyrn. You may recognize places or times she wouldn't," Corra reasoned.

They locked eyes. Something in their unspoken conversation weighed heavily in the room. "Alright then," he answered apprehensively.

"I have no idea what the hell I'm doing, so this could be a glorious waste of everyone's time. But if I can help narrow the search, I would like to," I said.

Cade sat across from me in the adjacent dining chair, seeming to dwarf it. Our knees were touching, and I grabbed his hands trying to stamp down the image of conjuring energy with Silas all those months ago. I closed my eyes and tried to relax. His hands were rough and callused from years of sword play. They felt warm and homey in mine.

I pictured sitting with him and telling him a story. Something stupid from my childhood or just the goings-on in a day. Pictured sharing the intimacies of a strong emotion. This could have been dangerous territory but there was a threshold I needed to surpass to let him in. I showed him the day Dad died. The complete and utter emptiness I had felt.

Showed him the desolation I had felt when I fled this dining room days earlier. He didn't respond other than tightening his grip on my hands.

I moved closer, knowing I may have been crossing a line more demarcated than the threshold allowing him in. Mental snapshots of how he looked to me as I watched him sleep in his room. The clenching in my gut as I stared at him. What I saw when he smiled, and the darkness with which he so often shrouds himself lifted from him. His hands began to shake in mine. I moved closer still. I shared the vision of the grotto and my father. The visions from the amazonite that struck me with electricity. The cloud forest. The humid land with the weathered hand. The robed arm with the candle. All of it.

He released my hands and held my face, pressed next to his, the heat from him seeping into the places that had gone so cold in me. We sat there for countless minutes until the last vision dissipated. I hadn't noticed that I had wound my arms around his waist as he held my face. Slowly, I extricated myself from him and shyly looked up. That mask was back. The unread– able, dispassionate mask. I had enough experi- ence to know what that look meant in a moment like this.

"Maybe you can make better sense of it all than I can," I said quickly, and walked out of the room so fast I had to grab the polished oak door frame to keep from careening into it.

I barely even noticed that Corra and Silas were conspicu- ously missing as I made my way to my room to change into running clothes.

"I CAN GO to Turkey and Bulgaria," I announced at dinner that same evening, pointedly not looking at Cade. Perhaps I was a coward. Perhaps he was as well, but I didn't have the courage to face fallout in that department. Three sets of nearly identical eyes looked to me.

"Not on your own. I'll go with you," Corra announced.

"It'll be a girls' trip. We can get drunk and run with wild horses."

I nearly laughed. The males shook their heads, Cade pinching the bridge of his nose.

I made an agreeable gesture to Corra. "Then that's settled. Let's book it, Corra."

"It isn't settled," Cade intoned. Oh? I'll be damned if I let him tell me what or where I cannot go. He ran a hand through his hair and stood abruptly. "For gods' sake, Neysa. I am not telling you whether or not you can go," he exclaimed at practically a shout. The others looked to him in surprise. "I know that's what you were thinking. I meant that Turkey may be a dead-end. Silas's idea of Bulgaria seems to be a more solid one. Make it a two-legged trip. For the sake of all that's good and holy, go. Get spit drunk. Run with the damned horses. Have a train of men following you both about. Be a tourist. Do what you want but make it worth the gods-damned trip." He pushed his plate away and stormed from the room.

The three of us stood in stunned silence.

"You do get under his skin," Silas teased.

I shot him an incredulous look. What had I done now?

"I think he wanted to be included on the girls' trip," Corra

giggled.

I took a deep breath for courage and left the room to find

the adult fae male who had just had a temper tantrum like a toddler.

Cade poked at the fire in a stance like that of a soldier measuring the battlefield. I supposed that was how I stood as well, taking measure of the battle I was about to face.

He loosed a sigh.

"Am I that difficult?" I asked.

"You're the one pondering the casualties of this encounter,"

he answered, not turning.

"I feel like it's one step forward, two steps back with you, Cade. Did you want to go to Bulgaria? Alone? With me? Did I miss something? I know I get under your skin. Silas even said so. I'm only trying..."

He whirled on me much like he did when we sparred. I was suddenly pinned to the wall beside the fireplace. His face was inches from mine. Distantly, I heard two chairs scrape on the flagstone floors. Footsteps hurried toward the sitting room but stopped short of entering.

"Trying to what?" he asked softly. My heart was pounding, and a look of frantic confusion was in his eyes. "Everything you are *trying* to do, you are doing. You treat me like I'm a lord of this manor, and I am not. We are equal, Neysa. Yes, you get under my skin. In more ways than you know. I get snippets of your thoughts and feelings." He placed a hand over my heart. "But I never know what is really going on in here."

He touched my head and leaned in, lips next to my ear. My knees felt weak.

"I have no doubt that you will be the one who figures this puzzle out, but I'll be damned if it doesn't make me sick worrying every time you take off on your own. Yes, I want to come to Bulgaria. No, I will not." He pulled back slightly, looking me in the eyes.

I brought my hand up and unconsciously brushed my finger over his full bottom lip. He closed his eyes and took a deep breath. "Then come along," I whispered. "We can all get drunk and run with the horses."

He laughed hoarsely and stood straight, again towering over me. His face regained that icy mask. "I can stay and guard the Veil. Your absence is bound to cause a stir in it."

As he stepped away, I felt cold.

"Then I'll book the trip."

With that, Corra and Silas walked in, both making a grand

point of not saying anything regarding the charged atmosphere in the room. I stared at Cade, willing him to look at me. He deliberately fiddled with objects in the room—the decanter, the dogs' ears, the curtains.

I suppose my lot in life is to always be a shade off normal. Is it so hard being close to me? I pondered to myself.

His head shot up, and he said to no one in particular, "It is difficult, Neysa. Yes."

Corra looked to me in an understanding that failed me. I drew my shoulders back and strode for my laptop. "Let's get this trip sorted, Corra."

She and I made our way to the desk to arrange the details of our excursion. Silas swiveled on his heels and vacated the room with a marked growl.

CHAPTER 15

On a hunch, we took a detour. It seemed to me that finding the black tourmaline, if that was in fact what we were looking for, would be more pressing initially than another stone. As such, I convinced Corra to travel to Peru. After retreating to my room for the night, we figured out the locations from my list, I decided that Vilcabamba, Ecuador, though widely considered a spiritual hub, had now become a lure for tourists. It no longer held a real link to its roots. Vilcabamba, Peru, however, is an isolated ruin of a lost Incan city and seemed more of a contender for our crusade.

We ultimately decided not to tell the males of our plan to forgo eastern Europe and instead head to South America. In my case, it was likely a long burning desire to not have to answer to anyone. To not have to explain my reasoning or the consequences if I happened to be wrong. Though in my bones I felt I had to be right.

Corra, bless her, would have followed me on an adventure to the moon for the sake of adventure and pissing off her brother and cousin.

"Why the bloody Spaniards thought it prudent to capture this blasted city given the terrain and all this muck we are having to go through is beyond me," Corra complained.

She pushed past a thicket of heavy foliage with her walking stick and swore at the skitter of beetles underneath it. We had seen more insects here than I ever want to deal with again. Despite the early winter, I found myself slapping my skin and brushing off the feeling of tiny beasts crawling on me.

Day three of our hike to this lost city and my certainty about the stone being there was starting to waver. Mid-November is the start of the rainy season, and while we hadn't had a downpour yet, the sky was increasing its density, sending my nerves on a collision course.

I had considered myself a seasoned hiker, having trekked most hikes in Southern California, many in Hawaii, parts of the Pacific Crest Trail, Appalachian Trail, and several world-wide with my father. Admittedly, I wasn't mentally prepared for five days in the high-altitude rain forest with only Corra for company. It was highly suggested we take a guide with us as the trail was long and treacherous. However, the nature of our quest made it tricky to have a tagalong. We pushed ourselves the first two days, leaving at dawn and continuing on well into the night when the terrain allowed. I wouldn't give in to the exhaustion I knew was longing to get its fingers into me. I knew from the map that we were close.

In an effort to capture the Incan region and maintain a stronghold on the area, the Spanish launched a campaign against the Incas, vying for Vilcabamba. The Inca fought for months to keep the Spanish at bay, and retreated deeper into the unforgiving mountains and forest, going so far as moving miles upon miles ahead of the enemy. Once the Spanish captured the bridge on the outskirts, it was only a matter of time before the heavily fortified army laid siege to the city of

Vilcabamba. On June 24, 1572, the Spanish stormed the city, only to find it abandoned, in ruin, and its people fled. Later referred to as a "ghost plain," the area maintained an aura of wisdom and pride, though it crumbled in its mossy remains. Here is where I felt we would find the tourmaline.

We stepped into the open plain leading to the ruins, and I took a long breath, feeling the quiet energy thrum through me. My senses reached out as I did on the plane from Los Angeles, trying to feel a link to that which we sought. Corra caught my hand in hers and as the skies opened up, I felt a pull to the north of the ruins. We followed the tug for several miles, panting and slugging through the banking mud. As we rounded a corner, Corra shoved me behind her.

"*Buenas, hijas,*" beckoned a small, crone-like woman, sitting on a plastic stool in a clearing. She was whittling a stick, unfazed by the downpour. "*Las he estado esperando. Bienvenidas hadas.*"

I was dumbstruck, and by the look on Corra's face, she was too.

"What did she say, Neysa?" Corra asked as the old woman smiled, waving us forward.

"She said she has been waiting for us. She referred to us as daughters and welcomed us. As faeries." I swallowed.

"Well, I suppose I shan't kick your ass for dragging me all the way here for nothing then." We moved toward the crone. She took my filthy hand in hers and sighed.

"My grandmother knew you would one day come, as her grandmother before her knew as well. I have kept it hidden for you. Know that the days ahead will be enrobed with trials. You will face more hardships, daughters. Your heart will be tested. Stay your course, and trust what is in here," she explained in Spanish, tapping my head.

I translated this somber revelation to Corra, and the old woman smiled largely and toothlessly.

"I am in your debt, grandmother," I replied.

She shooed me and stood with a groan, lifting her tiny pink stool. The site of that plastic rubbish here amidst the lush rain‐ forest made my head swim. She linked her bony arm through mine and led us away from the clearing. Shortly thereafter, we came upon a small tent and fire with no other inhabitants.

"*Sientate, hijas. Vamos a comer.*"

I was more than happy to oblige her in sitting and eating. Three days of dried meat bars and nuts had me dreaming of real food. Our grandmotherly guide placed bowls heaped with beans and rice in front of us, along with water and cloths to wash.

Once our bellies were full to bursting, she presented me with an object wrapped in a bright woven blanket. The pulsating vibrations from the object left me with no doubt as to its contents. I unwrapped it slowly. The crystal within was a pyramid shape of polished black tourmaline. In its flawless facade I could see my reflection staring back. Corra reached out to stroke it, and the moment both of our hands met it, I was thrust into a vision.

TALES AROUND A FIRE sung by tribal leaders. Battle cries of an outgunned warrior faction. Bodies falling hundreds of feet into rushing water. A young girl given this pyramid by her elder being told to run and keep it hidden. Large, chocolate eyes staring from a hidden copse of fern as her elder was gutted. The pyramid being moved with females from tribe to tribe and marriage to marriage, wove its tapestry through time. The eyes of our guide, though much younger, keeping the stone hidden beneath the grave marker of her grand‐ mother for many decades. Finally, the blazing blue of a cylindrical shaped agate in the hand of a man in a land with fluted mountains.

THE VISION COLLAPSED, and I gasped for air. Corra grabbed my shoulders and questioned me with her eyes.

"And now you know." The crone nodded at me.

She wrapped my hand in hers and muttered a blessing in a language time forgot. I held her hands in mine and thanked her for keeping it safe. Thanked her for her years of secrecy and solitude. She patted my cheek and smiled.

We stayed the night in her camp, delighting in another warm meal for breakfast before heading back on the trail to go home. Perhaps having the crystal in our possession made us physically stronger and faster. Perhaps the lure of civilization had the same effect. Either way, we made much better time on the way home. Our last night making camp, we settled into our bed rolls and groaned.

"You know, Silas will have my head for not telling him where we went," Corra mused. I smirked.

"And Cade?"

"Oh, he's likely pissed himself with worry," she answered. I snorted.

"Worry or anger?" I asked. I heard her turn to me.

"He's not angry in disposition. He takes everything upon himself and blames himself for what goes amiss," she explained.

I knew that. I don't really know why I had asked. I could see light in him, and some small part of me wished it shined for me.

"There was a time when Cadeyrn was wilder and more light- hearted than Silas. My brother can make Death herself smile, but he has a gift for feeling deeply. Cadeyrn has been burdened his entire life and used to shoulder it with more...devil may care —is that the phrase? After our parents and Solange, though, he internalized it all. One day, I fear that fire in him will erupt and take him with it if he does not lighten his load."

"And now I have added to that burden," I stated. "He knows I am meant to help with this puzzle, yet it's another burden to bear."

"He worries, Neysa. About you. He cares for you. It winds up Silas because my brother freely shows his heart, but Cadeyrn will stamp down his feelings no matter the cost."

I pondered that as I drifted off to sleep.

TRAPPED. My eyes sprang open at the feeling of suffocation. Corra was inches from my face, eyes wide, hand clamped over my mouth. She tapped her finger on my cheek three times and slowly lifted off me, placing my dagger in my palm. We silently got to our feet, collecting our absolute necessities. I had slept with twin small swords strapped to my thighs and the stone slung across my chest, still in its blanket sling. As I lifted the nylon strap of my canteen, I heard a voice behind me.

"You won't be needing that where you're going, *mamá*."

I met Corra's eyes. How many were there? Was that the three she tapped on my cheek? I heard the shuffle of two sets of feet to my rear. A flashlight shone outward, making Corra all but invisible to me, but I felt a shift in the air. If only her magic worked here. Realization hit that mine may.

"Good morning, sir," I drawled, not turning toward the light. "To what do we owe this visit?"

Laughter came from the far side. Three then. The one who had spoken first answered in heavily accented English.

"You should have listened to the travel agents," he said. "Young ladies in the wilderness don't last long. Especially when they carry such valuable cargo." My stomach turned.

"We are just tourists exploring the ruins."

Another laugh and a step forward. Corra looked at me and looked down. Her fingers splayed on her thigh, and she tapped her index finger with her thumb then signaled to herself with her thumb. I twitched my eyes in acknowledgement and she separated her index and middle fingers from the ring and pinky, then began to count down by tucking her fingers in one at a time. I closed my eyes and tapped into the tourmaline.

A swirl of darkness flowed around me, and as Corra tucked her last finger in, I heard the men swear. We launched. She took out the man hidden on the far side before anyone saw her move. I shot into the area between the sound of foot-falls I had heard and spun in a figure eight to separate the men. The torchlight dropped and rolled out of sight. By the sound of it, Corra was fighting the second as I took on the outspoken one. The sound of a handgun being released from its holster was not surprising, and I focused my attention on disarming him of that weapon.

We were close enough that I grabbed the front of the barrel and shoved it backward, disabling the gun from firing long enough for me to kick the legs out from underneath the mercenary. As he fell, he pulled my shoulder toward him, taking me down as well. I held the gun as we toppled and once we hit the grassy ground, I slammed his elbow until the gun released. He scrambled for it, and I kicked out wildly, sending the weapon into the foliage.

"*Puta!*" he screamed and knocked the side of my head with the back of his hand. My vision spotted. I rolled to the right and tucked my knees in, jumping into position. He pulled a fixed blade combat knife from his thigh and spun it in his hand. Perfect. This was my kind of fight. We parried in silence as the clash of metal sung in an arc behind us, Corra out pacing the other mercenary.

Streaks of silvery sunlight began inching across the sky, indicating dawn's approach. This needed to end now. Beck-oning to my opponent through the morning shadows, I smiled tauntingly.

"Let's be done here, sir. It's breakfast time."

He sneered and sprinted toward me. I dropped to a crouch just before his knife was in range and rolled, twin swords crisscrossing above me, finding their mark along his inner thighs. He screamed, and as he fell, I rocketed to my feet and pointed the blades at his sternum. A wet gurgle replaced the meeting of steel from Corra's end, and she was quickly by my side.

"Stay down," I commanded using the point of my sword for emphasis. He released a string of curses in Spanish. "What is your business with us?" He spat at me in answer to my question. "Look," I said. "By my account, you are not faring as well as you had hoped in attacking two women in their sleep. You can either tell me who you are and what your business is with me and my friend here. Or you can bleed out slowly and attract a whole lot of curious beasts out for their morning meals."

"The crystal does not belong to your kind," he breathed.

"I assume you use the 'your kind' lightly, as you've no idea what kind I am. Do you believe it belongs to you?" I asked.

"It is not to be used as a weapon between peoples," he said cryptically. "Your kind will find a way to destroy us all, and my men and I have been tasked with protecting it."

This was a new turn of events. I looked down at his injuries and realized they were grave. He had a few minutes at best. Panic started rising in me. I shot a look to Corra, whose eyes met mine quizzically.

"The realms are not meant to be crossed," he stated, breathing labored.

"We are doing our best to keep that from happening. Why attack us when we are on the same side?" I asked.

An arrow lanced his chest before he answered. Corra and I spun toward the trajectory and another arrow caught her just below the ribs. I screamed and blindly hurled my dagger in the direction of the arrow, distantly hearing it miss its mark. The tourmaline cast an obsidian shield around Corra and me as I centered myself, readying for the next arrow. It whizzed close. From within my shield, I could see the outline of a pale fae with a strung bow through the branches of a tree.

"Think, Neysa. Don't react," Corra gasped. I looked at her, seeing in the watery light, where the arrow had punctured. We were still a good few hours from town—a full day from the city. "I'll be okay. Get rid of Reynard, and we can move out of here," she said, trying to placate me.

"She won't be fine," that silky, amused voice called down from the tree. "The arrowhead was silver-coated iron. She's dead weight now, Neyssie."

I stilled as I heard the nickname my father used for me. A killing calm swept over me as I willed myself toward the trees. Sounds of Reynard dropping to the ground pricked at my senses, yet I kept the tourmaline bubble intact and made for the trees where I had kicked the mercenary's gun.

"Where are you going little mouse?" he trilled.

I stopped and dropped to the cloud forest floor in the blink of an eye, grabbed the weapon, and shot in the same fell swoop. He yelped and dropped his bow, clutching a bleeding shoulder wound.

"Oh, this, little mouse, will not go unpaid," he rasped before running. I broke for Corra, grabbing my daggers in the process.

"Let's go," I told her, hoisting her into a stand.

"I can make it to town," she said. "Beyond that we will need to pull the arrow out and assess the damage," she said. "Neysa, you need to be prepared to move on without me." I shook my head no. "Yes, darling. You need to get the crystal to my brother and cousin and stay with them."

"We are leaving," I said sharply.

I carried her for three successive hours and set her down just before heading into the small town. I wrapped a blanket around her to not attract attention, and I discreetly paid a taxi to take us to Lima. Corra stayed alert, if not waxen, the entire ride into the city. Once we arrived at the airport hotel, I began the job of removing the arrowhead.

"Do not seek medical attention for me. They will know I'm not human and that will cause greater issues. I need a fae heal– er." She looked at me pointedly.

I grabbed my charging phone. There were hundreds of texts and more than a few missed calls from both Silas and Cade. A knock sounded at our door. We looked to each other, exhaustion crowning every inch of my friend's elfin face. I looked through the peephole and saw familiar olive eyes peering at me. I whirled to Corra. She scented him before I could open my mouth.

"Open it," she wheezed.

"Are you certain it's not...not..." I couldn't finish knowing what the suggestion might do to her, given her feelings for Ewan.

"I guess we will find out."

I unlocked the deadbolt and let Ewan inside. He raced to Corra and dropped to her side.

"Gods, Corraidhín. What have you done to yourself?" he asked softly.

"I had a little help in the doing, darling," she said, making a grand effort to sound casual.

He looked to me and said, "I can remove it and staunch the blood flow, but she needs her cousin. We need to get her home. Without Cadeyrn or a fae healer, she won't last three days."

I nodded and again began to pick up my phone as Ewan laid the leather from his belt between Corra's teeth. "Here, *allaíne,* try not to scream," he spoke softly, stroking her matted auburn hair. I hit the call button on Cade's number. He answered immediately.

"Neysa," he stated nervously. I took a breath.

"Cade, we need you to meet us at the airport." I explained in short what had happened to Corra.

He said he would be waiting, and then tightly, "Neysa?" I squeaked at his tone of voice. "I am glad you are alright, though it was thoroughly irresponsible to not tell us where you had gone."

Prick. I hung up.

"He must really like you, madam, lest there would be harsher words for allowing his cousin to be taken out by an archer," Ewan said to me.

"I believe in this case, *'like'* is a very loose term, Ewan," I answered. He met my eyes with amusement. We both startled, looking at one another. His mouth dropped as I am sure mine did as well.

We both looked to Corra, who tried and failed to shrug.

"Can we discuss family dynamics after we have removed this gods-damned arrow from my ribs?"

CHAPTER 16

As it turned out, the arrow punctured her lung. Ewan was able to do a field dressing and magical stint. Our flight departed that evening, which left the ridiculous task of getting Corra, half-conscious from pain and blood loss, through an international airport and on to a flight. We wrapped and splinted her ankle, asking for a wheelchair without raising any eyebrows. Before heading through security, Ewan knelt beside the chair and leaned in close to Corra. I turned to give them privacy and heard only murmurs in the Aulde language.

"Safe travels, Neysa." Ewan half bowed. He would be taking a different flight, and I made it a point to ask later how he obtained travel documents. "I shall meet you in England and perhaps we can discuss with our friends," he delivered a pointed glance at the female in the wheelchair, "our uncanny resemblance to one another."

"I shall look forward to that discussion. Be well, Ewan." I shook his outstretched hand, and we both startled at the electricity between us.

IN THE LAST hour of our flight into Madrid, where we

were to connect to London, Corra's breathing became labored and wet. I fought the panic surging up and focused on keeping her calm. Were Ewan and I siblings, then perhaps I could use my gifts to stint her lung until we arrived in London. Trying and failing several times left me gasping for air. The pressure of descent had me doubting whether the next leg of our trip was possible at all.

We disembarked and were brought quickly through immigration. Standing waiting for us in the arrivals terminal in Madrid was Cade, who immediately took Corra out of the chair and into a waiting car. I didn't know where we were going and didn't care that we had missed our connection. The fact that Cade had showed up and was actively healing his cousin en route had me sagging with relief.

We were silent the whole ride, headed to the train station to travel via rail to England. I followed my companions into our train compartment and sat in uncomfortable silence the entire sixteen hours.

"Corradhin," Cade said softly. She opened her eyes and looked to him then flicked her gaze to me as I sat curled up on the seat in the opposite corner to Corra's bunk. "Libellula, I've closed the puncture in your lung. Ewan likely saved you. Your rib is chipped, so that will take me longer to heal, and I would rather do it once we are back home and comfortable. It will take some time for the silver and iron to leave your system, but overall, you will be fine."

He leaned over and kissed her brow. She patted his cheek and smiled weakly. My heart clenched. I had nearly lost her and mostly from my own stubbornness. Nearly cost their family the loss of her. The thought of that unit losing such brilliance, of Silas losing his sister, made me sick. Cade looked briefly at me then continued to ready the compartment for our departure. I couldn't even begin to imagine Silas's reaction to this fiasco.

Gods above.

NOVEMBER'S END snuffed out the light in Barlowe Combe. Dark skies hung low and heavy as we arrived back at the manor. I had still not spoken a word to Cade, and Corra was more or less asleep the whole trip. Leaving them at the front doors, I turned to head to my cottage. Not yet ready to see Silas, I felt like a disastrous interloper here. No one stopped me from going.

Relentless pounding brought me out of my dozing on the settee. For a moment, I was disoriented but extracted myself from the blanket over my legs. Biting my tongue from the sharp pain in my torso, I made my way to the door. The lock slid open, and Silas barged through like a storm cloud. I froze. He stared at me and caught my entire body up in a bear hug. I yelped at the pain in my side.

"Thank the gods you're alright," he said against my dressing gown, and set me back down, smoothing my hair with both of his broad hands.

I hadn't spoken aloud in so long my voice was gravely as I croaked, "I am so sorry, Silas."

"Ah, *Trubaíste*, for what? Making a decision, or for carrying my sister for twenty kilometers through the jungle?" He looked to me, and I straightened my dressing gown. "I am just happy you are both safe now. Have you eaten?"

I shook my head. Footsteps scuffed across the wet landing.

"I've brought dinner if you're hungry," Cade said, holding out a plate on a wooden tray. "Corraidhín is awake, Silas."

With that, Silas kissed my cheek and patted my shoulder, heading out.

"I figured you didn't want to be up at the manor with us. It's just a bit of meat pie and Yorkshires. Tilly saved the day," Cade said, attempting to lighten the mood. I stepped into the cottage, allowing him in, and shut the door while rubbing my arms, willing some warmth in them. "You're thinner. You should eat."

I scoffed. "It wasn't exactly fine dining where we were."

"No, I expect not. Not to mention your level of exertion must have been far more than what you managed to consume. Please, Neysa. Sit." He opened a bottle of cabernet and poured us each a glass.

In the short time it took me to eat, I felt Cade's eyes on me. I took the plate to the sink and tightened the tie on my dressing gown. My bare feet winced from the cold flagstone floors. He got up and began to light the fire in the sitting room, bringing both glasses with him. I followed, sitting on the settee upon which I had just recently napped. He sat opposite me, closer than I had been expecting. His hands went through his hair roughly, making the thick, straight strands stand a good inch above him.

"Why Peru?"

I guess that's where we are starting. I sipped my wine and fiddled with the silk of my dressing gown.

"We needed the protection stone," I rasped. "The more I thought about Vilcabamba, the more I realized it wasn't Vilcabamba, Ecuador. It seemed the right place to start."

He nodded. "Why not say so? It wouldn't have—"

"It was a hunch," I blurted. "I didn't want to second-guess myself if you lot thought it was dumb. Maybe I..."

"I wouldn't have thought it was dumb. I trust your judgment. Your hunches. I just wish you—"

"I know, okay? I should have said something. Had someone else there. It should have been me getting hit with that arrow. It was aimed at me."

"Stop." He put a hand on my knee and looked me dead-on. I met his glassy eyes. "The only thing I would have had you do differently is tell me. I...worry. I was worried."

"Did you send Ewan?" I asked.

"I did not. Silas did. We lost track of Reynard and thought Ewan might come in handy."

"Are we... is he my brother?" I stumbled on the word.

Cade scrubbed at his face and ran a hand through his hair again, giving it even more elevation. "I would rather you speak with him about it. Though it would seem likely," he admitted. You have similar scents."

I looked off, trying to stop my lip from trembling.

We sat in silence for a time, finishing our glasses. Finally, he asked, "May I hear the whole story?"

I looked at him, the firelight dancing on his features, and I wondered why we trip and stumble speaking to each other. All I wanted in that moment was to lean into him and show him the story in my mind. Instead, I steeled myself and told the whole tale. When I had finished, he was smirking.

"You took out two mercenaries and shot Reynard? With a gun?" he laughed. "Oh, please, show me if you will." My eyes met his uncertainly but reached out my hands.

Once the memory had finished, I started to pull away. He held tighter. "You can lean on me," he whispered. "I can stay and just be here. With you. For you." He dropped his eyes.

Slowly, I leaned forward and rested my head on his chest, stretching my legs behind me. He pulled the blanket over me and encircled my shoulders with his arms. Body nestled into his, it was the safest and warmest I had been in countless years.

"Thank you," I whispered back. His response was a soft kiss to the top of my head as I slipped into sleep.

UPON WAKING, my toes were frozen and the bruises to my shoulder and ribs were throbbing. A trick I had devised to quell anxiety in my waking moments was to recite currencies, languages, and capital cities. I started in the east and began working my way through Asia and into the Indian Ocean when the fog had cleared. That's about when I realized I was still in the sitting room, lying atop Cade, who at that moment was waking as well. Not sure whether I could sit up without support as my bruised rib was truly smarting, I stayed still, listening to his heartbeat.

"Mauritian rupee?" he asked groggily. My cheeks reddened where they lay against his black jumper. "I must admit I didn't know half the currencies you just read me." I squeezed my eyes shut and smiled. Neither of us moved. His scent had settled over me just as warmly as the blanket. "You didn't say anything about your injuries. I had assumed you were fine."

"I am fine. And you didn't ask. You didn't speak to me. I knew you were upset with me," I began but was interrupted.

He pulled his head back, careful not to push my shoulder.

"One, I was upset with both of you—upset that my cousin had been so gravely injured in a place I could not readily heal her. Two, *you* did not speak to *me*. The whole gods-forsaken trip. Even the thoughts that slipped past to me were quiet apart from one solitary mention of you being to blame for Corraidhín's injury." Though his voice did not rise, I felt an uptick in his heartbeat and the iciness was back in his tone.

To hell with my pain. I pushed off him and grunted indelicately.

"Why in all the realms would you move like that when your rib is cracked?" he barked.

I glared sidelong at his sleep-mussed face and realized I was still in just my dressing gown, which was rumpled and askew. I also hadn't realized my rib was cracked. That was likely why I had vomited repeatedly after carrying Corra. Which, of course, made it that much worse.

My pride overshadowing my good sense, I stood and yanked down on my robe, which had opened nearly to my navel yet kept any indecent bits covered. His incredulous expression softened a bit as his eyes dropped to my torso where I stood near the couch. I lurched back, unsteady on my feet, and his hand shot out to stabilize me. I yanked my arm back, which only had me yowling in pain from my shoulder.

"Are we back here then?" he asked hotly. I looked to him, pulling up my frosty reserve. He stood and said, "It's time I get back now. Come up later if you wish me to heal you."

He left quickly, and I shook, not knowing why I had reacted the way I did, mentally kicking myself for being so combative when all he was trying to do was help. I had been pushing people away for as long as I could remember. It's really no wonder that Caleb had affairs. Only my father stayed close to me. Only he saw the real me.

But in my frosty anger standing in the sitting room, I thought that perhaps here I had found others who understood me. Even understood me better than I did myself. If only I could stop being such an ass.

"STOP CLUCKING ABOUT, YOU GOOSE," I heard Corra snipping as I walked into the manor the following day.

"If you would sit still for a day and let yourself convalesce, he wouldn't be clucking about so much," Silas responded.

I rounded the doorway into the drawing room to see my friend laid out on the sofa with three males in a crescent around her. Bixby and Cuthbert trotted up to me. "Hallo, darlings," I cooed, kissing each hound in turn, trying to not let on how much pain I was in.

They sniffed at my shoulder and ribs, cocking their heads to the side in unison.

"Hallo, darling yourself," Corra called. I walked to her and kissed her cheek. She grabbed my hand. "Mother hen here says you were hurt. You should have said something!"

I rolled my eyes. "So, I've been told. I'm fine," I said.

"You carried me for four hours with a cracked rib! I might crack another just to punish you, you ninny," she scolded. "Go let Cadeyrn heal you. I don't want to see your pretty face back here until you're sorted out." I narrowed my eyes at her. "Off you go," she sang and waved her hands at me.

I turned to Silas and Ewan. "I like her better when we are fighting," I grumbled. They chuckled. "And it was just over three hours. Don't embellish." Then I looked at Cade, who looked like he'd eaten a lemon, and raised an eyebrow. He motioned for me to follow him into the other room.

For the first time, the pattern of the wallpaper in the dining room seemed thoroughly engrossing. Every swirl, leaf, and detail captured my attention as I entered and sat in one of the upholstered dining chairs. Cade sat in the chair facing me. He cleared his throat.

"From what I assessed, you have a T-shaped crack in rib number seven and the supraspinatus is torn, causing excess inflammation throughout the shoulder and bicep." He ran his hand through his hair and tugged at the tips.

I nodded. "I was pushed down onto my shoulder," I said needlessly. "Do whatever you need to do. I need to get back to work on this puzzle as you call it." There was silence. I finally looked at him.

"You need to remove your shirt," he said with what I detected to be a bit of embarrassment. *Ah.*

Stubborn as a mule, I pulled the oversized waffle knit over my head with a hiss and sat in my black balconette bra. He swallowed and tentatively reached out. I raised my arm above my head, giving better access to my rib, and bit my lip at the pain. A palm-sized bruise lay across my side where I had taken a boot to the ribs. A low growl escaped him, and his nostrils flared.

"Boot," I remarked nervously.

"So, it seems." He touched the tender areas and looked up at me, his finger at the edge of the band of my bra. "This likely isn't helping the pain, and I need to get to the skin underneath."

His sea green eyes stared up under a dark brow, full lips pursed. My own eyes met his, and I took a breath, attempting to reach behind me. Between the rib and lack of shoulder mobility, I stifled a cry trying to undo the clasp of my bra. He gently moved my arm back into place and reached around for me. As clinical as Cade was, this was more intimate than I had anticipated. After placing my arm over his shoulder to rest, he unclasped the hook and eye on my bra, then began to work on the area.

"I don't know how you managed to get that on. I've fractured ribs, and I think I didn't put on a shirt for weeks." He spoke distractedly as he had the day he healed my lip. I was breathing heavily from the pain and humility. "It drove my mother crazy. I went about the village bare-chested in the dead of winter."

I bet that caused a stir in the village.

"I didn't have anything to wear that doesn't go overhead," I admitted. His fingers moved like I was a violin he was playing pizzicato, fingertips light as mist over my skin. After a time, the unbearable pain ebbed away, and he leaned back into his chair, lifting my arm down to my lap. Signs of exhaustion lined that face I had seen every damn time I closed my eyes. I was trying to make this rift better, and every turn I took made it harder for him. For them. Cade's head lifted and met my gaze. *I was an abscess.*

"Give me just a moment, please," he breathed. "Corraidhín's injuries were quite consuming."

"You don't need to finish. Or at least not yet. I can go home..."

"I just need a moment. Please." Eyes closed, he sat back, shoulders slumped.

I concentrated on the energy from my clear quartz nestled between my breasts, hoping to transfer the fortitude from the quartz into Cade. The amethyst pendant had gone missing, so I had taken to carrying the quartz. Once in tune with the crystal, I pushed my knee against Cade's and reached for his hands with my good arm. His eyes snapped open. I knew I looked a sight with tears streaking down my face and the gaunt cheeks from days of little hydration.

"I have the amethyst," he announced. "You must have left it here. It showed up on my nightstand the night after we sparred."

Too tired to tell him I hadn't left the stone, I projected him an image of the illuminated stone leaving my palm as it had in my dream. With the pads of his hand pressed into his eyes, Cade bent over and took a deep breath. In sitting back up, he blew quickly onto my shoulder. Numbing, icy wind caressed the damaged joint.

"Why couldn't you do that to my rib?" I whined. A chuckle escaped him. "Trying to punish me for going off on my own? Hmph."

His head was close to my shoulder, inky hair tickling my chest. I was trying to think of anything but Cade's face next to my nearly bare chest. Reckless imaginings of diving my hands into that hair kept tugging at my mind. In an attempt to keep such traitorous thoughts from slipping past to him, I pictured laying a blanket over the thought, which truly didn't help, as it only reminded me of laying on the sofa the night before. A slight surge in his heartbeat where it ticked close to my arm suggested my attempts had been fruitless. Or maybe, just maybe, he could be trying to not picture me touching him as well.

"I could have numbed the skin a bit, but the structure of this joint is different to the rib area. It wouldn't have made a difference in the pain. Had I been able to take the pain away, I would have."

He pulled the shoulder back, and I screamed out as he clamped his other hand against the back of the joint.

"So sorry." He winced.

Breaths were short rasps escaping me. Where the shoulder met the bicep, his hands traced lines and ended up sweeping fingers across my open palm and off the tips of my fingers. With that, the immobility and pain released. I collapsed against him, and I had the feeling he did the same.

CHAPTER 17

T he intensity of weather in a place that is different
to where one has recently resided can be easily
forgotten. Though no stranger to the British Isles
and its penchant for being waterlogged, the fact was, I had
most recently wintered in one of the dry microclimates of the
Los Angeles basin. Being here in the northeast of England,
the days of late had taken their turn on the seasonal stage and
begun the long monologue of winter. Each time I stepped out
to see Corra or walk into town, the sodden weather raised my
spirits more than any cloudless, sunny sky ever had.

The shops along High Street in town had started putting
on their Sunday best, readying for Christmas. Rolls of wrapping paper and advent calendars filled the chemist and book-
shop. Little jingle bells tinkled on the door to Tilly's as I
pushed through, pulling in my large umbrella. To my surprise,
Silas sat on his own in a tiny corner table, pulling apart a
sausage roll. His chocolate-brown waves were slicked back
from the rain, showing off the chiseled structure of his jawline.
Where Silas was angled and rugged, Cadeyrn had a softer,

darker, more sensuous look that sat dangerously upon his warrior frame. What must the lay people of this town really think of this lot? My entrance was met with a broad grin.

"Knew I'd find you here, *Trubaíste,*" he said cheerfully. I took off the quilted raincoat and kissed his cheek. Tilly came around with a cup of tea and my usual scone, giving me a pat on the shoulder.

"Uh, oh. What did I do this time?" I asked.

"Apart from tearing through the countryside, stirring up trouble, and breaking hearts?" he teased. I tossed a crumb at his nose. It landed on the table where he picked it up and ate it with a grin. "You haven't been around much, and I missed my friend. We all have."

"I've been to see Corra," I protested. He quirked his mouth to the side. "And I've hardly broken any hearts."

"Well, you've not seen me nor Cadeyrn. I do believe Cadeyrn is missing his hounds as they seem to only be at home when it's feeding time." A dark eyebrow raised in my direction.

"They've become used to my peanut butter treats."

"Ah, and about that," he began. "My cousin seems to have developed quite a thing for peanut butter as well. He cannot seem to recreate the biscuits you had brought for tea so there have been several batches tossed in the bin." I laughed at that. "What have you been up to?"

After a long sip of tea and finishing my scone, I quietly answered, "I've been mapping out routes—possible routes to take to look for the next," I looked around and dropped my voice, "Item. I could show you what I am thinking, perhaps back at the house. If you want to know."

"'Course I do. Let's go." He stood in a smooth, cat-like motion.

I drank my tea down to the dregs and left money on the

table. Rain blew at us as we stomped home. Silas kept glancing at me expectantly.

"What?" I asked after the third or fourth glance.

"You aren't planning to go off on your own, are you? I mean...we haven't seen you much lately, and you're planning routes. I get it. I do. I just don't want you to..."

"I'm not. I wouldn't do that, Silas. I've just been trying to... not cause problems with you lot."

"Ah," he responded. For a while we walked in companionable silence. "I think you should come up more. We all feel your absence. It's too quiet. I mean, I know you can't be around me without wanting to jump my bones but..." I whacked him on the chest, and he laughed.

"Incorrigible male," I giggled.

MAPS, notes, and my laptop were spread across the low table in the sitting room. The two siblings and I sat around them, analyzing my thoughts on where we should look. In my father's ravings, both Cappadocia and Rila were mentioned, yet it seemed unlikely that two crystals would be in the same quadrant so to speak. Not implausible, but unlikely. However, as he was correct with Vilcabamba, we all thought it prudent to include both locations in the search. Tracing a finger down the map of eastern Europe, I explained how I thought the logistics of flying into Sofia, Bulgaria, first, then heading to Rila would be the best course of action. From Rila, we should travel south into Turkey.

A draft of early winter air entered as the sound of the heavy front doors preceded determined, heavy boot steps. Cade's shape filled the sitting room entrance and before I had a chance to look to him, the twins were at attention. Weapons were being shucked from Cade's fighting clothes, some landing with uncharacteristic disregard. Bixby and Cuthbert filed in and stood amidst the noise of their master's return.

"I take it the visit didn't go as planned?" Silas asked him. Until this moment it hadn't occurred to me to ask where their cousin was.

As he came farther into the light, I could see the blossoming bruise under Cade's eye and cheekbone, as well as a long gash from his upper lip toward his cheek. I stood then myself. His eyes flicked to me for the briefest of seconds then back to his family. I left to get supplies to clean him up.

"If you sit, I can clean it for you," I said nervously when I returned.

"It's fine," he grunted. "I can do it myself."

Gingerly, I set the first aid supplies down on the brass-topped table. "You're filthy. Let me clean it while you tell us what happened."

He held my eyes then rolled his own. And sat. Warm water laced with melaleuca oil soaked the gauze, and I dabbed lightly at his lip first, then moved on to the cheek. The bruising began to dissipate as I cleaned the wound.

"It's really something to watch the healing happen. Such a gift," I mused aloud almost to myself.

Silas cleared his throat. "So, you went to speak to the Elders..." he prompted.

"I did. After filling them in on some of the progress we have made and the threat of Reynard, I asked to speak to Ewan. They said he was otherwise occupied. I offered to wait or to help him. They asked me to leave. Perhaps I was less than diplomatic at that point," Cade continued. Silas and Corra both snorted. "They ordered me to leave, and as I was headed out, I caught sight of the lad. He looked worse than I do at the moment." Corra's intake of breath was sharp. Cade looked to her. "Not life-threatening, yet he had obviously been in a skirmish." Silas crossed his arms and growled. Cade continued. "I disregarded the escort I had and walked to Ewan, demanding what had happened. Cyrranus and Omnar," he turned to me, "guards—for the Elders—hit me before I moved. I took a knee to the gut and a fist or two to the face."

"I do hope you returned the favor," Silas said very softly. His cousin's smile was wicked.

"I slammed their gods-damned heads together and broke Omnar's arm in two— maybe three— places. Then I used Cyrranus' sword to pin his tunic to the rowan tree." He shrugged, and I smiled at him. Surprising me, he smiled back. Corra scowled. "Oh, don't give me that look. Of course, I made sure the lad was fine. It seems, however, that there is an ulterior motive amongst the Elders. I don't know when we can get back to Ewan, but my decision to keep our true acquisitions from Elder ears was a fair one."

He tugged a hand through his disorderly crop of hair. The dark strands were in a melee on his head, some parts stuck to his temple with blood. I used clean wet gauze and scrubbed it off. Curiosity shone on his face. The gauze was blackened, so the last spot on his earlobe I rubbed with my bare thumb.

"What have you lot been doing? This seems like a war committee," Cade asked us.

"Neysa has been outlining the route to take in Eastern Europe," Silas told him.

"I will go with you, Neysa," Cade announced unexpectedly. "You two," he motioned to the twins, "should stay here. Corraidhín, I expect you want to remain in case Ewan can cross. Silas, the crystals here and the Veil need your shield. Is that acceptable to you, Neysa?" I nodded. "Then, perhaps we leave as soon as you are ready to be back to fighting."

"Why? Do you plan on fighting with me the whole trip?" I teased before I had a chance to think about it.

He snorted and inclined his head to me. "You never know." He winked.

CHRISTMAS CANON STREAMED from the computer as I began pulling out what clothing I had. This would be my first Christmas without Dad, so I supposed it would be good to be away for the holidays. So far there were three piles of sweaters, two pair of jeans, fleece-lined leggings, and too many socks. Corra breezed into the cottage, so I called to her that I was in the bedroom.

"Your feet really are always cold," she greeted me, pointing to the socks.

"What does one pack for an open-ended trip to eastern Europe in the dead of winter? All I can think of is that my feet will be cold." Huffing, I sat on the edge of the bed. She dropped a small package on the duvet next to me. "What's this?"

"Yule gift. We always exchange, so..." she shrugged.

Tiny silk ribbon tied the paper together. As the paper fell away, an onyx trinket box was revealed. My index finger smoothed over it and caught the opening. Inside lay a double-horned pendant carved of polished black tourmaline. In lifting the pendant from its case and turning it, the back revealed that an amethyst was cut to the same shape, both stones set into gold bindings and strung onto a gold chain. Carved into the amethyst side of the double horn was a small eye at the tip of each crescent. The necklace vibrated a soft intensity. Both stones were powerful warding crystals.

I was dumbfounded at the thoughtfulness of the gift and looked up at my friend.

"The double horn, or what we call *adairch dorhdj* is a talisman to guide and protect. Wear the amethyst next to your skin to quell the anxiety. The tourmaline should face out to be your rampart."

"This is stunning, Corra. I've never seen anything so thoughtful. Thank you," I said, and kissed her cheek.

"Och. Wear it to dinner tonight so the boys can feel inadequate in their gifts," she said with a laugh.

YULE DINNER with a family of fae was not how I

would have imagined I would spend my holidays. To be honest, I avoided thinking about it. I never quite grasped how lonely the holi- days could be for those of us who had no family or, as was the case a few months ago, friends. However, what I had now was a softly blurred line of family and friends, and I found myself warmed at the thought of spending this dinner celebrating the entrance of winter and paying tribute to the gods of olde as we spent the longest night of the year. In my excitement over tonight, I had even bought myself a dress to wear as Corra remarked that it was the only time in this realm they ever really dressed up. Seeing as she and Cade were always immaculately dressed and even Silas made an effort most of the time, I had felt grossly unprepared for the occasion.

Evergreen boughs hung over the front doors and walking in, I found my senses lifted at the scent of pine and spices all around. No one was in the foyer, so, I took the opportunity to switch from my wellies to a pair of strappy black heels, etched with gold threading, which ran from the ankle straps and down the four-inch heel. In standing, I straightened the hem of the ebony silk and chiffon dress that skimmed down to just mid-thigh. The top half split into two sides joined over the breastbone with two scraps of material. It was soft and feminine, then tightened around the ribs before dropping to the gauzy black of the skirt.

I felt the ice-kissed air that had followed my entrance as it whispered against my skin where the dress was open down to the very low sacrum. The necklace from Corra sat just below where my collarbones met and was framed by the waves of my dark brown hair. Quickly, I checked the hall mirror, making sure my smokey eye makeup hadn't turned into a melancholic Goth look as I walked over from my cottage.

Candlelight and the scent of pine greeted me in the drawing room. A large Christmas tree stood proudly in the center with Silas next to it. All around the room were touches of winter. Berries and boughs, cakes and fruit.

"Happy Christmas?" Silas said with a question in his voice. "We don't celebrate Christmas as such, and this tree thing isn't really a Yule jobby, but I had an idea you might like one. For old times' sake, eh?"

"Then I must put all of your gifts under the tree," I said, giving him a hug. "That was very sweet of you, Silas. I appreciate it." I touched my hand to my heart after setting down my bag of gifts. He gave a low whistle and held me at arm's length.

"Oh, you are the Goddess Herself tonight, *allaína trubaíste.* This is a look that suits you." I blushed and thanked him as a yip sounded from Corra behind me.

"I am envious of every male who will ever have a chance with you, Neysa," Corra said with a pout. "Listen, even poor Cadeyrn's heart stopped for a second!"

Cade looked like he would rather have been gutted than for Corra to have said that, but he bowed slightly to me. "Neysa. Joyous Yule to you. May the days of light ahead sustain you in the darkness," he recited what I had learned was a traditional Aoifsing Yule sentiment.

"Thank you for having me," I said, rather more formally than I had intended.

Cade looked confused. "Of course."

He was the epitome of elegance in a tailored black velvet jacket over a white button-down shirt. Suiting trousers, which fit perfectly over his muscled legs, completed the ensemble. Night-dark hair had been smoothed into place yet still remained soft looking. Next to him, Corra radiated joy in winter white and gold, which made her garnet-touched hair stand out. Her dress was simple with long sleeves that started just off the shoulder, the bodice was cut on the bias and hugged her hips down to her knees. Cade handed me a warm cup of spiced wine. His eyes fell upon the necklace, and he raised an eyebrow to his cousin.

"It suits her, no?" she asked.

"I didn't realize you still had this, Corraidhín," Cade remarked. "May I?" he asked me. His long fingers gently lifted the double horn from my chest and examined the back of it. I knew he could hear my heart racing.

"Something I should know?" I was curious. He laid it back on my chest and touched the pendant again before pulling his fingers away, which made me realize I had held that last breath.

"It had been a gift from Cadeyrn to me when we were young," Corra began. I started, shocked to have been given it, and felt guilty. "Every time I thought of it, I thought it should be yours. I did have the eyes of the goddess etched into the horns to keep watch over you both. Since, you know, I can't be there to take an arrow for you this time." She winked, and I jabbed her with my elbow.

"Don't feel guilty," Cade intoned. "I cannot think of a better place for the *adairch dorhdj*."

"Makes my gift look naff," Silas complained.

"I love yours, Silas. You should see mine," I groaned.

From the bag I'd placed under the tree, I began pulling presents. In my head, I wondered where the dogs were, and Cade whistled for them and smiled shyly. To each hound I gave a deer antler with which they both hurried out of the room.

To Silas, I gave a book on the history of weaponry from the Greco-Roman Era through modern day. Corra received a cashmere throw similar to mine as I had noticed she was always eyeing it. When it was Cade's turn, I handed him two boxes. The first he opened having already detected its contents. His face brightened to that smile from which I couldn't look away. A double batch of peanut butter cookies with the recipe tucked inside. The next box contained a mint green and pink calico apron with ruffles along the ties. He laughed so loudly the dogs came running back in.

"I did say that was an immortalized image," I said with a smirk.

To my utter astonishment, Cade crossed over to me and ever so softly kissed my cheek. "At least I shall always live on in your memory, Neysa."

The longest night of the year was spent drinking spiced wine, eating rich foods, listening to stories of Yule past, and trying to not think about not all being together for an indefinite time span. Well past midnight, Silas passed out small river rocks to each of us. He explained that we each carve our names into the rock and imbue the essence of it with our hopes for the following year. We then throw them into the fire, and once the embers have burned and the fire has cooled in the morn- ing, the rocks are removed and the markings of ash and soot that adorn the rocks will be read to see what hints there are for the coming year. A bit like reading tea leaves I supposed. Silence descended on the four of us as we carved our names. One final toast for the evening, and we tossed the rocks into the hearth.

Head swimming with wine, I sat, one leg stretched to the side, elbows on my knees, staring into the flames as the rocks absorbed our wishes and sentiments. Corra sat behind me on the tufted ottoman, twirling my hair through her hands and braiding and unbraiding it. She was humming melodies to herself. It sounded like a mix of something ancient, berib-boned with what could have been 1950s doo wop. Silas was asleep on the sofa, having discarded his formal jacket. Cade sidled up next to me, pushing Corra's feet out of the way. For a moment he stared at the flames with me, our faces heating from the fire. After a time, he reached over and handed me a small parcel. Our fingers met as I took it from him, and I started at the feel- ing. One word popped into my head: home. I shook the thought away.

Sprigs from an evergreen bough were tied onto a muslin covered box with a wine-red velvet ribbon. I touched the wrapping. Not quite the kind you have done outside a department store. He ran a hand through his hair, disrupting its perfect style. The ribbon slid free and muslin came off to reveal a long box. Inside laid a dagger so thin and delicate it could fit inside a sleeve.

"That's the idea," he answered my thoughts. "There's a strap for your forearm and a holster for your thigh." I ran the tips of my fingers along the blade and touched the side, feeling the edge. I could have sworn he shivered. The hilt had an ergonomic grip that fit my palm precisely. So much thought went into this gift. As the firelight caught the metal, I noticed etchings in the steel. Turning it toward me, I saw it was a line of text from Aoifsing.

What does it say? I thought. He leaned over and touched the words.

"Chanè à doinne aech mise fhìne. Mise fhìne allaína trubaiste" A pause, as if second guessing telling me. "I am no one's but my own. My own beautiful disaster."

I swallowed. Words failing me completely, I laid my head on his shoulder and continued to touch the etchings on the blade. Corra's hands had stilled on my hair, her fae/doo wop rendition having silenced. I assumed she had fallen asleep like her brother. The same words echoed in my dream about my father.

"I am ready for tomorrow," I said thickly.

"Good," he said and patted my knee. "As am I. And...you do look beautiful tonight. More so. Than normal. I mean. Very nice," he stammered.

"So, do you," I said quietly and stood. "Goodnight, Cadeyrn."

CHAPTER 18

Humans are, essentially, pack animals and congregate close to one another for safety, trade, social purposes, and procreation. To have been far from your civilization, city, port, place of assemblage would have been detrimental to one's livelihood. It is incredible to see places of refinement in isolated places. The roads to the Rila Monastery were passable, though not forgiving in winter. Before the advent of modern vehicles and roads, the monastery would have been inaccessible for the bulk of the year. Even so, the attention to detail on this quirky sanctuary is a marvel.

Considering Rila is a much-visited tourist attraction and UNESCO World Heritage Site, it was strange that we had the grounds nearly to ourselves on this frigid day in late December. Byzantine frescos, Bulgarian Revivalist art and architecture shone around us. Black-and-white striped arches graced the facades of the cloister. We lapped the buildings inside and out.

I had been here once, years ago as a sulky teenager, and never truly appreciated the juxtaposition of cultures encased in this relatively small outcropping of structures. In all of the marveling I had been doing in this crossroads of history, culture, and faith, it hadn't escaped me that there was something very much lacking. There was no pull as I had experienced in Vilcabamba. Given the miles Corra and I had trekked once I had felt the tug for the tourmaline, it was obvious to me now that the crystal we were searching for was not nearby. Disappointment must have shown on my face.

"It's not here, is it?" Cade asked as the frosty wind swirled around us. I shook my head quietly. Cade pulled his hands from the deep pockets of his coat and breathed into his palms. Steam briefly rose from them as he considered. "Perhaps the cave?"

I shook my head again. "We can check, but I feel like the cave is close enough that I would still feel something."

Outward from the monastery, we walked through a frozen forest. Icicles dangled dangerously from tree branches, throwing light around us in glittering bursts. Our path followed a small stream that, though frozen along the edges and over the rocks, had the tenacity to keep its current going through the center. Feeling as though I were transported into a Russian fairytale, I wandered to a tree with a large heart carved into its trunk. Initials had been scraped out in a declaration of someone's love. Mindlessly, I touched the heart, which had a thin layer of ice over it, making it seem as if it were behind glass.

Images of the couple who carved the initials came into my mind. At first young and perhaps reckless, I could see them barely able to keep their hands off one another. I had never been loved like that. I wondered how long it lasted. As if in answer, another image of the same couple, clearly years later came to mind. Greying and moving slower, they stood before the same tree, hand in hand. There was good here. This was a place of belonging and love. I felt that the crystal had once been at home here, though it seemed it was no longer.

Cade looked at me oddly. "How often does that happen now? The ability to see images from objects?" he asked.

I pulled a lip balm from my pocket and covered my dry lips while I thought about his question. "Not...too often. But lately it seems that when I have a question in my mind about the particulars of an object, I get bits and pieces of an answer. Does that make sense?" He nodded in agreement. "Did you—were you able to see all of it? I don't know what I send to you or not."

"I think so. If I may ask...what question did you have in touching it?"

I turned a bit away, glancing again at the icy heart.

"I wondered how strong the emotion was that caused someone to want to carve the tree. And what it felt like to feel so strongly and so confident in the reciprocation." I wiped my hand across my numb nose and rolled my eyes at myself. "When I saw the couple, I wondered whether that feeling endured any amount of time." Admitting that much to Cadeyrn made me feel exposed. He studied me for an uncomfortable minute until I set back off on the trail we were headed. "Is that my gift then, do you think? What even is it? Psychic empathy? That sounds naff," I laughed.

"One of them," he answered. I whirled to him. "I am quite certain that you have a few tricks in there. Image retention being one. Electric conductivity being another. I'll bet good money that there are few we haven't seen yet. Or have yet to recognize."

"Image retention?" I asked. "So, am I like limestone? A little bit of emotion and suddenly I am projecting ghosts?" He chuckled. "That's not a bad description. Though, it seems to me that you simply connect with the emotive effect of an object through your empathy or your own raw emotion, and that delivers the images or visions to you."

"It's strange that I cannot connect with people the same," I mused.

"How do you mean?"

"I feel socially inept most of the time. People tend to give me a wide berth. Especially emotionally. And I can never get a good read on others' feelings."

"Really?" he asked. "I see you totally differently, I suppose. "You seem to attract energy. Perhaps you absorb so much that it blinds you to what seems obvious to others? Interesting."

I was a bit stunned.

We reached the cave mouth, and though there was a lingering vibration, I knew there was no crystal here. Nothing in the way of leading us forward. The temperature was dropping as we headed back toward the cloister. Frigid wind tore at us as we once again entered the gates of the monastery.

"Shall we see about a meal and accommodations?" I asked Cadeyrn.

He sucked on a tooth and tightened his black scarf. Nostrils flared, Cade whirled around. Two ancient looking monks strode for us, one of whom had a murderous expression on his face. Cade pressed me behind him, but I sidestepped and stood with him shoulder to shoulder.

"You cannot be here," the surly looking one said in flawless English.

"I thought the grounds were open until six," Cade answered smoothly. The monk scowled as his companion looked abashed.

"Your kind is not welcome here, heathen," he spat.

"I am quite sure you have mistaken us, Brother. My wife and I have come as tourists and were hoping to find accommodation."

"What you seek is not here, and I hope that you never

find it. There is no accommodation for you and your halfling wife."

I narrowed my eyes at the insult and sought the eyes of the quiet one. "Brother," I said to him, pleading with my hands. "If we may come in out of the cold before we go to the village, it would be much appreciated."

He smiled sadly and said something in Latin to his dyspeptic comrade. After a charged conversation, we were allowed to come in for a cup of tea before leaving the premises. The quiet one, Brother Mathias, led us into a small, wood- paneled chamber and poured us each a cup of tea and tipped a small amount of wine in with a wink. The disagreeable one had left to tend to his other duties and gave us fair warning to vacate shortly or the authorities would be notified.

Brother Mathias stoked the small fire and sat with us, pulling a ridiculously large book onto his ample lap. He flipped through it and settled on a page. My vantage point was not as good as Cade's as he was far taller and could see over the table. His frost-flushed face paled. The book was passed across to us. A watercolor portrait of my father stared back.

"Elías was a donor to our order. We were friends for a time. I liked to hear of his stories from places far from my knowl- edge." He looked to Cade. "I made a promise to a friend long ago." My hands began to shake, and I placed the teacup on the polished wood table. The scent of incense was overpowering, and I sank into a vision.

* * *

THE CLOTH-COVERED ARM HOLDING A CANDLE, shaking the hand of my father. I recognized the wedding ring, which now sat in the manor house in Barlowe Combe. Brother Mathias, much younger, placing a hand over his heart. Distant mountains and lakeside rock formations. Me, through my father's eyes, watching me *stand against a striped column in the cloister just outside of where I now sat, twenty years later. A blue stone and two eyes emblazoned in crag.*

GASPING, I came to, and both men reached for me. I said I was okay, though I suspected Cade knew it was far from the truth.

"Asparuhovo," Brother Mathias continued as though he hadn't just seen a half-fae female experience a very ungodly trance. "It is a village on the other side of the country. You may find what you seek. Your father could not reach it as it does not speak to him as it does to you, Mistress."

"Asparuhovo? Is it near Varna?" Cade asked. The monk nodded.

Footsteps sounded in the hall.

"You must go." He shut the book quickly and shoved it into a disorderly cabinet. We stood as the door was thrust open and the hostile Brother filled the doorway. Brother Mathias bowed to us, and we in return. He reached out and made the sign of the cross on my brow.

"Go with God, Mistress," he blessed me. We left without a backward glance at the monastery to which my father had evidently gone so far as to become a large donor.

As it was too late to secure transportation anywhere but the nearby village, we chose a small inn to stay the night and plan our next leg. Sharing one room kept up appearances of being married as well as it being a security issue. Especially as we had been noted as "other," and at least one monk was openly hostile toward us. I sat on the edge of the bed and groaned, cold all the way into my bones. My body had been shaking visibly since my vision.

"I'll take the floor," Cade announced.

I looked to him and waved him off. "No need. I can share. I won't bite, Cade."

In my head, I was squirming at the thought of sharing a

bed with him, but it was time to put my big girl pants on and not let him camp on the floor of a Bulgarian country inn. He stood his ground and began making a bed on the floor. Too spent to argue, I grabbed my clothes and left to shower. Once tucked into the thick quilt on the bed in the darkened room, a question arose.

"What's in Varna?"

"It's a seaside town on the Black Sea. Quite popular," came Cade's answer from the darkness.

"Have you been?"

"I have. Many years ago," he said, sounding tired.

I wondered if it was nice, like the beaches in Croatia and Greece.

"It's not so lovely as those," Cade answered. I really needed

to sort out what I broadcast, or I was really going to step in it soon. He chuckled and said, "Dubrovnik and Korcula in Croatia are far more attractive. Although, no sandy beaches as you have in California."

"I'm not one for sandy beaches." The only thing sand was good for, in my opinion, was for making my run harder.

"Then I would recommend Croatia for a summer holiday."

I laughed at his recommendation.

"I appreciate the tip. What's it like...in Aoifsing?" I had been

curious and afraid to ask.

There was a long pause, and the darkness filled the void.

"Home," he whispered. My heart sank. "It is terrible and magnificent. Sarrlaiche, where my family is from, is dense with forest. You would love it. I know you like to be in the woods. The trees canopy everything. They stretch between the mountains and open up only as the land falls into the sea." His voice took on a faraway quality and I felt as though

I could clearly picture this forest of magic that bordered the shore of a winter sea.

"There are other areas," he continued. "Maesarra is a more temperate region. That is where the island on which the royal summer home is. Where I was married." I stilled a bit at mention of his wife and was struck with a feeling of betrayal I had no right to.

"There are stunning villages throughout Maesarra. Clear waters to swim. The people are warm." He sounded so wistful.

"You do miss it then?" I asked softly.

"I do." His admission left a feeling in my stomach like I'd swallowed water whilst swimming.

"Do you wish to go back?" I asked. "Can you?"

He waited a long while before answering.

"I would like to go back. Perhaps one day to stay. There are

many reasons I am not certain I will ever be able to." There was a profound sadness to his tone. I wanted to reach down and squeeze his hand but knew better.

"I hope that one day, Cade, you will have less of a burden to bear."

"Neysa, if everything were to work out as it is supposed to, I will always have a burden to bear. It is what I was born to carry."

"Then I hope you have happiness amidst that weight," I said, and meant it.

"Get some sleep," Cade whispered.

I blew a very childish raspberry into the inky room and rolled over.

DAWN HAD us out the door and into the transportation we had booked the previous evening. It took half the day to drive to Varna and another hour to arrive in Asparuhovo. The attrac- tion here was what is called the Wonder Rocks.

Wind-shaped formations, which lined the shore of the Tsonevo Dam. The rocks looked like a castle hastily made of sand. We walked for hours as the sun set, and I was numb from cold. Searching in earnest for that tether to the crystal.

"Do you know what I wish right now?" I asked.

"If you are anything like me, it's for a large amount of alcohol and a hot meal," Cade quipped.

"I wish I were sitting with Cuthbert and Bixby. My toes are positively frozen."

"You miss them?" he asked with an air of astonishment.

"God, yes. They have been my allies this whole time."

"They do like you," he said with a tinge of disbelief. "Perhaps they are bored of me after all these years. Plus, don't think I haven't noticed their peanut butter habit." He had a smile in his voice. The only sounds beyond our conversation were the quiet crunch of gravel beneath us and light whoosh of wind.

"That's how I make all my friends," I said, bumping my shoulder into him. "How long have you had them?"

"Since they were pups. So, oh, thirty-odd years?"

"Thirty years!" I exclaimed. "Are they...from Aoifsing then?"

"Yes, of course. They normally travel between with me. I thought you knew."

"I am ignorant of quite a bit it seems."

"Yes, little mouse," came a voice in the distance. "You are." Cade and I both had weapons out and dropped low, all too

aware of Reynard's archery skills. Cade had a strong damper on his power at the moment, but I knew he still saw better in the dark than I could.

He pressed his mouth to my ear and whispered almost inaudibly. "There are five of them. Two behind you near the shore. Reynard in the cave mouth. Two have weapons pointed at me. Take out the two nearest you and run. Don't look back."

Like hell I would. I shook my head once tersely and whirled. My dagger shot from my arm holster and fit itself into my grip. Beautiful little thing. I pulled a short sword from my thigh that had been hidden by my long down coat, which was now billowing behind me as I ran full speed at the fae males who had crept up on us.

A shadow stood before me, broadsword spinning in his hands. Roughly a meter to his left, just at the shore, stood another whose weapon I could not see. I knew my steel wouldn't hold against a sword of that size, so my only advantage was to slither into his weaknesses. I jumped and hit the ground in a slide, which I felt tear through my fleece leggings and destroy my coat. Tiny rocks imbedded themselves into my legs, but I came at him quickly enough that he didn't have time to react.

Pulling him down, I grappled for purchase on his eyes, laying my dagger straight through one. He screamed, and his companion appeared before me. Still no weapon, and I hadn't seen him move. He reached for my dagger, and I twisted, knocking him with my elbow and kicking backward hoping for luck on the landing. Suddenly he was several feet away. *Ah. So, it's like that.* He had bright, honey-colored hair and golden skin that would have been gorgeous if he weren't hell-bent on killing me.

Centering myself, I looked inward at the protective stones I wore on my necklace. Once in tune with them, I knew the instant before this new adversary moved. We danced like that for several minutes as I heard grunting and clashing off in the distance. I wanted to be fighting alongside Cade. I needed to be nearer so the necklace could help him too. Just as the golden- haired assassin blinked into position in front of me, I pivoted and scissor-slashed out with both blades. It was a bit of a sloppy move as my arms were tired and frozen and the two blades were weighted differently. Even so, they found their mark. Although it wasn't a killing blow, he blinked away.

I sprinted for Cade, ripping off my cumbersome coat as I ran. He was actively fighting two large males who must be twins. An arrow whooshed too close to me. I stumbled and took a hard fall. Cade faltered a step and was slashed in the upper arm. Shit. He won't last much longer without a full functioning sword arm.

In my mind I said to him, *I will throw my dagger. It's lighter. Use that and I will take yours.* With that I hurtled the dagger at him, praying the message got through.

I heard an arrow piercing the wind, and I barreled into the smaller of the two males angling him to take the arrow in the neck. The unforeseen issue with that move is that he fell back– ward. Onto me. He was jerking, and I couldn't tell if he was dying or trying to pin me.

All at once, he flipped and rammed his overly large knee into my gut then kicked my legs apart. Pure terror washed over me. I was unarmed, as I hadn't had the chance to grab Cade's weapon. Despite the arrow lodged into the side of his neck, this brute was pulling open his trousers and ramming me into the gravel. I tried headbutting him, but he managed to pull back and smile at me grotesquely.

I felt him harden against me and bile rose up. *Shit. Shit. Shit!*

Stillness. His head lobbed forward awkwardly, and I registered two blades crisscrossed in the back of his neck.

Cade ripped the thick body off of me and lifted me to my feet.

We ran for a time until it seemed no one followed us. My nerves were frazzled. There were the lights of the town ahead, and without speaking, the two of us both bleeding, kept walking toward them. Once in the town, we wiped the blood from each other as best we could, and he staunched our bleeding so we could get a taxi into Varna. We needed a large city and airport access.

I HAD NEVER BEEN SO glad to see city lights and the inside of a hotel room. Cade pulled out the smoky topaz and began activating warding spells in the room. Once they were intact, he collapsed on the ground.

I stood, my arms dangling like they were broken toys fused to the wrong doll. I looked at my fingers, which had started twitching. That's when the full-body shaking started. My teeth were chattering hard enough that I had to press my lips together. A profound ache lanced my back from my shoulders quaking so violently. Cade looked up and tugged at my leg. I knew he had lost so much blood and was depleted. I couldn't move other than the constant shaking. He grabbed the mattress behind him, hoisting himself up on unsteady legs, then pulled me to him and onto the bed. I tried to wrench free, my mind rebelling at the touch of him. The touch of anyone after what I had just been through.

"Sshhh. You're in shock." He slurred a bit on the words. "Let me keep you warm."

I tried to still, but my body was vellicating with a huge amount of force. He pulled the blanket around us and wrapped his legs around mine, then placed his hands on either side of my face and closed his eyes. I knew he was using the last scraps of his power to heal me, and I began to protest but he persisted. The shaking slowed, and after a time, stopped all together. I was so cold and burrowed into the covers and into Cade for warmth. His heart was slow and breathing too soft. Still too tired to speak aloud, I spoke in my mind and wished he'd been able to respond.

Cadeyrn. I don't know what to do. Let me help you.

"Be...fine. Need...time. You...too." I felt his hand try to squeeze my back. An attempt at an encouraging gesture.

We lay there all night, not quite healing but falling in and out of sleep. As streaks of grey early morning sun filtered through the heavy drapes, panic rose up in me. The reality of the situation from the night before became unbearable. I couldn't breathe and needed to get up. Extricating myself from Cade's sleeping form, I stumbled to the bathroom and began vomiting until there was nothing left but dry, painful heaves. Gentle hands pulled my hair back and leaned over to turn on the tub. He seemed steadier but still wasn't speaking. Tears were coursing down my face, and I was heaving again. As the tub filled and steam rose up, he looked at me, assessing.

"Can you manage to bathe?" he asked. I nodded and used toilet paper to wipe at my mouth before flushing. Once we had both bathed, we crawled back into bed and nestled into each other again. Thank the gods I hadn't taken it upon myself to come alone on this trip.

"I knew you were thinking about it," Cade said. Oh. Pure exhaustion filled his words. "That would have been suicide." I knew it too. "Are you...are you alright?" he asked.

"No. I will be though. Just not yet," I answered.

He tightened his arms. "You gave me your weapon and left yourself defenseless. That was incredibly stupid," he scolded.

Well, great. Thanks.

"I would have taken yours but decided to shield myself, and you for that matter, from an arrow. I didn't think he would..." I trailed off. I didn't even want to think about what the brute had intended to do to me.

There was an unspoken apology in Cade's silence, like phantom fingers stroking my eyelids.

"Plus," I said. "I'm never defenseless. I was just vulnerable. I've never experienced that sort of rage in someone." I shuddered at the memory of the man on top of me.

Angry threads of energy thrummed all around us. I knew there was vehemence boiling in my friend on my behalf. I used my anxiety breathing to calm myself and tried to imbue the calm into him. It seemed, for a time, it worked.

"Can we not leave this bed for a long time?" I asked, and immediately heated from the possible implication. I felt him chuckle.

"Normally, that would be a wonderful proposition," he answered with amusement. I cringed.

"And now?" I pressed without thinking. *Ugh. Ugh. Why did that have to come out?* He laughed a bit more openly, which made me even redder.

"And now" he said with a smile, his toes prodding mine. "It is honestly just as appreciated. I am dead tired, and you have the coldest toes I have ever felt."

"Have you felt a lot of toes then?" I asked. *Really, Neysa?* Couldn't I just shut up and go to sleep?

"Loads," he said, with a slight growl. Oh. The toes in question curled under and dug into the sheets.

"Well, it's good to be esteemed for something," I retorted, less confidently than it was supposed to come out.

Quiet rumbling of his chest told me he was laughing at me, and I tucked my chin down into the covers. The pillow depressed slightly behind me as I felt Cade's chin press onto my head. Finally, I was getting warm.

CHAPTER 19

What stood out to me about Istanbul was the food. Food was everywhere and not in the sense of doughnut shops and drive-throughs. Enticing and assaulting aromas of street food, boutique hotels offering traditional Turkish fare with a modern flair, pastries releasing their taunting aromas from windows and carts.

We were in Istanbul for two nights before heading out to Cappadocia. Since the only time I had been there was at nine or ten years old, I was eager to peruse the gateway city between east and west. Though heavy rains and constant splashes of mud from tires threatened to keep us inside, we eventually made our way around the city and took in views of the Bosporous, experiencing being on the cusp of both Asia and Europe.

I began to feel a tinge of that familiar pull and shot Cade a look asking if he felt it too.

"Only through you," he remarked.

It wasn't as strong or pronounced. There wasn't that gingerbread trail to follow as there had been in Peru, yet I knew, somehow, that we were on the correct path. On a small, cobbled street a few blocks from the water, I ducked in and out of shops. We stopped for coffee at a corner cafe and the owner greeted us in English, asking where we were from. He told us how he had visited California in his youth hoping to meet movie stars and find a beach bunny to marry. We laughed, and his wife came outside giggling and whacked him on the arm with a towel.

They invited us inside their shop and showed us a modest collection of antiques and his jewelry counter at the back. We explained that we were not shopping for anything, though his wares were lovely. The couple looked to one another in a kind of parental-knowing glance.

The man brought out a pair of gemstone drop earrings and presented them to Cade. They were gaudy and old-fashioned. Perhaps styled before the dissolution of the Ottoman Empire. Large, pear-shaped yellow stones dropped from blood-red garnet studs. The yellow stone, he explained, was a Turkish diaspore or Csarite. It is a rare gem found only in Turkey. He brought the earrings from the muted sunlight of the window, deeper into the store where the incandescent glow of lamps illuminated the earrings. The stones had turned from a citrine to a delicate pink, like the stain of crushed raspberries on fingers.

"Wouldn't you care to purchase such beautiful earbobs for the lady," he asked Cade, gently thrusting the jewelry to him.

Just like that we had been lured into the tourist trap.

"Thank you, sir, but no," Cade said firmly, turning to leave.

As I moved to head out as well, a tug gave me pause. I looked inward and knew it wasn't the stone we sought, but there was a connection here with these gems. *Cade. I'm suddenly feeling the need for ostentatious earrings.* I said to him in my mind.

He stopped before the door. "Perhaps, sir, we can strike a deal..."

THE STONES WARMED my pockets as I carried the jewelry back to the hotel, the sun setting low and cold over the city. We didn't speak about the purchase on the streets, always on the lookout for eyes upon us.

Once we arrived, however, we decided to change clothes, wanting to have a nice meal in the metropolis before we left for the countryside in the morning. Cade changed into dark trousers and a matching fitted jacket. I knew from training with him that the bottom half of his ensemble were high-end men's activewear, but they looked appropriate with his jacket and black merino crew neck sweater. I unknowingly took that same cue and donned black leather fighting pants— which I wished I had had on when I slid through the gravel in Bulgaria—an olive-green silk camisole, and sky-high heeled booties. I topped it all with a large scarf and warm coat I had purchased that morning, having trashed mine in the scuffle.

As we walked through the lobby, Cade snickered. "Wouldn't a warmer sweater have been a better choice?" I flicked my straightened hair back from my shoulder and scoffed haughtily.

"Then I would miss catching you looking at me," I answered, wanting to catch him off guard but all it managed to really do was make me unsteady on my feet. Truly, I wasn't very good at this game. It was very sad.

"I'm looking at those awful earbobs and wondering if there's a wood sprite stuck inside," he teased.

I laughed despite myself. "I don't know what you're taking about. These are the height of fashion."

I touched the bobs for emphasis and felt an answering zing through me.

WE DINED at a trendy restaurant that served traditional mezzo and raki, the unofficial drink of Turkey. It is a beverage for celebrating life and healing loss. One only drinks it in partic- ular company. One shot—or tek, as they are called—and my warm layers came off, Cade pulling his arms from his jacket as well. We ate until stuffed and partook in two more tek of raki. His sleeves were pushed up, corded, muscular forearms braced on the marble table.

"The first time Silas and I got well and truly drunk, we had been in the home of a neighbor. There were five or six of us. Males and females. I remember lying with a female in one instant and throwing up on the rug next to her in the next. Silas fell on the way home, and I had to stitch his forehead and heal him before his father saw it."

"Did you clean the rug?" I asked.

He smirked. "Corraidhín turned it to mist for us then knocked us each square in the jaw."

We were both laughing harder than was warranted, curtesy of the alcohol in the raki.

"I do love Corra," I giggled.

"They are both very fond of you as well," he answered, more soberly than I was ready for.

I met his eyes and though they were the smoky quartz I had seen when I met him, and his ears were rounded when we were in public, his exquisite face had become so familiar in both forms. I was in that state of drunkenness where somehow it seems okay to simply stare. I took in his full mouth and high cheekbones, the soft lines next to his eyes that only showed in low lighting when the shadows from his dark lashes cast depth to his skin. A shiver went through me that had nothing to do with the cold. Our server appeared with the check, and I was shaken from my reverie, immedi- ately staring down at the constellation of freckles on the back of my hand.

Our hotel balcony looked out over the city, facing the blue mosque and the glow of streets which had seen a thousand years of worship, war, intrigue, and passion. We had brought up a bottle of wine and pulled on our coats to sit in the frigid night.

"I have always wanted to travel like this," I said after a long silence.

"Really? Like this? Getting kicked out of monasteries, fighting on the banks of a Bulgarian dam, and being stuck with someone like me?" he asked.

"Absolutely." I huffed a laugh. "Cruises are very overrated. Terribly boring and no exercise whatsoever. Plus, you're not so bad. You don't even steal the covers." I propped my heeled boot on the balcony rail and sipped at my wine, head spinning a little.

"Did you not travel? With your..." He waved his hand. "Caleb?" he asked.

I puckered my lips. "The farthest we came was to Italy a few years ago. He didn't like the idea of anywhere unpredictable. He worked a lot and didn't want to take a chance on vacationing pitfalls." As I said it out loud, I remembered that though that was Caleb's excuse, he worked far less than I had known, having girlfriends on the side for years.

I heard a sharp intake of breath from Cade, and I knew I had sent that thought along to him. My control over my thought projection was far less under the influence of alcohol than sober.

"You were meant for so much more," he said softly. "I suppose your father knew that as well."

I took a deep breath of cold night air and attempted to lift the mood. "Well, yes, and that's how I have come here now to traipse about the world on a universe-saving quest with a companion who couldn't stand me for the first few months."

I laughed, but he stilled then turned fully to me. Narrowed eyes, again that crystalline green, looked at me, his nose red with cold. "Do you believe that?" he asked ever so quietly.

I bit my lip. God, I had zero social skills.

Nervously, I smoothed my hair, setting the earring to swing. This is where I should have answered, but I kept putting my foot in my mouth and so, abstained from speech.

"I didn't realize you felt that way. I am...wary of...change. You came in so abruptly and seemed to fit our dynamic. Corraidhín adored you, of course, then Silas. You and Silas...it confused me. I am not always good with people." His hand went into his hair.

I was still sitting, dumbstruck and silent, willing myself to say something. Instead, I touched his reddened nose. He started a bit, but I traced his face with my fingers, brushing lightly over his slightly pointed ear tip. His eyes closed at this, and I thought I could touch those ears for eternity. I knew I'd had too much to drink, which gave me this brazenness. And I didn't care. Perhaps he didn't either.

I moved slowly to him and felt a tentative hand circle my back, inside my coat. My hand trailed his hairline at the base of his neck as I came closer and hovered my lips just before his, almost tasting him. In a blinding moment of clarity, I realized that his hand had dropped, and he was not moving to me in turn. I lowered my own hand and scooted back, embarrassed beyond function. I knew his eyes were still on me, yet there was a shuttered distance in his gaze. Cade cleared his throat.

"Don't," I said at last and got to my feet. He mirrored the motion and reached for me. I yanked away and walked inside, tossed my coat to the chair, and cursed the blasted single bed.

"You have had—*we* have had a lot of drink," he intoned in a maddeningly placating way, which made me see red.

I spun, the heel of my bootie ripping fibers of the

carpeting and stalked off. Gods, I was so naive. What did I think? That because I started to feel the stirrings of something for him, that he might decide to feel the same? Of course, he wouldn't. Especially not after Silas. Humiliation coursed through my veins.

Taking an extraordinary length of time showering and readying for bed, I left the earrings in, letting them warm against me. When it became too lengthy to be reasonable, I finally removed the gems and emerged from the bathing room and walked directly to bed, shutting off the light.

"Neysa," Cade called, voice soft.

I rolled further onto my side, facing away from him and spent the next few hours pretending to sleep.

CHAPTER 20

Ataturk Airport to Nevsahir by plane. Nevsahir to Ortahisar by car. We arrived in the center town of Cappadocia in the late afternoon. Beyond a muttered apology for stepping on Cade's booted foot, we had not spoken. He kept opening his mouth as if to say something, and I deliberately turned away each time like a petulant child to look out the window. Majestic flutes surrounded the town like peaks of meringue. Stalls and shops were brilliant splashes of color and texture in the snow-dusted town.

Determined to change my sour mood (and admittedly sour stomach and sore head), I told Cade, in a tone brooking no argument, that I was going to wander the town on my own. He closed his eyes once and pinched the bridge of his nose, hair falling out of place and over his forehead.

The earrings were too conspicuous to wear here, yet I kept them in my interior breast pocket of the fitted down jacket I wore with my leather leggings and Sherpa-lined boots. I took time this morning—more so to be alone in the bathroom—to heavily line my eyes with black pencil and sweep some blush across my cheekbones. The stalls dotted around were for the benefit of tourists, yet I found pleasure in making my way in and out as the sun started to set. The familiar pull of energy prickled up my spine, making me stop in my tracks and focus.

"Beautiful lady," a smiling voice called out in heavily accented English. "Come in and find treasure."

I saw him standing before a shop tinkling with hundreds of nazar, or evil eye beads. Large and small, the store was filled with blue glass beads swaying with the breeze. Dad's ramblings came to mind. *Gökçe munçuk*, he had said in the recordings. It was Old Turkish for 'blue bead'.

I walked in, to the delight of the shop keeper, feeling the pull through me. Again, it was not as strong as it had been with the tourmaline, yet perhaps the stone's energy was different. Weaving my way through stacks and aisles of beads, pretending to shop, it occurred to me that I should let Cade know where I was. That there was something here.

"Beautiful lady, let me show you treasures. Here," he said, holding out a velvet tray with even more beads upon it. The tug I felt swelled, directing my search to the back of the store, which was curtained off with a hanging rug.

Cade, I said in my mind, not knowing how far our connection reached. The tinkling of beads resounded.

"Sir," the shopkeeper called. Cade stepped next to me.

The shopkeeper bowed. He looked to the door nervously then motioned for us to follow him to the back. Maybe I should have been annoyed he was so close by. Following me even.

I can feel it. I said to Cade in my mind. *It's here somewhere. Blue. Of bloody course.* In my peripheral, I saw his cheek lift in a small smile.

"Lady, my grandfather told me to watch for you. For the beautiful lady with the stars written upon her." He indicated to the back of his russet hand. "And the male who was other with the stars at his back." His large almond eyes implored me.

Energy pulsed all around us. I couldn't imagine how everyone else didn't feel it. Slowly, I drew off my gloves and held out my freckled hand to him. He nodded and smiled broadly then motioned for Cade. I looked at him, confused. Cade swore under his breath and unzipped his jacket then turned around, lifting his shirt to reveal a perfect replica of my freckles just above his left shoulder blade. Though, I supposed mine were a replica of his, given our age difference.

The shopkeeper bowed low again before turning away. From a locked cabinet, he pulled an object wrapped tightly in heavy woven purple and red fabric. He bent on a knee and presented the object to me.

"Go with God, lady," he blessed me. Then to Cade, "Battle King. Restore our worlds."

We made a quick exit and nearly ran back to the cave hotel in which we were staying. Once inside the pale stone room, which curved up and around feeling like a womb, I unwrapped the object. A pillar of blue lace agate sat glowing in my hands. It was roughly a foot in length, yet looked severed at the ends, broken and incomplete.

Cade's face was pinched in concentration, and I could hear him stop breathing. Distantly, I filed away being able to hear his heartbeat and the moment he stops breathing.

"I have the other half," Cade breathed. I widened my eyes to him. "That's why it's been so hard to find. The energies have been truncated."

"Why didn't I ever feel it back home?" I asked, mentally kicking myself for calling Barlowe Combe home. He touched the agate.

"Because it's not there. It's in Aoifsing." He looked at me, a look of devastation on his face.

I sat.

"Did you know we have matching markings?" I asked, suddenly feeling very tired again.

"I did," he bit out.

"You didn't think it was worth telling me? I mean we have these twinsy freckles...Wait. Oh, God. *We* aren't..."

"No! Gods above. No. We are not blood-related." He actually laughed nervously. I did as well and put my face in my hands.

"Thank bloody mother earth for small miracles," I said to myself with a shudder.

"I think it's time for a drink, don't you?" he offered. "Oh, yes," I agreed. "Just not raki. Never raki."

IN THE PALE light of the sickle moon, the white-washed fairy chimneys of Cappadocia stood in anticipatory regard from the view we had from our terrace in the cave hotel. Cushions and rugs were strewn over the extension of our suite. Frost hung expectantly over the valley. An uneasy truce settled between us. I honestly could not look at him without seeing my lips so near his and his wordless rebuke. The need to be comfortable had me change from my travel clothes into the cashmere dressing gown I had packed. At this point it didn't matter in the least how I appeared in front of Cade. So, sitting on the cushioned ground in my dressing gown, feet tucked under, suited me just fine. We were avoiding the conversation that needed to be had. I cradled a large glass of red wine between my cold hands as I looked out into the valley. The entirety of the area radiated a feminine strength, perhaps enhanced by the Crone's moon.

As a little girl, my father used to tell me stories about the moon. It represented the many faces of the goddess. In the new moon, you made intentions and affirmations. The half-moon meant you act upon your intention with focus. During the full moon, we are full of emotion, energy. Lit from within and volatile. The Crone's moon is wise. It is more darkness than light, and the dark absorbs and understands more than the maiden light does. It is a time for surrendering to feelings or letting go. One either plants new seeds like bringing into one's life another person or releasing those who are not one with our soul.

Looking up at the Crone now, I wondered where that put me. Had I attempted to forge that new bond when really what I should have done was submit to letting go? Perhaps all these things I was meant to do and who I was meant to be were encased in the reality of being somewhat alone. Maybe I wasn't meant to find love like others were. Unlike the couple from the tree in Rila, perhaps I was meant to be unloved. Stars flickered above me, and I wasn't sure I was ready to believe that.

"Where would you like me to start?" Cade asked, sitting close to me, his knees bent, chin resting upon them.

I clenched my jaw trying to not want to touch him. I didn't know why I reacted this way with him. Why could I barely control the need to touch him?

"I noticed your hand when we first met," he said. "I had wanted to pass it off as coincidence, but deep down I knew I had recognized your scent, and it started to drive me a bit mad." He stopped for a while and drank his own wine. "Corraidhín had me by the balls quite often for how I acted around you. Silas hit me once." He laughed humorlessly.

I turned my face in his direction, laying my cheek on my knee, yet still could not look at him.

"It certainly was not because I couldn't stand you. I was afraid for you. Afraid of what it all meant." His breathing hitched. "You were so..." He pinched his nose again and pulled at his hair. "And then you and Silas." He stopped talking and drained his glass. I squeezed my eyes shut then drank my own. Cade refilled them both.

"I don't judge you for it," he continued. "Or Silas. I

under- stood. I do. It was really none of my business, but it affected me. Corra realized why I acted the way I did. The way I still do, I suppose. Silas took longer. I am sorry if I was horrible. Your life is yours and simply because you have had the misfortune to fall in with us doesn't change that."

The oil lamp on the low table near us flickered, and he turned the dial on it to regulate the flame. I was mortified to feel warmth from my eyes slipping over my knees.

"I still do not understand why we connect the way we do and why the markings. I would assume that you and Ewan are of the royal blood line. So, you can, in fact cross through the Veil. If you wish to," he added after a pause.

I raised my head and wiped at my eyes, trying to not smudge the mascara even more. A sort of dread started in my gut, praying to whatever merciful goddess happened to be observing tonight, that he wouldn't conclude this speech with a verbal version of the dismissal I had gotten last night.

His hand lifted toward mine and halted. "May I touch you?" he asked softly.

I sniffed loudly and shook my head. "Please, no," I managed. He nodded absently. "May I ask why?"

"Because I am not sure my heart could take it right now," I answered in complete honesty.

A look like he had been slapped crossed his face, and his fingers clenched. "I don't understand," he admitted finally.

I leaned my head back and pressed my lips together, staring at the star-speckled night sky as my eyes kept filling. This was not supposed to happen. This was not how this day, this trip, was supposed to go.

"I can't even look at you without wanting to touch you, Cade," I said to the stars. "When you are near me, there's a buzzing inside me. Quite literally. If you touch me right now," I took a deep, shuddering breath, rallied my courage, and dared to look at him. "It might break me when you pull away." I lay my cheek against my knee again, my hair falling heavily across my shoulder. There. I'd said it.

He was so quiet. We sat in silence for a great deal of time. Finally, I pushed from the cushion to stand and walked over to the low wall that looked out from our terrace. In the instant before I reached the wall, Cade was there and grabbed my hand.

"Don't," I whimpered, and hated every inch of myself for the weakness in my voice.

He held tighter and pulled me closer to him. "What if I don't pull away?" he asked shakily. "Gods know I don't want to."

"And tomorrow? Or when we get back?"

"This is not new for me, Neysa. You are like this great ocean, and I had fought to stay up above the water, but all I want is to drown in you."

I knew my heart stopped, and I couldn't remember simple things like how to move.

"Then why? Last night, I—"

"Because I'm a shit," he said cutting me off. "Because we were drunk, and I was afraid that would be an excuse. Because I didn't know if you wanted me only because you are stuck with me here." His hands pulled from mine, one moving up my arm, the other circling my waist, pulling me closer. I roamed my hand up his chest and moved my thumb across his jaw.

"I can't think straight when you touch me like that. I thought I was going to die when you cleaned my cut the other day." His voice was rough and lowered to a rumbling bass.

My thumb moved across his lips then across his eyelids, feeling the soft flutter of his lashes. He buried a hand in my hair, moving me closer still, cupping the back of my head as it tilted back. Thumb trailing along his temple and down the side of his neck, I moved my other hand to his waistband, anchoring him to me.

"Not pulling away?" I asked in a rasp, which sounded nothing like my voice.

"I don't think I could if I tried." He leaned forward and touched his lips where my ear and jaw met, sliding over my cheek and kissed my eyelid before moving back to my throat.

I might have burst from my skin. Featherlight strokes made their way up my sides and around my back. He made a whisper of a trail from my clavicle straight down over my stomach to my bellybutton. Whether I moaned out loud or in my head, I don't know, but his answering growl gave me reason to dive my hands up under his shirt. Each muscle I had tried to not watch when we sparred, rippled under my touch. I sent my hand up his stomach as well and went onto my toes to kiss the base of his throat. Both chests beat together as if grasping for purchase.

"Can I kiss you?" he asked.

"I think I might kill you if you don't."

He chuckled at that. "I'd like to see you try, lady. It could be

fun."

"Maybe tomorrow," I breathed.

"Then I will be awake all night worrying and will need to fill the time." He moved his mouth back across my jaw.

"So really we are back to square one," I reasoned.

"Indeed."

His lips fastened to mine in a proprietary claim. Lips, which I stared at when he spoke and teased me with each smile. He swept his tongue inside, meeting mine. Palms smoothed along my sides and pulled open the shoulders of my dressing gown then lifted the strap of my bra before bending to kiss the top of my shoulder. We backed to a low sofa but missed it and ended up softly falling on to the cushions again. Legs astride his lap, I sat with my dressing gown completely open, in my black sheer lace bra and panties.

"This bra," he muttered, voice dripping with what I felt. "You were cruel to wear it when I healed you. That was a calculated attack." He pulled the straps from my shoulders and dropped his hands to the sides of my breasts, pushing them in together and then bent down to move his mouth over the cleavage. *Holy gods*. He looked up with heavy-lidded eyes.

"Needed to use a weapon. I have very little in my arsenal," I countered breathlessly.

"You are the gods-damned armory." He moved his mouth back to mine and nipped my bottom lip, which made me want to explode.

I pulled at his shirt, taking it over his head, so I could feel his skin against mine. He swore and unclasped my bra, tossing it across the stone. "That was very expensive," I complained with a giggle.

"I'll buy you ten more, so I can rip them off you too."

"Isn't it just typical that just when you're about to get your fix, plans change?" a voice drawled from the door. My hands were still buried in Cade's hair and his face pressed against mine, but the heat in him rose so quickly, I drew back feeling my bare stomach burn.

Reynard was leaning against the rounded cave archway, picking at his nails with the tip of an arrow, the full quiver strung on his back. Cade pulled my arms from around him and scooted back, throwing his shirt to me. I quickly slipped it over.

"Oh, don't do that for my benefit, mousey," the alabaster-faced male purred. "Perhaps I should have waited a few more minutes and enjoyed myself."

Eddies of rage were pouring off Cade, but I knew as well

as he did that there is no way Reynard came alone, and we had to first figure out where and who was accompanying him.

"Reynard," Cade said smoothly, and stood to his full height. Reynard's piercing eyes roved over Cade's shirtless torso, and he bit the bottom of his lip. I could actually have been sick on the floor for the look he was giving Cadeyrn. "Can I help you with anything in particular, or were you just trying to get in on the fun I was having with Neysa here?"

His stone-cold mask was back, and I felt more naked now, sitting in his shirt than I had moments earlier, exposed to Reynard and whomever lurked about. Our visitor breathed in deeply and looked at Cade with unmasked longing and a sneer of hatred.

"Mm. If I weren't on such a tight schedule, Cadeyrn, I may take you up on that—but no. You don't tend to favor my type. Let me ask you? After my sister, you seem to have declined many offers of female companionship. Is this halfling really bewitching you?"

I stood and gathered my discarded dressing gown around me.

"We were simply bored, Reynard. If you need to discuss matters with me, let's do so while the girl gets dressed." Cade made a dismissive gesture toward me. I swallowed, not knowing where this was headed.

"So, she isn't the one who is turning you away from an eternity of solitude after you butchered my sister?"

"Gods, you fool. This," Cade waved at me, "is a plaything. Can we get on with why you are in my hotel room?" Cade said with an annoyed tone.

I felt sick and stumbled back a step.

Reynard casually strode toward Cade, and I wanted to shout.

"No need, *brother*," Reynard smiled, full of malice, reaching his long fingers out at Cade like he wanted to stroke his chest. In an instant, he had me pulled against him with a dagger at my throat. Four other fae surrounded us with bows pulled tight, the arrows pointing at Cadeyrn. "I will be taking the mouse with me. The Elders would like a word. And with your little display the last time you came, you can understand that you aren't welcome there."

Cade took a step forward. I widened my eyes in warning at him.

He cocked his head to the side. "All of these antics? Why not say so from the beginning? Take her. I don't care," Cade said with an air of haughtiness. Though my practical mind was telling me he was being dismissive for my benefit, the emotional side of me was warring with whether I wanted to cry more or kick him in the groin.

Reynard's arms tightened around me. For one so slim and nearly sickly looking, he was quite strong. His hand smoothed down the side of my dressing gown as he licked the tip of my ear. "Oh, I love cashmere," he purred, then sent the roving hand into the fold of the robe.

I squirmed and tried to elbow him, but his arms held fast. I felt the simmer of fury off Cade and caught his eyes as they calculated the odds of taking on the four sentries.

It's not worth it, I said in my mind. Let this demon violate me to get a rise out of him. *I will kill him myself as soon as I can*, I promised Cade as much as I promised myself.

Cade's eyes followed Reynard's hand, and his own hands were clenched in fists. I went utterly still, my stomach churning wildly, wanting to be away from this. Just before the hand went any lower, I slammed my head back as hard as I could, shattering Reynard's nose. He kept one arm about me.

"I will come with you," I said. "But if you try to touch me again, I will remove every extremity from your body." I pledged.

He snickered, but his nose was still gushing blood.

Before I could say anything else, we were moving faster than I ever had. The scents and colors of the sentries moved in a blur alongside us. When at last, we came to a stop, I emptied the contents of my stomach in a recurring retch.

A glimmer in the night air looked similar to the haze in the wood of Barlowe Combe, and I knew in my heart we were about to pass through the third Veil. This was the one that was close to closing. One shove from the sentry, and I went flying through the haze and emerged on the other side gasping for air.

Casting a glance around me, I was suddenly certain that we were not in Saarlaiche where Cadeyrn and his family were from.

PART II

CHAPTER 21

Sharp, angular rocks jutted from icy ground as far as my eyes could see. Winds tore across the landscape, biting against my skin. Countless hours had passed as we walked across this plain of unforgiving stone. I stumbled and took a hard fall onto my knees, ripping open my dressing gown. The sentries snickered as my backside was exposed to them. It had been nearly a full day since I had eaten and hours since I'd had a drink. A boot poked under my rear and lifted, humiliating me, though I wouldn't give them the satisfaction of showing it.

In front of me, Reynard sighed and turned. "Get up," he barked. "Keep moving. It will be dark before we reach the shite bucket Paschale calls a residence if we keep this pace."

I took a deep breath and tried to stand again, though my head spun from exhaustion, hunger, and thirst. The boot poked again at me, and when I couldn't stand, he then pushed me clean over.

"By the gods, Omnar, was that necessary?" Reynard snapped at the guard.

I knew that name. Omnar was the Elders' guard whom Cadeyrn had retaliated against for Ewan.

Ewan. Likely my brother. He was trapped by the Elders. I had to keep going.

Reynard lifted me under my arms and straightened my dressing gown. My limbs were numb. He swore and took his own cloak off to wrap around me.

"Thank you," I whispered through chattering teeth. He seemed surprised at my gratitude but quickly sneered.

"You're slowing us down," Reynard said, waving off my thanks.

"I need water. Food. Haven't eaten," I chattered.

The guards behind me sighed.

"Omnar," the pale demon of a fae commanded. Give her your ration and canteen." There was a pause then a guttural rebuke. "Listen, you useless piece of shite." Reynard got right in Omnar's face while saying it. "You are along to serve me and your masters. I have no desire to bring a dead female to the palace. Unless you would like to offer your own hide as meal and sacrament to Paschale in penance for killing our charge, I suggest you hand over your ration and canteen."

With that, the canteen and a hunk of dry bread and hard cheese were shoved in my face. I ate both as quickly as I could, not wanting to delay finding shelter any more than they did. Not to mention, I was getting less and less keen on this Paschale the more I heard of him.

I knew that exposure could kill me faster than hunger. However, the more sustenance I could get in me, the better I could make my numb feet obey and get us away. Having not looked at my feet, I couldn't be sure of where I stood frost-bite- wise, but the throbbing, consistent pain had subsided to a sickening numbness. I couldn't even feel the stones beneath my feet, tearing into my soles. That was not good. I debated not saying anything, but it seemed that losing my feet would not serve the greater purpose either.

"My feet. I think..." My words were sloppy. Reynard looked down and swore. "Frostbite," I managed.

He looked me in the eyes and seemed to wrestle with some- thing. He then glanced at the guards behind me. "Cyrranus," he called. "Carry her, and make sure her feet are wrapped in your cloak." Cyrranus wordlessly lifted me, cradling me in his arms gentler than I had expected. Omnar snickered from beside us. "Omnar, by the damned gods, one more fucking remark, and you will be giving her your boots. Now, can we please get on with this? I would like to be home before spring."

Though the wind still howled around us, gnashing with its icy teeth, I was surprisingly warm being carried and, at some point, fell asleep. Distantly, sounds of metal groaning and multiple sets of feet shuffling on the ground began to spear through my consciousness.

Cyrranus must have felt me start to wake. "We are passing through the gates to the castle in Festaera, lady," he whispered.

My eyes opened and took in the surrounding area. Open bonfires blazed and half-feral folk warmed hands and food before them. Most of these folk did not look like my friends or even my captors, but were overly tall and thin with skin the pallor of fish from ocean depths where the sun never reached. I shivered. Their stares followed us as we made our way into the stone walls of the main keep. Once inside, the temperatures not much different to the frigid air outside, we were shown to a large stone room, which held only battered wooden furniture and a single unlit fireplace.

Reynard hopped onto the table and crossed his leg over a knee. He eyed me appraisingly.

"Can she not stand?" Reynard asked.

"Likely not," Cyrranus answered, still keeping me up. "I can set her on the chair, but she may well fall over."

Reynard grunted in response as a white shadow entered the room. Arms tightened on me.

Mostly, I had come to realize that people, fae and creatures in general, are frightening when their disposition becomes so. A wolf is not frightening to look at but strikes fear from both knowledge of its predatorial nature or if it has become aggressive. The person, if one could call it such, who walked in was frightening in the most base and primeval sense. White, wispy shadows danced around a face as long as my forearm and nearly transparent in its skin tone. If the folk outside the keep were pale, this creature was a thin sheet of vellum barely covering the bones and veins inside. It strode for us, opening its maw in what may have been a smile but showed double rows of elongated, pointed teeth. Christ, who was this?

I heard Reynard swallow, but his voice was steady as he said, "My lord, Paschale. Here is the halfling the Elders Council requested I bring."

"Is she ill?" Paschale asked.

I could have answered, yet wisely remained silent.

"She has not eaten, my lord, and her feet and hands have taken the frost sickness from the journey."

The monstrous one stood in front of us, two heads taller than Cyrranus whose heart I heard do an uptick.

"Yes," he drawled. "Well, fortunately, you are here now. I shall take her farther on tomorrow."

Panic surged through me. I did not want to go anywhere with him. I tried over and over to quiet my mind and reach out to Cade, but there was roaring empty silence, and I knew he couldn't hear me.

. . .

"No need, my lord," Reynard said casually, waving his hand. "We will be on our way back to the palace in Veruni and are happy to oblige the Elders in her transport."

"Hmm," Paschale hissed through those teeth. "I might like to have her on my own first. My mate is fascinated with humans and would love to inspect her."

Reynard laughed in his maniacal way and twiddled his fingers together. I saw a panicked gleam in his eyes as he smiled at Paschale who smiled back. My stomach turned, and I felt Cyrranus's arms tighten even more. Perhaps he would fight for me, as useless as it may be.

"Oh, I do think that sounds fun, my lord," Reynard trilled. "Regrettably, in her current delicate state, I believe that perhaps she might be best transported with Cyrranus as it is his heat that has kept her alive this day past. Analisse was quite clear that the girl," he spat *girl* like it had a bad taste, "remain well, whole, and untouched. As it was, I nearly killed Omnar here for his insubordination in regard to her. With your excellency's permission, I wish to shelter here the night and continue on my mission with the girl at dawn."

Paschale did not answer but ran damp fingers down my face. He pulled at the skin under my eye and looked into my eyes so close the world was filled with his bulbous white irises. He pulled my left arm from under the cloak and sniffed the length of it.

"She smells of Cadeyrn," he hissed quietly.

"Yes," Reynard smiled. "He was making sport of her when we arrived."

Paschale chuckled darkly, then faster than I could register, he tore my inner arm open from elbow to wrist and licked at the well of blood that surged to the surface. I cried out, and Cyrranus pulled me back. Paschale lifted his blazing white eyes to the guard.

"Am I not your superior, Cyrranus?" he asked, blood

leaking through his teeth. I felt Cyrranus nod. "Then surely you are not pulling my subject away from me?"

"No, my lord," Cyrranus answered. "The girl jerked back. I moved instinctively. Apologies." Paschale smiled.

"Good," the monstrous one answered. I wanted but a taste of this trouble that has been brought to my door. Oh, how my mate would like to taste her," he mused, his tongue sweeping across his sharp teeth.

"Yes, well, my lord, Paschale. My men and I have had a long journey and beg your leave to rest before we set out in the morning."

"Very well, Reynard."

We were dismissed. Blood began to clot where he had licked my wound, and as hungry as I had been, nausea roiled in my gut.

We were shown to rooms in the keep, and I didn't know whether I was more afraid to be alone in this hideous place or to be behind closed doors with any of these three. In the end, I shared with Reynard who did not speak a word to me the entire evening, which allowed an uneasy sleep as my body tried to heal itself.

TWO HORSES and a wagon were procured for the rest of the journey. Reynard and Omnar would ride the horses which would pull Cyrranus, another guard whose name I had not heard, and myself. The roads were unforgiving, yet the alternative of having to sit atop a horse or walk were far worse. Frostbite had indeed set in, but a healer tended to my wounds before our departure. As long as I held my hands and feet near Cyrranus, the sentry's heat would keep the healing process going.

As my only clothing had been Cade's shirt and my dressing gown, a fresh set of clothes were laid on my bed when I awoke. A large woolen sweater, likely a male's, and pants that seemed to be a sort of riding breeches, combined with a pair of thick socks was my outfit. Though I was far from clean or warm, it was a vast improvement.

I tried not to think of my friends and whether they were in danger on the other side of the Veil. From Reynard's chatter early this morning, I heard that the Veil we had passed through collapsed completely in our wake. While the separation of the realms is ultimately our goal, the violence of a complete collapse signified a total destabilization of magic between the realms.

Cyrranus's eyes were on me as I looked out of the wagon while we descended a steep mountain pass. There was a sharp drop to our left which looked closer than I wanted to think about.

"We are descending the Vascha mountain range, nearing the the Festaera border," Cyrranus explained.

I felt the heat coming off of him and tried to not think about Cadeyrn. About what we had started and what I was forced to leave behind.

"Where are we going?" I asked.

There was a snort from the other guard who was sharpening a blade across from me.

"No need to for you to know, girl," the guard said. "We are taking you to the Elders, and that's all you need to know." I let the canvas flap back down and looked toward them both, then focused on Cyrranus. Surely, he was my safest bet for an ally.

"I know that the Elders are normally at the point where Veruni, Prinaer, Saarlaiche, and Naenire meet," I began. "Rey- nard said we are headed to see Analisse in Veruni." It was not quite a question.

"Again," the guard sneered. "It is of no concern—"

"Correct," Cyrranus said, cutting him off. "Analisse is a seer and wishes to assess you before you go before the Elders. She can then report to them what she gleans from you. It is not so far out of the way. Rather than head south through Prinaer and Naenire to Veruni, we have moved west toward Saarlaiche first." The trepidation and fear must have shown on my face because he went on to say, "No harm should come of you there. Analisse is fair."

Still, the thought of Analisse seeing what we had researched and planned. Seeing into my mind or heart. I rested my cheek on my hands and squeezed my eyes shut. For now, I was remotely safe. Warm. In a covered bloody wagon traversing the geographical landscape of a fae realm on my way to be judged by a seer and a panel of ill-intent elders, but safe and warm. For now.

Wheels squeaked to a stop and the sounds of two males dismounting the horses had me jumping to the opening to take care of my own business. The landscape had indeed changed, slipping from the barren rocks and whipping winds of Festaera to the mountainous forest of northern Saarlaiche.

As I squatted beneath frost-covered holly, my heart leapt a bit knowing I was in the province of Cadeyrn's family. I wished I had thought to ask about it. About where their village had been. Distances and anything that could help me escape and get word to them. I didn't even know exactly where the Veil was which led to Barlowe Combe. Stupid, stupid, Neysa.

Perhaps Cade or the twins would know where we would travel. Perhaps they might intercept us. Likely not, I argued with myself. Their assumption would be that we were headed straight to the Elders. My feet had healed enough to pull on the boots that had been left for me, and I made myself useful gathering wood and pine needles for a fire.

We camped the night, my only warmth from Reynard's cloak, which I still wore. Dawn saw us packed up and on the road again. Two more days until Veruni if the weather held. Taking mostly isolated roads, we passed only a few villages.

That first day we stopped at a pub in one of the villages, the males in my party joined the other patrons in mugs of ale. On the third round, I stood and announced that I would get myself one as well. Reynard pushed a coin to me, and I headed to the bar where the barkeep stood, wiping the wooden surface.

I ordered my mug and quickly pushed over an additional silver piece I had found in Reynard's cloak, as well as a flat stone on which I had etched a dagger and an eye. Using a discarded arrowhead I'd picked up from the forest floor the night before, the etching came to be under the cover of darkness. I'd scratched at it while seeing to my business in the thicket of foliage outside our camp. The eye reminded me of the blue beads in Turkey, the dagger, the gift Cade had given me. I could only hope he understood.

I looked at the female behind the bar and said once, barely above a whisper in the noisy pub, "Cadeyrn." I pleaded with my eyes as I took my mug from her hands.

She laid a flannel over the stone and the additional currency and swept it off the table before I turned around. The males huddled in the pub entrance, complaining about the mounting weather. Cyrranus stepped aside, making room for me to pass through and out to the wagon where Reynard waited.

Canopies of trees blotted out the winter sun in this eastern part of Saarlaiche. Though I felt comfortable in the dimness of the forest, this area was the forest of warnings and nightmares. Heavy mist and persistent, fat drops of rain pooled on the top of the wagon, and though I had no love for the males on horse- back, I was empathetic to their misery. Our party pressed on well past dark and came to an inn just after moonrise. My heart surged at the opportunity to perhaps try to get another message to Cade.

"We are stopping for the night. The rain is too heavy to camp comfortably."

Staying the night complicated my plan. Too many opportunities to rat me out to my companions. So, I waited until breakfast, and as we were leaving the tables, I plunked another etched stone into my half-eaten porridge, along with the last of the coins I had pilfered from Reynard's cloak pockets which hung heavy at my sides. Taking it upon myself to clean up the dishes from our party, I brought the bowls to the bar. From beneath lowered lashes, I looked at the older barkeep and gambled with my options.

"Thank you for your hospitality, sir," I said quietly, handing him our bowls, mine on top. His eyes narrowed at the stone and coin half-submerged. "Cadeyrn," I murmured, and prayed the people of Saarlaiche were loyal to their Battle King. As I turned to walk to the door, Cyrranus was standing right behind me, arms crossed.

I knew my heart was audibly thumping faster and faster. If I had been in a physical fight, I would have reacted efficiently, yet here I was, cornered by a sentry with whom I had been trying to build trust. He raised an eyebrow at me and stared for a long moment. The barkeep went about his business.

"Do you always clean up after everyone?" Cyrranus asked.

I nodded and swallowed. He looked me over once more and ushered us out into the downpour that hadn't let up overnight.

By our third day on the road, the guards had become testy and even Cyrranus gave me short, clipped answers. I hadn't figured out whether he had heard my encounter with the barkeep and had kept quiet for whatever reason, or whether he really had come up only seeing me bringing dishes over.

Our camp on the third night was just over the Veruni border. There was a steady light rain that kept a chill inside my bones no matter how close I sat to my sentry. Cyrranus used his gift to start a small fire, which was impervious to the rain. The two other sentries were able to catch dinner after finding a warren of rabbits nearby. My mind balked and protested eating the creatures, but I knew my survival depended on keeping my strength. As the rabbits turned on a makeshift spit over Cyrranus's fire, I excused myself to see to my business and wash in the trickle of water coming off a close hillside.

As I stood and pulled up my breeches, twigs snapped closer than was comfortable. I froze and immediately crouched into a defensive position. Thankfully being in Aoif-sing had begun to heighten my eyesight and hearing, so I saw the shadow lunge for me as I dove to the side. Thanks as well to my heightened sense of smell, I knew it was Tomas, the second guard who traveled in the wagon with us.

I jumped to my feet and his hand shot out to grab the front of my sweater. "A word, girl," he seethed.

"Go to hell," I spat in his face. He slapped me, and I grunted.

"I saw what you did back at that inn. You are leaving notes for that impotent sole born. I could have you flogged for that. I could do it myself," Tomas threatened. My mind raced. "The funny thing is," he mused. "My fellow sentry was standing right behind you. So, if I heard you, then I'm sure he did as well. Yet, he didn't say anything. Why do you think that is, girl?" he asked. "This information could very well put me in a better position with the Elders. I'm sure Reynard would be very interested to know you are leaving clues about our whereabouts."

I jutted my chin out and tried to struggle against the dagger that lay across my neck. A warm sensation ran down into the funnel of my sweater.

"So, tell them. What's stopping you?" I asked with a

feigned mask of calm. He smiled, and in the dark of the forest I could see his eyes darken then turn to a glowing yellow like a wolf. Oh, shit.

"You see, I'd like to propose a deal," he crooned. The hand not holding the dagger grabbed at my matted hair.

"I have no deal to make with you," I said through clenched teeth.

"Oh. I think you might." His eyes looked wildly around the forest, and I noted glowing eyes surrounding us. "I can call on the Lupine Kingdom to aid me. Your options are slim. So, you can turn around like a good girl and let me pound you like the whore you are," he said into my ear. I spat in his face again, and he tightened his grip on my hair. "Or we can let my brethren take care of the camp. Hm?"

I slackened and sniffed like a child then nodded.

"That's a good girl now," he crooned and slowly pulled the dagger from my throat and began to turn me. Golden eyes kept their watch from a distance. "I have waited for this since I saw you tumble through the Veil, the scent of that bastard all over you."

The sound of his sword belt hitting the ground was my key. I twisted around with my hair still in his grip and punched him solidly in his groin. He doubled over, dropping the dagger, yet did not release my hair. My shoulder shoved into his ribs as his elbow slammed into my ear. The world fizzled, and I slumped to the ground, coming back to myself as I hit the mossy earth. I had landed on the dagger and though it poked into my back, I had just enough maneuverability to roll and pull it out as he began to lay atop me. The dagger jammed straight through his ribs, and I screamed as he pulled it out and lifted it above his head. *What the fuck?*

"Not so easy to kill, I'm afraid." *Holy gods above!*

The dagger gleamed in the reflection from his eyes and though his legs had me pinned, I pulled the spoon from my morning porridge out of my breeches and stabbed it into his throat as hard as I could muster.

Boots trampled through the thicket and all three were standing there staring as Tomas ripped the spoon from his throat and tried again to lift the dagger. Within that split second, Reynard was there and had shoved an arrow through Tomas's temple. Reynard's exceptional speed may have been the only thing that kept Tomas's dagger from my face, and for that I was eternally grateful. Cyrranus kicked the corpse off me and, in one fell swoop, severed his head from body. I collapsed, panting. The golden watchful eyes began retreating to the forest.

"What is he?" I breathed.

"A disloyal piece of shit," Reynard answered. "Apart from that, he was what is referred to as a lupinus. He can call on wolves and can draw life from them if and when his is threatened. Fortunately for us, once the head's off, the game is up."

Reynard kicked said head and stalked off. Cyrranus lifted me off the ground and led me back to the wagon.

Needless to say, I refused to eat or drink anything for the rest of the night and refused to relieve myself in the morning as well.

"I will come with you and stand two strides away. Tomas is dead. You cannot possibly hold it in any longer," Cyrranus said, attempting to assuage my panic. Finally, I agreed, and we continued our journey once I had relieved myself.

"Are lupinus common?" I asked. As in, is this something I need to be preparing for regularly?

"As a rule, no. Most of the Elders try to keep at least one in their charge as they are, as you witnessed, quite difficult to fell. They hail from an ancient clan deep in the center of Prinaer."

"Are they like other fae who are born in pairs?" As in,

should we expect a vengeful wolf fellow to seek us? He looked at me inquisitively.

"They are not. They are single-birthed and live shorter lives than the rest of us. However, they can procreate more and tend to inbreed." I shuddered at the answer. He nodded. "That in itself tends to make them a couple of arrows short of a quiver. I was not happy that Tomas was sent with us. That is why I insisted on being in the wagon with you."

"Thank you, Cyrranus," I said honestly.

"As for whether we can expect retaliation," he went on. "I doubt it. They are half-feral and keep to their region, killing even their own children and siblings in power struggles. Every generation, Nanua, the Elder from Prinaer, takes a unit into the lupinus lands to select a few for Aoifsing."

"Can you tell me about the Elders? What I should expect?" I asked in a small voice. He stared at me for a few long moments, no doubt figuring out what advantage the information will give me. "I am scared, Cyrranus," I said. "I have been taken from my realm and been beaten, humiliated, and threatened for no reason I understand. At least if I know who and what I will see, I can prepare myself."

He sighed and held up his hands in surrender, his eyes softening. "Paschale you have met. He is by far the most terrifying. The people of Festaera are isolated and uncivilized. They are miners though, and many of our resources come from Festaera. Prinaer and Naenire are twin provinces. Nanua of Prinaer and Camua of Naenire are siblings who were born on the border a millennium ago. They still reside on the threshold between their lands, governing as a unit. Both provinces are interwoven with rivers rich with fish and surrounded with wildlife. There are many caves and mines, which contain precious gemstones."

He raised an eyebrow at me. Ah yes, those. I would file that away for later.

"Dunstanaich," Cyrranus continued. "Is an area of steep hills and sheep farmers. Soren's is the smallest province. Below Dunstanaich is Laorinaghe. It is temperate and coastal. They have olive groves and fertile lands. Lorelei is its representative. Analisse of Veruni, as I have said before, is very even- tempered. The land is green and within her borders is perhaps our largest city in Aoifsing. From what I have seen of the human realm, the city of Bania is still quite small in comparison, yet it is a center of commerce. Another city is Laichmonde in Saarlaiche, which is governed by Turuin. That is where your...friends...are from. Laichmonde is not as large as Bania, but it is well-kept and many wealthy folk reside there. What did I leave out?"

"Maesarra," I interjected.

"Yes, Maesarra is warm and temperate. Even in winter, it is rarely cold. The coastal waters are clear, and its people are happy. Feynser is the Elder representative there, though Queen Saskeia is in residence, and it takes clout away from Feynser. Don't say I told you that," he said with a wink.

"Where are you from?"

"Maesarra, lady." His smile widened, and I realized he was handsome in a classic, rugged way. His olive skin glowed, and he had friendly hazel eyes. "My parents were fisher people, and my mother would free dive in the ocean and collect pearls. Her centuries have affected her lung capacity, so it is no longer a livelihood fit for her, but my father still takes to the seas each day." He looked wistful and softer.

"And you became an Elder Guard." I couldn't help the distaste in my question.

"I was born with the song of the sea in my heart, but I wished to forge my own path. I wanted more than what my family had settled for," he answered tightly.

"I can understand that more than you might think. Did you find it? Your more?"

"I think I may have," he answered and held my eyes. I looked away.

Voices sounded outside and Reynard slowed the horses. Gates closed behind us, and looking out of the canvas flap, I could see buildings and houses on either side of us, stretching up the hillsides, sprawling outward. Everything was constructed from a reddish clay and glowed despite the cool temperature. Markets and towers flanked us, shops and cafes snaked down the streets that bisected the main avenue on which we rode.

At last, we came to a stop in front of a palace that seemed to be a part of the hills themselves. Pale red marble rose in simple lines to form towers, and lower levels were carved and adorned with birds of varying species. Staff helped us from our wagon and ushered us inside where we were greeted by whom could only be Analisse. She radiated beauty from skin as dark and smooth as espresso. Her equally dark eyes shone as she approached us with a warm smile. Reynard and my two sentries bowed swiftly, clicking heels together. Belatedly, I bowed as well.

"Welcome, child," she addressed me, and took my filthy hands in hers.

Her simple, raw silk gown was a column on her lithe frame, and though I should not have felt inadequate standing before Analisse, as I had been abducted, I felt like a street urchin. She cocked her head and leaned in to me. "I will personally show you to your room, and my ladies shall help you wash and dress. I would wager you are ready for a bath and hot meal."

"Yes, my lady," I confirmed. Was that an appropriate term of address?

She grinned.

"I thought there were four of you, Reynard," she asked, turning to my captor.

"There were, milady. We had trouble. Tomas was our lupinus, and he both attacked the girl and threatened my men."

Her eyes widened. "I do not like their kind. I trust he was taken care of?"

"Of course, milady."

She nodded and took my arm, leading me through the palace to the upper levels where a large room awaited me.

I knew I should be angry. Should demand from this Elder that I be sent home. I knew all of this and yet she was being kind, and I was so very tired and hungry. I had never known hunger or feared for my safety. My training was sport until recently. Yet here I was, calculating who I might ally with and wanting nothing more than to shower and sleep for a long, long time.

Windows opened behind the bed, looking out onto what appeared to be apple or pear orchards. The sounds of another set of feet scuffled around the wood floors and splashes of water came from the adjacent room.

I spun, looking longingly for the water.

Analisse laid her hand on my shoulder and led me to a handmaiden. "Ama will help you. Rest and we shall speak of things at supper."

She turned and walked away.

"Thank you," I quietly called after her.

TINY PINPRICKS of heat lashed into my feet and ankles as I lowered into the bathwater. It had been five days since I was taken from that cave hotel in Cappadocia. Five nights of fitful sleep encumbered by frostbite, Paschale's bite, raging hunger, bone numbing wet and cold, bruised and battered body, and filth. Ama had first insisted on scrubbing me down with warm wet cloths soaked in what smelled like lemongrass. Flakes of blood and dirt dropped from the cloths to the tiled floor. Once she deemed me worthy of the bath, I eagerly stepped in, heed– less of the heat, and hissed. Ama chuckled.

The bath was deep enough to submerge completely and there was a lip at the back from which to hang my head. My handmaiden pulled my hair back from the lip and apologized when the touch on my ear and sensitive scalp made me wince with pain. Incredibly gentle fingers poured warm water over my scalp and rubbed lavender oil over my head, then washed my hair for me as I soaked in the tub. Finished with my hair, she moved to clean my caked-up fingernails and toes and tutted at the scar on my forearm. I finally left the tub and crawled into the cream-colored sheets without any regard for clothing. I didn't have any, and I was too tired to worry about it.

Sleep the previous nights had never been deep enough to dream. Asleep in this warm bed, I dreamt I was calling out to Cade. Dreamt of talking to Silas on a riverbank. Dreamt of being stalked by wolves and beasts and Cade being chased down and beaten. I was calling his name and drawing my power from the earth, pulling him to me. As hard as I pulled, the beasts would pull him back until he was a speck in the distance, reaching his hands to me.

I awoke sobbing and out of sorts. Panic rose in me, and I counted my breaths to calm down. My chest felt tight, and my breaths were shallow. A hand was clutching mine and shushing me like a baby. I focused on Ama, and she looked at me with such kindness and sympathy, I fell to pieces again.

"Now, girl," she said. "Let's get you dressed and down to dinner. A hot meal makes everything better." I hiccupped and let her pull me from the bed, wrapping a blanket around my naked body.

On the chair opposite the bed was an emerald-green gown. It seemed like dinner was more of a formal affair then. Though the dress was both long-sleeved and full-length, it was anything but demure. The neck opened to the middle of the breastbone and nipped in at the waist. From there it flowed to the ground and pooled around my slippered feet. The sleeves were tight and belled at the wrists.

Ama asked if she could brush out my hair, promising to be extra gentle. I agreed and once she was finished, my hair was left loose. Any contraction on my scalp would have me in tears after the way Tomas had yanked me around by my hair. I knew my eyes were red and swollen, and for that I was thankful. Let them know I am not sitting pretty in captivity.

Just before I walked to the door, Ama handed me something. So quietly, she said, "I found this in your undergarments, girl. Best keep it hidden. While you slept, I sewed a small pocket on the interior of your skirts. I will do my best to do the same to each garment while you are here."

I looked at her in stunned silence, noting the double horn she placed in my hands. The chain was missing but the talisman Corra had given me was unmistakable. My heart clenched that the charm couldn't keep me from being brought here. Couldn't keep me from not knowing where Cade was and whether my friends were safe.

"Do not lose hope."

With that she placed a hand over her heart, and I instinctively did the same. "Thank you, Ama."

Dinner and scrutiny were waiting.

CHAPTER 22

Plastered walls and dark wood floors lined the hall outside my chamber. Stationed at the end of the hall, was Cyrranus. Clean and well-dressed, he seemed so at odds with the ruffian I had come to know these days past. In seeing me, his eyes went round, and his brows lifted. I supposed I looked less the bedraggled urchin myself. He bowed deeply at the waist and offered his arm. In taking it, I noticed his scent of greenery and musk and a soft lavender from the soap offered in this place. By the sidelong glances I was getting, I knew he was itching to say something.

"What?" I demanded.

"Pardon, lady?"

"What is it you want to say, Cyrranus?"

"Simply that you are lovely this evening. Being clean suits you." He laughed and tried to smother it with his free hand.

I snorted. "Yes, well, covered in blood and filth isn't my normal look. You clean up well yourself."

He ducked his chin.

After descending a back flight of stairs and winding

through corridors, a plastered archway frescoed with climbing vines opened up to a dining room that bridged both cozy and formal. Seated around the dark oak table were Analisse, Reynard, someone whom I immediately took for Analisse's twin sister, and a male I hadn't met. Analisse stood, a welcoming smile on her face, and gestured for me to sit.

"My sister, Julissa," Analisse introduced me to the woman seated to my left. "Lord Dockman." She waved toward the stranger seated at the opposite head of the table to her. I tucked a strand of hair behind my ear as I nodded in greeting. "Reynard, I believe you have already been acquainted with. I do apologize for the behavior of Tomas. It was unexpected and, of course, unacceptable."

"And the behavior of Lord Paschale?" I asked defiantly, raising my chin high. "What of his threats and tearing my arm open with his teeth?" I raised the arm, allowing the belled velvet sleeve to fall back, revealing the angry scar that ran the length.

Analisse's eyes shot to Reynard, who had the sense to look somewhat abashed. I could feel my face heat with anger, and my breathing started to hitch. Cyrranus, seated on my right, placed his hand on mine on the table where my palm was flat down, fingers splayed. I jerked back, but the gesture had been a soft reminder to calm and watch my tongue.

Lord Dockman snickered as Reynard raised an eyebrow, then cleared his throat.

"My lady," Reynard began. "Lord Paschale had wanted to hand the girl to his mate for...*inspection*." Analisse snarled. The sound was so at odds with her soft-spoken warmth that I started. "Cyrranus was keeping the girl from frost sickness when Lord Paschale tasted her."

The memory had me shaking. Not from fear, but from an intense rage at the violation. The violation of the sentry who had tried to rape me in Bulgaria, Reynard pulling me from

Cade's arms, the exposure walking through Festaera, Paschale, Tomas, even being here against my will. Ama's risk of sewing a pocket for the talisman into my dress centered me.

I straightened in my seat, establishing an air of displeasure but not weakness.

"Neysa," my host began quietly. Her softly pointed ears were turning from her normal lovely dark brown to a russet, which matched the angry flush on her cheeks. "There are some here who are less benevolent in nature. The Lord of Festaera is one. On behalf of the Elders of Aoifsing, I extend my apologies. I do not tolerate violence against women for the sake of dominance. Those in my province who act as such pay a very steep price indeed." As she spoke, wine was being poured and bowls of soup brought round.

"I accept your apology and am grateful for sanctuary here. I must ask, however, the purpose of taking me against my will from my own realm." A slight gasp sounded from the end of the table and a boot gently knocked into me from my right. I didn't care.

"Girl," came a high-pitched voice to my left. "My sister is kind. Do not press her generosity."

I turned fully to Julissa and stared into her brown eyes. "Forgive me, lady. I am not questioning her generosity. I ques- tion the manner in which I was brought here. I was hunted and captured. Perhaps, had I been given an invitation to dine with your *kind* sister, I would have come of my own volition rather than face the trauma I have endured these weeks past."

"Please," Analisse announced. "Let us eat and begin anew. For after we dine, a guest will be with us for drinks."

I resolved to eat as much as possible, and though I knew I couldn't train as I'd like to, I would work my muscles to main- tain my strength back in my chamber. The meal passed with mostly idle chatter between Analisse, her sister, and Lord Dockman. As pudding was brought round, I decided to implore the stranger. He appeared older than most I had seen in Aoifsing. Most folk looked barely above thirty years old.

"Lord Dockman. Are you from this province?" He seemed taken aback to be addressed.

"I...dwell along the coast of Veruni."

"In what capacity do you come to Bania?" I asked.

Reynard cleared his throat, and the same booted foot, along

with a solid thigh, pushed against the side of mine. I knocked my knee into his as if to say, "bugger off."

Analisse answered.

"He is my captain of trade and maintains the port and waterway that runs from Bania to the sea. Though he is here to discuss business, he is also my friend, whom I have invited to share our meal." There was a slight bite to her answer that told me she was displeased with my question.

Good. As friendly as she was, I am not such a fool to believe there is not an agenda here.

Acting as though I understood my place, I looked to him. "I would love to hear of the coast and port, my lord. Forgive my curiosity. In my realm, I worked as a scholar of sorts and studied trade."

He gave me a tight-lipped smile, and the room relaxed somewhat.

"Veruni's coast is rugged but has a large, open harbor. I have several merchant ships, each trading with a different province. We trade pearls and glass with Maesarra; food provisions such as wine, fruit, and textiles with Laorinaghe. Dunstanaiche has woolens, Saarlaiche has cattle, lumber, and arts. That ship is the largest as it houses larger animals, lumber, and often people."

"Slaves?" I asked with unmasked revulsion.

"Certainly not!" Julissa spoke up. I turned to her. "There are some provinces—Festaera," she listed. "Prinaer, and though Naenire keeps very few they are still participants in a slave market. We in Veruni abhor slavery both institutionally and privately."

"What does Veruni have to offer the other provinces?" I asked, genuinely curious.

The three local denizens looked to one another as though waiting to see who would answer. Lord Dockman held court. "Produce. Apples, plums, danafruit, spirits, hides from beasts found mostly here." He paused and sipped his wine, eyes on me. "This evening I have brought a shipment of excellent wine and oils—olive and lavender—and will be off in two days' time to pick up a shipment from Saarlaiche."

"Well, it seems you live a life on the go, Lord Dockman. The wine is most pleasing. Thank you all for sharing with me."

"I go with the tides, lady," he stated cryptically. "I have always felt the moon's pull upon the sea." I quirked my head to the side.

"Lord Dockman travels by night only. He is most sensitive to light." Reynard interjected. Dockman motioned his agreement. Curious.

With that, we moved into a drawing room of sorts, though it was the largest I have been in outside of the castles in Europe.

A fire the size of a modern walk-in closet roared in the center of the room, flanked by stone columns, all plastered with reliefs of the same birds I noted on the pillars outside.

Library shelving covered the north end of the room while a wall of windows was the south end.

I walked toward the books, curious of the reading material in this realm. With a pang, I missed the library of crystals in Barlowe Combe. I missed reading alongside Bixby and Cuthbert and seeing Cade's military novels. I missed Cadeyrn and what we had started between us.

Tracing the gold-leafed title of one book and reading the name, pictures flashed in my mind.

THE LIBRARY OF CRYSTALS, the stone altar with the beautiful woman turning toward me, shock on her face. Blood splattered. So much blood. Flashes of light. Deep, deep sadness and loss. A man whose back was to me. Not any man. The constellation of freckles on his shoulder blade told me it was Cade, though lashes marred the panes of muscle.

JUST AS FAST, I was back in Analisse's drawing room.

"The visions get easier to handle," she said, placing a hand on my velvet arm. "Will you tell me what you saw?" I shook my head, realizing tears were freely falling. "I understand. I hope that one day, Neysa, we can be friends. I knew your mother

and would be proud to call her daughter my friend."

Shock. In all of my years, I never thought I would find anyone who knew my mother. Dad rarely spoke of her, and we

had moved away, I had assumed, from anyone who knew her. Analisse gave me a sad smile and walked to the doorway.

I stifled a sob and turned back to the books, hoping to see

again, what was happening to Cade. Was it a warning or had he already been beaten?

"OUR GUEST HAS ARRIVED," Analisse announced.

"Pleasure to be here, Lady Analisse."

I whirled at the voice I knew so well. There stood Silas. My knees nearly gave out. I looked at his face, unmarred. He gave me an ever-so-subtle shake of his head, yet walked straight to me, taking my hand in his.

"And thank you for keeping Neysa for me."

Something in his eyes told me to be quiet as he leaned down and kissed my cheeks lightly on each side and squeezed my hands. Instead of stepping back, Silas wrapped one arm around my waist and pulled me tight to his side, brushing his hand over the velvet of my hip. I looked up at him not knowing whether I was waiting for a cue and found his eyes on me. Someone cleared their throat across the room.

"And what of your meddlesome cousin, Silas?" Analisse asked. Inside, I began to squirm under the heat of his stare, yet he still did not take his eyes from me as he responded.

"Detained for now. He shouldn't be a problem, my lady." Not sure what role was being played here, I simply looked back at my friend. "The collapse of the third Veil weakened his abilities, so he is healing slowly. Once Neysa has recovered from her ordeal, I will escort her to the Elders myself. If it pleases you, my lady, I will retire with her for the evening."

"That, sir," piped in Cyrranus, "is my task. I am to escort her to the Elder Palace." Ever so slowly, Silas pried his eyes from mine as he turned to the guard.

"Yes, Cyrranus. I appreciate your loyalty, but the task, as you call it, is now mine."

"I disagree. I shall return her to the Elders with you. I will not abandon my post."

The two males were in a standoff. Finally, Silas nodded and turned back to me. He tucked a strand of hair behind my ear, making me wince in pain. Anger briefly flared in his eyes, but he simply turned and walked us toward the door.

"Silas," Analisse called. We stopped, and he half-turned to her with a lazy grin. "I expect to see you later for a debriefing." She smiled at him, her eyes heavy and hooded.

"Of course, my lady," he answered, that grin still on his face. With that, we left the room.

As soon as the door shut to my chamber, Silas's shield came up around us. We both began talking at the same time.

"What is the plan?" I asked.

"Where are you hurt?" he barked at the same time, his hands roaming over my head, feeling for what made me wince. "I'm fine. Or healing. I fought with a lupinus. He had me by

the hair."

Silas growled and stalked closer. He leaned in and sniffed me.

"You smell like someone has marked you," he spat. I held out my arm and pulled back the belled emerald sleeve to reveal the tear in my forearm. He grabbed it and began to shake from anger. "You were bitten by the lupinus?" His words were deadly calm, and thunder rumbled beyond the window.

"No. Paschale."

While his anger still boiled, Silas's shoulders dropped a bit in relief. He leaned in and kissed my mouth. It was almost chaste. Almost. Until he pulled back and gave me a lopsided smile. I whacked his shoulder.

"Cadeyrn asked me to kiss you for him. He didn't specify where."

I laughed despite myself and threw my arms around him.

"Please tell me he's coming. Or that we are leaving. Tell me the plan."

He circled his arms about me as well and said into my neck, "Not yet. Be patient, Neysa." I started to protest, but he patted my back. "I know patience isn't your virtue, *Trubaíste,* but trust me. He turned his head into my shoulder and sniffed along the exposed skin. "This a very nice gown." I began to feel a bit awkward and started to pull away. He leaned into my ear and spoke quietly. "Cyrranus is outside the door. There is a raven on the tree outside the window who answers to Analisse. I have to bring down the shield slightly to allow them to hear and see bits and pieces. I am here to supposedly be taking you from Cadeyrn for myself. Because you already smell of both of us, the ruse is easy, but you must play along."

His shield dropped. I stiffened a little as his lips moved over my jaw. My mind flashed to Cade's mouth having traveled that same path.

"Silas," I said. "Bed, please."

He stopped, scooped me up under my knees and carried me to the bed. We lay down side by side, and as he leaned over to kiss me, he flicked his hands and the curtains drew closed, shutting out the raven's view. He growled and thunder clapped outside, and I felt the shield click back into place.

"I am so sorry, Neysa. Analisse knows me as a bit of a cad," he said with a smirk, moving away. "It was the easiest way we could think to get one of us in here."

"How long do we have to play this game? Where's Corra?" His hands played up and down my arm and leg, fiddling with the velvet. I whacked his hand again.

"Sorry," he laughed. "This gown is so soft." I rolled my eyes at him.

"Cad indeed."

"Corra is meeting us later," he said, and I swallowed. He brought his hand to my face. "I will get us out. You will see him again. I swear it."

I nodded into his hand and turned into it to kiss his palm.

"Thank you for coming for me." I tucked myself into his body and closed my eyes.

"You know, this whole ruse would be easier if you were naked," he teased.

"I'm sure it would," I laughed as I stood and began to change out of my gown and into— into what? Ama left a thin chemise on the chair for me, and while his back was turned, I quickly slipped it over my head and walked back to the bed.

"You and I have already gotten ourselves into enough trouble, don't you think?" He shrugged, and for a minute I thought I detected a hint of regret. Of sadness in his aura. Outside the window, the raven squawked as a soft rain began falling.

"Silas?" He wouldn't look at me.

"You know, I think Cyrranus out there is a bit overly protective of you." He slid his eyes to me briefly and looked away again. I wasn't distracted. "You have a way with males it seems."

"Silas."

He still didn't turn fully. I climbed over the bed and kneeled in front of him, turning his face with my own hand.

"Come now, *Trubaiste*," he said, still not meeting my eyes. "You're a canny lass."

I dropped my hand and sat back on my heels. What had I done? I didn't have the words to say to him, and so I remained quiet as I put my hand over his heart and brought his hand to mine. He slowly looked at me, the rain falling harder. His mouth quirked into a sad smile. "It's okay," he whispered. "I always knew. You and Cadeyrn were like lightning from the start. I knew, and Corraidhín knew."

I hadn't. About him. About Cade. I was so socially inept; I couldn't see anything but for the glaringly obvious.

"You're always, always, in my heart, Silas." I covered his hand over my heart with my free one and squeezed. "You brought me back to life. With your friendship. Your teasing."

"Yeah? What else?" He grinned up at me and folded his free arm behind his head.

I laughed again.

"Your magnificent male body and its infinite capabilities with the female body." I batted my lashes and he barked a laugh. I leaned down and kissed him on his brow. He had brought me back, and I would forever be grateful to my friend for that.

"Now, there," he said. "No pity party." I laid my head on his shoulder and curled my legs around his. "We never talked about that night. After everything got complicated." He made a sound of dismissal, but the rain kept coming down. "I thought about it for weeks. It was...incredible, Silas. You can't know how much it meant to me. I am sorry if things worked out differently. *But*. I will always remember it. Quite fondly."

He wrapped his arm around me and kissed the top of my head.

"I will too, *Trubaíste*."

CHAPTER 23

With the curtains still drawn, watery light was slowly creeping in through the window as I hit the floor, face down.

"Ugh!" I groaned and popped back to a crouch and dodged the next kick. "You need to work a little harder to get me this early in the morning," I said with a smile.

"How much harder, lass? I thought I was already working quite...hard." Silas responded with a wink and flipped forward into me, pulling me off my feet and on top of him.

I yelped as he laughed and flipped me. His hands pinned my arms overhead, and he dug his nails into the wooden floorboards.

"Cade said you never appreciated the sight of me under you." I was goading him as I slowly moved my leg into a bent-knee position.

Silas growled and pulled back just a little as I hoped he would. "Did he now? Too bad I'm the only one who's actually had you under me," he said with a very male, guttural rasp. "And on top of me."

With that, I brought that bent knee up and used my foot

and shin to dislodge his arm from mine, finally able to roll out from under him. Until he tackled me on my side and locked all four of his limbs around me. I was matched. We were breathing heavily, and I had sweat soaking through the chemise I was wearing. Completely impractical for fighting but I had few options. I needed to talk to Ama about my wardrobe. Silas licked the back of my neck where sweat was running freely down it. I yipped like an injured coyote.

"It's been too long. I've missed these daily romps," he breathed into my ear. To the listening ears outside, we knew it all sounded and would smell like our morning activities were completely different to what they were, and it gave us the opportunity to get me back in shape. "I have a present for you."

He unfolded from the floor with a low moan. From a satchel, he pulled the amethyst dagger and my Yule present from Cadeyrn and presented them to me. My smile was broad when I stood.

"I'm going to head down to eat while you bathe. Walk me to the door."

I did, and before he headed down the hall, Silas turned and kissed me for Cyrranus and the other two guards to see. Cyrranus looked daggers at Silas, and his nostrils flared as he passed him. The door clicked shut, and I slid against it.

Gods above, I wished Cadeyrn were here.

THE ORCHARD in midwinter was skeletal and layers of ice lay upon mud where last night's rain had frozen. Silas had to meet with Analisse, so I walked with Cyrranus through the dormant orchard. Ama had left out a midnight-blue gown that buttoned up the front yet opened at hip length. I wore it with fitted breeches made of thin, black leather-like material. They were stretchy enough to move with me, yet thick enough that I knew they were a hide of some sort. The dress was a light wool with cuffed sleeves that hid my dagger well.

Against my left breast was an inner pocket where Ama, as promised, had sewn a small pocket for my *adairch dorhdj.* Feminine yet practical lace-up boots in an off-black color came to mid-calf. Atop the entire ensemble, I wore a cloak pinned at the chest with a golden bird.

A clearing in the orchard appeared ahead and there was a table set with tea and biscuits. My companion motioned for me to sit. Flicking back my cloak and the tails of my gown, I sat on the iron stool. He remained standing.

"Cyrranus, sit, please." He hesitated for a moment then sat stiffly. I made to pour his tea, but he grunted, taking the pot from my hands. "I *can* pour tea," I bit out, "May I pass you a biscuit, Cyrranus, or is that a bit forward?" He rolled his eyes and took the plate from me.

"Is there a problem?" I asked him when the silence had stretched on longer than was comfortable.

He seemed to wrestle with saying something but finally blurted, "Are you really with both Silas and Cadeyrn?"

I shifted in my seat and sat up straighter. "That is none of your concern."

"Do you even know where he is right now?" he asked, and I pulled down the cuffs on my sleeves and flicked a piece of biscuit crumb from the table before he continued. "He is seeing to Analisse."

"And?" I asked.

"He is *seeing* to Analisse. Just as he was seeing to you this morning from the sounds of it. Does that not bother you?"

234

I cleared my throat. It did bother me. It bothered me that Analisse would engage Silas when he was supposedly mine. My mind was spinning with the issues at hand. The games being played and the risks being taken. The dismay on my face was not feigned, but Cyrranus didn't know what I was actually upset over.

"I am still a prisoner here, Cyrranus. There may be pretty clothes for me and a soft bed, but the fact is that I have been taken from my home, my friends, my life and kept here against my will. Do not presume to judge my choices of company to keep." I pushed at my nose that was feeling traitorously red and swollen.

"If you do not want to be with him, I can keep him from you. My orders are from the Elders. I can take you away today."

My demeanor softened at that. He was kind. I looked off into the bare branches of the trees, picturing them as they would be in a couple of months, covered in blossoms. The breeze would flit about, and the tiny flowers would rain down, covering the grass in pink-tinted white petals. The sun would be shining, and lazy clouds would float in and out of view. People would walk amongst the fallen petals.

A WOMAN IS STANDING. She has long dark hair and is holding the hand of a small child, tucking a blossom into the child's braid. The woman turns and looks to me, standing in my winter apparel, my face too thin, too pale. Her eyes widen and drop to the child at her side who is facing away. The woman looks again to me and covers her mouth with her hand before she scoops up the child and runs off with her.

* * *

I BLINKED and was back in the wintery clearing. Cyrranus was staring at me wide-eyed as the teacup shook in my hand. I dropped my eyes to the table. In my mind, I tried to reach that bond with Cadeyrn. How close did he have to be to hear me?

Cadeyrn. I don't know where you are or if you hear me. I don't know what the hell is happening. If it's just a puzzle, then why is so much at stake? I...I need you. With me.

"Was it a vision?" my sentry asked quietly, as if he were

keeping it out of listening ears. I nodded once. He placed a hand over mine. "I can protect you."

"I want to go back to my chamber."

"EITHER YOU ARE FAR MORE fun than I initially thought, little mouse, or something is afoot," Reynard said.

I hung my cloak on a peg by the door and walked into my chamber.

"What do you want, Reynard? Hoping to catch some action again? Go find yourself a plaything of your own."

He chuckled and breathed deeply. "It certainly smells of sweat and desire in here. I wonder which of you is playing the other?" he mused. "The last I saw, Silas was attaching himself to Lady Analisse's face as they went to her chamber."

Energy crackled in my fingers, and I felt heat rise in me. The hairs on my arms and the fabric of the bed linens and curtains began to stand on end with static. My fingers curled into the hide of my pants, and I pulled at the fabric. Reynard's eyes crinkled in amusement.

"Do you like the aphrim skin pants? I suggested them for you. Nasty beasts, the aphrim. Makes for lovely clothing. Breathable, light, moveable, water-tight..."

"What. Do. You. Want. Reynard?" I asked again, light pulsating from me. I felt the glow of the amethyst strapped to my back.

"Apart from your lovers?" He laughed. "I want to know what you are up to and whether it will get me killed." He breathed in my scent and shook his head. "Still both those males. Have you thought to take them both at the same time?" Light erupted from me, casting the room in a near white-out glow. "Save that light of yours for the dark seas ahead," he rambled.

"Get out." I thrust my arm toward the door, and it swung open on a phantom wind.

Cyrranus stood there staring in at Reynard, and Silas

rounded the corner, his wavy chocolate-brown hair mussed, clothes askew. Reynard snickered and left. Cyrranus snarled at Silas as he passed.

Before I could register it, Silas had the guard pinned a good three feet above him, against the plastered wall. One hand was around his throat, the other bending his sword arm back.

"One, I am going to assume your snarl was misplaced and rightfully directed at the rat who just left this chamber. Two, may I impress upon you that not Reynard, nor *anyone* who is not Ama or myself, is allowed into Neysa's chamber. Are we clear?"

"What about Analisse?" Cyrranus asked with a smirk. Part of me was slightly impressed he had the gall to ask.

"One would think the lady of this manor would have the good graces to knock." Silas released his grip, and Cyrranus dropped to the floor, his sword clattering next to him. With that, my friend walked into our chamber and slammed the door.

He stunk of male muskiness and Analisse. It made me feel sick. I walked to the window and looked out upon that orchard where I had seen the vision of the beautiful woman and her child.

We were silent in the room that was still buzzing with static. I knew without turning that Silas was sitting on the edge of the bed.

"Cadeyrn was attacked." My heart stopped as I turned to him.

His head hung low, and that sweet, rugged male looked for the world like he wished he were dead. His shirt hung open and nail marks were striped down his chest. He noticed my eyes going to them and clamped the shirt together. "She told me while I fucked her. I never knew her to be cruel. She was one of the better ones. Maybe...maybe we played this wrong. Perhaps since she wanted me, it made her jealous enough to hurt you. I don't know."

"Is he..."

"Alive? Yes. He was captured outside of Bania. I don't know where he is now." I wanted to go to him, but I couldn't stand the scent of her on him. "He was here. Nearly made it here."

"Go and bathe, Silas." I turned back to the window. He left the room and came back after bathing, steam billowing out of the bathing chamber.

"Does it bother you? That I bed her?" I was silent for a long moment, not knowing how to answer.

"I don't know. Yes," I confessed.

"Why?"

"I don't know, okay? Maybe because I care for you. You're my friend, and it makes me sick that she would use you." "What if it were more consensual. Would it bother you?" he

asked, and it hit me like a kick to the gut.

I scrubbed at my face. "I don't know, Silas," I whispered. "I don't like this situation. I want Cade here. Your being here makes me miss him more, and everything is muddied in my head because of memories of us, and sometimes I want you too but—"

"But only because you miss him."

"I was taken from his arms!" I screamed, and the sound bounced off the invisible walls of his shield. "We were *together*! I wanted him so much, and I think...I think he wanted me too. They took me from him. I was exposed and abused, and I'm here and you're safe and I'm exhausted, and I want to burn this gods-damned place to the ground and rip the realm to pieces to find Cadeyrn. And Corra. I want you all back with me. And yes, the smell of that woman on you makes me sick. Maybe I want to be in bed with you, but it's only because I love you as my friend, and you're safe and I'm so shattered at the moment, and..."

He pulled me to him and held me.

"We found each other, Silas. It could have been right with Cade and me. And now it's all fucked, and I don't know what I'm doing. I wanted it to work with him," I sobbed. "Do we stand a chance of getting out of this?"

He didn't move his hands, only held me tightly. "Yes. We do. We will go on here like nothing has changed. In two days' time, we will leave. I will find my cousin and he had better make you the happiest female alive or I will kill him myself."

I snorted into his chest. "I will always be jealous of any girl you have, Silas. You are beautiful, inside and out." I kissed his chest once, then brought his face to mine and held it between my hands. His sea glass eyes bored into me. Eyes squeezed shut as though he were in pain, he crushed his mouth to mine once, like a final farewell.

JULISSA HAD BEEN BAITING ME THROUGHOUT dinner. She was well aware of her sister's conquest. As pleasant as Analisse came across, Julissa was a conniving syco-phant and was playing me against her sister to gain the atten-tion of Lord Dockman. Reynard watched closely, not as amused as I thought he would be.

"And was your tea in the orchard this afternoon pleasant, Neysa?" Analisse asked, sweet as honey. "I trust Cyrranus was companionable."

I dabbed at the corners of my mouth and swallowed the last of the bacon-crusted fish.

"Very much so. I can only imagine how lovely the orchard is in spring."

"And have you seen it so?" Analisse asked.

"I have only been here this one time," I answered.

She smiled at me. "But have you seen the orchard in spring–

time? Did you smell the sweet apple blossoms and feel the breeze tickle your neck as the blossoms rain down?"

I took a large sip of wine. There was silence round the table. If these goblets weren't so large, I would have gulped the whole glass to buy time.

"I have, my lady." Cyrranus caught my eyes from across the table. His own were bloodshot, and his neck was rimmed red and bruised where Silas had held him up. His face was a mask of sympathy for me. *I can get you out,* he had told me.

"You were permitted to be here prior to going before the Elders because I am to sort through your visions," Analisse explained.

I started. Were they mad?

Julissa scoffed. "What, girl? Did you think your stay was a luxurious gift?"

Holy Christ, I wanted to throttle her.

"Julissa!" Analisse reprimanded. "You are out of line. Neysa is our guest. There are conditions for her stay, however."

Silas's knee pushed into mine. A warning and a comfort. Bide my time. Fair. Everyone described Analisse as fair. In what sense? A give and take perhaps? I present her with adequate information, she allows me to stay here? She uses Silas as I eat her food? Gods above, I can't wait to meet the others.

"How do you plan to sort through my visions? Do you go into my head?" A tinkle of laughter. A cough from Lord Dock– man. Silas threaded his fingers through mine and held them at his lips, playing the game well.

"No, dear. You tell me about them, and I filter through. I can clearly see intention. It shines for me like your aura.

Yours is determined and burns hot." She gave me a knowing smile and a sultry one to Silas.

"I am not comfortable telling you of them amongst so many," I answered, my chin high. Another snort from Julissa.

"Leave us," Analisse waved to everyone but Silas and me.

Reynard began to protest and was silenced with a flash of those deep chocolate eyes.

And so, I told her. I left out the crystals, the woman I had seen both before the altar and in the orchard. I left out my father. She asked about the magic I had inadvertently used this afternoon in my chamber with Reynard. Apparently, it was felt throughout the manor. It was late into the evening when we were heading to our chambers. I knew she was going to ask Silas to come with her and, as such, I took his hand and looked her in the eyes.

"Thank you for your insight," I told Analisse. "I am feeling quite raw at the moment and would like to turn in with Silas."

Her beautiful ebony skin shone in the sconces as she looked me up and down. Finally, she took my hand and kissed it, bidding us both a goodnight.

IN THE CORNER of my chamber sat a satchel, half-obscured by my boots. Silas noted it as we entered. A heavy grey cloak was neatly folded on top. Ama. Packed inside the satchel was another pair of those aphrim skin pants, a close-fitting tank lined in fur, and a mid-thigh length jacket, all in the same skin. In the folds of the clothing, lay a knife small enough to tuck into my boot, strips of dried meat wrapped in a cheesecloth, a skein of water, lavender oil, and a pouch of coins.

I looked to Silas. "We go tonight," he stated as a soft knock sounded.

Ama opened the chamber door. "Is there anything you require, lady?" She asked, her eyes darting to the satchel.

Would she be safe here? I took her hands in mine. "Thank you, Ama, but no. We are fine tonight. Get some rest yourself."

I placed a hand over my heart and bowed deeply to her. She echoed the movement and left.

CHAPTER 24

The guards at our door would be a problem. None of them had been unkind to me, and Cyrranus especially had gone out of his way to be my advocate. Weapons buckled and boots laced, I slung the satchel across me, the amethyst dagger wrapped inside. My fingers found the *adairch dorhdj* and warmed against it. I muttered some plea to whomever listened to such things and slipped it into my interior pocket. I pulled the door open slightly and left it that way. As expected, one of the guards peered around and called for me. When I didn't answer, he stepped in.

Silas knocked him back with a single blow, and I pulled the guard behind the slipper chair, binding his limbs and fastening a gag around his mouth. We slipped out the door and headed for the stairs at the end of the hall. Boot steps sounded. Silas pushed me against the wall and bent his head into my neck. I kept one hand ready to eject my dagger and one around his waist as he had one braced on the wall behind me and the other, farthest from the stairs, on his sword belt.

"Your chamber is footsteps from here," sneered a voice I knew to be Omnar's.

I looked up with sleepy eyes and Silas growled, thunder clapping outside. That really was a neat trick he had. Omnar walked past us, rolling his eyes, and Silas whirled, knocking the side of his sword into the guard's back. Omnar rolled with the blow and stood, sword out. Shit. We really didn't want to make noise.

Pressure from the gathering weather outside pressed upon me, the stray bits of hair that had escaped my braid stood on end. Winds howled as we tried to silently parry with the guard. He made to yell out and however I was able to use my powers —whatever they may be—the sound was drowned by current of electricity. While his scream was muted, the fact I had drawn upon so much energy was bound to be noticed. In a split-second decision, I stuck my dagger through the neck of the guard who had laughed and kicked me when I had fallen. Who had stood by and watched as I froze to death. I sent a whisper of gratitude to whatever benevolent force had Cyrranus off-duty this evening.

Our feet were near silent moving down the corridors and toward the servants' door at the back of the manor. We passed through the kitchen and grabbed two loaves of bread as we slipped through the door to the mudroom where we both came to a stop.

Reynard looked us up and down, noting the skins and weapons, the blood on my hand, and the weather outside. I braced for a fight. Silas spun his sword. The pale-faced fae quirked a smile at us and put a finger to his lips.

Hit me, Reynard mouthed and mimed the motion.

I really didn't need to be asked twice, remembering the arrow that nearly killed Corra and the hands that had pulled me from Cadeyrn. One solid strike shattered his nose and had him running, dropping a quiver of arrows and his bow.

For the briefest of seconds, Silas and I looked to each other then grabbed the bow and quiver and set out at a run.

The skies opened up as we tore across the grounds. Snarling erupted behind us and the sound of dogs giving chase made me pick up my pace. I hadn't trained fully in over a month, unless you count the Bulgaria incident. My muscles were straining as we ran, dodging rocks and puddles forming from the deluge.

"The bow!" Silas yelled.

"I'm not an archer!" I screamed over the rain and the sound of the wind. I passed it to him, dropping an arrow in the process. He knocked an arrow and released it, a yelp sounding in its wake. Gods dammit, I hated the thought of having to kill the dogs. Another arrow was released and one more set of crashing paws dropped away. The gates ahead loomed before, us and I knew there would be sentries waiting. I prayed it wasn't Cyrranus. Silas sent one last arrow out, and we were in the clear to the gates. There were three sentries, weapons drawn.

Silas looked to me as if willing our training together to manifest into some perfect choreography. We aimed for the middle guard and each rolled in the opposite direction, kicking out toward the flanking guards. I discharged the dagger from its forearm sheath and grasped it around the hilt, aiming into the hip crease of the guard before me. He madly swiped out at me as he fell. Clearly, they hadn't expected my capabilities. Silas took the third after dispatching his initial mark.

We made for the gates as Cyrranus came running through them. Both of us stopped dead and stared at one another. His eyes were devastated, mouth pursed tightly. I heard Silas spin his sword.

"I would have gotten you out," Cyrranus whispered as the rain was pelting us.

"You would have taken me to them," I responded.

He shook his head. "Go," he said with something of remorse in his voice. He turned to Silas and held his sword aloft. "Take me down and get her away."

Before he had a chance to say anything more, Silas knocked him sideways and drove an elbow into the soft spot between Cyrranus's neck and shoulder then took the guard's weapons and dragged me away.

The dirt road we had traveled on by wagon was now a sloppy mess, and we veered off it into the fields and trees that lined the carriageway. Less than a mile away was the Bania city proper. Pink-tinged buildings began popping up.

Still moving, though at more of a steady trot than a run, we weaved in and out of streets and alleys. My foot caught a pothole obscured by rainwater, and I went down hard. Silas yanked me up and pulled me behind a building. We were out of breath and soaked through. In the distance, the sound of horses running at a clip caught our attention. For the moment we were safe to catch our breath. My knee was skinned under my leggings, but the material held up. We had to get out of the city. My knowledge of its layout was minimal, but knowing the basic defensive layouts of ancient cities in the human realm, I would bet there were ways they had of locking the place down, sealing us in. No to mention the magic that would be involved.

"We head north out of the city and get past the foothills. It'll be a day's hike into Saarlaiche. Can you manage yet?"

I nodded and stood. He peered around the building and deemed it clear. A thought struck me, and I grabbed his arm. "Wait. Reynard said something," I blurted.

"That little shite bucket talks out of his arse."

"Yes, but the fact is, he helped us. He helped me in Festaera too. Before you came in earlier today, my magic was coming out." Was that just today? Gods I was tired.

"Everyone noticed. *Trubaíste*, we really need to get going. Tell me as we move." The sounds of booted feet running edged closer.

"No. When light erupted from me, Reynard said, 'save that light for the dark seas ahead.' Maybe...maybe he meant for us to go by sea?"

"That's quite a big assumption. We will likely get ambushed at the harbor. Dockman's ships are there, and they will be securing all outlets to and from the city."

"Yes, but," I pressed on. "The first night. At dinner. I asked about Lord Dockman's trade. He described what he trades and where. He looked me in the eyes and told me he had a ship leaving for Saarlaiche in two days' time. That's today."

Silas swore. He looked skyward. "We may have missed the tide. I don't know what time it is now. Did he say anything else?"

"He only travels by night." I shrugged.

"Gods and shite and fuck it all to never," he swore, pinching his nose in a gesture so like Cade. "Let's go catch a ship."

And so, we ran, scaling walls, ducking under washing lines, even slinking across two adjoined terraces to private homes. The brine of the harbor wafted toward us a few blocks out. Shouts and hoofbeats were all over. Silas motioned for me to go before him, daggers out, while he covered from the rear with Reynard's bow. We walked in a low squat for a few hundred meters, my thighs burning.

Large wooden crates provided us some cover as we slunk along the seawall, headed for the docks. The nearer we drew, the louder the voices. There's no way we could get past all those males. I peeked around a crate and bit back a cry as I was inches from the back of an armed foot soldier dressed in homespun rather than livery.

I reached over and stuck the small blade Ama had gifted me into the base of the guard's skull. The slip and crunch of the knife displaced me, making the situation seem like I was moving through the bars of music—not quite here yet forging on. I didn't know what or who that made me. A monster maybe. Or a trapped beast.

Silas touched my shoulder, acknowledging the severity of what I had done.

There were guards stationed every few crates. Silas took out a couple with arrows until he ran out. As we neared the only ship large enough to transport livestock and people, I locked eyes with a familiar whitewashed face.

Reynard smirked and jerked his head toward the ship then ran toward where we had just come. He whistled and tossed pebbles into the water drawing attention away from us. By all that's good and plenty, whatever his impetus was, he had helped us several times. I just hoped he wasn't leading us into a greater trap.

Once the dock was cleared of guards, we launched ourselves onto the deck of the ship and found the darkest, foulest corner to tuck into. It wasn't until we felt the boat pull away from its perch along the harbor, did I exhale a breath of relief. Then quietly and thoroughly emptied my stomach, adding to the feculent stench of the place. I closed my eyes and leaned into my friend as he took first watch. For three nights, we took shifts sleeping. Bits of salt pork and stale bread were rationed between us.

The morning of the fourth day greeted us with gull cries. Silas shook my arm. "Time to get moving. I hope you can swim, *Trubaíste*."

As the ship pulled in, we dropped straight into the harbor, my limbs locking up from the sudden cold. Twenty or so meters were all we needed to cover. The pale light of dawn gave us a shroud of conspicuity as we swam toward a neighboring boat.

Silas rammed his sword into the hull as hard and high as he could manage, then pulled up onto it until he reached a fishing net draped over the side. Legs outstretched from where he held onto his sword, hands dripping with blood, he tugged the net free with his feet. Once it dropped, he released his grip and splashed back into the water. My legs were barely able to keep me aloft in the frigid winter harbor as he pulled me toward the boat. I knew he was losing blood, yet his strength hadn't faltered.

We both climbed the fishing net, much slower than we would have liked, and finally hauled ourselves over the side and onto the deck. A young greenhorn was standing, staring at us as though we were mythical creatures. He opened his mouth as if to call out.

"Wait! Please," I stuttered with cold. I reached into the soaked satchel and pulled out a coin to hand to him.

The boy eagerly took it and wordlessly pointed to the exit.

Saarlaiche's harbor was minuscule compared to that of Bania. It was easy to see why. The inlet was flanked on either side by massive cliffs and against those behemoths, crashed wave after wave. It took a relatively short period of time to traverse the docks and make our way into town. Both of us shaking and not speaking, I kept an eye on Silas as his face grew more and more pale, his hands still dripping blood. He was walking on autopilot, steering this way and that until we came to a small structure on the outer edges of the town. We walked into the stables of an inn and a female appeared from behind the stall.

I sobbed and ran into Corra's arms.

"You two," she scolded. "Have made quite a mess of things." Silas and I looked at each other, guiltily remembering our conversation from days earlier. "Och, brother, what in the name of every old god have you done now?" She took his hands, pulled the cork from a bottle of spirits, shoved the cork into his mouth and poured it over his bleeding palms.

He roared through the makeshift bit in his teeth as the cork was pulverized. Once his hands were cleaned and bandaged, we sat on bales of hay, huddled together in horse blankets.

"H-How d-d-did you know we would be here?" I asked, shivering.

"I had a hawk stationed on the southern border. Elder guards came through yesterday with no sign of you. I made my way here, only arriving a couple hours ago. Figured you came by sea."

She winked at me and handed me the spirits. It tasted heavily of apple and burned fiercely going down. However, the warmth steadied my speech and shaking.

"Cadeyrn?"

"I don't know," she admitted. "He was attacked and taken outside Bania. I assume they would take him to the Elder Palace. We do know they want you, Neysa. The hope is that they would hold him as a means to draw us out. Rumor has it you two put on a good show in Bania though, so who knows." She eyed her brother speculatively, narrowing her eyes.

He waved her off.

"Have you tried to contact him?" Corra asked me.

"Only before when I was being taken to Analisse. I left notes, so to speak."

"Yes, I know. We did receive those. Clever of you. What I

meant though was through your connection to one another. Have you tried to contact him?"

"It's not a phone, Corra," I snapped. "He could hear some of my thoughts and read my feelings I think, but I couldn't hear him." Her eyes implored me. I sighed. "I would say things to him, yes. Sometimes. Just in case."

"Can you try to tell him where you are and where we are headed?"

"And where is that?" I asked.

"Laichmonde," she said and tore a piece of salt fish with her teeth and handed it to me. I gagged but forced it down. "We need to get lost in the city and gather information. By the way, how did you ever come across aphrim skin clothing?"

"It was given to me at Analisse's. I had a servant who was very helpful."

"It is very expensive and rare. A servant wouldn't just pick that up. It's made to order. Think carbon fiber Chanel. Reynard's family made its fortune harvesting the nasty beasts. Change into what I brought you whilst yours dry, but I would suggest wearing them again as they are akin to armor. Which I brought as well."

"You do think of everything, sister," Silas mumbled, half asleep against the stable.

"And I've done so for three centuries, brother." She kissed his head and stroked his hair as his eyes dropped closed.

My heart clenched. "It's so good to see you, Corra."

"I missed you too, Neysa." She kissed the top of my head as well. "You two smell like shite and death."

I mumbled something about that being about the measure of it and tipped my head back to sleep before the sun was fully up.

MOVING inland from the port in Saarlaiche toward Laich- monde would typically have been a day's travel with small villages all along the way linking the sea and the capitol. As we were staying under the radar, we had to skirt the direct route and move through the forest to the north of Laich-monde and enter from the northwest of the city. As Cade had described whilst we were in Bulgaria, the forest here was dense, the coastline unforgiving. It did remind me of parts of England and Scotland—of the rocky beach in Barlowe Combe where I had first sparred with Silas and where the thunder rumbled overhead.

"Tell me about your gift, Silas," I asked quietly in our camp that night.

It was too cold to not risk a fire, but Corra was able to use her power to reflect the light in a different direction. Silas looked up from where he was poking the flames with a long stick.

"My shield?" He continued to poke it.

His demeanor had become more downcast this evening. I noticed him almost sulking when I came back to camp after changing back into my skins. Corra had been speaking quietly to him, her hand on his shoulder. *It will get easier*, she told him, before I came into view.

"Well, that too, yes. Though I think I've got that figured out," I said with a smile. "The atmospheric changes. The weather." I honestly loved trying to figure out how the magic here corresponds to the science of things in the human realm.

Corra snorted. "Och, you should have seen him as a child. The skies would open up every time our father said no to him." She rolled her eyes.

I smiled and wondered if one day I would hear all their stories. If we would have that time together.

Silas gave a half smile and continued to prod the kindling. "There's not much to tell. We," he gestured to Corra and himself, "can become mist, rain, any moisture in the air. Corraidhín more so than I. She quite literally loses her corpo- real body. I, however, fade a bit but can command changes in the pressure systems. It's difficult to explain."

"So, it's always at your behest?"

"No. I can consciously control it. Keeping it at my behest, as you say. But our magic—all of ours," he said making a broad sweep of the three of us and, I was certain, including Cadeyrn. "Is controlled by our emotions. It's easily the hardest part of training our gift. We often allow our control to slip when we are in a heightened emotional state."

"When Reynard came to my room. He was trying to incite my magic. Make it surface, do you think?"

I saw him nod.

"Your gift is strong, Neysa," Corra piped in. "I have felt your power since long before you knew what we all were."

We. She included me in the we. I missed Barlowe Combe. I missed the cottage, the manor, the dogs, Tilly's shop, peanut butter cookies. However, I realized, sitting here, half-frozen with these two, that home was with them. Wherever we all ended up, my friends were my home, and I would fight for my home. I really did miss the dogs though.

"You commanded the storm when we were fleeing Analisse's?" I asked.

"Yes and no. I was worked up anyway, so the weather, as you may have noticed, had been volatile since I arrived," he said with a lopsided smile. "I may have made the storm a little angrier though." He winked at me.

I thought of the soft rain outside the window in Veruni.

"I have no doubt you will be able to control your gifts soon," Corra said to me. "You are quite focused and able to compartmentalize. Better than I ever was. I know that in the human realm it sometimes worked to your detriment. That control had you facing anxiety attacks and not allowing the openness we see in you now. But you're becoming who you were always meant to be, and I am proud to see it."

My eyes pricked as I blinked and murmured, "I dreamt it." "Dreamt what, *Trubaíste?*" Silas asked.

"My father came to me in my dreams. Back in my cottage.

He said, 'You are becoming who you were always meant to be.' Verbatim what you just said, Corra." I looked at her in surprise. She smiled, wide and lovely, then flipped her braided hair back over her shoulder. "So, it is told, so shall it be. The moment we met, I knew you. Like I'd known you my whole life, darling."

I remember feeling the same way. The same way I'd felt meeting Cade, and it infuriated me. I felt like I should be afraid, yet I wasn't. Felt as if I were always angry with him, but I couldn't place why. *You were like lightning from the start*, Silas told me. Perhaps my tapestry was more tightly woven than I had anticipated.

"Look up," Corra instructed. Above us, the night sky was pinpricked with stars. Some clustered so closely and densely, it was a thumb smear of light on black canvas. Corra took the index fingers and thumbs of both her hands to make a circle and moved it upward. "See that?" she asked, indicating a band of stars. I gasped and looked at my hand. My freckles, barely visible in the firelight. "That is the constellation known as *Adairch a Taeoide Gaellte* or The Horn of the Promised Tide. It is a double horn if you see. The stars cluster to form light on the one side of the horn, and the stars outline to form a negative space on the other side. They are said to meet in the middle and bring about change to our world."

The clearing where we were camped had just enough opening in the tree canopy to see the night sky. The others were quiet as I stared above me, unsettled and a bit sick if I were honest. Sounds of bedrolls laying out and the shifting of my companions as they readied for bed pulled me out of my skyward trance. Silas looked to me as he removed his boots.

"Don't give me that look, *Trubaíste*," he said with a slight smile in his voice. "Before you ask...did I know about the *adairch* on you that matches my cousin's?"

"And the stars in the damned sky, Silas. Don't forget those. Such trivial details," I said dryly.

Corra snickered, likely opting to stay out of this part of the discussion.

"Yes. I did. We all did. Cadeyrn tried to come up with a hundred different ways it could all be a coincidence."

"And so, you and I?" I really didn't know how to finish that question.

He sat forward and pursed his lips while he stared me down. "What?" he challenged me. "Do not pin this on me. You, and only you, are the master of your fate. At the time, both you and my cousin were hell-bent on pissing each other off, because you refused to even look at one another. It took that night to ruffle his feathers."

My eyebrows shot upward. "Did you...did you do it to..."

"Fuck the gods and all that's holy. No! You are not that daft. You know," he said pointing in my face. "You know how I feel about you. I also know how you feel about Cadeyrn and he you. But trust me, *Trubaíste*, if it were anyone, *anyone* but my cousin, I would be fighting for you. So, don't ask a bullshit question like that."

With that he turned and slammed himself into his bedroll, turning away from me.

I caught Corra's eye. "And the pendant you gave me? The *adairch dorhdj?* Is that a coincidence?"

"Oh, I suppose it was once upon a time. I was surprised when Cadeyrn gave it to me all those years ago. He was never one to give jewelry or frivolous gifts. But I realize now that it was never really mine. It was always for you." I touched the breast pocket of my coat where the double horn sat and slid into my bedroll. "I'll take first watch," Corra called. Then ever so quietly, though I knew Silas could hear, "You will find each other again. I swore it to my cousin, and I swear it to you."

"He missed it here. He wanted to come home, I think," I said more like a question.

"Home is with you. Wherever you are together," Corra answered gently.

"Funny, I just thought the same thing about all of you." With that I rolled away from the firelight and tried to sleep.

CHAPTER 25

Laichmonde was, to my surprise, not a walled city. The forest thinned to pockets of houses and businesses crafted of stone. Some roofs were thatched, others solid, and most of the homes had detailed stained-glass windows. We arrived by nightfall, having spent the day sparring in the woods.

As we passed each home, I was charmed by the glowing lights from within that shone through the colorful windows. The pocket neighborhoods became closer to one another as roads formed and led into the city center. Several temples dotted along the road, interspersed with schools, shops, and immaculately kept townhomes that would be at home in Belgravia, London.

Cyrranus had been correct. Though Laichmonde was much smaller than Bania, this city was awash with restrained beauty and so very clean. Corra had said they all maintained homes here, but it was not safe at the moment to try our luck in them.

The *Taempchal a Aimschire* or Temple of Weather sat atop

a steep hill in the center of town. As we lumbered up the steps to the temple, I muttered a complaint.

"It seemed fitting to reconnoiter in the structure dedicated to my particular gift as we plan our next move. No?" Silas asked, poking me in the ribs. He had a point.

Five elements were recognized in Aoifsing as worthy and necessary to pay homage. The sea, weather, greenery, fire, and love each had temples in Laichmonde dedicated to the element. Wind-stripped pillars of stone stood in a circle in the center of the temple, protecting the inner sanctum from the elements. Texts were inscribed in the floor, scuffed with age making them illegible.

Silas unpacked leaves on which he had scratched words. The leaves were placed in a copper pot on the stone altar then lit using a flint.

"It's handy when Cadeyrn is here to light the fire for us," Corra remarked.

Once the leaves had burned, the siblings muttered an adulation to the elements and sent the ashes in four directions on the wind. We then waited as the ashes settled back into the pot, having gathered along the side of the copper.

The twins peered in. "Southwest," they said in unison.

"He is at the Elder Palace," Corraidhín explained. "We will head out the day after tomorrow." I would rather go now. She must have read my discontent as she said, "We are just as eager to retrieve him, but we must gather supplies and rest. There is a long road ahead. Trust me."

BOTTLES of every size and color lined the walls and shelves in the apothecary we entered. Darkness had settled on the city. Some shops were closing up for the night while restaurants and cafes were opening, spilling warmth and light onto the wintry streets.

"*Aimserre deird*," called a soft voice from the back of the shop.

"Closing time for everyone?" Silas crooned.

The sound of something being dropped preceded a female's dark head popping around the pocket door to the back.

"Silas?" she exclaimed.

"It's a three-for-one special, I'm afraid," Corra chimed.

"Corraidhín! Och, and I am a positive mess." She walked to us and embraced my friends before giving me a hard stare through piercing blue eyes. "Lady." She inclined her head to me in greeting. I rallied a smile.

"Lina," Silas began. "This is Neysa."

"It is a pleasure to meet you, Lina," I said.

She shook her head, eyes pinched together like she was shaking off a pesky thought.

"We require assistance and supplies," Silas admitted.

"Of course, you do. I am still waiting for that dinner you promised me, Silas." She tugged at his jacket.

"Soon," he promised with a wink. "At the moment, however, there is a matter of a sensitive nature. Can we trust your discretion?"

"Och, you know you can. Come on back."

We followed her through the storage room and up a narrow stairwell into the upper levels of the townhouse. Scatered carpets covered the wood-paneled floors. Leather settees faced each other in the center of the room. Book-shelves ran the length of the two main walls, a small stove and sink sat at the back of the room near a large window, which looked out upon the street below. We sat at a worn table, that looked like it had once been a regal dining table, as she brought us tea and began to cook something on the stove, not allowing us to tell our tale until we had eaten.

"Tomorrow is my market day. I apologize I don't have more to offer you." She placed the largest serving of what looked similar to a ratatouille in front of Silas, then passed dishes to Corra and me, placing a loaf of crusty bread on the table.

We ate in silence, and as the dishes were scraped clean, Lina placed her arms on the table and asked for our tale. The twins took turns giving the barest details of our situation and what we needed of her.

After a time, she sat back and looked to me. "You smell of both Cadeyrn and Silas. That does not bode well with me."

"Lina," Corra warned.

I remained silent. Really, I was worried I would start spewing light and electricity if she pissed me off.

"Cadeyrn belongs to Neysa," Silas jumped in. "I have been with her these weeks past. If you do not wish to help us, Lina, then we shall take our leave."

Her head snapped to him.

"Don't be daft, man. Of course, I will help." She pushed the dark hair behind her slightly pointed ears and closed her eyes briefly. "Stay here tonight and tomorrow. We can gather your goods in the morning. I have an extra room upstairs. You can sleep in there or out here. Consider this your home."

"Thank you, Lina," I said.

She mustered a small smile that didn't reach her eyes.

LINA WAS UP BEFORE DAWN, shaking Corra who slept next to me. They dressed quickly and set out to go to the market stalls before Lina had to open her shop. Though I knew I should get up, the comfort of sleeping in a bed and not a bedroll or the underbelly of a ship was too tempting. I was also a bit afraid to touch anything in Lina's home.

The mattress sank beside me.

"Good morning, princess," Silas teased. "Better be up soon or Lina will think worse of you."

I threw the cover back and glared at him. He chuckled and looked again like the Silas I knew.

"So, you two?" I asked through a yawn.

He tipped his head from side to side.

"Why? You jealous?" He smiled and waggled his eyebrows. I whacked his arm and pushed off the bed to get dressed. "Well, we had a thing years ago. She and I—I think we would kill each other."

"She seems more inclined to kill me on your behalf."

"True. It's a very good thing you are Cadeyrn's then."

I rolled my eyes.

"I am no one's." It came out more of a bite, and he put up his hands in supplication. "Seriously, Silas, she seems to be enamored with you. And she is beautiful."

He ran a hand through his mass of brown waves. "She is that. Perhaps one day, *Trubaíste*." He stood as I made the bed and walked around to the bathing chamber.

On the far side of the room, a bronze mirror hung on the wall. My reflection caught in it as I passed and I backed up, shocked at my appearance. My face was a bit too thin, my eyes rimmed violet with fatigue. I brought my hands up to my face as if making certain it was actually me. My hazel eyes sparkled from within as if a light burned behind them, reminding me of the stained-glass windows we had passed. My mouth parted in surprise as I touched the tips of my ears, which were slightly elongated and came to a soft point. I couldn't stop staring at myself, turning this way and that, looking at my ears, eyes, even noting a subtle extension of my incisors.

After a time, a gruff voice asked from behind me, "Had you not seen yourself? Since you have been here? Crossing must have triggered the final uncloaking."

I turned to him and breathed a response. "I had been cloaked? By whom?" I exclaimed.

"Likely your father." The door clicked open.

"My father was human." The two females came inside the townhome.

"We had thought so too," Corra began. I was shaking my head. "The trace of human scent on you is gone. Silas didn't detect it when he came to you. Did you notice how any of the guards or Analisse's household did not refer to you as human?"

I sat down hard.

"Why were we not here? My father..." *Those fae not of the two bloodlines would experience consequences in crossing the Veil. The magic was reduced, and they became ill with a wasting sickness.* He didn't have to die. He could have come back.

I put my head in my hands. Two sets of hands were on me, but I was somewhere else.

A LITTLE GIRL, not more than five, dark hair flowing behind her, running along a beach that sparkled with smooth stones and colorful shells. My feet, crushing into the shells as I ran. A boy the same age, standing in a boat moored in the shallow tide pool, his feet wide part, rocking side to side and laughing. The woman from the stone altar and the orchard stood looking at the children, a sad smile on her face.

A window to the sea, a lovely blonde female dancing in the dying light of day. She walked closer. Hands were reaching out to her.

Cadeyrn placing hands on her hips as she swayed before him. She spoke, but I couldn't hear her words. Cadeyrn brought his mouth to her belly where she stood in front of him. He breathed out, and she arched back and into him, sighing in pleasure as she put her hands into his hair and pressed his face closer to her.

GASPING FOR AIR, I snapped back to the present, the room bathed in light so bright I couldn't see my companions around me. Every hair on me, every loose thread and soft material in the room was standing on end, crackling in warning. I knew where I was and who I was with, but my mind was reeling from both visions. The subtle memories that washed in with the vision on the beach had tears streaming down my face. Cadeyrn and the female had me seeing red, my heart pounding.

"Corra," I sobbed. She was by my side in an instant though the light still bright enough that we couldn't see each other. "I was a child here. I had a brother. A mother. I've seen her." She placed a hand on my back. "I saw Cade." Her hand stilled. "He was with another female."

Thrashing and screaming were in my head as though some living being had awoken, fighting for its voice inside my mind. Hollow ringing sounded in my ears, drowning out the voices in the room. I have been hunted and hurt, and he was taking another female to bed. I wanted to call out to him. I knew we hadn't had that much time together, yet it had felt real. Signifi- cant. I had gotten my hopes up, but a pain lanced through my veins as that beast within me snarled.

I willed it to quiet. Willed the light to subside. We had work to do regardless of my relationship to Cadeyrn.

Silas was shaking his head, the wind outside picking up, and dark clouds blotted out the sun. "He would not do that, *Trubaíste*," he said softly, an edge to his voice. "I know my cousin, and he is not that sort of male."

I looked up at him, his sea glass eyes blazing. Then to Corra whose own eyes, the twin to her brother's, softened.

"I saw him with her," I said. "There was no alternative for what they were engaged in." Lina walked out of the room and distantly I heard the sound of the kettle and cups being set out. The siblings, for once, were out of responses. "It doesn't affect what we have to do. Let's move on." The last of the light eddied into me, the beast inside settling with a final indignant growl.

TINCTURES, tonics, oils, and powders were all used in healing, protection, and magic. What seemed like a simple apothecary was a vessel for power. Lina catalogued each vial in her shop. She told me she had spent the past century and a half mastering her skills. Born with a gift of healing like Cadeyrn, though not as powerful, she had educated herself in all the intricacies and nuances of magic and protection. She was a wealth of information and practical application of such knowledge.

Wavering light and the tinkling of bells had everyone's heads turned toward the door, Silas and Corra closing in around me. A male walked in, wiping his boots on the mat. My friends opened their protective circle around me and relaxed.

"If you two are here, there must be trouble," the male quipped lightheartedly as he came toward us. Silas clasped arms with him, and he bowed to Corra and me before kissing Lina on the cheek. "I haven't had the pleasure, my lady," he said to me.

"Magnus," Lina gestured to the dark-haired male. "This is Neysa, a friend to these two and under our protection. Neysa, my brother, Magnus." Magnus bowed again and held his arm out to clasp. I did so, and his nostrils flared.

"And where is Cadeyrn? Your scent and his are entwined," Magnus said.

I stiffened.

"Our cousin has been taken. Likely to the Elders. We are preparing to get him back." Corra spoke before Silas had the chance.

"Then you are preparing for war?" he asked without judgment or reservation.

We three nodded.

"If it comes to that, then yes. Our cause is for the good of Aoifsing and our cousin," Silas answered.

"Then you will need steel and transport. I will join your cause." I liked him already.

"Of course, you will, Magnus." Corra winked. "We have

saved your arse countless times. Plus, I have never known you to run from a fight."

"My brother? He more likely runs headlong into it. Especially if the odds aren't in his favor. It's a miracle he has lived these two centuries!" Lina distributed a concoction she had been mixing between two mortar and pestles and a glass vial, amongst small blue glass bottles and corked them. "Here," she said, handing them round. "These are *draíchnhud aemdifnaíd*," she explained.

"Magic shield?" I questioned aloud, though immediately was embarrassed.

"*Trubaíste*, you have picked up some of the Aulde language!" Silas patted my back.

"More like a protection for your magic, but yes, technically it is a shield of sorts," Lina clarified for me. I had heard Silas describe his shield as *aemdifnaíd*. *Draíchnhud* was in countless texts I had poured over back at the cottage. "Each of these," she said, tapping the bottle in my hand, "should last a few weeks. Take it daily." Into our respective satchels we placed the bottles along with tinctures for wounds and provisions.

Magnus left to procure a wagon and weaponry for us as we wandered through the streets of Laichmonde. Each street had its own style. Even in winter, vines climbed the walls of town- homes, bare trees lined the sidewalks. It must be stunning in warmer months when everything was green. There were small parks with ponds and benches where parents sat while their children ran in circles—some being able to hop their peers, others blinking in and out of existence, causing both laughter and tears in their companions. I must have stopped to stare because Corra took my elbow and gently led me away from the park.

Sweet breads and pastries lined the windows of a small shop we passed, and my stomach growled. We stopped in for a light breakfast, eating as we walked farther along the city streets. Human cities were never this clean and peaceful. As much as I loved London, Paris, Oslo, these cities had the edge that was lacking in Laichmonde. In so many ways, fae seemed human. Yet being here, amongst the people whose cities were so kempt and had raw magic rather than technology, the difference in species was glaringly apparent. Something in this city was so very much like Cadeyrn in its elegance and antiquity. Its simple beauty. Trying to banish from my mind the vision of Cade with the golden-haired female, I looked about the buildings feverishly.

"Have faith, Neysa," Corra whispered, laying a hand on my arm. The wool of my coat stiffened as the threads all stood on end, crackling with my emotion.

We turned before a white townhouse complex and walked up the stairs. Silas had a shield around us the entirety of our walk, and I felt it strengthen as we walked through the polished ebony door into the building. An immediate assault of scents hit me. Sun-warmed stones and icy rain. Cadeyrn. The entirety of this place was awash with his scent. I squeezed my eyes shut briefly, not allowing the emotion to affect what we needed to do.

The twins quickly took stock of the downstairs rooms, then we made our way up. On the edge of the bed, just in front of the footboard, laid my cashmere wrap, folded neatly, a handwritten note atop. I was touching the wrap before I registered moving, the siblings beside me.

Silas picked up the note and handed it to me, both of them reading over my shoulder.

Disaster always finds me in every realm. The soft place in my heart you occupied is no longer. Family once held love, peace. You and I are never meant to be. Apart from always staying here, I wish to never see you again. Silas can have your faith and love now. Our brotherhood time is up. Go with the southern wind.

Chanè à doinne aech mise fhìne.

— Cadeyrn

The note was hastily written, the hand rushed and angry. I swallowed once and did not wipe at the tears running down my face. Silas wouldn't look at me, nor I him. We all stared at the note. The dismissal. The beast in my heart howled, pulling inside the pain and vulnerability. My hands clenched into the cashmere, the fibers fraying under my fingers and releasing his scent.

Silas pried them free and held my hand. His voice was rough as he spoke. "This," he spat, "is bullshit. It's not Cadeyrn." He turned to Corra who was staring, pinch-faced, at the note.

"Clearly," I said, speaking past the lump in my throat. "It is."

"No." Silas shook his head and whipped it at his sister. "Corraidhín." His eyes pleaded with her.

I took the note and re-read it, each line ripping a wider hole in my heart. As with the vision I'd had, it was irrelevant my relationship—or lack thereof—with Cadeyrn. We were on an ever-tightening schedule to get to the Elders, and we still had to head to Magnus's estate.

"Whatever his childish grudge is, it can't affect our mission. I'm sorry to have made trouble for your family, but I still plan to see this through," I announced, far more steadily than I thought I could manage.

A jog to the north from Laichmonde took us to the small estate belonging to Magnus and Lina's family. While it delayed the mission by two days, it was where we could load with transport and steel. Their mother was a jeweler. The front room of her estate had been transformed into a showroom of her bobbles. Corra explained to me that Magnus and Lina's father had been a blacksmith and that after his death when the twins were quite young, their mother put the forge to use and began a business making jewelry. As time grew on, her career bloomed, allowing them to keep the estate. Magnus came of age in a tumultuous time in the realm. After soldiering alongside many fellow Saarlaichians, he apprenticed to become a smithy like his father and expanded the family business.

Our arrival just past sundown was greeted by Baetriz, the family matriarch. She gathered my friends in an embrace and narrowed her cerulean eyes at me over their shoulders. Pushing my own shoulders back, I met her speculating gaze head-on. Though saddened to my core, I was in no mood to be picked apart by someone I not only did not know, but who had no real impact on what I needed to do. Should she forbid her son to allow us use of his own weapons, I would find another way. Problem solving was my wheelhouse and the gears have been turning relentlessly lately. It was Corra who pulled away first and introduced us. Baetriz sniffed, indicating she scented both males on me and didn't approve. I couldn't help but roll my eyes. Silas tugged on my braid and gave me an amused smile.

"I do love the Laoringhan glass bottles you gave my Lina, Silas. She takes great care in using them," Baetriz said to him with a pointed look at me. Was it too soon to roll my eyes again?

"I noticed she had them up in her shop. Happy to get them. Now, Auntie Baetriz, there's no need to pepper our *Trub*— Neysa—here with your *aerth maíthaer* looks. We are all family and working on the same side. Give her a chance, and you just may like her." He leaned over to her and whispered, "And if you feed her, she may take to you as well."

Family. I pondered what Silas told his "auntie" while we made our way farther into the house and sat in the large open kitchen. A casserole was dished up alongside crispy potatoes covered in gravy. Only Magnus spoke as we all filled our bellies.

The vision of Cadeyrn kept haunting me; the note he wrote was a sick love song stuck in my head. We could have been family, I supposed. My food began tasting like nothing the more I thought it over.

Baetriz's eyes still pinned me. The disproving mother bear gig was wearing on me. Regardless of anyone's feelings about anyone, this was a job. A directive bigger than moony love songs or the stars in the sky. We needed to figure out where Cadeyrn was, so we could aid in freeing my brother and exposing the Elders. Magnus's deep voice chattered away, filling us all in on his smithing, who is running around with who, and how a bad batch of barley crops had made an entire town nearby go slightly mad.

"You should have seen it!" he told us. "Tea totalers were screaming the gods' vengeance. Females running about with their bosoms bouncing." Baetriz swat his arm. He smiled at her and kissed her cheek. "Sorry, Mam. But 'twas a sight. Ye remember old man Boris? Och, he wore a stag's antlers for four days and claimed the gods had granted him rule of the forest!"

"It was quite the fiasco," Baetriz added. "Once a few of the townsfolk were sober, they looked into the ale and found it had turned. Everyone has been mighty quiet since the incident." She turned a dark metal ring on her middle finger. Protruding from the nearly black band were claw set diamonds. She looked so much like her daughter with large marine-blue eyes and jet-black hair with only a single streak of silver running its length. "Lina's childhood friend, Sara, told anyone who would listen that she had been held by Festaeran thugs for days on end in caverns across the border." Given my experiences with the Elder from Festaera, I wouldn't have been surprised in the least. "Silas, you remember Sara, don't you?" she asked sweetly. "When my children were young, you lot spent so much time together. Or was it Cadeyrn who was here all the time? Yes, it must have been Cadeyrn."

Corra must have felt me simmering because she placed her foot on top of mine under the polished wood table. Ever so briefly, I closed my eyes to regain my composure, and the vision I'd had flashed behind my eyes. Even if I had been told Cadeyrn was with another female, it wouldn't be as cruel as my having to *see* them getting steamy.

"Excuse me," I muttered, standing so quickly I knocked the chair back onto the slate floor.

Not even stopping to pick it back up, I left through the kitchen door and out into the garden. Moonlight shone down giving just enough visibility to make my way to the tree line. From my boots I pulled two small throwing knives and flicked them at the center of a thin-trunked tree. Knots ran along the pale length of the trunk, and I had aimed for one knot about four feet off the ground.

Both blades hit the mark. I retrieved them and before I reached my spot about five meters away, I spun and pulled a larger hunting knife from my belt and threw it at the tree. I then chased the knife with the two smaller ones, hitting just above and below the serrated blade. Cadeyrn's letter sat like a hot knife itself in my jacket pocket.

"You now, I watched a documentary about those witch trials in early America," Corra chirped from behind me. "Did you know that there was a time there that hops or wheat went moldy and sent the villagers into a hallucinogenic state causing accusations of witchcraft? Funny it should happen here, too. At least we fae know witchcraft when we see it. Humans are funny things," she mused. "So quick to panic at anything out of the ordinary, yet completely averse to the idea of magic." I huffed a non-committal response, though I agreed with her. "Darling, don't let Baetriz get you in a fluff."

I had walked farther away from my targeted tree and took off at a run, flipped, and threw all three knives. One whizzed clear of the tree, landing somewhere in the leafy blanket of darkness.

"We need to be moving," I said quietly. "We need to get the weapons and move on so this can all be ended."

"Yes, I'm quite certain the poor tree would like for you to move on as well," Corra chided. "Baetriz prepared our rooms, and the males are readying the weaponry as we speak. Come, darling."

I fussed about, searching for the lost knife. A sharp pain in my finger let me know I'd found it.

I brought my finger to my mouth, tasting the blood. A flood of memories, visions, and remembered words filled me so quickly, I staggered.

Corra grabbed my shoulders. "You can tell me all about what you've seen once we get to our chamber." She led me back to the house, leaving behind flickering images of people as though they were ghosts in my wake, watching me leave.

Dark wood paneled the walls in our rooms. A simple bed with thick tapestries hung about it sat in the center of the chamber, surrounded by worn rugs. A maid was turning sconces on, turning the coverlet back, and finally lit a small candle on the bedside table. I sat heavily on a wooden chair. Corra kept a wary eye on me while I wiggled on the purgato- rial seating contraption. Thudding footsteps drew closer and Silas knocked once and entered, giving the maid a small smile as she left. He shut the door and told us we were outfitted for a decent battle. Corra was still looking at me when Silas noted the uncomfortable silence in the room.

I rolled my eyes and told them it had been a flood of

pictures and words. Nothing specific. Just a reminder really of the fact that I was still a pawn in the whole game.

Sighing at their silence, I began taking off my jacket. The note fell from the interior pocket and shimmied to the dented floorboards.

Silas and I reached down for it at the same moment.

"*Trubaíste*," he said softly. "Something is amiss. Perhaps my cousin sampled some dodgy ale as well. This letter," he said, knocking the paper with the back of his hand, "is not Cadeyrn. I just...I know him. It just isn't."

"Silas," Corra warned. "You two were very convincing if the entire province of Veruni were to be believed. Cadeyrn could very well be hurt enough..."

Silas was shaking his head. "Gods-dammit, Corraidhín," he growled. "I know him like I know myself!"

I laid the note on the table and pushed against the paneled wall. Reading it for the millionth time hadn't changed the nausea-inducing sadness it gifted me. But what if...I let myself consider an alternative. Reading it again, I reached back and grabbed their hands, squeezing once.

"You're right," I said, focusing my gaze as I stared at the words. The siblings turned to me. "It's...I think it's coded. The vernacular is off from his normal speech pattern. The hand- writing is less controlled. I know he may have been rushed, but between the alteration in the vernacular and tone and the change in control, I think it's meant to be a message."

They re-examined the text. I hoped I was right and not just wishfully projecting. I was not known for my social skills, yet I had written a dissertation on wartime code-breaking for the purpose of exchanging currencies. While understanding people and emotions failed me, financial motives and political intrigue did not. Perhaps Cade had gambled on my recognition of both the subject and his choice of fiction material. In that fractured part of my heart, I clung to the hope that I was right. I wanted so much to be right.

"I must admit, I am not familiar with this type of thing," Corra said carefully.

I smoothed the note flat on a polished surface and took a pen from the leather hammock hanging in front of the table.

"Most skip codes use numbers or letters. For instance, you would replace A with D, D being three letters past A. Then continue on for the rest of the word, thus having a coded word that looks like a jumble of nonsensical letters. However, what Cadeyrn has done, it seems, is encoded the skip into his words. He wanted it to be less obvious that he was encoding it. That's why the vernacular is off. He placed words deliberately within the text to hide the real message."

"So how do we suss out the message?" Silas asked.

I stared at it. The most common skip codes involved threes. Every first and third word. I tried that first, but it made less sense than Cadeyrn's telling us to piss off in the literal text. I bit my lip and focused again, trying to feel for a pattern.

During World War II, a nearly unbreakable code was used by the British in communication with embedded POWs. The prisoners passed messages through German soldiers, who were none the wiser. It was also used to navigate the transfer of money between countries during wartime. While many of the codes are still unbroken, a repetitious one was found to ascertain the message by singling out every fourth and fifth word of the document.

I tried to tap into my feeling for Cade. I let the memory of his scent surround me. I breathed him in as I hadn't let myself do when he held me in my sleep in my cottage or when he healed me. I refocused. The fourth and fifth words still produced nonsensical results. Finally, I touched the words and while not necessarily code-breaking in its truest mathematical, algorithmic sense, I sensed the emotive drive in the words, and my eyes popped open.

"The first, third, and fifth words." I blurted as I circled such words.

Silas grabbed another pen and paper and rewrote the words that I had circled.

Disaster, Find, In, The, Place, My, Family, Held, Peace, You, And, I, Never, Apart, Always, I, Here, Silas, Have, Faith, Our, Time, Is, Up, Go, With, The, Wind.

Quiet. Complete and utter quiet filled the space between the three of us. Silas and Corra both interrupted the silence at the same time.

"*Trubaíste*," Silas spoke while Corra said,

"The place my family held peace, Silas." I raised my eyebrows in question. She continued. "In our culture it is custom to pay tribute to the elements as you saw yesterday. In our village, our family paid tribute in a forest grove rather than a temple. It was a place of peace."

"So," Silas wrote on the same paper. "I would assume he is writing to you in the initial word." A smirk.

Disaster (Trubaíste), Find (what?) In The Place (where) My Family Held Peace.

"The blue lace agate. We found half of it in Turkey. Cadeyrn said he had the other half here in Aoifsing. He wants me to find it. Perhaps it's there?"

"Yes," Corra agreed. "He was frantic about finding it when he returned after you were taken. It was his priority in coming here."

We dissected the note further, Silas writing, *You And I (are) Never Apart. Always I (am) Here.*

"One would assume he is still speaking to you, *Trubaíste*," Silas went on, scrubbing at his face, a light scrape of stubble piercing the silence.

"What if..." I turned the paper toward me. "Rather than 'I

am always here,' he meant, 'I always *hear.*' As in, he can still hear." My voice broke a little. "Hear my thoughts."

It was a stretch. A hopeful stretch. Like training up to twenty miles for a marathon and letting a hope and prayer take you the last six miles.

"So," Silas began. "The next part seems meant for me. To have faith." He growled.

Corra placed a hand on his shoulder in comfort.

An oily feeling settled in my gut. "What exactly does he mean by 'our time is up'?" I asked.

"It's a call to arms. He is invoking his birthright. We fight," Silas confirmed.

"And 'go with the wind'?" I asked softly.

"I think here the code is dropped a bit. I do believe he means the southern wind. We become our powers. We head north with the wind and go to the Elders. Go to Ewan and Cadeyrn, and protect the Veil."

We rewrote the message.

Disaster (Trubaíste), find in the place my family held peace. You and I (are) never apart. (I can) always hear (you). Silas, have faith. Our time is up. Go with the (southern) wind.

"*Chanè à doinne aech mise fhìne,*" I added. "I am no one's but my own."

"And yours," Silas whispered.

"Mine," I concurred.

Corra sighed, long and suffering. "Well, it was almost easier when he was telling you lot to fuck off, no?"

CHAPTER 26

R eally, it was difficult not to compare the ease of travel in the human realm versus what we had to do to get from point A to point B here. For the most part, the lack of technology and infrastructure was actually easy and preferable to me than the hustle of whence I'd come. Due to the amount of magic in constant use, nothing was truly lacking in this realm. Apart from the travel issue. Our wagon bobbed along, far more quickly than a human wagon would have traveled, through back roads toward the village where Cadeyrn's family grew up.

Having a sound directive in our undertaking lessened my anxiety. In the quiet moments, however, when we all stopped our chatter and the winter hush lulled my senses, my mind drifted toward Cade. What if I was wrong about the code? What about the vision? Whatever his activities with the beau- tiful female, her small frame and golden curls made me feel like a giant galumphing troll due to my height and muscular build.

I tugged at the neck of my aphrim skin jacket, needing air

to get in. Corra's eyes caught mine. She and I were sitting in the carriage on this leg. Silas and Magnus were in the driver's seat.

"I can see in your face what you're thinking about," she said, eyes narrowed to slits. I waved my hand dismissively. "Do you want to tell me about it?" she asked.

Yes. No. If I say it out loud it makes it more real. At this point, I thought to myself, I was a thirty-five-year-old child hiding under the covers.

"So, you two never completely..." She trailed off suggestively.

"No."

"That might explain..." She stopped, as if catching herself. I turned slowly to face her.

"Explain what exactly?" I knew the tone I used dripped with acid. It wasn't directed at her. She knew that as well.

"Forgive me, Neysa. I am your friend, but it is not my place to discuss certain things with you at this time. For the record, though, Cadeyrn is as much my brother as Silas. I have known him for three centuries. How he feels for you is no small thing, and as Silas said, he is not the sort of male to disregard you in such a fashion. And, in any case, he knows Silas would well and truly kill him for it if he does hurt you like that."

"And yet," I insisted, my eyes rolling skyward. "Every time I close my eyes, I see his face pressed to her, her hands in his hair. Feel him...responding to her." I didn't like admitting that.

"Where are they?" she asked quietly. I pulled at my own hair.

"In a room with curtains blowing. I can't hear anything, but she was dancing for him. He was shirtless and bandaged. I could feel him. Feel him want her."

We knew he had been attacked. I had visions of him having taken a lashing.

"What kind of bandages?" Corra's question was flippant as she swigged from her skein of water and handed it to me.

"They surrounded his back and ribs. He looked thinner. Less built."

She leaned forward and placed her hands on my knees. "Tell me about her." I turned my head as she spoke. "Neysa. What did she look like?"

I growled. A sound like nothing I've heard from myself. "Blonde. Tiny. Regal. Everything I am not."

Corra smiled broadly. I nearly slapped her. If my muscles hadn't been screaming from our swordplay this morning, I may have tackled that smile right off her elfin face. Silas's head popped through the front flaps on the wagon, a smile on his handsome face that matched his sister's.

"Solange," he said.

It took me a second to register the name.

"As in his *wife*?" I asked, wondering why they were smiling. "As in his scheming, banshee of a wife who is most definitely dead," he clarified. *Oh.*

"You simply saw a glimpse of his past," Corra said.

The beast inside me settled back, becoming once again my breath and heartbeat, slumbering until I had need of her. I placed a hand on my chest, marveling at the near sentient nature of the beast, then sat back and closed my eyes.

Cadeyrn, you are in trouble when I find you. I could have sworn there was a whisper of amusement in response.

COMING THROUGH SAARLAICHE FROM FESTAERA, the woods felt ominous, oppressive, and sinister. I had remarked upon that to Corra on the second day of our journey as we came closer to Aemes, the village where her family once resided.

"You were in the company of a lupinus," she reasoned. "You were watched and stalked, and the forest likely felt abhorrent because of it. Here, we are in the lands of our people. We are mist dwellers, and the landscape itself welcomes us."

Indeed, it did. I found my breathing easier as we neared the village center. Stone manses and homes, carved from what looked like a collection of small mountains, were set all around the tight cobbled streets. A stream ran through the village, ducking under stone bridges and meandering through gardens and fields as if in a constant round of visitation. Trees leaned inward seeming to listen to one another, while the smell of woodsmoke scented the crisp winter air. The village itself seemed like an artist's representation of Silas. Brush-strokes of allegory painted a picture of my friend, from the beautiful, rough-hewn edges to the woodsmoke and cedar scent.

We disembarked and passed the wagon and horses to young fae who were jumping in their boots with excitement to see the twins. Faintly, the sound of crashing waves called to me, luring me with its siren song. I suppose I had always been drawn to the sea. As a child, my father could never keep me from splashing into any body of water, no matter the tempera- ture. Beyond the watermill and distillery, the road became lined with groves of trees that were surely a crop here, yet I didn't know what. The leaves sparkled in the soft light, shining silver on one side, gold on the other. It was like walking through a chandelier.

"Araíran-aoír nut trees," Silas remarked, noting my wonder. "They will be heavy and ripe in the autumn." I gazed around with delight.

"They are found only in this region. Our family has tended these groves—the only ones in Aoifsing—for nearly a millen– nium. We three are the last of our line. Thus far," he said with a smile. "So, we hire both the townspeople and those from the islands who are in need of work after the summer months. We have always tried to tend the land and its people. It has treated us well and we mean to always reciprocate." Silas smiled proudly at the groves around us while I walked farther still toward that siren song. "You are just like him," he laughed.

I turned to him. "Who?"

"Cadeyrn. Always slinking off to the sea. It has called him in every province, every climate, each realm. Funny enough, you always smell like the sea." He shook his head, and I looked at him, a bit shocked. "Wild like wind and open water, salt and sun." I hadn't known that.

We reached the end of the road. A wall made of piled and mortared boulders stood before us, guarding the village from the sea beyond. Waves churned and lashed at the rocks far below, spraying upwards the hundred or so feet. Salt spray raked through my braided hair, lifting my senses.

"This place," I said.

"Hmm?"

"This place. Your village, the sea, even Laichmonde. They feel like home. I felt Corraidhín in the city. Here is you."

"How do you mean?" he asked cautiously.

"The essence of the place. It feels like you. Laichmonde felt like Corra. They both felt like home."

"Do you feel Cadeyrn?" he asked a bit more carefully.

"I feel him everywhere," I whispered, not sure he had heard. I felt, rather than saw Silas smile. He put his arm around me and shook gently. "Then let us get on with this and get him back, no?"

"Lead the way, my friend."

IN THE END, it was I who led the way. We entered the

forest clearing where the village folk and centuries of mist dwellers paid tribute to the land, and I immediately felt the tug of the agate. As it was in Turkey, the tug couldn't have called me from miles away, yet it was strong enough to warm my senses, leading me on.

In the clearing, small altars were built, interspersed with tree trunk bases a half meter off the ground. Into the top of each trunk were carved symbols from the Aulde language and family names. As the pull of the agate took me to the last trunk, I saw the carving upon the top. Amidst more names and symbols was the *Adairch a Taeoide Gaellte*. My fingers automati– cally reached to touch the engraving of the constellation.

"That has been carved into that tree since before our parents' parents," Corra told me.

In my mind, I could see them. Not like many visions, which sweep me away from the here and now, but gentle pictures in my mind like a long-forgotten photograph. Their grandpar– ents exchanging wedding vows in this circle, flowers strung from both their hair, hands pressed against the other's.

I smiled at Corra and held out my hand for the spade she carried.

Digging near the trunk, I could feel heat as though a radi– ator was buried in the dirt itself. My hands thawed at that warmth and eventually touched an object.

Wrapped in felt, I lifted the broken piece of bright blue lace agate. It pulsed and throbbed, leading me like a divining rod to another spot just outside the clearing. High in the tree canopy was a small platform made of wood and thatch. I handed the stone to Corra and swung up into the tree, pulling myself up into thick, ancient branches. Atop this platform was a steel bowl, likely to keep a small fire, a rusted old dagger, and tucked up against the tree itself was a hatch made of bark and thatch. It opened with a crack, the metal and wood fastenings a bit ornery with age.

Inside the hatch lay the missing end of the agate. Veins of white and grey streaked the cobalt. At my touch, they glowed, and the stone itself pulsated, urging me to bring it to the other piece. I slipped it into my jacket and began the monkey busi- ness of lowering myself down the branches.

I had always been good at compartmentalizing my vulnerabilities and emotions. Perhaps this was because I was always displaced and, as Cade once said, wearing the skin of another beast. These past few days, since I'd had the vision of myself as a child, I had pushed the contempla- tion to the back of mind, focusing solely on getting to this crystal.

Warm and comfortable for the moment, sitting in Cadeyrn's manse in Aemes, with his scent and the feeling of his presence all around me, my mind drifted to that vision. While I had no further insight, I started to wonder where in Aoifsing it was. It seemed temperate. Maesarra, perhaps? Was I from there? Is it in fact Ewan in the memory? Where was he now? I had never longed for a simple life. However, it seemed all I have been forced to endure and accept is taking it a bit far.

I was curled tightly into the settee in Cade's cozy sitting room, watching the flames dance in the fireplace when I heard Silas's boots come in the door with two companions. I quickly set down the wine goblet as four sets of paws came bounding at me. The hounds and I were on the carpet, enjoying our reunion.

I finally looked up to see Silas standing, arms crossed across his chest, shaking his head. "I thought you lot would be happy to see each other," he said, grinning.

I was now completely covered in Cuthbert slobber, as he was both the most promiscuous and the sloppier of the two, yet Bixby simply wanted to lay his enormous head in my lap. I really had missed these two.

That night I slept better than I had in the past month, snuggled up with Bixby and Cuthbert in Cadeyrn's bed. The following day, I kissed them each between their furry ears and promised to bring Cadeyrn back, then set off to fight for their master.

CHAPTER 27

Thirty-six fae were willing to stand beside us. In leaving Aemes, more and more began to show up from villages and towns around the province, pledging to support Cadeyrn. The twins and I went on ahead as they were able to use their gift to transport the three of us while the others followed at a slower, albeit much faster than human, pace. It was quite a thing being lifted across forest and meadow by the mist and wind itself. A trip that might have taken three days was accomplished in one. I made a small camp just outside the sentried borders of the Elder Palace lands, at the point in the very center of Aoifsing where Saarlaiche, Veruni, Prinaer, and Naenire met. The siblings had not yet been able to shift to their corporeal form as they had spent much power on moving me. So, I risked a small fire to keep from freezing to death.

Just before dawn, I secured the straps on my blades—twin swords across my back, the dagger on my forearm, another along my left thigh, two knives in my boots, and a throwing star on my belt for good measure. I murmured gratitude for the skins I wore and set off for the palace. Where the manor in Bania had been classically elegant, refined and stately, the keep in Festaera was a shrouded edifice of odium, The Elder Palace was majestic. The grounds sloped down from rolling hills to a clear lake, the palace itself built along the shore. Long terraces and balconies jutted out over the glassy water. Pillars of white marble held mezzanines and promenades, most open air, allowing the sun or moonlight to blanket the structures. Mossy stone steps ascended to the front gates.

I walked closer and closer, waiting for the guards to come at me. Silas and Corra drifted at my side, barely visible in a ghostly translucent form. As we neared, the guards began to file behind us, herding us into the compound. As anxious as I was to be here, part of me marveled at the magnificence of the place. Lamp posts cast a warm glow, and the gentle lap of water could be heard from the lake behind. We climbed more steps to the upper promenade where a courtyard sat before what looked to be a sort of throne room.

Leaning against the iron gates was Reynard, adjusting the cuffs of his skin coat.

"I suggest you lot play nice," he said to us. "Not one of them is very happy with you." He looked at me and smirked. "Lady Analisse is particularly eager to see you, little mouse."

"Then let us get on with it," I responded. He shrugged as if to say, *'Your funeral'* and led us past the courtyard with its bubbling fountain to another open-air room wherein sat a dais large enough for eight.

Flanking the Elders were two sets of guards, swords at the ready. Cyrranus would not meet my eyes as I stared him down before turning to the congregation ready to mete out judgment on me. Paschale stood and walked toward me, his moon-white skin pulling back into a hideous grin. He licked his bloodless lips.

"If you try to touch me," I said coolly, looking him in the

eyes. "This will end very quickly and very poorly for all of us."

I heard snickers from a few of the other Elders and even caught the ghost of a smile from Cyrranus.

"You are in no position to make threats, halfling," the female half of a set of twins—Nanua, maybe—said, hissing her words through disturbingly long, sharp teeth.

"But look," her brother said sniffing at the air between us. "She is not a halfling at all." All seven of the others leaned forward and sniffed. I stifled a gag.

"No, she is not," Analisse spoke. "Neysa was my guest. Yet, dear, you caused such a disruption in my home."

"I have a history of doing that," I retorted, and Silas chuckled.

Scuffling and shifting in the background told me there were guards filing onto the piazza. The air was heavy with ozone, clouds forming.

"Such theatrics, Silas," Analisse said to him. The thought of outright killing her for simply speaking to him crossed my mind. Perhaps I was more protective of Silas than necessary.

"Allow me to narrate this scene," Nanua chimed in, teeth slipping back and forth across her lips. She and her brother might have been alluring and beautiful, had I not immediately seen them for what they were: monsters who you allow into your bed before realizing you are prey. "You have something that belongs to the realm. Something that should not have been in human hands. Return it, and we will let you go."

"And you will allow the Veil to dissolve, causing the destruction of the human realm and loss of magic amongst your people?" I asked, rising an eyebrow. "No, thank you." I widened my stance, feeling the twins rally their magic on either side of me. "I have come to take Cadeyrn back to his people."

There was a snort from the dais.

"He hasn't been there for *his people* in a hundred years. He has hidden in that hovel of a realm you call home. *His people* lost faith in him long ago," said a man who looked older than most of the fae here. He sat looking like he was the emperor. Snapshots in my mind showed me Cade throttling him, one of the other males waiting a bit then deciding to interfere. So, this must be Feynser of Maesarra.

"You can have him. If there's anything left," Feynser scoffed. He motioned to Cyrranus, who left the terrace.

Ozone picked up, my skin rising in goosebumps, the air around us snapping and sparking. Fat drops of rain began to fall, and where Corra had begun to regain her body, she was once again fully mist, nearly impossible to see.

"Take care, girl," a female with deep olive skin and sapphire-blue eyes stood from her place on the dais. She was voluptuous and sensual, draped in sheaths of cobalt velvet. The only other female. Lorelei—I racked my brain—of Laorinaghe. As she strode toward me, her scent of salt and wine rushed over me. "One would say it is unwise to challenge the Elders. For we have outlived most fae. These lands belong to us, and we will defend what is ours."

Behind me, the sound of boots and dragging had me spinning. Cyrranus and two others dumped Cade onto the tile. Cyrranus gave him a kick in the ribs to turn him over, then one of the others backhanded him, sending a spray of blood and saliva from Cade's mouth.

My stomach flipped and something inside me snapped. The entire arcade became ensconced in white light. There was only Cadeyrn visible to me. It was as if we were the only two there. Blood ran down his face as he knelt in his fighting leathers. A rapidly healing bruise under his eye was outlined by ribbons of blood drying as the cut itself healed. He was hurt yet healing.

Though battered and bloody, he looked up at me from

under his glassy eyes and a slow, wicked smile crept across his face. Warmth bloomed low in my gut, and he tilted his head to the side.

And now? I asked him in my mind.

He turned and spat a wad of blood on the tile, loosened his neck, and said, "Bulgaria."

Without a second to consider, I pulled the twin swords from my back and the white light dissipated. Cadeyrn easily broke free of his bonds and jumped from his knees to stand back-to-back with me, the siblings joining us.

Guards swarmed in around us, and my bowels turned a bit watery as I considered our odds.

"The crystals cannot be taken from you, Neysa," Cadeyrn said quietly, taking the sword I handed him. "They must be given willingly. They won't kill you. You keep fighting and do not yield."

It took me a moment to register what he was saying. "If you think I will let you get yourself killed, you're more of an idiot than I thought," I barked at him.

He laughed as the first of the guards began to stalk us.

Before we had a chance to clash swords, Corraidhín was a crushing river, drowning the males in one fell swoop. She took out at least twenty in one go. The sheer amount of power in that act blew my mind. We rushed the next line of guards, slashing and stabbing. Cadeyrn moved like nothing I had ever seen. In the human realm, he was graceful and fast. Here, he was movement itself. It was as though his body followed the lines of sound and light. Water began to rise under us. I turned to see Feynser lifting his hands and walking along the edge of where we fought.

Cade, get the other two onto the next balcony. Now.

Thankfully, he did not hesitate, I spun, grabbing Silas and seemed to absorb Corra as they blinked from existence and appeared over us.

You never said you could do that.

Amusement rippled through me. I turned to Feynser and slammed my sword into the tile beneath the shin-deep water, willing my magic. Electricity surged from me through the watery conduit, turning everything in its path to ash. Feynser had but a second to register his surprise before falling victim himself. The rising water evaporated leaving a terrace of steam and the Elders, high upon the dais, wide-eyed with shock.

Analisse sat with a cat-like grin and rubbed her palms together.

Swords clashed around us. Despite my friends' power, the odds of the three of us versus the numbers against us were not good. To kill the beast, cut off its head. Finally able to embrace my speed, I set off toward the dais.

"Bloody fucking hell!" I heard Cade yell after me. An arrow whizzed past my ear, making my heartbeat speed up even more. "Oomph."

It was as though I had been hit myself. I felt the arrow hit Cade in the stomach while he took on another set of guards. Where was Reynard? I couldn't see him anywhere. Where did the arrow come from? Across the slick tile, I spotted Cyrranus, bow in hand, charging at Cadeyrn. I stopped my forward progress as I watched the guard I thought I could trust try to take down Cade.

Cadeyrn ripped the arrow from his abdomen, bits of leather and skin coming out with it. He was doubled over in pain despite the healing, and in my head there was nothing beyond getting to him. Cyrranus lifted his sword above Cadeyrn, and I threw out every ounce of magic, strength, and speed. His sword turned to ash, his body was thrown across the terrace, hitting a marble column with such force, the column itself fractured. I didn't take the time to see if he was dead as I rushed to Cade. Blood seeped from his mouth and nose, and the beast inside me unfurled, roaring its own pain.

What do I do? Do that blinking thingy, and get us out. Please. I pleaded with him in my head.

He looked at me.

"I'll be fine. Run. I'll hold them off." He coughed and more blood came out. Fuck.

Silas was next to me, covering us in a rapidly weakening shield. "Shit, Cadeyrn. What did you do to yourself?"

Cade coughed again, attempting to laugh. He rasped a breath and the wet, struggling sound made me snarl.

The beast within me shed its cover and great wings spread from my back as I pounced atop Cade just before Silas' shield dropped.

"Holy Gods, *Trubaíste*," Silas breathed. Shock must have shown on my face too.

"That's my girl," Cade said.

I wrapped my wings around him, blocking him from anyone while he healed himself. Though alarming in their sudden appearance, the wings held fast, their weight solid and familiar. As though I'd had them my entire life. As though the child in my father's stories truly was me.

Silas's sword knocked two arrows away from me. Heat rose between Cade and me as his body became more flame than physical, burning off his wound. An arrow hit my wing, and I rolled, howling in pain then skipping to my feet.

Nanua dropped the bow she had in hand and looked to Analisse, who held a dagger to the Elder twin.

Reynard appeared, standing next to Cade and Silas. He nodded to them and turned to fight alongside my friends.

"Who *does* hold your leash, Reynard?" Silas asked, as the three of them fought back-to-back.

Distantly, the sound of a wave building had me look to the

lake where Corra, it seemed, was drawing power to fell the soldiers below us.

"It's not really that simple," Reynard answered, skewering a soldier. He ripped the blade out of the soldier's gut.

Cadeyrn turned to me, and his eyes widened. With that clever blinking trick, he was before me and had severed the head of a particularly large male. "Watch yourself, lady," he growled at me, teeth snapping.

I reached for him and pressed my lips to his instantaneously before whirling back to fight the battle.

Camua, the male Elder from Naenire, appeared before me, eyes glowing. I recognized that glow, but in the heat of the fight, couldn't place the recognition. He spun a chain, readying to whip it at me. I knew they wouldn't let me die but holy gods would that hurt. I dove down, feet first, aiming to take out his legs, but my wings caught on the tile and possibly a few soldiers. Fuck, that hurt!

He lashed the chain at my leg, and I screamed. The chain came at me once more, and I struck out, slashing across his midsection with my narrow sword. He grabbed at the opening, pushing on the innards, which were spilling over his hands.

A female scream came from the dais. In the same moment, Cadeyrn finished the job and removed Camua's head, a choir of howls sounded across the forest and plain.

"Neysa!" I heard Cade scream as a body collided with mine.

Long, claw-like fingers wrapped around my shoulders, and the world started to darken. I hadn't felt any pain at all but saw the look on Cade's face. Complete devastation.

"Get your hands off my daughter," intoned a deadly calm female voice.

My vision was spotting, electricity fizzing and popping from my hands. The claws released me, and I slumped to the ground. Cadeyrn waved his hands, dropping the cloaking spell from around us. Surrounding the lake and the palace itself were hundreds of fae, male and female, all ready to fight. The female who had caused Nanua to drop me nodded to him. There was a brief collision of metal around us before everything around me turned to black.

HAD I known I would end up in a hand-to-hand battle with millennia-old fae of varying magical abilities, perhaps I wouldn't have invested quite so much in my academics. Maybe two postgraduate degrees were unnecessary. Dad had never hinted at my not needing to further my schooling. Granted there was no subtlety to his pushing my skills in fighting.

As I lay in a state of semiconsciousness listening to the din of voices in other rooms, I wondered where I was and who was there. Did any of my friends survive? My body felt battered and heavy but not broken. It was a struggle to swim through the murkiness of my mind. The vision of me as a child kept appearing, except I was now fully the girl on the rocky beach.

I GIGGLED and yelled to my brother to be careful. He yelled back that he was the captain of this ship, and he was crossing dangerous waters. I threw a glob of washed up seaweed at him, and he toppled over the side of the dinghy, splashing in the shallow water. I laughed and told him the captain went overboard. He jumped from the water and started to chase me down. I zigzagged along the shore calling him Captain Booboo Kitty.

"Neysa!" My mother scolded. "Stop taunting him. Neysa. Come here. Come now," she called, softer this time.

THE MURKINESS SUBSIDED, and I was looking into the face I had repeatedly seen in my visions. The fair, freckled face, long dark hair, hazel eyes, and a beatific smile that sent my beast into a low growl within me.

Daughter. She called me daughter. The mother I had

thought was dead was sitting here. My mother. A flicker came to me of the fact that dad never explicitly said she was dead. It was always "your mother is no longer with us" or "she is in the next realm." It always held a sort of religious mysticism to me, like people who believed in heaven. Yet, really, she was, quite literally, in the next realm. And he was dead.

The female bit her lip and squeezed my hand. I tried to pull it away, but she held tighter.

"You let him die." It was the thought at the forefront of my anger. Not that I grew up without a mother. Not that my brother and I were separated and couldn't remember each other. Not that he had been enslaved to the Elders. The primary flame in my burning anger was that my father did not have to die. Anger boiled in me.

"I did not know," she answered, tears rolling down her face. "Bullshit."

"The last I had seen him was just after you both had left here. I crossed and showed him the amethyst. He told me to not cross again as it would put you at risk."

"And Ewan? You knew where he was! Did you plant him there? Were you using my brother?" I sat up in the bed, wincing from the pain in my neck and all the protesting muscles. She sobbed.

"No one knew about you two. Only Analisse. We stayed on the island until...until you left. No one knew we had children. It was safer to keep him hidden."

"Why didn't you send him with me? Do you know—do you know how lonely I was? Did you know I spent half my life with anxiety, unable to breathe?"

"When you two were together, you were too powerful," she cried. "You glowed and played in the light. It was a risk we could not take." She was openly crying, and my own tears streamed down my face. "I will make it up to you. I will..."

"Where is he now?"

A heavy door opened.

"I'm here." Ewan walked in, Cadeyrn on his heels.

My chest felt lighter seeing Cade, but at the moment my focus was Ewan. Our eyes locked, faces so similar. He was tall and lean with a smattering of freckles across his cheeks like mine. Like our mother.

I smiled at him, and he returned it. "Captain Booboo Kitty," I said, wiping my eyes.

All the memories from our very young childhood came rushing back.

"Are you ever clean and unbattered, Neyssie?" Ewan asked.

Cadeyrn chuckled in the back of the room. Ewan sat on the edge of my bed. I couldn't wait to be out of it and walking around, but I knew my body well enough to wait a little longer. The room was silent but not uncomfortably so.

"I would have come for you," I whispered to my brother. "If I had known. I would have burned them all to hell and come for you."

He wiped at his nose, shaking his head. "I know. It wasn't bad. How I grew up. I wasn't mistreated."

"You were kept," I stated. My beastie began to rumble. I would definitely need to revisit the beastie issue.

"It wasn't terrible. I swear it." He grabbed my hand and squeezed.

"I'm sorry I threw the seaweed at you," I cried, hugging him.

He laughed and hugged me back. "I think it was being called Captain Booboo Kitty that pissed me off more. So, one day we will have to talk about things. Tell me about our father."

A small sniffle came from the other side of the room where our mother sat. In the memories that had come back to me, I could see how much they had loved each other. I knew it from my father's tone when he spoke of her. I had felt the emotion in the wedding rings. My heart broke for her loss as well. I couldn't make sense of everything that had happened, but I had no room in my heart to hate her. I had seen the threat the Elders posed.

The thought had me looking to Cade.

Silas and Corra? I asked him.

"They are fine. Resting. Not quite in their stubborn, fleshy form yet." he answered.

"How did it all end after I was attacked?"

Cade looked to my mother and bowed at the waist. "Her Majesty, Queen Saskeia. She caused quite a diversion. I was able to uncloak my warriors. Nanua, however, was able to slip away," he growled.

I was still stuck on the Queen Saskeia part. I looked among the three of them. Ewan had his hand on the back of his neck, and he was wearing a look of faint satisfaction.

"Apologies, Princess," Cade said with a twinkle in his eyes. "Perhaps I shouldn't have put you up in the gatehouse."

I threw my pillow at him.

APPARENTLY, it was Reynard who put it all together and arranged for my being taken to Analisse rather than directly to the Elder Palace. Analisse knew as soon as she scented me, as she and my mother had been friends for many years. Reynard intercepted Cadeyrn and swore to bring Saskeia. Soon after, Cadeyrn had himself captured and brought to the Elders.

"Now, why in the hell would you do something like that?" I asked.

"How else would I easily slip two hundred warriors into the compound unnoticed?" he answered with an air of innocence. "Plus, I needed to secure this lad before anyone else got wind of it." The two males looked to one another.

I needed to get out of this bed and move. Layers of duvets

and quilts dropped off me as I swung my legs over the side. I also very much needed a bath.

"I can help you," Saskeia offered sheepishly.

I agreed and let her lead me to the bathing chamber. Cadeyrn said he would be out and about dealing with his legion and healing some of the warriors. He was solemn and cautious with me. I didn't know what to make of it.

WE WERE STILL in the palace, all the previous occupants having fled. Around the grounds were the hundreds of warriors we brought as well as quite a few Elder guards who had either surrendered or refused to fight. After bathing, I joined Saskeia for tea on a veranda overlooking the lake. Sitting in waiting, we found Analisse. I stiffened, but she bowed to both my mother and me in turn.

Late afternoon sunlight gilded the two impossibly beautiful women. At the moment, I was very glad of my ability to compartmentalize my feelings as I had absolutely no idea how to deal with everything. Analisse claimed she had had no intention of turning me over to the Elders. She did everything she could to keep me safe in her manor yet allowed for dropped hints for safe passage should we leave. I asked her why she had sought out Silas, knowing how it would make me feel.

She blushed, making her ebony skin light up.

"I suppose that was an abuse of power, but I have had my eyes on Silas for many years. Oh, stop," she chided. "You are so clearly in love with Cadeyrn. I had no qualms about slaking my lust." I sat back abruptly, feeling like I had been hung upside down by my toes. Analisse grinned in a serpentine manner. "Perhaps you need to take a hard look at yourself, my dear," she said.

"What of Cyrranus?" I asked. He lives, she told me. "He tried and nearly succeeded in killing Cadeyrn. If he were loyal to you, then why?"

"Because he has a grudge against me," Cade remarked from the archway behind us. I turned to him. He had cleaned up as well. His hair was a bit longer than when I had been taken, and when he ran his hand through it as he always does, it stuck straight up like a wave of raven feathers. "Cyrranus had been in love with my wife, Solange, long before she and I met. They knew each other growing up." Ah.

"I am afraid all of that is my fault. I tried to forge a union between the two families," Saskeia admitted.

"You didn't know my sister was a two-faced, collusive bitch?" Reynard spat from the archway. Cade looked at him quizzically. "What? You really thought I was avenging her this whole time? How base. Besides, you really are too beautiful to kill," he said to Cadeyrn.

I coughed a laugh that had both males looking at me.

"I would have to agree," I said, and my two female compan– ions nodded as well.

Cade rolled his eyes and walked away. I laughed again.

Flight risk, I teased in my mind. I heard his bootsteps stop, the sound of his hand smacking the marble wall, fingers drum– ming the stone, then he kept walking. I laughed again, wondering when it had become easy to do so again.

Analisse and Saskeia were staring at me, jaws dropped. "Yes?" I asked. Reynard chortled and left.

"Nothing," they said in unison.

I drank my tea watching the sun descend little by little. My companions took their leave, allowing me to sit on my own. The temperature was dropping, yet my heavy dress was warm enough that I stayed out as the sun moved lower and lower, turning the lake from deep blue to shades of burnt orange and magenta. Gems from the edges of my open cuffs caught the light and glittered, throwing reflections like fairy lights across the midnight blue velvet. I moved my arms this way and that, thoroughly entertained by the light show it was casting on the open V-neck and down the skirts.

"You know, there are dying warriors down there, and you are playing with pretty dresses," my own warrior said, appearing in the space beside my seat. I slammed my arm down on my lap. Cade sat in the chair opposite.

We were timid with each other again. I supposed with everything that was going on, that was okay. As long as he was safe.

"I didn't like seeing you covered in blood," I blurted.

"No? Huh. For a second there..." I groaned at his suggestion and threw a biscuit crumb at him. His magic flicked it away before it came close. "You're always throwing things at me, Princess."

"Do not call me that, lest I throw heavier things at you," I threatened with a half-smile.

He chuckled and sat back, surveying the landscape ahead. "You were impressive in battle. I was impressed. Scared shitless. But impressed," he said. His hand shot through his hair again.

I chewed on my lip and fiddled with my dress. "When Silas found me in Bania, he saw my bite from Paschale and asked if it had been from the lupinus who had attacked me. He seemed relieved it wasn't." Cade continued to stare out. "Nanua is one, correct?" He nodded. "And what does that mean now? For me?"

"I don't know," he answered quietly. I nodded. "I am not sure what all your gifts are. I haven't seen you in ages." He lolled his head to the side and gave me a lazy grin. "However, the wings? The snarling within you? Perhaps your mother has more insight on that."

"Does it bother you?" I whispered almost inaudibly.

He turned slowly and braced his arms on his knees. He

was still for so long, staring at me as I stared out, but I was not seeing, just feeling like I could throw up.

"Let's be clear about something," he said coldly. My stomach clenched, but I forced myself to look him in the eyes. Gods above those eyes. "The only thing that bothers me about you is your lack of self-preservation. If there is a beastie inside you who needs to take a walk every once in a while, then she can get in line with the dogs because the way I see it, they will take more issue with it than I do."

I looked down at my hands and sniffed a laugh.

"What happens to others when they are bitten by a lupinus?"

"Wolves are drawn to them. For now, while Nanua lives," he began in a tone suggesting that Nanua would not enjoy that privilege for much longer. "She will be able to locate you through them. Especially as you are linked to her brother's death. I would advise against being alone outside until it is sorted. I know that will be hard for you."

I groaned and hung my head over the back of the chair.

"Ugh. Bloody hell. It can't be easy can it?" I asked the darkening sky above me.

"If it were easy, it wouldn't be worth fighting for."

CHAPTER 28

Three of the four protective crystals were in our possession. Black tourmaline, amethyst, and agate. Locating the whereabouts of the fourth would be our next priority. In theory, it should be in the human realm, though there was a strong possibility it was here in Aoifsing. The collapse of the third Veil, the weakening of the second, and the fact that half of the agate was here, all hinted at the possibility of it being hidden in this realm.

Based on the contingent of guards who crossed over to kidnap me, we were sure that the Elders had a thumb on the pulse of many illegitimate members of the royal family. We were all in agreement that staying on here and looking for it took precedence over going back. Additionally, none of us were under any illusion that the remaining Elders would be staying away for very long.

After dinner the following day, and after the twins finally woke after a long, regenerative rest, we convened for our next plan of action. Our unit would not split up this time. Saskeia had offered her foot soldiers, scholars, and healers to aid the greater cause that was both Aoifsing and the human realm.

Ewan and Corraidhín had been agitated with each other. One was stealing glances, whilst the other looked away. I caught Cade's eye and stifled a giggle when we noted Corra biting her lip while watching Ewan describe the different manor homes of the various Elders. As soon as his eyes fell on her, she casually flipped her mass of auburn-tinged brown waves.

I would be lying if I said I hadn't taken a decent amount of time to fall asleep the night before, hoping Cade would come to me. A silly thought, I suppose, given how much had changed, where we were, and the fact that he was now responsible for hundreds of fae warriors. Still, as I did start to drift off, I sent him a soft, *Good night* and a memory of my floating the amethyst to him.

Thinking that the two halves of the agate must need to, at some point, be fused together, I held them each, concentrating on the task as the others left Cadeyrn's chambers. The sun had all but set, the room now lit by sconces and small lamps. Tiny flickers of campfires and torches from the fae outside dotted the landscape beyond the closed windows and veranda doors.

After what could have been an hour, I set the broken crystal down on the coffee table, next to the other two stones. The others had filed out of the chamber. A glass of wine I hadn't seen Cade pour sat in waiting. I sat back on the small settee and sipped at it, enjoying the thick warmth.

Cadeyrn stood staring out the windows, no doubt thinking of the legion outside.

"I'm thinking of you, actually," he said, still facing the window. Alright then.

"How often...I mean, how much of...me, I guess...do you hear? Or did you hear while we were apart?" For whatever reason, heat crept up my face.

He didn't turn. "Quite a bit, I think. I knew when you

were hurt and scared. I saw you give the stones to the innkeeper." He pulled one of such stones from his pocket and tossed it to me.

"At least there's not porridge on it anymore," I tried to joke, but my voice sounded hollow.

His cheek lifted. "I saw your visions. Some of them at least. The messages you meant for me to hear. I knew when Silas was with you. You were calmer. You're often calmer when he's around. I heard you yelling at him for bedding Analisse." Oh.

This was a good time to keep my mouth shut as I knew I would surely just end up with my foot in said mouth otherwise. So, I kept the glass of wine pressed to my lips.

He stayed by the window. "I heard you when you figured out the letter." He turned slightly then and gave me a half smile. "You believed it at face value?" I wasn't sure it was truly a question.

"After the vision I had..." I didn't really know how to finish that.

He nodded.

The vision that awoke the beast within me. That must be an important piece I am missing. I set the now-empty glass down. The split skirts of my green-and-black brocade gown spilled open as I crossed one leg over the other. I wore the aphrim skin leggings under the open-skirted gown, keeping my daggers strapped to my thighs. Both of us were silent. My own silence stemmed from a complete loss of what to say.

When I couldn't stand the quiet anymore, I got up and walked to him. Rallying my courage, I looked straight at him while he looked out. Pounding, roaring blood sounded in my ears. Mentally, I traced his beautiful profile, smoothing his creased, dark brow, his nose, his full lips. His eyes closed briefly.

I knew Silas had said Cade belonged to me. I knew Corra

believed he thought of home as wherever I was. I knew these things, and I also knew they were my friends and wanted me to not be hurting. To not break. Everyone needed me to not break. As such, I couldn't face him as I said aloud before leaving, "It was always you." *Every gods-damned second. It was always you.*

He was pivoting me so fast I didn't register it. Our bodies pressed up against the marble wall. Hands were in my hair and on my waist. His thumb brushed my jaw and ran across my bottom lip. I had both hands on his hips, shaking with nerves. Every ounce of his attention was on my face. His peridot eyes glazed over as they zeroed in on my lips when they parted for his thumb.

"Did you know," he remarked huskily. "Your eyes almost glow here? And these really suit you," he said touching my ear.

He brought his face close to my ear and touched the pointed tip with his own lips, then buried his face in my hair. My hands moved up his muscled back and grabbed hold of his hair as well. His arms came around me, and for a moment we simply stood in an embrace, breathing each other in until it wasn't clear where his scent ended and mine began.

Ever so slowly, his hands pulled back and began unbuttoning my dress until it pooled around our feet. He moved his mouth down my chest and stomach then unstrapped each dagger from my thighs, deliberately grasping my inner thighs. Fingers unlaced the waist of my leggings and pushed them down over my hips while he moved his mouth down my hip, thigh, and inside of my calf, sliding the pants free at last. I should have felt exposed standing in front of him, completely unclothed while he was fully dressed and taking me in with predatory intent. Yet, having him see all of me was what I had craved for so long now.

I met his stare, breathing heavily. Cadeyrn placed the flat

of his palms on my hips and smoothed them up my sides. I made a sound of impatience, and he chuckled darkly while scraping those calloused hands over my chest, shoulders, then down the length of my arms until our hands met. Fingers intertwined, he moved against me, my back pressing against the wall.

I yelped from the cold, and he laughed an apology then heated the wall itself. Our mouths met with a fury I couldn't have anticipated. I pulled his lower lip with my teeth and ran the tip of my tongue across the small wound. He growled, the sound shaking the wall behind me. With that I tore at his jacket, needing to feel his skin.

Cadeyrn.

"Hm?" he mumbled against me, sending vibrations through my lips. I groaned again, my legs going limp. He processed it and slowly lifted me to the bed.

There was a rapping on the chamber door.

"Go away," Cade growled.

I smiled against him, my legs wrapped tightly around his waist. We stared at each other, not moving more than hands slipping up and down each other's arms and chest. Just to touch him freely. To not be self-conscious or afraid of a rebuke. This is all I've wanted.

"Can we not leave this bed for a very long time?" he asked me, placing small kisses along my collarbone.

"I feel like I've heard that somewhere before," I answered wryly. He shifted his body on me.

"Yes, well, only a complete imbecile would not have agreed," he said.

I muttered a swear and said something along the lines of there having been quite a few imbecilic moments. Cadeyrn's hair tickled my stomach as he dropped his head, laughing quietly.

"Every day we were away, every time you looked at me,

every time I held you sleeping, every time you made fun of me, I wanted you. And it killed me," he said.

I lifted my head to kiss him slowly, thoroughly. Cade's hands held my face as he returned the kiss, our bodies pressed against one another, not yet joined.

Another knock, then Corra's voice. "Cadeyrn. I'm sorry, but it is urgent."

His head dropped onto my chest, and he swore viciously.

"Of course, it is," he muttered, sliding from the bed. I ducked into the bathing chamber to dress while he opened the door. She whistled and apologized again. "What. Is. It?" he ground out.

It seemed that five males were dragged from their camp into the forest by wolves. A plum-sized lapis lazuli was left in their place. The males were heard screaming as the wolves howled and yipped. The legion was terrified as the eyes of the wolves could be seen blockading the tree line.

When I emerged, fully dressed, Cade was standing, still shirtless, holding the tear-shaped lapis stone. The light caught the base of the stone. I traced my finger over carvings in the blue stone. In my mind, I could see Nanua and Paschale. The two Elders had Lorelei and Soren tied to a stake, surrounded by wolves and the unsightly inhabitants of Festaera. I shuddered, Cade's arm steadying me. I knew he had seen what I had. This was a message.

"Bring everyone in here," he ordered Corra. "We need to figure out a strategy." The female twitched her lips. "What?"

"Cadeyrn. Perhaps we should move to another room. One with less..." She cleared her throat and waggled her eyebrows. He threw up his hands in submission. "We will see you down shortly." Corra peered around her cousin and apologized to me before leaving.

Cade turned to me, and I burst out laughing. It was a

completely inappropriate reaction, but I couldn't contain it. He shook his head and rolled his eyes.

That's my Cadeyrn. Always rolling your eyes at me.

"Mine?" he asked, pulling me to him and starting to strap my daggers back onto my aphrim skin–covered thighs. I cocked my head quizzically. "You said 'my.'"

My heart raced. I knew we needed to get downstairs. That we were in the middle of a huge conflict. Yet, I felt like I couldn't let this go, and I couldn't breathe. I didn't know how to respond and had no intelligent responses left in me. My God, I wanted him so much. He stood and pulled on his shirt and jacket, strapping the long sword across his back. I bit my lip so hard it drew blood.

"When this is resolved," he said with a dangerous quiet. "I plan to find out exactly what it means to be yours." My toes curled. "Then, perhaps, we can at last have some undisturbed time together. Until then, if there is a question, the answer will always be that you are mine."

As you are mine.

He pressed a kiss to my lips before we left to join the others.

CHAPTER 29

There was an ensuing argument as to whether I was to be out in the camp while the threat of the wolves loomed. No one but Ewan was willing to allow me out there, despite my ability to look after myself. In the story of Aoifsing, there had never been a war between the Elders and the folk of the realm. In fact, the very idea of the Elders came about in a divisive plan to have representation from each province and keep the royals or an individual from gaining too much power or influence over the realm. When the corruption began was a matter for debate. According to Saskeia, it was there from the beginning. Analisse insisted that though a few of the representatives were shady individuals, there had been a time that they truly had the best interest of the realm in mind. I personally could never see Nanua and Paschale interested in anything but personal gain, but I was a child in the minds of this lot, so I refrained from putting my two cents in.

The twins felt it was time to form ranks in the legion, with Cadeyrn as the leader. Having brought everyone together and his impressive cloaking trick, there was little balking in regard to Cade's position. While they talked, I worked on how some of my thoughts slipped past to Cade without my knowing.

Cupcakes and cashmere.

He stopped, mid-conversation and looked at me with closely knit brows. I pressed my lips together. Well, I guess that one got through. I shook my head.

Festering footsteps in flood water.

Cade paused and looked over his shoulder again.

Sorry. They were discussing demarcating the lines and sending different groups to various locations. Perhaps I should have focused on that rather than blocking my thoughts, but I had a plan, and for me to successfully act on it, I couldn't very well be broadcasting to Cadeyrn what it was. Ewan looked at me suspiciously, even turning his palms up as if to ask what the deal was. I shook my head.

Corra and Silas were to head one regiment, working specifically with a handful of fae who possessed gifts, which could be beneficial in battle. Analisse was to call in her seafaring unit led, unsurprisingly, by Lord Dockman. His entire brigade moved only by night. I made a mental note to ask Cade about that later. My underlying thought was questioning whether there needed to be a battle at all.

Battle schmattle.

"Neysa," Cade barked. Dammit. "Is there something on your mind?" Er, well, yes, I thought to myself. But I'm trying to figure out how to *not* tell you. Next to me, Ewan snickered.

"Let me go down there and feel for things," I said. Five fae in the room immediately said no. Reynard shrugged his shoulders, and Ewan remained quiet. I squared my shoulders. "I may be able to sense something. Have a vision or reach out. To someone."

"To *whom*? Do you have a death wish?" Cade whirled on me 310

and got right in my face. "If you think for a minute I would sanction your going down there alone..." I stood, flapping the skirts of my brocade dress back, and poked him in the chest. His eyes flared, and he stared down at my finger. His chest puffed in and out.

"Do not get in my face," I bit out. "There is no rank in this room, and I certainly do not answer to you."

"There most certainly is rank. You, *Princess*," he said with a sneer. Silas winced. "Are under our protection." Corra muttered a plea to the gods. "You have not dealt with the likes of this situation before, and we have many more years on you."

Wrong thing to say.

"Oh, take your cantankerous, geriatric hierarchical bullshit and shove it up your ass, Cade. I am no more under your protection than you are under mine. And! Do. Not. Call. Me. *Princess*." I poked at him harder, and he snarled, baring his teeth and taking a step toward me.

Silas was there in an instant, a hand on his cousin. Cade swung and hit Silas on the cheek, blood spraying from my friend's mouth.

"That's for the comment about being under her. And do not think I would ever lay a hand on Neysa in anger, cousin." Cade stormed from the room. Corra and I saw to Silas's face. He wore a smug smile that nearly made me hit him myself.

"Cadeyrn is like a dog who hasn't had his balls cut off yet. You should really take care of that, Neysa," Corra said. Ewan choked. "You. Don't speak." She pointed at my brother.

"What the hell is wrong with all of you?" I questioned as I left the room hoping to not run into Cadeyrn. I had no desire to see him at all right now.

Ewan was on my heels as I turned down a balustrade, looking for a way to get out of the palace.

"Heading down there?" he asked, shoving his hands in his pockets.

"Yep."

"Want some company?"

I pulled one of my twin swords from my back and tossed it

sidelong to him. He caught it without a glance, and we made our way, side by side, down the stairway into the kitchen gardens of the palace, the open skirts of my brocade gown flapping behind me.

Is there a plan? Ewan asked mind to mind. We both stopped short, both surprised. I cocked my head to the side and replied in my mind.

Threads of a plan.

He nodded.

I'm in. Just...let's figure out what we say to one another mind to mind, and what you say to Cadeyrn. Because, ugh. I laughed, despite the boiling anger in me.

LACK OF SELF-PRESERVATION was about the long and short of it. The fact of the matter was that I was here for a reason. I could be their wild card—being useful where it wasn't expected.

We walked straight into the center of the camp. Where I had the ability to cause a white-out around me, blotting out any and all darkness, my brother could blur the lines between light and darkness, cloaking us in pockets of dusk. This was a handy parlor trick when we were walking into a camp at night, attempting to be stealthy.

In the middle of the tents and braziers, we came to a stop.

I reached my mind out to anyone around receptive to me. Tendrils of my power stretched on for miles, thinning out the farther it went. I felt and saw the wolves. They prowled closer, the encamped fae getting twitchy. Just before my power dissolved into nothing, it touched upon a seething malevolence. The signature on the power was cold and ancient. It spread for miles across the forest beyond the mountain. Within the coldness stood a gathering force of fae who hunted in the dark.

Just before I pulled back out of the ghostly army, the Elder representative from Festaera seemed to look directly at me. His colorless face and bloodied mouth stretched into a vicious grin. I jerked back, Ewan catching me. His cloak dropped from around us putting us in full view of Cadeyrn's legion. Hundreds of wolves happened to be in on the secret as well. A call went out to archers and males and females nocked arrows in their bows. Horses began to whinny, anxious at the predators in their midst. Ewan and I exchanged glances. I began walking toward the tree line, my brother beside me.

Distantly, my name was being yelled, and the air was shifting with speed and warmth. I threw my light behind me, blinding anyone in the camp and palace. No one else needed to be in danger. Roaring anger fused through my bones. I knew Cadeyrn was incensed and trying to get through. I felt Silas's shield over others, and Corra's essence was there as well, seeping through the light in her non-corporeal form.

Hungry, glowering, yellow eyes multiplied in the night. I willed them closer.

I hope this is part of your plan because we are severely outnumbered on this one, sister.

Take one step back, please, Ewan. If any get past me, you will be the second line of defense.

He did as I asked like a good soldier. Magic built and

swelled within me. As I had done in the palace above, I stabbed my sword into the ground, sending my current of electricity through the roots and straight into the infantry of wolves. Only a few sensed the oncoming threat. Ewan put up his shield again and fended off the stragglers. Interspersed with the wolves were nearly translucent beasts snapping their maws at us, the wolves, and anything in front of them with a pulse. Ewan and I swiveled, lunged, spun, slashed and fought them off using both skill and magic. Once I was certain the annihilation was complete, I joined him in fighting the remaining wolves who were pressing closer to the camp. Light and dusk dropped like the curtain on a stage, and we both bent at the waist, gasping for air. He looked to me side-long and smirked. I echoed his look with my own, and he clapped me on the back.

"You stupid shit," Corra screamed at Ewan, batting at him with her fists. He grabbed them and pulled her face to his in a possessive kiss.

I turned away only to see Cadeyrn staring at me with unmasked rage limning his features. I could feel him not breathing, hear his heart slowing in controlled distemper. I knew what I had done wasn't fair. Maybe I could have told him my plan and he could have helped. If I were being honest with myself, I had wanted to do this on my own. Ewan and I having accomplished it together was an added bonus.

I understood his anger. All of their anger. I could feel Silas seething in the background. I knew I would get it in the ear from Corra once she was unfastened from my brother. I understood it all, yet I was wholly unapologetic. Still, I couldn't bring myself to meet Cade's stare. Ripples and surges of heat and fury flowed right at me.

Turning tail, I stalked off. Gathering fae in the camp stepped aside for me, some commenting to each other on what had happened. Many mentioned my belonging to Cadeyrn.

Some of it piqued my attitude, most I brushed off. At the bottom of the mossy steps leading to the marble palace, Saskeia stood in her wine-coloured gown. I didn't want to speak to anyone at the moment.

She allowed me to pass but called softly after. "I am proud of you, daughter."

My feet stilled. So much loss filled me with anger and resentment. Yet it meant something. It meant something for her to offer that pride. It meant something for Ewan to accompany me, no questions asked. It meant a hell of a lot that Cadeyrn was angry with me because I knew, deep down, that his anger was from fear of losing me and not bruised ego. Well, I knew all of this, yet I wasn't ready to face him or anyone else, so I kept walking.

Dawn was close at hand, and more than anything, I needed sleep. My very bones were weary. As I began pulling back the coverlet on my bed, I sensed him outside my chamber door. I waited to see if he would open it, as I'm certain he waited for my invitation. I focused on my breathing, trying to not allow any thought to slip past. There was heat coming through the door, as if he had pressed a hand to the wood. I turned the lamp down and slipped under the covers. His footsteps faded.

PARRY, duck, slide, clash.

Though we had grown up apart, parented differently, fed, trained, loved differently, Ewan and I moved similarly. We danced in our sparring. Over breakfast we talked about our father and Los Angeles. He laughed at the stories I told of the people and the film industry and traffic. He was completely baffled by the idea of getting a fake tan. We spoke of Barlowe Combe and the forest and running. He told me he had a wet nurse who cared for him until she left to tend to another when he was twelve. A little boy with a broken heart roamed this palace and the many different outposts he was shifted to depending on who was visiting.

Every mention of him lonely made my heart ache. I had been lonely and different. Always a shade off from my peers. Yet I had my father and his absolute love and support. My brother, who was the product of love just as I was, never had that. It was unfathomable to me.

Tears ran freely from my eyes. He grasped my hand. "Och, all is well that ends well, *áoín baeg*," he said. I didn't know the translation to that, so he said it meant "little one."

I snorted.

Once we finished our tea and porridge, it was time to train and after a time, Corra and Silas headed down to join us. They both only raised an eyebrow at me but said nothing of my rashness the previous evening. Silas always had a good head for letting me get on with it. He squeezed my shoulder and told me to remind him to not get on my bad side. None of us had slept much in the early morning hours, so after an hour or two of training, all four of us were ready to rest.

Only lingering threads of Cadeyrn's scent remained. While I lacked the nerve to go to his chamber, I knew he was not in it. I walked the hallways and terraces of the palace yet found nothing of him.

"The first time we met, little mouse, you told me we could get together and talk about boys." Reynard leaned casually against the marble wall, examining his nails.

"Yes, then you bit me."

"You stabbed me! Twice!" He affected offense.

"And you shot my friend, brought a bunch of brutes to attack us in Bulgaria. Oh, yeah, and then kidnapped me. You are the worst at girl talk, Reynard." Despite the horror of it all, this slick weasel of a male had warmed himself to me. How, I really did not know, but he had.

"Nature versus nurture. My nurturing was terrible. You should have met my sister. Our mother was just the same." I rolled my eyes at him. "If you're looking for Cadeyrn," he said. "He's gone. Ran off this morning."

"Where did he go?" I asked in a panic.

Reynard made a dismissive gesture.

"My guess is the Hollow."

He knew I had no idea where that was, so I tapped my foot in annoyance.

"If you are sending me on a fool's errand, I will hurt you. If it gets me killed, I swear I will haunt you until the day you die." He had the good sense to pale at that yet stuck to his assumption.

THE HOLLOW WAS a half day's walk. Reynard accompanied me the first few hours then directed me to keep going, saying it was a sacred place and only those anointed could enter.

It sounded like utter horseshit, but I trekked on, pulling thorny branches away from my leathers and hair. Up ahead, there was a cave mouth. I swore but moved forward. As the opening neared, I began to recognize Cadeyrn's scent. It pulled me like the tide before a storm, surely ready to drown me once I was fully in its grasp.

All I want is to drown in you, Cade had said to me on that balcony in Cappadocia. It seemed like a different lifetime ago.

The cave wasn't a cave at all, but an entrance to a repository of natural wonder. Acres of lush grotto spread before me. Individual pools of varying size dotted soft moss-covered ground. Stone rotundas stood near the pools. Large, weeping trees shifted as the breeze tickled branches over the tops. It had gotten dark out as I made my way through the woods, yet in here, there were tiny lights hanging from the trees. Globes of phosphorescence, illuminating the enchanted Hollow. Age-smoothed boulders lazed about on the shores. Against one such boulder sat Cadeyrn, one knee bent, the other stretched out in front of him. He picked at small pebbles, tossing them gently into the nearest pool. Each time one hit, the splash reflected the light above, sending facets of aquamarine across the smooth surface.

Stubbornly, I stood watching him. I knew he knew I was there. He could sense me as well as I could sense him. Eventually he looked to me out of the corner of his eye and shifted ever so slightly on the moss. An invitation. I hoped. Heavy feet took me to the spot where he sat, and I lowered myself down. I knew it had been an age sitting there, as my rear end started to go numb. I wiggled around, trying to get some feeling back.

"I am not used to this. This feeling." He likely hadn't spoken since the night before as his voice was raw and scratchy, like it had been every morning I had woken up near him. My stomach flipped over.

"Which? What feeling is that?" I asked delicately. He pushed his hands on the top of his knees, splaying his fingers wide. Soft sounds of the breeze flitting through the leaves was the only other movement around us.

"Of feeling like I can't see beyond wanting you. Wanting you safe. With me," he said with a wobble in his voice. "I can't even breathe, thinking of you." Useless limbs hung stupidly from my body as I lost my grip on all sense of myself.

"I needed to do it." The words tumbled out of me. Not the sexiest interjection to the conversation, but it needed to be discussed.

"You could have told me."

I tried. I told him.

"You didn't. You *tried* to go out to 'reach out to someone.' What does that even mean? What you *tried* to do was test how well you could keep your thoughts from me."

"I am not sorry that I did what needed to be done."

"Of course, you aren't." He pinched the bridge of his nose before continuing. "It's just like Peru. You decided what you need to do and that's the end of it."

"You didn't let me finish," I started. He huffed. "I am not sorry to have done what I did. I am sorry. So sorry that it... affected you."

"*Affected* me? I am in love with you, Neysa! You were courting suicide, and I would have died alongside you. Twice now in two days, I have watched you nearly get killed. Yes, it affects me. It *kills* me." His long fingers tore at his hair and scrubbed at his face near violently.

Slowly, I entwined my fingers with his, feeling the thick ebony of his hair. I lowered our joined hands and looked at him. His clear sea-green eyes were red and tired. Tiny lines fractured the smoothness of his skin around his eyes and mouth. So beautiful.

Love? Bringing myself to say it out loud was too difficult. "Of course," he whispered. "What did you possibly think?"

I hadn't. I hadn't let myself think what it all meant. Mine.

He was and I intended to keep him. Why was this so hard for me? Why could I not just let him in fully? I had admitted so much to him in Cappadocia. Yet, not this.

"I didn't know what it was. To love. Until this. Until you.

From the day we met, I felt like—you could destroy me. From the inside. Every part of me is so stupidly in love with you," he said, voice dropping at the end.

A weight had been pulled from my chest. Cadeyrn turned his full attention to me and cupped my face with his hands, then kissed me. Leisurely at first. The satiny feel of his lips against mine, his tongue brushing my own, sent that electricity that lives within me surging. It rose and met with his heat, brightening the Hollow for an explosive moment.

There better not be anyone interrupting this time, or I may kill on sight.

He rumbled a laugh against my mouth. I unbuttoned his jacket, smoothing my hands over his chest and the rippled plane of his stomach. He growled, a low bass that went from my toes to my ears. Deft fingers unhooked each eye of my aphrim skin jacket. It was fitted enough that I wore nothing underneath, and as the last hook unlatched, my breasts spilled out. That mouth of his was fastened to my breast in an instant.

The world was sparking around us. My head hung back as he flicked at my nipple with his tongue. Cade's hands moved down along my sides and pushed my pants down. I returned the favor, wanting to get him fully pressed against me. Near-painful eddies of warmth and pressure built in my core. I pulled his face away to look him straight on. From the errant hair that fell out of place onto his forehead to the tips of his ears and the mouth I always wanted to be attached to, I nodded in encouragement.

He reached a hand between us, guiding himself into me. My breathing hitched as we moved together. Heat bloomed the further he moved.

"I am so in love with you, Cadeyrn."

We both broke at the same time and collapsed onto the moss. As though a bell were chiming within me, something unfurled like a wing or petal. It reached from me to Cadeyrn. An answering interlocking of ourselves. The beast in me was content. I laid my head on his chest, breathing him deep inside me. I could hear every beat of his heart, every pulse of blood, and...

"Did you say something?" I asked, pulling back to look at him.

"Hm? No. I was just thinking."

"That the stars must have been right?" He sat up.

At the sight of him, I nearly hopped on top again.

Can you hear me? he asked in my mind. I smiled, bright and wide.

Loud and clear. An answering smile had me biting my lip.

That smile. *When I first saw you smile like that, Cadeyrn...That was it for me.*

"Gods above, you have no idea how much I had to restrain myself," he growled.

"Mm," I said, protesting. "You certainly restrained yourself well."

I'll make it up to you. Many, many times. He stroked my stomach in idle circles. *Repeatedly. Until you can't walk if you wish. I am at your full disposal, my lady.*

And...that was it. I straddled him, not caring whether he was ready again yet. Though I found, happily, that he was. Heat, electricity, pure white light, all surrounded us, as we spent hours with each other like this.

As the sun began peaking its wintry grey rays through the trees, we dressed and prepared to walk back to the palace.

KNOWING the others would realize what we had done and experiencing the reactions were two very different animals. In order to avoid the chatter as long as possible, we made straight for my chamber to clean up. Of course, as soon as Cadeyrn pulled off his clothes to get into the bath —quite honestly, just him standing there shirtless in leather fighting pants with his dark hair wet from sweat and getting caught in the rain—I had my legs wrapped around him, and we were pressed against the marble wall. My God, I could lose myself with him for eternity.

"For the record," Cade said into my hair as he lowered me down. "When you were pushing me and poking me in the library, I wanted to rip off your clothes and have that wicked little mouth on me. I was so turned on by you giving me shit." He nuzzled my neck.

Holy freaking Gods. Will this ever stop? I wriggled against him.

"I think we have to get downstairs eventually, lest they come after us with torches and pitchforks."

WRINKLES WERE ALREADY PRESSED into the silk skirts of my charcoal-grey gown from continuously pinching my fingers into them on our way down to dinner. Cade eventually grabbed hold of my hand to still the fidgeting.

Deciding to wear a dress came as a result of both my leathers being wet and filthy and the fact that it was highly unlikely in the months to come that I would have the luxury of being this feminine. The top of the gown gathered in the middle then criss-crossed across the chest to fan over my shoulders with beaded chiffon dripping down my back. Cade wore a dark jumper with wool trousers that tucked into his boots. Butterflies fluttered in my stomach looking at him.

Stop that or we will never get this over with, he said to me.

I smiled and stroked my thumb over his hand. He leaned over and kissed me softly. Taking a reassuring breath each, we walked into the dining room. Everyone stood around drinking wine and chatting yet stopped when we entered.

"Thank you, merciful Mother Aoifsing," Corra intoned. "Feeling better, you two?" I pursed my lips at her in mock disdain.

Saskeia looked uncomfortable, yet Analisse spoke. "Then it's complete? The *Cuiraíbh Enaíde?*"

We all looked to her.

"Excuse me?" I asked. Saskeia looked abashed so I directed my question to her. My mother. "Am I missing something? Cadeyrn?"

He looked as confused as I was.

"It is a plaiting of souls," Saskeia explained. "I have only sensed it twice before in my lifetime. You two have it, but you must have fought it for some time. One may now assume the plaiting between you has been solidified." Sorry, no. Not understanding. Again, I looked at Cade, who looked like he might throw up.

"What, in simple terms, please, does that mean?" I asked. It was Corra who told us that it means there has been a link between us forever. Perhaps that is how we found each other. The stars knew. Anyone around us could sense it. We had both been too stubborn to see it. The bond sat waiting, frazzling us until we gave in to each other. I really didn't like the sound of that. Silas had said something similar. That we had been like lightning from the start but too bullish to recognize it. However, what I didn't like was the idea that it was all predetermined. Did we ever really have a choice? Was that what Silas had given us? A choice in this. I shook my head, as if to dislodge the confusion. Cadeyrn reached for me.

No, I didn't know, he said.

I grasped his hand, needing to feel him. He put his arms around me from behind.

"Tell me," I asked no one and everyone. "Do Cadeyrn and I have a choice in this or is it like an illness that lies dormant?"

"Everyone has a choice," Silas spoke. "As I said before, you are the master of your fate." He and Cade were looking straight at each other. "What you two feel for each other is real. It is your doing. The thing that connects you is your anchor." Cade nodded at him from behind me. My arms covered his as they wrapped about my waist.

I am confused, but I love you. I see no reason that is wrong, I told him. He kissed the top of my head.

And I you. We could duck into another room down the hall and try to work out some of that confusion if you think it would help. Cheeks heating, I whacked his arm.

"Ugh. Here we go. Can we eat before the rest of us lose our appetite?" Corra teased.

CHAPTER 30

Steel upon steel was the chorus the following morning. Encamped soldiers below the palace had been divided into regiments and had begun training within their units. Corra and I decided to join them. Both of us picked a random male on opposite sides of the camp and sparred, slowly moving from soldier to soldier, until we met in the middle. Loads were untrained, having volunteered out of solidarity to both their realm and Cadeyrn. Many, however, had been training since childhood. Which, in fae terms, could very well mean hundreds of years. Still, I was not without skills, speed, strength, and now, I had almost fully come into my magic. We each spun and clashed, kicked and punched from one opponent to the other, leaving a trail of bewildered fae in our wake. When at last, Corraidhín and I reconnoitered in the center of camp, there was a huddle of males with shit-eating grins plastered on their immortal faces. She and I spared a glance for one another and launched onto the nearest. I hooked my legs around the neck of a moderately tall fellow and dropped backward, pounding his elbow with the hilt of my dagger, making him drop his sword. As he fell to his knees, I rolled off, narrowly avoiding him grabbing hold of my legs. That roll, however, put me right in the path of two sets of boots. One second I was in control of my fight, the next I was flat on my back with a knee in my chest. I thrashed before realizing it was Cadeyrn who had me pinned.

"Do you yield?" he asked with a smirk. Stirring warmth distracted me for a moment, yet my pride won out, and I brought a knee up straight into his groin and flipped him over, my knees now on either side of his chest. How I managed to not have my way with him that day in the forest in Barlowe Combe was beyond me. As it was, I could have taken him right here, in the middle of hundreds of watchful eyes. Cade's face was red with the blow to his manhood, yet he grinned at me and propped himself up on his elbows.

"You two were that bored?" he asked. I looked around for Corra. She was kneeling beside a female warrior, both of them out of breath, Corra's narrow sword lain across the female's chest. I smiled at her, and she returned it, standing and helping the feminine warrior up from the grass.

"No sense in wasting our talents. Plus, these guys needed a little shaking up."

A few of the soldiers grunted. We made our way through the camp, several males clapping us both on the back. A female with golden-brown hair inclined her head to me in deference.

"Felicitations, my lady," she said softly. I looked to her in question. "On your *Cuiraíbh Enaíde.*" Her eyes went wide, hand covering her mouth. "I apologize if it..."

"Gratitude, *cólleínhe.* My lady simply has not yet been accustomed to the attention." He bowed at the waist. I forced a smile. She seemed relieved and placed a hand over her heart before turning to leave.

Does everyone know? I asked him.

It would seem so. I am honestly surprised the males would fight you knowing though.

Did you know her? You seem to call her by name.

I did? He asked me. *Oh. No. Cólleínhe means girl. It is a form of address.*

Why did she call me my lady?

Because you are. Her lady. You are both the daughter of her queen and, for lack of a better term, my queen as well. Or, if that makes you need a glass of wine and cake from Tilly, you can think of it as being simply deferential to you.

I had stopped walking. He was right. Ewan and I were the children of a queen. Of *the* Queen. Cadeyrn is their Battle King. The chosen one. And we had chosen each other. This had always been about more than us. Clearly, every stitch in the tapestry wove us deeper into the greater story. Maybe a month ago, a week ago, three days ago, this revelation may have bothered me. Made me feel trapped. But now it did not. It empowered me and gave me greater motivation to rectify the mess that had befallen the realm. Lifting my eyes to Cadeyrn's, I placed my hand over my heart and bowed to him. Emotion swam in his own eyes as he placed both his hands over his heart and bowed deeply to me.

"While extremely touching and oddly formal, based on the animalistic scents you two put off, I have some startling news." Reynard stood with Analisse and my mother near the lower level patio. The sounds of Silas's boots and a few other sets of feet closed in.

"Speak, weasel," Silas commanded. Reynard tisked.

"I had been tasked with visiting my lovely parents to garner support for our cause. They had already pledged the subsidy of one hundred aphrim," Reynard informed us. "To Festaera, Prinaer, and Naenire." Silas and Cade swore. "While I am not their favorite child and seeing as I now pledge loyalty to the family who killed their favorite child, as awful as she was, they refused to listen to me."

"Then we prepare our legion to fight the beasts," Cadeyrn spoke with military precision.

"Weeellll," Reynard squeaked. "It seems as though the aphrim are able to cross the Veil. Soooo, we may have a problem."

"I need a regiment at both Veils. Send two scouts to each right now to report back to me. We prepare to ride out as soon as they return," Cadeyrn said, slipping on his cold mask as he gave orders to each of us, from provisions to armor. To Saskeia he said, "You must go to Eíleín Reínhe. You are safe there with its sea borders and wards. We need you to remain unscathed in this. Analisse, you may choose to stay and fight or go to the queen's island."

The twins were off, reiterating orders to their regiments before I had the chance to turn to them. The rest of us walked inside and up to Cadeyrn's chambers. I had the crystals out and began readying them for transport as Cade and I would go to the main Veil. Ewan was looking at the agate in its fragmented state.

"May I?" my brother asked. I gestured to go ahead. His long fingers plucked the initial piece that had been given to us in Cappadocia. It began to glow at his touch. The others ceased their chatter and looked on. Saskeia walked to us. I could feel these crystals from miles away. I knew their presence, and they often throbbed with energy, so it wasn't a stretch that the stone responded to Ewan.

"Pick up the other half, darling," Saskeia said softly. I did what she asked and the half I held glowed as well. My brother and I looked at each other. "Try to get closer to one another, please. But do be careful," she added. We took a step toward each other. There was a magnetic pull between us now. It was a fight to stay separate.

"Neysa," Cade growled in concern. Ewan and I both gave in and let the pull close the distance between us. The two halves fused together and all three crystals in the room began to glow and pulsate. A shock of power ran through the room and seemed to suck in a breath before shooting from the room in all directions. No one spoke or moved. Ewan and I replaced the agate onto the flannel wrapping I had laid out. I looked at my— my what? My lover? My partner? I sent the question through to Cadeyrn yet plodded on with what I had been about to say.

"We need to find the fourth stone," I said as though no one knew that. In order to secure the Veil. Think of the damage if fae, humans, weapons, and beasts can cross." At that moment, Silas and Corra burst in.

"What in the fucking Gods was that?" Silas exclaimed.

"Power. It seems Neysa and Ewan are able to channel their power," Cadeyrn remarked. Saskeia smiled at us. She reached a hand to my brother and me. Neither of us pulled back, though the feeling was odd.

"We need to find the last crystal," Corra reiterated.

"We will. We will take care of the aphrim problem and get back to the crystal search." Cade asserted his dominance. I looked at him sadly. It occurred to me what I needed to do.

"I will go. Alone." I'd made up my mind.

"No," he answered, pursing his lips, eyes flaring. Silas swore in the background.

"Cadeyrn," I began, grasping his hands. "Your people need you here. You've started something essential to this realm. You cannot leave now. I have to be the one to go."

I've started something with you, he whispered in his mind. I squeezed his hands feeling like I was about to die seeing the look on his face.

"You are everything to me," I told him aloud, not caring

that everyone could hear me. "But without the Veil, that everything is in danger."

Don't do this, he pleaded.

You know as well as I do that I have to.

His eyes closed, tears slipping out. There was a sound as my

heart broke seeing him like this. Like the buzz of an electrical transformer as it explodes in the winds of a hurricane. Every- thing I had worked these months to become, all I had been meant for, was here. Yet, as a cruel turn of the stitch in the tapestry, I would have to give it all up in order to save those I love.

"I will go too. We will work quicker if it is the two of us." Ewan stepped forward and laid a hand on Cade's shoulder.

"If you succeed," Corra added, barely audible. "If you bring the stones together, you will be stuck there. The Veil will secure itself by closing completely." She was speaking to everyone yet looking at Ewan. He hung his head. Our mother made a small sound of distress.

"I've only just gotten you both back. Please. There must be another way."

I looked at my friends. My family. Each, in turn, lowered to one knee.

"Go with grace, my lady. My lord," Reynard declared. Saskeia was openly weeping now. Corra left the room. I nodded to Ewan. He walked out to prepare and to no doubt find Corra.

THAT NIGHT, Cadeyrn and I moved about somberly. I couldn't keep from touching him every chance I got, whether it was handing him a glass of wine or pulling back the covers of our bed. We lay in the darkness, my back pressed to him as we had lain in Bulgaria. When I had realized my heart belonged to him. Our coupling throughout the night was slow and laced with regret. He told me about all the time he had spent in the human realm, searching for something and not truly knowing what. I shook in his arms, preferring to die right there than having to live with the pain that was sure to come when we had to be apart. We would be, quite literally, ripping our souls apart. Yet, we both knew that it was the only chance there was for the realms to go on without apocalyptic consequences.

We rode to the main Veil at first light. The oily scent of beasts thickened the closer we came. Scouts had returned in the middle of the night, reporting that the aphrim were halfway there, moving slowly. Perhaps a mile or so out from the Veil, we left the horses and moved on foot. Reynard and Corra crossed, as they were the fastest, fighting through the beasts in a blur of movement and mist. I assumed they had taken care of any that had crossed, as they returned shortly, covered in sickly blue-black blood. Cadeyrn, Silas, Ewan, and I fought back to back slaying the beasts. While enormous, thick-hided, and strong, their gangly limbs and overly large, long-snouted heads made them slow and clumsy. They were meant to be a dispos– able infantry—one we happily disposed of in a relatively short period of time. Magnus and Lina arrived shortly after the fight, and with their help, we loaded the carcasses onto several wagons to take back to a tannery. This infantry would allow many soldiers to wear aphrim-skin leathers. We scrubbed the blood from our hands and faces at a nearby stream. On the off– chance Ewan and I ran into humans once we crossed, it would call too much attention were we covered in creature blood.

Squatting next to me by the stream's edge, Silas wiped off his blades. My hands shook so badly I wasn't able to hold the flannel any longer. He gently set his blade on the leafy ground and folded me into an embrace.

"You'll be okay, *Trubaíste*," he told me, shaking a bit himself. "You are a survivor despite that heart of yours." I was openly sobbing, the light around me springing into ribbons of white heat. Heat was crowding around Silas and me like we were in a sauna.

"I don't think I can go, Silas. I don't think I can leave." He was stroking my back but passed me gently to another. Cadeyrn's warmth enveloped me. His face was pressed into my neck. I knew by his heartbeat, that he could barely breathe, yet he comforted me.

"You can do this. You will. And you will live. For me. Do not ever regret or stop living, Neysa." He put his hands on my face and pulled back to look me in the eyes. Everything. Every- thing I wanted was here. So, because I could not stay, I would figure out how to save him. All of them. I'd be damned if I wouldn't figure out a way. He saw the resolve on my face and gave me a lopsided smile.

Chanè à doinne aech mise fhìne, he said to me. I am no one's but my own. But that wasn't true. I am his. I am theirs. *You are yours alone. Go cause some trouble, my beautiful, beautiful girl.*

Ewan laid a light hand on my back to say it was time. I stood, still holding onto Cadeyrn. He kissed me and released my hands. I backed away, not taking my eyes from him, memorizing every line of his face. Every crease near his peridot eyes and brushstroke of his dark hair. I felt my broth-er's arm around me, and we crossed the Veil.

PART III

CHAPTER 31

March moved in, still cold and wet. Ewan and I fell into an easy routine of training together, researching, and attempting to make what little magic we had in the human realm cohesive. He retained knowledge as soon as it was given to him. Texts that were read, conversations had, faces met. He held onto all of it. Even when completely inebriated from alcohol. We went to the pub in Barlowe Combe one evening after a particularly grueling day of outlining our father's journals and ancient texts written by monks with a penchant for circuitous circumspection.

"This is not ale," Ewan spat after sipping the pint he had ordered. I laughed and explained the difference between different types of beer. Caleb had been a connoisseur of beer, and we had frequented microbreweries and breweries often. I told Ewan that what he had ordered was a pale ale and might be a bit more bitter than what he was used to. Slack-mouthed and ready for a challenge, my brother decided to try one of each type of beer in the pub. The barman raised his eyebrows and I shrugged, ordering myself a gin and tonic to sip. Drinking but the smallest amount had me feeling melancholic and desperately missing Cadeyrn. I spoke to the stars each night, hoping they would give him peace and that he could be happy. It had been nearly a month since we crossed, and though routine made it bearable, it was not easier.

After nine types of beer, Ewan declared that the only two he was willing to have again were a malty brown ale and a stout. The latter earned a second round. Ten pints and two gin and tonics later, we stumbled home. Fae tolerance for alcohol kept him upright and without alcohol poisoning, but he was clearly drunk and acting goofy. Leaving the pub, my brother began softly singing a bawdy tune which got louder the farther onto the country road we walked.

It was a once
I was a-way
Far too gone to make a play
That lassie had my bollocks a clutch-ed
Made me lose my mind...
So, what diiiiiiid
I do whens I was a-way?
Made a run for the light o' day
That lassie's male came a callin'
A trough of shite I had a fall-in
Alls because I got my prick
In desprate need of a stick

I was laughing as he sang, deep and serious, while spitting through the words.

As it turns out, Ewan was quite adept at doing impressions of people. His disinterested, highbrow impression of Cade had me roaring then sniffling a bit. We each fell silent and said good night. I slipped back outside to my nightly routine, holding the double horn *adairch dorhdj* where it lay against my chest. The door clicked behind me, and I felt Ewan sit next to me. He reeked of beer, but I turned to him and saw the loss on his face and knew he needed to be out here with me as much as I did.

"What do you think we would have been like growing up together?" he asked me. I smiled despite the reality of our being apart for thirty years.

"I probably would have tormented you," I answered. He huffed a laugh and hugged his knees in.

"I am older you know." I hadn't known that. I turned to him. "Saskeia told me. She said that whatever we happen upon, she and our father wished for us for a hundred years and loved us more than life itself." I swallowed repeatedly, trying to get past the lump in my throat. Dad used to say he had wished on the stars for a hundred years for me. I always rolled my eyes and told him he was old but not that old.

"I wish you had been with me and Dad. Or at least with Saskeia. Nothing will ever make that right. You deserved more. And then you came here now with me." I shook my head. He punched me lightly on the shoulder.

"Couldn't let you down, could I?" His accent was so similar to Cadeyrn and the twins. Something like invoking a song in the dead of night. Had I once sounded similar? We were silent as I stared heavenward. He inhaled deeply, chest puffing out. "I told Corraidhín to move on. It had always been different for us. Not like you and Cadeyrn. She gets bored easily, and I didn't want her to think she owed me anything." I could see in the sagging of his shoulders that he had been holding onto that.

"Do you love her?" I asked. He shrugged and nodded. "She wasn't with anyone else in the time I have known her. Only you." I tried to ease his pain.

"And yet, sister, here we are." I laid my head on his shoulder.

"Thank you for coming with me, Ewan." He turned and pressed a kiss to the top of my head.

CHAPTER 32

I t was Ewan who suggested looking at the material composition of the stones we possessed. He thought that perhaps there was a complimentary makeup to each of the crystals, which could lead us to what crystal we should be looking for. So, we looked up the mineral composition of black tourmaline (also known as Schorn), amethyst, which is in fact a type of quartz, and agate, also a microcrystalline form of quartz. Both the amethyst and agate were composed of silicone dioxide and, as such, were the more closely related of the three. The black tourmaline is a sodium, iron, aluminum, boro silicate. Now we just needed to find another crystal or semi‑ precious stone with a similar composition to the tourmaline. Of course, that was much easier in theory than practice.

Two days later, our search was fruitless, and as we sat in Tilly's, I remarked to Ewan that it was our birthday today. Tilly, pouring tea for an older couple sitting near us, turned and asked why I hadn't said anything. She brought out a slice each of the Victoria sponge Cadeyrn always ordered. My heart clenched. I hadn't celebrated my birthday last year. Dad had just died, I was recently divorced, and it was pointless. This year I was heartbroken and on a deadline, but I had my twin brother. So, I ran down to the off-license and bought a bottle of champagne. Ewan and I celebrated our first birthday together since we were five in a small English tea shop, eating Victoria sponge and drinking champagne from a teacup. We spoke of our parents and the thirty years we were apart. Of Ewan's twenty-seventh birthday in Prinaer when he reached his full maturity and was given an anonymous gift of an engraved sword. For my own twenty-seventh, Dad gave me a powder-coated narrow sword to go with my collection. He made such a fuss that birthday and at the time I couldn't fathom why. As with Ewan's, the gifts were our coming-of-age presents.

"I can give you their wedding tokens if you'd like," I offered to Ewan.

"I would love to see them."

"You should have them. Dad left them, and I'm sure he would want you to have them. A necklace as well. It's the constellation that's on my hand. And Cadeyrn's back." The champagne was kicking in, starting a tingle at the base of my spine. I pulled out my phone and showed him a photo of the rings and the necklace. "You see the tiny aquamarines that act as stars? Those are our birthstones."

"Birthstone?" he asked. I explained that each month has a specific gem attributed to it. "And ours is aquamarine? And that's in both pieces of jewelry?" I nodded. He grabbed my phone, having become proficient in using the phone and basic computer functions. His thin fingers moved over the glass, and he turned it to me.

Chemical composition of aquamarine: Beryllium, Aluminum, Silicate. It was the closest we had come to finding a match. I pulled my notebook from the ever-present tote bag. In it I had written:

Blue Lace Agate: stabilizing and strengthening properties
Amethyst: Healing, Protective
Black Tourmaline: Most powerful protection stone. Also has pyro electric properties and can attract and repel hot ash.

Ewan typed something back into the phone and placed it on the table. I copied it into my notebook.

Aquamarine: Stone of Courage and protection. Truth, trust, and letting go.

I tapped my fingers on the table and ticked the pen irritatingly. He plucked it from my grasp.

"So, the question is whether these tiny stones are what we need, whether they are smaller parts of a larger stone we need, or whether it's just a hint and we need an entirely different aquamarine."

"That's three questions," I pointed out. He narrowed his eyes at me. "I say we put them all together and see what happens." A nod in agreement.

The library was a bad idea. There was too much energy in there. So, we decided to put the stones together in the sitting room. Every time I looked at the couch, I missed the dogs. As selfish as it seemed, I wished they had come with me here. I knew Cadeyrn would eventually make it back to Aemes and be with them, but they had become my co-conspirators here. Maybe once this whole explosive crystal business was over, I would seek out a rescue and adopt a dog. Maybe a bulldog who just wanted to sit on my feet and eat peanut butter. Or a leggy thing who likes running with me. Or both. Maybe I would be that woman with a whole pack of dogs to fill the void in my life. Just not a cat.

We placed all the crystals on the dining table, in close range of one another. Thrumming, powerful energy vibrated from the stones. The table shook. The stones formed a bond of white light between them, the light reaching out as if to find something. After a time, the lights subsided, and the vibrations stopped. We both made sounds of disappointment. I had my hands on my hips, examining the stones while Ewan scratched at his deep cocoa hair.

"Why is it that we can cross and not others? I get why humans can't. I understand why Cadeyrn's family can, as they become magic itself. But why can we? It's not just a special royal decree. It's physiological," I stated. Ewan twitched his nose and mouth side to side in contemplation, making him look like a giant rabbit.

"It's the Veil itself, correct?" he asked. "Somehow passing through it is the disruptor?"

"Yes and no. Crossing through disrupts, but being here, our physiological make up is so different to humans and the world here. Humans breathe, heal, pump blood differently than fae," I responded.

"So, what is the difference?" he asked as much to himself as me. "What is the physical difference in our abilities to heal, procure magic, and pump blood as you say?"

"Fae are sensitive to iron?" I asked, and he made a so-so movement with his hand.

"It slows healing, so weapons are often tipped in it." I opened my mouth, but he held up a finger. "I am not reactive to it. Are you?" I didn't know and said so. "What if," he contin- ued. "Our bloodline was different quite literally because of our blood and its chemical constituency?"

"Okay. I'm listening."

"Most fae have very high iron content in their blood, which is why iron delays our healing. It causes corrosion in the body. If an iron-tipped weapon remains in the body, the body begins to waste. That, as I'm told was the end result of fae who crossed the Veil," he explained.

"Apoptosis. Cell death," I remarked. He shrugged his shoulders. Right. Human science.

"Cadeyrn's family, as you said, are magic personified.

Every part of their body holds magic like grains of sand. Corraidhín dissolves into her magic." He turned beet-red from his collar to hairline, and I didn't want to know what memory Corra's dissolution triggered. He cleared his throat. "Cadeyrn is healing in its basic sense. He has the line of mist fae as his cousins do, yet his healing is in unto itself. It likely is the starting point for a new era. His offspring will be even stronger because of it." He stopped, realizing what that implied to me. I felt like a battering ram had hit my stomach. "I...I didn't mean to..." I held up my hand.

"I know. It's true. You're right. It...just hurts. I feel like my soul has been torn from my body." I hadn't thought of it until that moment, but of course, Cade would have to move on to produce offspring. It was his birthright to be the lodestone of a new era. Because of that, he needs to uphold furthering his line. Everything I had eaten turned to acid in my stomach.

"Do humans have iron in their blood?" I nodded my head in agreement to his question.

"They need iron, yet too much is toxic. It actually takes very little excess iron to be toxic. So, what are we looking for?"

He slumped into a dining chair and held up his hands. I sat as well, fiddling with the crystals. What do the crystals have to do with the Veil? If we took magic out of the equation and replaced it with human magic. The magic of science. What is the question?

"What do the crystals have to do with the Veil?" Ewan asked, saying exactly what I had just asked myself. "How does the composition of each one affect the strength of the Veil?" Ah. And we have arrived. I looked at my watch to check the time and figured out that it was morning in Los Angeles. I excused myself and left the room to make a phone call.

Shannon was my roommate at university here in England, and she was now a professor at a highly regarded university in

Southern California. I shot her a text to ask if she had a minute. My phone buzzed immediately.

"Neysa? What's up?" It was good to hear her voice. We had been close as undergrads. Or as close as I had ever been to anyone I suppose. Yet, we lost touch over the years until she came to work in LA. Shannon was the only friend who came to Dad's memorial.

"Hi, Shannon. I'm sorry to bother you. I have a professional question for you."

"Oh, phew. I was worried. Okay, shoot." How do I ask this without sounding like a crazy person?

"Alright, bear with me here. If there happened to be an area of relatively high volatility that had certain elements crystallized in stones near it, could these stones, or the elements therein, act as chelating agents and help to stabilize the volatility?"

"Do you know the cause of the volatility?" she asked. Magic of course. Obviously, I couldn't say that. Especially not to a scientist.

"I believe it's an extreme concentration of iron. So high, that those around it become ill with iron toxicity."

"So, in theory, yes. There could be certain stones of differing physiological makeup that could, theoretically, help to counteract the toxicity. As you say, they could act as a chelating agent, pulling the excess iron from the soil or whatever. There would be, of course, a limit to the stone's abilities based on the levels in the contaminated area." I breathed out. "What are you up to, Neysa?" She laughed. "I thought you were still pirating the global Forex market?"

"Ha. Yes, but I've taken on a special project here in England. Something my father had started." She made an agreeable sound. "So, what can accentuate the counteractive properties of the stones themselves?"

"Well," she pondered aloud. "It would be the moving of

electrons and stabilizing the ions. For instance, free radicals attach to tissue to stabilize themselves and it damages tissue in the process. Electron exchange would help stabilize the free energy. I'm not sure if high levels of a certain metal would still be toxic if a stone was making sure these were neutralized. Do you know the cause of there being such high iron levels? Usually there would be a secretion of acid, which lowers the pH levels of an environment that causes the increase in iron. You might need to find out what causes the acid secretion."

"Would abruptly removing the chelating stones cause a knee jerk sort of secretive reaction?"

"Hm. Possibly? I would have to have soil or tissue samples to confirm. Measuring the levels would be important. Try finding the pH levels of the area as well as the calcium and magnesium levels. Both of those are important in binding iron. Sorry, Neys, I have to go teach."

"Of course. One more quick question. If the high levels of iron, which cause the volatility causes corrosion in the environment, could the cellular death spread? Almost like a cancer in the earth?"

"Absolutely. Think about all the court cases where contaminated groundwater has sickened entire communities. People died, crops were ruined. Gotta go. I hope I could help a bit."

"You are a star. Thanks, Shannon."

"Take care, Neysa. Maybe I'll drag the family back across the pond and revisit my inner Anglophile."

"I'd love that," I told her honestly. Especially now that I knew just how we were going to close the Veil. I turned from the fireplace where I sat to see Ewan leaning against the doorframe.

"That sounded promising." He grinned, and I smiled. It finally felt as though we were getting somewhere. The only thing I felt we needed was a stone that had a high calcium and magnesium constitution.

LAST AUTUMN, when I had visited Christ Church in the village, there was a small plaque on the wall. The original limestone front of the church had fallen into disrepair and there were pocks of limestone breaking from the front wall of the church. At the time of said disrepair, limestone was being quarried to be used to purify the tanks of drinking water for the troops in the Second World War, so it was unavailable to be used to make repairs. Dolomite had then been used as a substitute to fill the spots. It was found that the dolomite was too soft to last long, so eventually, the holes were filled with memorial bricks for the fallen soldiers.

I looked up dolomite. It is nearly all calcium and magnesium. What's more, it is used to stabilize pH levels in soil. If we can gather the stones at the Veil and the electron exchange between the stones would buttress the free energy, we may have a chance. Once the stones act together and the calcium and magnesium are bound to the area, then in theory, the Veil should collapse or at the very least, close. While knowing that collapse will mean our permanent exile here, so to speak, it would be a kind of closure. I wondered when Cadeyrn would move on. When he would have children to carry on his line. I had a feeling that Silas was bedding his way across Aoifsing. A stabbing sort of curiosity had me asking whether Cade might be as well. If not for anything but a distraction. I wouldn't fault him for it. I just didn't know if I could ever move on myself. I suppose that every broken heart in history has felt that way. Though, not every broken heart had its soul torn apart as well. As if in answer, the beastie inside me purred in misery.

CHAPTER 33

Since returning to Barlowe Combe, I hadn't had the heart to set foot in Cadeyrn's room. Enough of the house felt like him and smelled of him that I couldn't bring myself to be in his room. Eventually, I knew I would have to. There was no sense in having an empty house. I didn't even know if we would be able to stay there. I left Aoifsing in such a hurry, we hadn't discussed things like the house and any possessions they had here. At this point, however, we had to search the house in case there was the dolomite we were seeking. It was a common sedimentary rock, but I felt as though I needed to feel some- what of a pull toward it. The library held the largest selection of stones, and we picked through each one, which took the entire night. Our heads were bobbing with exhaustion in the predawn hours, so sleep became more of a priority.

In my dreams I saw my mother—our mother—standing before the stone altar I had seen so many times before. She turned to us as she had turned to me previously, yet this time there was recognition. Pride, love, and a deep well of sadness was in her eyes. Beyond her was the sea, rough with spring

. . .

WEATHER BUT NOT THE WINTER SEA OF SAARLAICHE OR
England. The hypnotic, tumultuous sea of an oncoming
storm stretched before her. She laid both hands on the altar
and pulled the sea from its bed, creating a canvas of slate-blue
water. I squirmed in my sleep, worried for her. The wall of
seawater approached the altar, and just as it would have
crashed upon Saskeia, she pulled the water into her very
being, falling back in the process. I awoke, sweating and out
of breath. Ewan came crashing into my room, soaked to the
skin with sweat. I knew he had seen the same thing. What it
meant, I had no idea, but I felt it prudent to continue our
search. During a very long, hot shower, I felt a fluttering of
wings moving within me. I hadn't had time to talk to anyone
about the beastie. Was she me? Was she a part of the braiding
of souls with Cadeyrn? I spread my hands over my stomach,
wishing I knew more about myself. What I had become and
what I always had been. How do I keep the cloaking spell
going for my lifetime? Would Ewan and I live indefinitely, or
would being here curb our long-lived fae lifeline? I took
longer than usual to dry off and dress, as though I knew what
the day would hold, and I would need to be strong for what
was to come. It was thankfully dry for early spring, yet the
winter chill still lingered in the air. I pulled on fitted jeans
with a grey, boxy sweater. Once my hair was dried and pulled
back into a low ponytail, I zipped up my knee-high combat
style boots. Wellies would have been better for the forest, but
the maneuverability of rain boots was minimal. At least five
minutes passed with me standing outside the door to Cade's
room.

"I could go in for you if you want," Ewan offered. I shook
my head. He had been in and out of all the rooms but

Cadeyrn's. He said as a child he had roamed palaces and manors out of boredom and gathered enough incriminating

details on important people in Aoifsing to have set him up for life. Of course, now it was all moot as we knew we were royalty and were in another realm. I took a deep breath and walked in.

He had been so tidy. I touched the grey duvet cover and leaned into his pillow, breathing in his rain-kissed scent. The room was in need of airing yet was clean and had me nearly doubled over with longing. Even his stupid military novel still sat on the side table where he had slept while I healed. A small writing desk sat near the window, a neat stack of papers next to a thick fountain pen, his laptop off to the side. I put a hand on the desk and felt an answering buzz. My eyebrows shot together, and I pulled my hand back, then replaced it on the desk. Another buzz. It wasn't the pull of the other stones, but something wanted me to keep my hands on the desk. There were two small drawers on the front, which held basic office supplies and what looked to be two jade pendants in the shape of dogs. Closer inspection, I realized that they were to be hung from the hounds' collars. I smiled and slipped them into my pocket to keep close to me. I wondered when and where he had bought them for my floppy-eared friends. The deeper drawer on the right of the desk had two stacks of file folders. On the top of one sat a jagged, white stone. It was perfectly spherical in the middle and on the bottom but jutted up at the top like the Dreaming Spires of Oxford. The rock buzzed, and I lifted it from its hiding place as an ordinary paperweight. We had all the pieces, and for all intents and purposes, were ready to bring them to the Veil. I made my way across the room but stopped in front of a small mirror near the door. My nose had reddened with the strain of trying to not cry, which made my freckles stand out on rosy cheeks. I missed seeing my pointed ears and the color my eyes were meant to be, but I looked like

THE SAME NEYSA I HAD ALWAYS BEEN. YET THERE WAS something more refined and perhaps a little more beautiful. I touched the mirror.

I know you can't hear me. We are going to the Veil now. I want you to be happy. And I miss you more than anything. I could have sworn there was a brief startled reaction. The beast in me tried to reach out and just as soon as it happened, the feeling disappeared.

SPRING HERE WAS an arrangement of color and soft-ness from the budding grass to the blooming trees. Sun miraculously dappled through the branches, adding to the disorienting feeling as we neared the Veil. Just as I had the day I'd first run into Reynard, my boots slipped and grappled for purchase as the leafy ground sloped downward to a sunken meadow. On the opposite side was the hazy barrier that marked the demar- cation of realms. It was where we had come tumbling through last month, and though it was wider than before, the feeling of wrongness still held.

"This isn't a discussion I am willing to have, Ewan," I had barked at him earlier whilst we discussed the order of events for the day. "I will place the last stone closest to the Veil. One of us needs to be able to finish it if the other falls, and I want to take that upon myself."

He growled at me, and I growled right back. Our identical almond-shaped hazel eyes were in a standoff, willing the other to back down.

Please. If something happened to you too, I might not make it anyway. Please, I begged him. His eyes softened, and he agreed.

I pulled the dolomite out of the sack first, placing it in

the most distant area around the Veil's abhorrent atmosphere. There was dying plant life all over the vicinity. All the stones had begun pulsating from being so close together. I could feel we had a definite timestamp on this endeavor. My brow beaded with sweat despite the cool air, and I unzipped my thin down jacket. I set the aquamarine jewelry from my parents on a handkerchief closer to the Veil, slowly forming a sort of arc to the barrier. Nodding to Ewan, who held the amethyst dagger, he laid it out on the dead grass after the aquamarines. We looked to each other and tried to summon encouraging smiles. I touched the tourmaline and amethyst *aadairch dorhdj* on my chest trying to feel for Corra's strength, then walked to the very edge of the haze, just in front of the Veil itself. The stones were sending out beacons of light and energy, thrum- ming through my heart as though I were standing next to a large speaker. It was time.

I started to set the tourmaline on the ground. It sparked and pulled at the other stones and away from me. Its magnetic properties were severely elevated and started to erupt. There was fire and light, and Ewan was sprinting for me, water forming from his hands, his face a mask of shock. From my own, shot veins of uncontrolled electricity, and I screamed trying to pull back and not hit my brother with them. Our gifts were out of our control, responding to the properties of the stones and the Veil. All of the crystals had converged on one another, relaying both pure white light and charcoal darkness, which swirled around us as we fought to keep the elements Ewan and I each possessed from harming each other. Ulti- mately, the tourmaline dropped from my hands out of sheer lack of control, and it tumbled directly into the haze of the Veil. It was much like the night the amazonite had exploded in the library. There was an eruption of light and electricity, water and ash, that all seemed to form a vacuum into the Veil. I was finally able to grab hold of my twin's hand, and as we did so, I felt the Veil violently combust around us and the ensuing quiet told me it had faded from existence. I was still blinded by the light, and the air was so thick with smoke and ash, my breathing became difficult. In squeezing Ewan's hands, relief washed over me as he squeezed back. Through the fumes, my eyes struggled to open, though tears ran down my face from the loss that we had just caused. I knew that because we had exiled ourselves here and closed the door to Aoifsing, I had saved so many. I had saved Shannon's family and Tilly's and even Caleb, wherever he was. I didn't have room in my heart to even resent him anymore. Yet, all I felt in that moment was profound heartache. We were coughing and struggling onto our knees, still grasping each other's hand, when we crawled far enough away that the smoke had cleared somewhat. In the near distance, I could hear birdsong and a bubbling stream and the gentle rustle of the wind through the forest canopy. I squinted at a pair of booted feet in front of me, then looked up.

"I knew you could do it," my mother said with a full, beaming smile. She reached down and hoisted both Ewan and me up from under our arms with surprising strength. I had never seen her in anything but a dress. Yet here she stood in what looked to be homespun trousers and a leather tunic with a full baldric of knives strapped across her chest, a strung bow on her back. I steadied my breathing and looked around. We had crossed into Aoifsing.

"It collapsed though," I managed.

"It most certainly did. You two became conduits for the energy."

"The tourmaline." Ewan coughed. That was the last piece. "Because we conducted the electricity and the ash, the magnetism of the tourmaline pulled itself—and us because we had connected to it—into the Veil as it imploded, thrusting us through to this realm." I mused aloud, amazed. It very nearly killed us.

"How did you know when to find us?" Ewan asked, his voice hoarse.

"I began to sense you both on your birthday. I sensed you had the jewelry." Her eyes shuttered for a split second. "I knew I had to imbue my gift to you, my son, in order to get you back. And so, I made my way here soon after. No one knew I was coming." She looked at me as though realizing what I was searching for. I swallowed the breath I had been holding, then embraced my mother. Her entire body sagged into me as though she hadn't been held in...thirty years. I could feel tremors of her weeping and held her still, Ewan eventually putting his arms around us both. She finally pulled away and laughed.

"You both stink of ash and ozone. Let's find an inn to bathe." And so, we did. I washed out my singed sweater and hung out my jeans, scrubbed at my skin and hair until the layer between worlds was washed away. By morning we had set off again. Saskeia told me, with a gentleness that made me sick to my stomach, that no one had any hope of our coming back and it had been so long— nearly two months. Only she had thought there might be a way but said nothing to the others. Over a month and Cadeyrn had been soul-sick and ensconced in battles. She alluded to the very real possibility that he may have moved on. If not moved on, but perhaps, had taken comfort with another. Or many others. I knew it was a reality. I hadn't expected to cross back either, so my own two months of sleepless wild thoughts often came back to that possibility. Still, I hadn't thought I would have to face him

. . .

AFTER THE FACT. IN LIGHT OF THE CONCEIVABILITY OF Cadeyrn having been with another female, I decided to keep my emotional outpouring and the thoughts I sent to him in complete shut- down. I needed to see him and gauge his reaction to me. The beastie growled in protest, wanting to reach out to him, but I chose to wait.

It was a day's trek from the Veil to Laichmonde, where Saskeia heard Cade had been most recently. We arrived by midday, having left the inn in the wee hours. Saskeia waited outside in case I needed her, Ewan having gone to Lina's shop to ask after Corraidhín. I knocked on the door to Cadeyrn's flat, and it opened to Lina, wrapped in a dressing gown. My eyes darted back and forth, at once confused and utterly panicking. Her own azure eyes grew huge, and she threw open the door.

"Neysa!" she exclaimed. "By the Gods! I felt the Veil collapse. We thought surely..."

I was shaking my head, feeling filthy and bedraggled, with Lina standing pristine in Cadeyrn's flat, mostly undressed. I backed away.

"Excuse me," I mumbled. "Don't...don't bother telling him I came." I turned on my heel and darted back down the steps.

"Wait! Neysa, please. It's...I can explain. It was the final battle..." Yet anything she would say I knew. I had my answer, but I didn't want to wait around to see the answer on his face. Especially as I was looking like a drowned rat after the events of the past two days. Having tried to prepare myself for the reality and actually experiencing it here, I realized I wouldn't be able to get past him with someone else. I never shared well, and I knew, in that instant, that I could never be with him knowing he had been with another. Even if it were just for comfort. Even though I did not fault him for it. I knew in my heart I couldn't get past it. I should have combusted along with the Veil.

I told Saskeia I wanted to go to Aemes and pick up the dogs, then I would go to Eíleín Reínhe, The Queen's Island, with her. Ewan chose to seek out Corra and promised he would see us soon. I rode alone to Aemes, needing to think by myself, letting my previous travels and the draw of the sea guide me back to the village where I had hoped to one day live. Pipe dreams of a happy life. The horse under me rode under the near flight of the beast within me, pushing us faster, until we skidded into the village proper just after nightfall. I dismounted, preferring to walk and realized I didn't even know where to stable the damned horse. Hands shaking with anxiety and exhaustion, I stumbled down the cobbled street until the horse whinnied from the sudden arrival of Bixby and Cuthbert. I dropped to my knees and let them nuzzle and lick me in greeting. I was sobbing like a bad drunk, rubbing their bellies and heads as they rolled around, obviously pleased to see me.

"By the fucking gods. You are hard to catch, *Trubaíste*," Silas bellowed, out of breath. He pulled from the mist he had become and walked to me. "That beastie in you give you wings?" While I was happy to see him, I was so out of sorts I felt like I didn't want to be around anyone.

"I'm going to take the dogs with me, if you don't mind," I spoke so quietly, trying to not break again. Christ, I was equal parts unerring strength and complete and utter sob case. So, I raised my chin and squared my shoulders. He folded his arms and smirked. Had I eaten today, I would have right hooked that fucking smirk off his face.

"And how will you do that? Are you planning to walk to Eíleín Reínhe? It's a loooonnnng way on foot," he drawled with

. . .

BIG EYES. WELL, I HADN'T THOUGHT THAT FAR. WHICH, admittedly, was dumb. But I could. I had no deadline, and no one waiting for me. Not really. I would make it a road trip. On horseback. With dogs. "Okay, *Trubaíste*. I see the wheels turning in that pretty head of yours. I have been staying at Cadeyrn's flat the past two nights as I graciously allowed Reynard to let mine in the wake of he not having a place anymore."

I pulled my shoulders up about to retort when he started waggling his eyebrows.

"And?" I asked, impatiently. He smirked again, taking a step toward me.

"And I have had company these past two nights."

"Lina?" My voice broke a little.

"Lina," he confirmed with a heartbreaking smile. I wasn't

ready to smile yet. I stammered about, not knowing what to say, the dogs whining and pawing at me. "He's here," Silas said, voice soft. I looked up, my eyes lined with tears. Silas's thumb brushed the wetness from my cheeks. "You know he wants only you." I sobbed once, knocking my hand against my heart.

Night had fallen completely. Lamps came on magically, sending small pools of yellow light onto the cobblestones. Warm lights flickered in homes and businesses. I looked around me, at a loss as to what to do next. So, I stood, looking at my friend with pleading eyes, yet not knowing what I asked of him.

"Come, *Trubaíste*. Let's get you cleaned up. I know you aren't feeling your normal princessy self at the moment." I didn't even have the spirit in me to hit him as I once would have. Silas handed the reins of my horse to a nearby male, and we walked through the village and up the tree-lined drive to Cadeyrn's home. There was smoke billowing from the chimneys, lights in the windows. The dogs sprinted ahead and pounded their enormous paws on the door. I smoothed at my windblown hair and tugged uselessly at my burned sweater. It was then that I let the damper off the bond between us, and the beastie purred.

Even the dogs jumped back as the front door flung open and Cade stood there staring in disbelief. It was as if the night dropped away around us. Broken sobs caught in my throat, realizing he was really there.

Surprise? I said in my mind. Surprise? Really, Neysa? One second he was atop the steps at the front door, the next he was so close, we shared breath. I wanted to touch him, but he hadn't moved at all. It reminded me of that night in Istanbul. So, I stepped back, trying to breathe over the panic that maybe he had gotten over me. His hand shot out and pulled me by my waist, the other went into my matted hair. I felt his breathing speed up as did mine.

"How are you here?" he murmured. "I felt the Veil collapse. I felt you...leave. Then nothing." His eyes went wild for a moment. "Ewan?"

"He's fine. We did it together. Our mother... she helped. Ewan went to find Corra. It's a long story."

"One I would very much like to hear. Later perhaps? Cousin, last I knew, you were in Laichmonde."

"Yes, I was there until this *paítherre moincháí* let her beastie move her on horseback from the city out here," Silas answered. Cade looked at him like he was crazy. I was now embarrassed and wished he would just shut up. "She came to your flat, Cadeyrn. And Lina answered." Ugh. So embarrassed. "And I was not in at the moment. I believe assumptions were made."

Oh, for the love of all that's holy. Shut up, Silas. I squeezed my eyes so tight, the hair on my head strained. Cade's fingers were under my chin lifting it.

"Thank you for clarifying, Silas. Good night."

Silas mumbled something along the lines of his being happy to ride all the way back to the city in the middle of the night.

Suddenly, Cade's mouth was on mine, and he kissed me so thoroughly, my knees wobbled.

He led the way to the warmth of the house, shutting the door behind him.

"I have one question." His hand rested over my heart, lightly pushing me into the stonewall, our bodies melting into one another. "Have you not learned your lesson with the grey jumpers?" He pointed to my sweater and the many snags and crisp singed holes. I gave him a lopsided smile.

"It was for old time's sake," I answered, finally feeling more like myself.

"I would assume you might like to bathe?"

"I know I stink. You don't have to hint." I was having trouble all of a sudden, keeping my head straight, looking at him. His hands reached under me, lifting my legs around his hips. Each place where our lips met sparked like embers. Through the tight walls, he carried me before setting me before the copper tub. Long fingers pulled each article of clothing from my aching body, his calluses rasping over my hips and thighs. When I stepped into the tub, half-thinking I really didn't care about being clean anymore, he pulled up a stool.

"I thought you might want help with your hair." His hands moved into my long, tangled mass of dark waves, lathering a peppermint scented shampoo in and scrubbing it into my scalp. I groaned with pleasure, and he chuckled, sliding his hands down my neck, working out the kinks. The room was quiet, bar the sounds of water.

"Did you really think I would have been with Lina?" he asked me in a gruff voice, still scratching his fingers along my scalp.

"It has been a while, and I knew you had fought and may have needed release or something. So, I—"

"Everyone told me to take another to bed," he blurted.

"And did you?" I was still facing away from him, the bath going cold. "I won't judge you." The words he had said to me in regard to Silas. His hands stilled.

"I lost a bit of myself in battle. Did things I am not proud of." I was thankful I hadn't eaten. My stomach turned to concrete. "What I will never lose, Neysa, is the fact that there is no one but you for me. So, no, I did not."

I stood from the bath, the water dripping from me, and sat atop him, soaking through his clothes. Grabbing the back of his head, I tipped it back, giving me access to his throat, which I licked up the front. His body shuddered under me, responding in turn. My hips moved automati- cally, and I pulled his shirt over his head, groaning at the feel of his skin once again against mine. His hands moved up my back, calluses scraping deliciously over my wet skin. Heat burned around us, cradling our bodies in a pocket of warmth. I pulled his bottom lip into my mouth and ran my tongue over it, wanting to taste all of him. I slid down and unlatched his trousers, pulling them off revealing every sinful bare inch of him. I held him in my hand, then brought him to my mouth. He made a very non-warrior-like sound and leaned back, grab- bing the chair for support. I continued this game until he swore and pulled me away then lifted me off the ground and had me on the bed simul- taneously.

"No wonder human lovers had questions," I teased him. He

grunted, looking up at me from where he was hovering over my chest.

"If you have any, I am happy to answer them for you," he growled, the sound low and guttural. It was completely inhuman and nearly not fae. He was pure male, adhering to no species. I felt his lips close over my breast and bite gently, making me yelp and push my hips up into him. He laughed and brought a hand down to me.

"Shall I take the edge off your impatience?" When I couldn't stand it anymore, I flipped him on his back. He looked at me through heavy-lidded eyes. I bent over, riding him slowly, and kissed that mouth I could watch all day. I couldn't believe it was real, and I was here. If I could do anything at all for the rest of my life, it would be to be here with him. I climaxed as he sat up and pulled me in tight.

I would spend it with you as well. If it's all we did though, we might have to get truly creative in here. He answered the thought I hadn't realized I transferred.

"I love you," I told him. "More than that. You are my every– thing." In saying so, the beast in me unfurled its wing and reached out to Cadeyrn. He looked surprised, and I felt an answering unfurling in him. There was an ancient, satisfied purr deep inside him. I smiled, unable to stop kissing him.

"No one else," he breathed. "There's only you."

Purring inside him called out to me much like my *baethaache* felt within me.

"What are we exactly, Cadeyrn?" I asked, peering up at him, spotting the slight dimple that rarely made an appearance.

"In regards to?" He swirled the skin around my belly button, making me shiver. I didn't really know how to answer that, but I saw him swallow, cheeks brightening in the dim light. Was he nervous?

"To each other. With the *Curaíbh Enaíde* our souls are plaited. With the baethaache, our inner beings or whatever are linked. What does it mean?"

"I believe," he said, the cool voice taking over. Instead of thinking it was patronizing, I realized now—and for some time now—it meant he was unconfident. He cleared his throat and I smiled, a little giddy at making him nervous. "I believe we mated. We are mates." His body was a tight coil under me.

"I suspected as much," I answered, laying my head back on his chest, kissing over his heart.

"And is that what you want?" His question hurt my heart.

"I want every part of you. You fit every dark space. So yes, it's what I want."

"It seems every bond and attachment from the depths of fae lore, we have managed to amass for ourselves," my mate laughed, kissing the unruly hair on top of my head.

"We're nothing if not thorough."

CHAPTER 34

The shoreline of Eíleín Reínhe was perfection. The harbor itself was tiny. Only large enough for one or two ferries to dock. The rest of the island seemed lined with beaches and coves, caves and cliffs. Atop the highest cliff, looking toward the west, sat the palace. It was a sandcastle made real with flowering vines climbing the many pillars and turrets. I marveled at the structure as seeing it started the memories rolling in of running on the beaches, my brother and me tossing grapes onto unsuspecting passersby from our terrace. I knew there was magic we could use to traverse the steep steps to the top. Magic coded in our blood. But I was content to move, climb, and take in everything I hadn't seen in thirty years. My first home. Where I had two parents who loved me. A brother to play with.

The queen welcomed us all to her isle for the summit to reform Aoifsing. Cadeyrn, I noted, was unusually quiet. Even for him. I tried to put my hand in his, and he gently pulled away. Pangs of rejection settled in my belly, but I ignored them. There was a lot going on, and I also knew he was rallying his power for this summit. Silas bumped my shoulder and slightly shook his head as if to say don't worry. I mustered a small, confident smile knowing he wasn't fooled.

The afternoon sun had dipped low and the terrace faced due west, allowing a spectacular view of the slowly setting sun. As the light warmed from the brightness of day to the gold and burnt umber of sunset, I knew Cadeyrn wasn't coming down. Saskeia caught my eye from across the blue and green mosaic tiled terrace. She crossed to me.

"I am sorry. For..." she looked out at the sea. "For not realizing who Solange was and what she wanted from him." It was like a sack of bricks hit my face. Of course. This place was full of horrors. For all of them I realized. Corra and Silas lost their parents, Cadeyrn, his mother. Then he was gravely injured and wed to Solange who betrayed him. All of it here. The situation made me sit suddenly on a chaise. Silas walked over and lifted my glass from my hand, as it was tipped at an alarming angle. I look up at him, anguish coating my features.

"Silas. I hadn't realized what it must be like for you all here." I placed my hand over my heart and bowed. In respect.

"Och, *Trubaiste*. We have made peace with our past. Go to him. His situation was different to ours, and if I know my cousin, he will still be brooding and beating himself over the past."

Our balcony opened with French doors and sheer curtains. Just as I had seen in my vision. I shook myself free of the gnawing aggression at having seen *her* with him. Cadeyrn sat on a wide, semi-reclined wooden chaise, bare foot propped high on the wrought iron railing, his toe toying with the blooms of a flowering vine. From the back, his hair was sticking up at all angles, likely from his hands pulling at it. Beside him, on a low bronze table, sat a half-empty bottle of pinkish liqueur, a tumbler of it dangling between his long middle finger and thumb. I wondered if he saw the waves and the sunset or saw only images of his tattered past. I slowly made my way to him.

Assessing the casualties again, Neysa? There was a cruel note in his voice that I didn't like one bit, and while I shouldn't take the bait, I was never one to back down.

"Playing brooding Lord of the Manor, then, Cade?" I asked snarkily. He downed the rest of his glass and slammed it on the table before refilling it. I snatched it out of his hand.

"Oh, please. Give it here." He waved his fingers and snapped. The snap did it for me. I tossed the contents of the glass down my own throat and set the glass down. "I hope you're planning to refill that," he bit out.

"I'll go. But just so you know, every one of us down there has been through some pretty phenomenal shit. I know being here rehashes memories. But brooding over some conniving bitch from 115 years ago, then biting my head off for checking on you, is a pretty shitty thing to do. So, figure out how to get through it or fuck off for a bit because I'm not rolling over for it." Plus, whatever that liqueur is, is not doing anyone any favors.

I went back downstairs and must have looked like a storm cloud rolling in because Silas muttered an "uh, oh" and used the wind to carry me a fresh glass of sparkling wine.

"So?" he laughed. I glared back and drank deep, immediately regretting it as a massive hiccup rocked me. Silas threw back his head, chocolate-brown waves dancing in the light and roared, then slapped me on the back. I hiccupped again, and he swiped at the air and the hiccups stopped. Neat trick.

"He's being a shithead. I may bunk in with you, Silas. That'll get his knickers in a bunch." Silas was still laughing.

"Always welcome to," he retorted with a wicked grin.

We watched the sun sink down, playing its final farewell

of the day, and toasted our glasses to being together and forging a new world. I felt him behind me before he said anything.

"I'd rather you not bunk with Silas, but I suppose I deserve it if you do." There was a thread of amusement in his tone. I smirked despite myself.

"You would," I answered.

"I agree," Corra chirped from next to me, then reached around and pinched her cousin.

"Okay, fine," Cadeyrn said, raising his voice to everyone. "I apologize. We have all undergone some, as Neysa so delicately put it, 'phenomenal shit' here. So, I will try to not monopolize the brooding. Everyone, feel free to mope and bellow at will." He bowed dramatically. I whacked him on his tousled hair. "Ow."

I stood staring out into the darkening water, feeling its movement in my bones. A hand slipped into mine.

"You have the filthiest mouth when you're angry," Cadeyrn said into my ear and nipped at it. The rocking feeling of the water, the wine, and his nearness had my knees wobbling.

"Oh, I wasn't angry," I answered a bit breathlessly.

"Oh?"

"Nope. Just putting you in your place." I tilted my head, giving him better access to my neck. He smiled against it and ran a few light kisses up the length of skin.

"I suppose I rolled over then?"

"Of course, you did."

"Ugh, just go and spare us all," Silas said waving his hand in front of his nose.

CHAPTER 35

Pine needles covered the ground along the back stretch of sand on the far side of the island. Memories of this island were as though they happened yesterday, and others I could be convinced I hadn't experienced at all. I remember the feel of the pine needles underfoot. How I would come in at the end of the day with itchy toes. Getting me to wear shoes was a constant struggle for my parents. I liked the feeling of the ground beneath my feet as I ran across sand and rocks, moss and grass. Cadeyrn left breakfast before I got downstairs, but there was a note to come find him. I followed the scent of my mate down the palace steps and across a courtyard onto the beach.

Where are you? I asked him. No answer came, but I could sense a smile. I walked for a mile or more along the shore then followed a path up the cliffs and into a forest of pine trees. There was a clearing ahead, within it hung a swing, Cadeyrn idly moving back and forth. The breeze picked up here and ruffled through my loose hair and dress as I walked to the swing. He opened his arm for me to nestle against his warmth.

"You look like a goddess this morning." He pointed to my dress. Light silk dropped from a halter neckline to mid-calf. The soft powder-blue color reminded me of a winter morning. I smiled and reached up to touch his face as we looked out through the trees. "I want to show you something I found." He took my hand and led me to one of the trees. On its trunk was carved a large heart with "E & S," Elías and Saskeia, carved into it. Then within the heart, lower down, "E & N," Ewan and Neysa, in a smaller heart. I reached out and touched it, tracing the indented letters with my index finger. Pictures formed in my mind as I felt the letters and the emotions with which they were carved. Early on in my parents' relationship. She stood barefoot in men's breeches, her hair wild, face flushed. Dad didn't take his eyes off her as she looked out to the sea. Another, as he carved the heart and sunk down to his knees and took her hands in his, as her hazel eyes smiled. Another snapshot: the two of them standing before the tree, the new smaller heart having been carved, my mother holding two babes. My father placing the constellation necklace around her neck, kissing her clavicle then pressing a kiss to each child. The last was my mother, in a black gown, sitting against the tree, alone, crying. I dropped my hand and turned to Cadeyrn. His eyes bore into mine. I knew he saw what I had seen, and there were no words. The sadness imbued in the images left me breathless. They had been so happy once. So in love. My mother spent the last thirty years completely alone. Each corner I turned on this island opened up a new memory. I could feel my *baethaache, the beast who is a part of my being,* wanting to let go. Cadeyrn took my hand and led me to the next tree and walked around to the opposite side. I half- laughed, half-sobbed. He had carved a large heart with membranous beastly wings and "C & N" within it.

I turned to him, a question bubbling up. "When is your birthday?"

He leaned in close and whispered in my ear, "The same as yours." I pulled back, wide-eyed. "Only 275 years apart."

"You're positively ancient," I teased.

"Oh? Shall I demonstrate my stamina? I have a few years on you to show some finer points of being as old as I am."

"Here we go with the geriatric hierarchical hoopla again," I said biting my lip, wanting very much for him to demonstrate that stamina. His eyes crinkled.

"Marry me," he blurted. His hand grabbed at the back of his neck, then shot through his hair. He lifted his eyes to mine. God, I could get lost in those eyes. "Marry me, Neysa," he asked again in a whisper that was echoed by the wind itself. He dropped to the pine needle covered ground and held both my hands against his chest.

"Of course," I said, pulling my hand from his and running it through his hair. His eyes closed, and he turned his face, pressing it into my hand.

"I don't have a ring. Yet." I shook my head. "When we can begin our lives again, I will have you dripping in jewels. Preferably naked."

"I don't need jewels," I said. "Only you." I pulled at his shoulders so he would stand. "Preferably naked."

CHAPTER 36

Four of the eight remaining Elders were expected to be at the summit. Though the Elders as an institution was no longer, the position of these four would be considered. Each representative would be weighed individually to assess their commitment to Aoifsing and its folk. Cadeyrn seemed to think Turuin of Saarlaiche was both a fair representative and would be amenable to the restructuring of the ruling body. Lorelei was seen as somewhat of a viper, but honest and committed to her citizens. Analisse had reservations about Soren. He was the youngest now that Camua was dead.

Twiddling my thumbs and tapping the tabletop as we sat discussing this over lunch, I became antsy.

"Something wrong, Neyssie?" Ewan asked. I stilled my hand.

"I was just thinking how I could have scoured their earnings and funds management back in the human realm and seen just how well the provinces fared. There's a saying, 'follow the money.'" Ewan made an agreeable sound, and I knew from working alongside him that the wheels were turning. Records are kept to balance coffers, of course, but anything damnable would be destroyed or moved.

"Then we look for the holes." Ewan followed the thought I hadn't realized I'd projected to him. "Your thoughts are spin– ning out of control. I grabbed that one like catching a leaf in a windstorm," he laughed.

Silas spoke up. "Look into who and from Cadeyrn was able to procure soldiers. If the three of us were being paid a trace– able wage by the Elders for so many years, surely anyone else's salary would be noted in ledgers as well. Also look to see who had tails on us. All the insurgents we took out when they crossed the Veil. Start there. Everyone had armor, weapons. Each should have been specific to a certain region. Find a common thread amongst them. Who moved more provisions during the past year? Your Majesty, would you be willing to question Lord Dockman?"

"Of course. Do you question his allegiance?"

"He has a vast network that traverses every province and beyond into the lands across the seas," Silas answered. "There may be some in that network for whom allegiances are purely profit. Festaeran steel turns a fair coin." Saskeia nodded at him. I was more than a little bit impressed by Silas's calcu- lating efficiency.

"Who is holding Festaera?" I asked. Maesarra had the queen in residence so Feynser's death hadn't created a hole in its government. "What of the provinces lacking Elders?"

"That is precisely what we intend to ascertain tomorrow," Cadeyrn spoke up. My head was already pounding. I wasn't sure I played well enough with others to be a part of this summit. Ewan smirked as though he agreed with me.

I COULDN'T SLEEP. I had a sneaking feeling I needed to figure something out before everyone arrived tomorrow. Cadeyrn breathed evenly beside me. On soft feet, I rose from our bed and tiptoed across the room to retrieve my dressing gown from the chair near the door, donning it as I slipped out of the chamber. In the library on the lower level of the palace, I turned the oil lamp to a soft glow and lifted it to peruse the shelves. Tentative fingers brushed along the spines, allowing impressions to flash. After a few minutes, my head was reeling a bit from a constant stream of foreign images. My head hung down as I breathed deeply, taking a break.

A scuffle of feet rounded from the hall into the library. Though masked in shadow, I knew Silas's scent.

"Couldn't sleep, *Trubaíste?*" he whispered. I shook my head in response. "What are you looking for?"

"Ledgers ultimately," I explained.

"In the library?"

"Not exactly. I was looking for both indications of who had

been here as well as military histories from Aoifsing."

"To what advantage?" he asked, starting to scan the shelves. Silas never doubted that I had a sound reason for the things I

do, even when they seem dumb to anyone else.

"More for my understanding so I can be more useful. I

wanted to see what provisions and goods were used or required in previous wartimes. The idea stemmed from what you said yesterday."

I blew out a breath, which lifted a strand of hair from my face. Silas pulled a few volumes from the high shelf and dropped them on a table behind me. I touched one and images of Lord Dockman appeared in my mind; he was handing a tome to Saskeia. She in turn locked it in a cabinet in her office.

"Silas," I said. "Saskeia has a ledger from Dockman in her office."

"She sent word yesterday to have him bring all his account details from the past few years." He leaned in close to my ear and said quietly, "Forgive me, as she is your mother, but I had scouts follow the messenger just to be sure of them." I pulled back to look him in the eyes in the dim lamplight. "I am loyal to her, but in order to do my job, I need to cover every possibility."

"I agree." I opened the volume that sent the images and sat. Silas placed a paper and pen on the table and sat next to me. There seemed to be a thick silence. "What else, Silas?"

He drummed his fingers.

"I don't trust Analisse," he said almost inaudibly. "I know she's your mother's oldest friend, but...I just don't."

I sat back and pushed my hair behind my ears, then looked him straight in the eyes knowing what haunted him. I knew I didn't trust her either. I had tried to ignore the feeling because I was always so distrustful of people in general. Her taking Silas to bed would always be a blight on her personality.

"And Reynard?" I asked.

"Oddly enough, I trust him. Or his self-interest rather. His family has disowned him. By keeping his loyalties to us, he knows he will always have a place with us. The little weasel."

"Good. I agree. I just feel I may not always be the best judge of character," I added.

"Och, you do just fine."

"Do you think Saskeia will be offended by our asking to see the ledgers?" I asked, feeling guilty second guessing my own mother.

"I believe she is loyal enough to the cause to make no fuss about it whether it offends her or not." I nodded absently.

We poured over the volumes on the desk. Historical accounts of past wartime talked of the bedrolls the soldiers used, the water skeins, food shortages and the necessity of producing more wheat and oats to use for rations. Nothing out of the ordinary. Silas mentioned having scouts in each province. He smiled and told me that he sent word to his scouts after our discussion yesterday to "follow the money." He flicked my nose.

In the last volume we pulled, there was a smaller, hand-bound one tucked inside. I flipped it open and saw that it was a record of Ewan's and my birth. The spelling of his name was originally Eóghaín, mine, Neíysa. Locks of our hair caught along the spine next to a hand drawn portrait of us with our parents. On the back page was a blessing written by our nurse– maid, someone named Elíann, and Analisse. I touched the notes one at a time. Elíann had a calm face with bronze hair and deep brown eyes. Just like my father, Elías. I looked to Silas, who shrugged. My fingers felt the note from Analisse and a buzzing, like the one from the drawer in Cadeyrn's desk in Barlowe Combe, shot up my arm. I held my hand firmly atop the lettering and closed my eyes.

Analisse kissing the brow of both babies, holding her hand in a hover over my face and closing her own eyes. Analisse meeting with Turuin of Saarlaiche. Meeting with Soren of Dunstanaich, trailing her hands down his face as he pulled away from her. Analisse privately entertaining Lorelei of Laorinaghe. Finally, My parents drinking wine with Analisse, my mother in tears while the Elder of Veruni held her hand as she cried.

I slumped back in my chair, drained, and slowly turned to my companion.

"Your face betrays nothing, but your silence has me worried, *Trubaíste*."

"I assume there will be wards up tomorrow?" I asked quietly. He tipped his head to the side.

"You assume correctly. Is there anything in particular you are concerned about?"

"I'm not sure yet. I know that I have felt malevolent feel-ings from Analisse, and from what I have gathered, there is no one who knows this place and my mother better. With everyone coming together tomorrow..." I put my face in my hands. Sleep would have been glorious.

"What is it, *Trubaíste?*" He squatted down and took my hands.

"Ugh, Silas. I don't even know where to start. I think the intention or the purpose of what I saw was to show me that Analisse went directly to the other Elders as soon as Ewan and I were born. Something isn't right. Is there...I mean, was anything off when you were with her?" He shook his head and curled his lip.

"I knew I should have said no. I just wanted to be able to get you out."

I remembered the scratches down his chest that made me see red.

"Silas." He looked up with a haunted look "I'm sorry to ask, but what did she—when did she scratch you? On your chest." It was embarrassing to ask him. He gave me a lopsided smile.

"She was not the only female to have clawed me in the throws, *Trubaíste*," he answered, making me blush a bit.

"But she is a seer," I pointed out. Blood magic was a powerful entity. His face blanched.

"She licked it," he said just above a whisper. I wanted to start throwing things. Had he told me this at the time I may have burned the damned place to the ashes. I squeezed his hands, still in mine as he crouched in front of my chair. "We were close to finishing," he began and growled. "She sniffed at my chest and said I smelled of you. Then she tore her gods-damned nails down my chest. I was too far gone to, you know, stop." Thunder rumbled across the sea outside the window, rain started to pour. He swore, and I could see even in the low light that his face was flushed.

"It's okay. It's just me," I told him. He huffed a humorless laugh and kissed my hand.

"She sat up and licked all the way up the gashes and drank from me. Fuck. I just wanted to get out of there. It didn't even occur to me—" I pulled him a bit closer, my heart breaking more.

"You're going to hate me," I began. "But can I see the scratches?"

"The scars are gone. They were mostly gone soon after. Then when I was impaled..."

"You were *impaled?*" I exclaimed in a whisper. "By whom? When?"

"The final battle. It was Paschale. Just before Cadeyrn destroyed him. Cadeyrn would have been killed with his injuries as well if it weren't for that gift of his."

Holy gods.

"I think I need more details of what transpired while I was gone." He leveled a look at me, which I couldn't read.

"No," he said. "I think perhaps, you do not." File that away for later. In any case, I needed to see where Analisse mauled him.

"May I see anyway? Perhaps I can sense something?" I asked timidly. He pressed his lips together and released my hands to pull off his shirt. My fingers were drawn to the left side of his chest where the scratches had been, pulling in lines from his collarbone, across his pectoral, over his heart, and stopped near the indentation where his ribs met. Though no scars remained visible, a ghostly echo of them showed me exactly where her nails had been. I placed my palm against his chest over those ghostly scratches and was flooded with images.

Silas in the throws, then Analisse smiling as she dragged her nails down and fastened her mouth over the welling blood. Simultaneously, images of Analisse and Lord Dockman in a similar situation, the male walking away from the encounter dazed. Analisse laying atop Lorelei, the Laorinaghe female enjoying herself. Then, finally, Silas walking away and slamming his hand through a wall while thinking of me—of us together—trying to clear the image of Analisse from his head.

I was gasping, my head against his chest, my fingers curled under where they had gleaned all that information. Silas's hand clasped around my free one. He and I were both sweating, and the weather outside had grown ferocious. Analisse was a monster. I didn't even know what to say to him.

"Perhaps, you could start by telling me what this is about?" questioned Cadeyrn's cool voice from the doorway. I squeezed my eyes shut briefly, realizing how this could look. Silas jumped and tried to pull away. I stood and made sure my dressing gown was in place. Cadeyrn watched me walk to him.

"I can go," Silas said, not meeting Cadeyrn's eyes.

"Why?" his cousin asked flippantly.

"Oh, please," I said and rolled my eyes at my mate. "Analisse

is not who she seems," I stated succinctly. "We need to prepare for complications."

"And did you discover this while wrapped around my cousin?"

"Cadeyrn," Silas said sternly, "You are making assumptions with no merit." Cadeyrn whipped his head to him, eyes flaring.

"Then you are not in love with Neysa? You were not showing her images of you and she in bed—or the floor as it seems?"

Silas hit him square in the face, a spray of blood covering the wall. Murderous rage limned Cadeyrn's features as he loos– ened his neck and took a step back.

"Whatever you think of me is one thing, cousin. Do not debase your mate with such claims."

Cadeyrn spit blood onto the floor.

"If anyone understands your love for her, it's me, Silas. However, this is—" I stepped in front of him and shoved my hands against his cheeks, flooding him with every image I had seen this evening. Silas walked out. Cadeyrn swallowed, and I knew it took all of him to meet my eyes. I knew mine were mournful. I didn't think he would believe anything so base of me or Silas, regardless of Silas's feelings. He opened his mouth.

"Don't bother," I stopped him. "My heart belongs to you, Cadeyrn. Don't villainize Silas for caring about me. We have a true and close enemy to face, and rest assured I, nor your cousin, are the enemy. Please excuse me. I need to speak to my mother." I left him standing there and from the outpouring of emotion, I knew he felt like an ass. I could understand. Yet, in some ways, I could not.

CHAPTER 37

Within the hour, Ewan and I were looking over the ledgers that our mother had graciously, and without hesitation, agreed to let us see. She sat close by in case we had any questions. The bulk of profit here on Eíleín Reínhe was from silk and moonstone pearls. Most of the ledgers listed the constant import of food products and livestock. Five years ago, export profits shot up. Cross-referencing production logs from just one of the silk mills, it seemed production had increased.

"Some time ago, I began to sense a downward turn in the state of things," she explained. "I decided to increase production of our goods in order to prepare for what may be coming. There are so many good folk here on this island, and I knew Feynser thought us all expendable. Two years ago, I employed Lord Dockman to procure me foreign steel. Most of what we have here comes from Festaera and much of it is forged with magic interwoven so as it cannot be used against the Festaerans. As such, I entrusted him with a great sum to procure that for me. Half is here in the armory. Half has been moved to my estate in Maesarra. Last year, I arranged to personally go to Prinaer to harvest crystals. I took one trusted guard with me, and we were careful to keep our movements hidden, using only small coin and trade items."

"What is the purpose of the crystals?" I asked.

"Protection, location, strength," she answered.

"Did Analisse know of your ventures?" Ewan asked. She pursed her lips.

"I began to suspect her ulterior motives and tried to keep it all from her. That was why I endeavored to find these crystals." "So, you do not trust her either?" I asked.

"I trusted that she would see you safely from the Elders. I trusted her in everything so far as she would think she remains in my confidence, and perhaps she has that which to gain. However, sadly, I have come to terms with my oldest friend now being my enemy."

"Why would you allow her back here?" Ewan bit out.

"My choices were few," she answered. Ewan and I looked at one another. I nodded to him.

"How do her powers work?" he asked. She looked up and sought my eyes, panic registering in them.

"I had visions." I then told her of all that I had seen, giving only the barest details of what had happened to Silas.

"I do not think she works with anyone else. I believe her to be purely self-motivated. Those who work with her are enthralled. That was the main reason we sent you away."

"But Ewan was here!" I squeaked. My brother patted my hand.

"I did what I could, daughter." There was a steel note in her tone.

"I want access to your armory. Now." She nodded tersely in agreement to my demand, and Ewan and I walked out.

BOUGAINVILLEA TWISTED and draped columns and fountains, intertwined with jasmine. My hair was instantly matted to me, rain sluicing from my leathers. As the courtyard opened up onto a promenade, Cadeyrn and Silas sat shoulder to shoulder on a tiled ledge looking toward the sea. Cadeyrn's arm slung over Silas, neither caring that the skies emptied on them in the rising dawn. Both males' backs were rounded and heavy. Cadeyrn turned his head briefly to glance at me. His mouth was still puffed and bloody from the blow Silas had given him. As though he kept from healing himself.

"I'm opening the armory," I said to them and kept walking across the promenade. Saskeia stood just inside, having taken Ewan through a separate entrance from her private chamber. Shelves ran the length of the building, all stacked with weaponry. Hooks covered the walls where maces, handheld battering rams, swords, and bows all hung. I marveled at them all, turning in circles.

"Do you have inventory of all of it?" I asked. Saskeia pulled a rolled paper from the satchel at her hip and handed it to me. Ewan came round to read over my shoulder. I recalled reading the provisionary stores on her ledger. As though following my thought, she handed me another folded paper.

"There is not enough in the stores for both open battle and for laying in for a siege. As queen, I wish to hold provisions for those here. The weapons are yours. The lock is coded to your bloodline," she said to my brother and me. Cadeyrn and Silas entered upon Saskeia leaving, and her hand lightly touched Silas's shoulder. He gave her a look as if to say it was okay.

The night of not sleeping and heightened tempers had me constantly trying to refocus my eyes. Cadeyrn hadn't spoken to me yet and was keeping a distance as we perused the armory. I decided to get a couple hours of rest before everyone arrived, otherwise I may start channeling electricity from Silas' storm to incinerate the whole lot of Elders. I tripped on my own feet and Cadeyrn caught my elbow, righting me.

"Thank you," I muttered. He nodded, and though his eyes showed all three centuries of his existence and his face was still battered, I walked away, desperate to close my eyes.

SAILS HOBBLED along the rough sea, heading for the island. Saskeia stood with Ewan and me on the veranda, watching the boats come in. Footsteps filed in behind us, and we three turned to face the cousins. Cadeyrn's eyes found mine, and he bowed deeply, the others following suit. I met his eyes, my emotions a mix between my stubborn idea that needed to still be pissed off with him and wanting to simply go to him and put it all behind us. He stood in his diplomatic finery, which skimmed every honed inch of him and only bulged where I knew he had blades strapped. In his eyes swam thoughts he wasn't sending to me, and I realized I must have shut mine down to him as well. Behind my ribs, my beastie purred and perhaps it was the rumbling thunder outside that still had yet to let up, but I thought I could hear his as well.

"Your Highness," Corra chirped. "You are looking quite regal and sexy this afternoon." I laughed and waved at her own dusty lilac gown that had her fair skin and auburn-tinged hair standing out. Her refined beauty had to have people underestimate her all the time.

"No more than you, Corra," I told her and kissed her and Silas's cheeks before turning to Cadeyrn. He swallowed audibly as did I, making us both chuckle.

I'm not sure why I found it hard to speak, but I stared at his face, latched onto his glassy gaze, and simply stood. He reached a tentative hand for mine where it hung at my side. The others moved away toward my mother. We had but a few minutes before the contingent of dignitaries were upon us, and I couldn't even get a single word to come out of my mouth. Anxiety bloomed, my heartbeat quickening, and my breathing shallow. That familiar ache between my ribs started, and spots were forming in my vision. Cadeyrn led me just beyond the veranda to the hallway. I couldn't breathe. My counting was useless, and the pain rose as I realized that soon there would be two boat loads of fae coming to discuss our strategies and strength to lead. And I was breaking down. Cadeyrn's free hand came to my face, and he blew lightly, freeing up my airways. He leaned in and kissed me. Not the soft, tentative kiss I had expected, but a fierce, claiming one that turned my anxiety on its head. Our beasts did in fact reach out to each other then, and our bodies pressed into a single line where we began and ended with each other. His scent wrapped around me like a welcome fog.

I'm sorry, he said, holding my face still. *It's no excuse, but I am not human, and I descended to feelings beyond reason. I would never doubt you.*

I stood there, holding onto him. We were both so damned stubborn. I knew he didn't doubt me. It was how he treated Silas that ripped something open in me, and I said as much. He put his head on my shoulder and kissed the exposed collar- bone, then dropped to his knees.

Your Highness, he said, and I laughed, about to whack him but saw a determination in his eyes that made me pause. *If you'll still have me...* He pulled the ring from his jacket pocket and slipped it onto my finger with endearingly shaking hands. I stared down at it—the white gold that matched the diadem atop my head, the tiny gems that were hammered into the band and met in the middle with a diamond so clear I could see where an aquamarine had been set in the band under the diamond. As a streak of light caught the stone, it shone just for a moment, like the light in his eyes.

"I told Saskeia I wanted to find a jeweler, and she gave me this band, which I had altered for you. The diamond was my mother's. Fitting that the band was yours. Each stone represents the regions of Aoifsing. Will you wear it?"

I really was trying to not destroy the little makeup I applied, but tears slipped out regardless. "Forever."

He rose, and I kissed him, feeling relief pour off him in waves.

I wonder if this summit will break for dinner, because I need to see that crown from a different vantage point, Your Highness.

And what vantage point would that be, Your Majesty? He quirked a lopsided smile that sent a whole host of butterflies to my stomach.

"I'll show you later. Top secret," he whispered with a peck to my cheek.

EACH DELEGATE TOOK a seat in the semi-circle that had been laid out. Reynard made his way to us.

"Weasel," Silas addressed him.

"God of the Forest." Reynard nodded back, and I laughed. Silas clapped him on the shoulder.

"Ugh," Corra groaned. "That's definitely going to his head."

Two people kept glaring in our direction, and Cadeyrn gave them a curt acknowledgment as he sucked his cheeks in, a muscle feathering along his jaw. I slipped my hand in his, my engagement ring facing out. He lifted my hands briefly to brush a kiss to my knuckles before turning to address Turuin.

"My Lord," my mate said.

"Cadeyrn," he responded. "Before this all begins, I would like you to know that you have my full support, but there are certain delicate matters we must address." His eyes shot to mine and away again, landing on Analisse. "My loyalty is to the people. Regardless of our past, Cadeyrn," he continued. "We have a common goal."

Ewan sat beside me, Corra to his left. Silas flanked Cadeyrn. Reynard looked a bit peaky as he made to sit next to Corra, and she gave him a saccharin smile that had amusement rolling off my brother.

Saskeia called the meeting to order with two guards on either side of her, hands on their swords.

"Thank you all for attending. I know it was a hardship for many of you to travel here, but I felt that it was the safest location at the moment." She paused. "Many of you know my daughter by now, Princess Neíysa of Aoifsing. My son," she gestured to Ewan, "whom most you may recognize, Crown Prince Eóghaín of Aoifsing."

It was so quiet, the hush was nearly tactile. Eyes were upon us as Saskeia turned it over to Cadeyrn.

He explained the overall goal for Aoifsing. The need for a council that did not hold as much power over the people as the Elders had, so that the people of the realm would feel confident in their leadership.

"No one lost confidence in their leadership, Cadeyrn," a female, whom I hadn't met, piped in. "No one sought to over- throw the Elders before you." She sat back with a smirk.

"With all due respect, Bestía," another unidentified male interjected, addressing the outspoken female. "I have been general for Naenire for roughly eighty years. I myself have thwarted two coups, have been alerted by the guards of several assassination attempts against various Elders, and most unpleasantly, and with regret, brought dissenters to the Elders to Nanua as bait for her lupinus."

"Are we then to allow sovereign citizens to run amok in our territories without the promise of discipline?" Bestía asked, looping a thumb through the belt on her dress. I wished I had been given pictures of everyone coming. Bestía looked as though she were from Festaera, though I did not know her position and I didn't appreciate the question she presented to Cadeyrn.

She's baiting me to open the floodgates. Bestía is on our side.

Cadeyrn said to my mind. She still gave me the creeps.

This new question, which having lived my known life with freedom to disagree with government and support ideals as I liked, rankled me.

"And by sovereign citizens," I questioned. "Do you mean someone who believes in something different, or someone who simply disagrees with you or what you personally stand to gain?" Everyone turned to me. The female sucked on a tooth and responded.

"If individuals were to constantly question the governing body, we would have outright chaos, my lady," she answered.

"Your Highness," Corra corrected, looking straight at Bestía.

"Pardon?" the female sneered.

"You speak with the princess, Bestía. As such, you will address her as, 'Your Highness,'" Corra answered. The female snorted.

"Your Highness," Bestía said and bowed mockingly from her seat, platinum hair falling forward. Silas and Corra both stood on either side of me. I lifted my hand subtly, and they sat. Everyone in that room saw the gesture and noted it.

"I believe," I began, impressed with my own ability to keep my cool. "It is our responsibility to the citizens of Aoifsing to allow them to feel they can question the motives of their governing body. To live in fear of tyranny does not endear the council or monarchy to the folk who live, work, and support the realm."

"And you know so much regarding our folk and the running of a ruling body, *Your Highness?*" The male whom I assumed to be Etienne, Reynard's father, spoke up. I sat a bit straighter, knowing he also fathered and doted on Cadeyrn's former wife.

"The princess," Cadeyrn addressed him, "is an expert of

foreign trade and government. So, Etienne, I would say she does."

"Yes," Etienne responded smoothly. "In her realm. Tell me, my queen," he continued. "Why did we not know of these heirs to the throne until now? And while we are on the subject of absence, my son-in-law has been hiding out in that realm since my daughter's murder. Why do we now answer to him at all?" And there it was.

"Oh, but many of you did know about my brother and me," I said sweetly. "Isn't that right, Analisse?" I felt the tension rise in my companions.

Saskeia jumped in before Analisse could respond.

"The lives of Elías and my children were threatened from the day they were born. We kept them on this island for five years until the threat was deemed unsurpassable, and I was forced to let them go."

"You yourself, Majesty, arranged for the marriage between Cadeyrn and our daughter, Solange. Do you take no responsibility whatsoever of the fate which became her?"

"I take full responsibility for endangering the lives of Cadeyrn and his family. My arrangement was a well intenioned mistake that resulted in the murder of Cadeyrn's family and very nearly the murder of Cadeyrn himself."

"Lies!" Reynard's mother, Francoise, yelled. Her pale eyes widened in her face, and her mouth was pulled back in a sneer. "You murdered her in arranging that union."

"I took her life," Corra said. "I slit her throat." There was a hushed murmur. "My brother and I found her winding a dark spell around our cousin and holding a knife over his heart. Your daughter, madam, was a witch and murderess."

"These are the people we are looking to lead Aoifsing?" Etienne asked the room. "Assassins and cowards who hide their children? I would sooner bow to Paschale. Alas I cannot. He was killed by this lot as well."

"Paschale, may he rot in twelve festering realms," Reynard spat. Everyone looked at him in shock. "He ran a province of tyranny and tortured for sport. He tore open Her Highness's arm to drink from her and tried to offer her to his mate for inspection. I myself was once held for the so-called inspection of Paschale and Ascha. My body was used and cut open for countless nights. The amount of blood loss I sustained assured that I will never fully recover my coloring."

"Be quiet, useless son," Etienne spat. "You have whored yourself enough to last three lifetimes."

"I was whored by my sister for her own personal gain. She used me to become proficient in the Aulde dark magics. She indentured me to the Elders, for whom I worked when I was tasked to intercept the princess and open the Veil."

The room became a cacophony of noise. Everyone was talking, shocked to hear Reynard's admission.

"I knew of the children," Turuin spoke up. "Lady Analisse informed me soon after their birth." Analisse shifted in her seat but did not alter her serene expression.

"I was told as well," added Soren. "I felt it a betrayal of the queen's trust. It seemed that should the queen herself think it prudent to keep her children hidden, then the cost of exposure would surely be too great."

Saskeia acknowledged him with a quick hand to her heart. All eyes turned to Analisse.

"Her Majesty is my oldest friend. It was never my intention to betray her. I felt it prudent the Elders knew of the children in order to protect them even if Her Majesty could not."

"I am sorry, my lady," Lord Dockman said, sweat dripping down his wind-weathered face. "I must say I was informed of the birthday as well. And witnessed..." A choking sound came from his throat. He sat gasping for air. Analisse was stock-still.

"She has enthralled him," I spoke up. "Using his blood."

"I have done no such thing!" Analisse feigned shock.

"What proof do you have?" Bestía spat. Cadeyrn moved to Dockman and tried to free his breathing, working around the spell.

"She tried to enthrall me," Silas said quietly. "She tore open my chest and drank from me." That admission had cost him; I could feel it and wanted to tear Analisse's head from her body for what she had done.

"I would have loved you." An olive-skinned female with bright blue eyes spoke. We looked to her. "Analisse," she said. "I could have loved you. I hadn't realized all this time you were trying to control me."

"Lorelei," Analisse said, a note of genuine regret in her voice.

"Analisse," Saskeia spoke, her queen's tone ringing in the room. "You will no longer represent Veruni in our council."

Analisse screamed in indignation and launched herself at my mother. Cadeyrn intercepted her, and Analisse thrashed at him. My beastie protested and tried to reach Cadeyrn. His own seemed to claw out to mine, and Analisse paused and swiped at him, pulling his beast from him. I watched in horror as my mate's face slackened and the beast became him.

It was not the freeing spread of wings I felt the time I fought to save him. His was an eruption of his fire and wild, endless power. The wings tore from him, claws shooting out like knives, his head rocking back in a scream, fangs and snout extending from his beautiful face.

I couldn't breathe. The world went white, and in the achromatic room, the only one who could come near me was Ewan. He held my shoulders as I insisted on running to Cadeyrn. I tried calling my *baethaache*, hoping she could reach out to his, but I couldn't make my magic work. I couldn't think beyond getting to Cadeyrn. Ever so slowly, his scaled, snouted face turned to me. His eyes, the same shade, between aquamarine and peridot they always were, alighted on me. There was a spark of recognition, but he shook his head, and in one beat, those enormous wings took him above the crowd as they stood stunned and terrified. Those wings took him from the room and out into the sky above the sea. Away from me.

ACKNOWLEDGMENTS

I want to thank my family—India and Phineas for understanding when I needed to finish a scene and the tortillas got burned. You lot are my inspiration & the reason I use both last names and annoy everyone. Coco, my own familiar—my baethaache--for never leaving my side. Damian, for understanding that sometimes I have to be in another headspace. And for loving me so completely anyway.

Endless thanks to my Mommy who never stopped believing in me. To my big brother, Lars, who would totally fight wolves with me. If we could both get rid of tendonitis.

Thank you to my original Alpha reader, and ride or die, Heidi. I hope this version is much better than the drooling, infantile one you read. And to Poppy. Always.

Thanks to my betas: Meredith, Robin, and Margarita. Love you all.

Thanks to Shannon Patel (she is real!) for the organic chemistry lesson, and for not batting an eye when I asked if I could close a Veil between realms using organic matter.

Thank you to my mother-in-law, Ming Sai, for her support

and for having the cottage which initiated the inspiration for the story.

Huge appreciation to all who have read and believed Another Beast's Skin.

OTHER GENZ PUBLISHING FANTASY TITLES YOU MAY ENJOY

Lycan's Blood Queen (Randolph Duology #1) by Catherine Edward

Lodestone by Katherine Forrister

Printed in Great Britain
by Amazon